THE BRIDGE TO NEVER LAND

THE BRIDGE TO NEVER LAND

By DAVE BARRY
and RIDLEY PEARSON

Disney • Hyperion Books
New York

SUSTAINABLE FORESTRY INITIATIVE — Certified Fiber Sourcing — www.sfiprogram.org

THIS LABEL APPLIES TO TEXT STOCK

For Michelle, Marcelle, Sophie, Rob,
Storey, Paige, and Bishoppe

ᏇCKNOWLEDGMENTS

This book was born on an airplane. We were out promoting our fourth Starcatchers book, *Peter and the Sword of Mercy*, and one morning, waiting to board a flight in Seattle, we got to talking about trying something a little different, possibly even a little weird. We had the germ of an idea, and on the flight we talked about it some more. By the time the plane had landed, the germ of an idea had blossomed into a full-grown flower of an idea. Or possibly a vegetable of an idea. Whatever germs turn into.

We put our idea into an e-mail and sent it off to Wendy Lefkon at Disney • Hyperion. She got right back to us: *Go for it*, she said. So we went for it, and here it is. Thus, the first person we want to thank is Wendy, our champion, who has always encouraged us to go for it.

We're also grateful for the help and support of many others at Disney, including Jennifer Levine, Deborah Bass, Frankie Lobono, and Nellie Kurtzman. We love working with you guys, and not just because of the free park passes and behind-the-scenes tours.

Speaking of which: We thank Chris Ostrander and Alex Wright for helping us with the Disney technical stuff. We also thank Catherine Steventon for helping us with research on the Tower of London. Any errors in this book are totally our fault, and not the fault of the people who helped us. We also accept full responsibility for global climate change.

We thank Judi Smith and Laurel and David Walters for their careful reading, perceptive questions, and thoughtful (we mean this in a positive way) nitpicking.

We thank our agents, Al Hart and Amy Berkower, for their wise guidance.

We thank our wives—Michelle and Marcelle—for their unflagging support and hotness, and our children—Rob, Sophie, Paige, and Storey—for being great kids as well as tax deductions.

Above all, we thank our readers, especially the young ones, both for buying our books and for asking us to write more of them. We have never had so much fun, and you're the reason why.

—Dave Barry and Ridley Pearson

TABLE OF CONTENTS

BERN, SWITZERLAND, DECEMBER 1905

THE WOMAN MADE HER WAY carefully along the icy sidewalk, pulling her long wool coat tight against the harsh winter wind and swirling snowflakes. Night was falling quickly; she had to stop and peer through the gloom to make out the building numbers.

Finally, she found her destination—Number 49 Kramgasse Street, a stone apartment house with an arched entranceway.

She entered quickly, brushing snow from her coat, grateful to be inside. She pulled off her scarf and shook her long brown hair; her cheeks were bright red from the cold. On weary legs, she climbed the stairs to the second floor and knocked on a door. It was opened by a twenty-five-year-old man, still in the frayed, plaid suit he had worn to work. He had a soft, round face accented with an unkempt moustache and framed by an unruly mass of curly brown hair. His dark brown eyes sloped down at the corners, giving him a look of wisdom beyond his years and a hint of sadness.

He welcomed her into his flat and they exchanged introductions. He offered her tea, which she gratefully accepted. Sitting close to the warmth of a small coal-burning fireplace, they made a bit of awkward small talk about the weather. They spoke in German, the woman with a thick British accent.

"I'm sorry my German is so poor," she said.

The man waved a hand. "Your German is far better than my English," he said, smiling.

She smiled briefly in return. "Thank you for agreeing to see me," she said. "I know you're a very busy man."

"I am honored by your visit," he said. "But I confess that I am also puzzled."

"Puzzled? Why?"

"It's quite mysterious, the letter I received from Doctor Pratt. I understand he is an associate of yours?"

"Yes, an old family friend."

"His letter was very complimentary about my papers in *Annalen der Physik*, and of course I was flattered to attract notice from a man of his stature. But I also could not help but wonder why a distinguished professor of history at Cambridge would be so interested in papers on physics published by an academic journal in Germany. And my curiosity deepened when Doctor Pratt inquired if you—with all due respect, a nonscientist—could come to Bern to meet with me personally about an extremely urgent matter, a matter he could not discuss in writing."

"Yes, I imagine it does seem rather mysterious," the woman said.

The man nodded. "So," he said. "What is this extremely urgent matter?"

The woman leaned forward, her face somber. "What I am about to tell you will likely seem impossible," she said, "but I swear to you that everything—*everything*—I will speak of is true. I cannot compel you to believe me, but I ask that you give me time to fully explain myself before you pass judgment."

The man smiled. "I am quite familiar with the problem of trying to explain that which seems impossible," he said. "Please, take whatever time you need."

"Thank you," said the woman. She took a deep breath and began talking. She spoke for the better part of an hour, stumbling occasionally, wrestling with the difficulty of expressing certain concepts in German—but for the most part she spoke quickly and precisely, having rehearsed her speech well.

The man listened intently, saying nothing, his dark eyes fixed on the woman's face. When she was finished, he sat perfectly still for quite some time. Then, without a word, he rose and went to the window and drew the curtain aside. He peered out at the darkness for what seemed, to the woman, an eternity. When he finally spoke, he did not turn around.

"I understand now," he said, "why you thought I would not believe you."

The woman's face fell. "I see," she said. "All right, then. If you would be so kind as to get my coat. I apologize for taking your time." She rose.

The man turned around.

"I didn't say I didn't believe you."

"Then you do believe me?" she said softly.

"I didn't say that, either," he said. "But I am intrigued. I would like to know more."

"Of course. There is so much more I can tell you, and show you. And there are others who . . ."

The man held up his hand. "Yes, I will want to hear everything," he said. "But there is something I need to know first."

"What is it?"

"Why are you telling me these things? Why has your organization decided that I, of all the people you must have access to, should be given information that you and your people have worked so hard, for so long, to keep secret?"

The woman took a step toward the man.

"Because we have a problem," she said. "A grave problem that threatens to cause terrible harm, not just to us, but to many people. Perhaps all people."

"All people?" asked the man, arching an eyebrow.

"Yes. I don't mean to sound melodramatic. But yes."

"And you come to me because . . ."

"Because we believe that the work you are doing may hold the key to solving this problem."

"You want my help."

"Yes. We want your help."

The man looked out the window again. The storm had worsened; the whistling wind pelted wet snowflakes against the windowpanes. The woman stared at him anxiously, awaiting his decision. Finally, he turned back to her.

"All right," he said. "Tell me about this problem of yours."

A smile of relief flooded her face; her green eyes shone with gratitude.

"Thank you," she said.

"I haven't done anything yet."

"But you're willing to listen," she said. "And we have nowhere else to turn. We believe you are our only hope, Mister Einstein."

CHAPTER 1

THE SECRET COMPARTMENT

*A*IDAN COOPER SPRINTED UP THE STAIRS. From behind he heard a voice, choking with fury, shout, "I'm going to *kill* you!"

Aidan reached the second-floor hallway, crowded with antique end tables and chairs, its walls covered in dark oil paintings. He heard footsteps creaking up the stairs. He hurried down the hall and ducked into his father's study, closing the door as quietly as he could.

The footsteps reached the top of the stairs.

"You're dead, you hear me!" called the voice. *"Dead!"*

The voice belonged to Aidan's sister, Sarah. She was very unhappy because Aidan had just swiped her iPhone, which he now clutched in his hand.

He heard a door open and shut, then another. Sarah was checking the upstairs rooms one at a time. Sarah was methodical. Her room was always neat, her weekend homework done before Friday dinner. What worried Aidan more was that she was also quite a good puncher, having taken six years of karate.

"I'm going to find you, you little snot!" she said.

Aidan looked around frantically for a place to hide, his eyes lighting on a massive oak desk. It was a new addition to the household; Aidan and Sarah's dad, a serious collector of Victorian furniture, had bought it recently at an auction. Aidan dropped to his hands and knees and crawled into the space where the chair was supposed to fit, between two walls of drawers.

Sitting cross-legged under the desk, he activated the iPhone screen and opened the text messages. He scrolled quickly through them, looking for the name of the girl he was deeply in love with, at least this week (Aidan fell deeply in love a lot). She was a friend of Sarah's, Amanda Flores. Like Sarah, she was seventeen, and in eleventh grade. Aidan was only fifteen, a lowly ninth-grader. He wasn't dating Amanda; the truth was, he had never actually spoken to her. But he had hopes.

These hopes had soared a few moments earlier when, reading over his sister's shoulder, Aidan had spotted a text from Amanda saying—at least this was what Aidan *thought* it had said—that Amanda considered him cute. He had tried to see more, but Sarah, annoyed at his spying, made the phone's screen go dark and told him to mind his own business.

So Aidan had snatched the phone and run upstairs. At the time it seemed like a good idea, but now Aidan sensed that it might have been a mistake. First, his sister was really mad. Second, as he scanned the iPhone texts, he realized that Amanda had not been texting about him at all, but about a boy named Aaron. Aidan didn't know Aaron, but he was pretty sure he hated him.

The study door burst open. Three seconds later, Sarah was crouched in front of the desk, red-faced with anger.

"Give me my phone back right now," she said, the palm of her hand extended.

"Okay," said Aidan. "Don't get—"

"I said *give* it to me!" yelled Sarah, lunging toward him.

Startled by his sister's lunge, Aidan jerked back and banged his shoulder and head, hard. Then three things happened.

Aidan said, "*Ow!*"

Sarah grabbed her phone back.

And a hidden door appeared in the desk.

It was a wooden trapdoor about the size of a DVD case. It hung down between Aidan and Sarah from the underside of the desk, revealing a dark opening.

"Huh," said Sarah, suddenly more interested in the door than in killing her brother.

"Weird," said Aidan, relieved that his sister was at least temporarily distracted. Trying to prolong her interest, he said, "What is that, anyway?"

"Duh," explained Sarah. "It's a secret compartment."

"Cool," said Aidan. He reached up and pushed the door shut. There was a soft click as it latched. The grain on the door matched the surrounding wood exactly; the fit was so tight that the seam was invisible.

"Wow," said Aidan. "When it's closed, you can't even see it."

"Right, nimrod," said Sarah, "but you also can't see inside. Open it back up."

Aidan tried to pry it open, but his fingernails couldn't fit into the seam. He banged on it, but nothing happened. He ran his hands over the surrounding wood, but found nothing that would open the door.

"I don't know how," he said.

"You are such an idiot," said Sarah. "Let me see." She crawled under and felt around the door as her brother had just done, also finding nothing.

"You must have done *something* to open it," she said.

"I hit my head."

Sarah pushed the panels above them. Nothing happened.

"I also hit my shoulder," said Aidan.

"Where?"

He pointed to the sore spot on his shoulder. She punched it, hard.

"Ow!"

"Not your shoulder, idiot! Where did you hit the desk?"

"Oh . . . the side, I think."

Sarah made a fist and pounded it. Nothing.

"I hit it really hard," said Aidan.

Sarah frowned and gave the panel a karate chop.

The trapdoor popped open.

"Excellent!" said Aidan, reaching his hand up into the hole.

"If there's money in there," said Sarah, "we split it."

Aidan groped inside the opening. "I don't feel any—wait! There's something in here!"

He withdrew his hand, which now held an envelope. It was letter-size and yellow with age. Aidan turned it over; it had no writing on either side.

"Open it!" said Sarah.

Aidan frowned. "Maybe we should tell Dad," he said.

"Absolutely," said Sarah, snatching the envelope. "After we open it."

Before Aidan could protest, she slid her finger under the flap and opened the envelope. She pulled out a piece of flimsy paper, folded into thirds. She unfolded it carefully, and Aidan leaned in to look.

The paper was so thin that it was almost transparent. On it, drawn in black ink, were random-looking lines, some straight, some curved, not forming any obvious pattern. Below the lines, handwritten in the same ink, were the words:

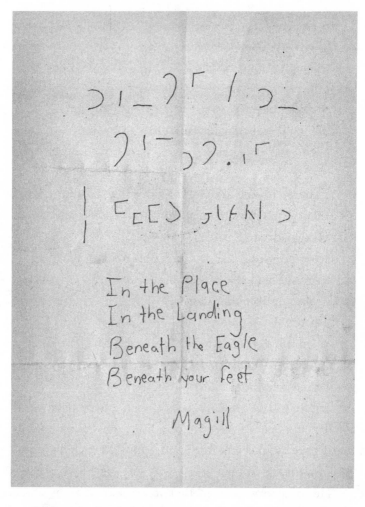

In the Place
In the Landing
Beneath the Eagle
Beneath your feet

Magill

"What the heck does that mean?" said Aidan. Sarah was staring at the document.

"Magill," she said.

"What about it?"

"I think I know that name."

"You know somebody named Magill?"

"I don't know. I'm not sure I actually *know* him, but I've heard that name somewhere." She continued staring at the document. Fifteen seconds passed.

"Can I ask you something?" said Aidan.

"What?"

"This guy Aaron? Who Amanda likes?"

Sarah looked up. "What about him?"

"How old is he?"

"He's a senior."

Aidan's shoulders slumped.

Sarah smirked, enjoying her moment of revenge for the iPhone theft.

"He's also very cute," she added.

Without a word, Aidan slouched out of the room, heartbroken. Sarah turned back to the document.

"Magill," she whispered softly.

At 11:40 P.M. that night, she remembered. She had turned off the light and was almost asleep when it suddenly popped into her brain.

"Magill," she whispered, sitting upright in bed. Fumbling in the dark, she found the switch to her reading light and turned it on. She got out of bed and crossed her bedroom to

13

a shelf jammed to overflowing with books. She searched the titles, stopping finally on a fat hardcover book. She pulled it out and began impatiently turning pages; she flipped most of the way through before she found what she was looking for. She read a passage, then read it again.

"I knew it," she said. She sat on her bed for a few moments, thinking. Then she returned to the bookshelf and pulled out another fat book. After flipping through it as well, she found a particular passage and began reading.

"Yes," she said. She bookmarked the page and moved ahead to another chapter, reading with growing excitement. She opened the small drawer on her bedside table and withdrew the fragile document they had discovered in the desk. She reread it, standing as she did, too excited now to sit.

She paced her room for a minute, the book in one hand, the letter in the other. Then she collected both books and, holding tightly to the document, quietly left her room and crept down the hallway to Aidan's room. She eased open the door without knocking and closed it softly behind herself. She switched on the light.

"Psst! Aidan, wake up!" she whispered.

"What?" he said, squinting and blinking at the unwanted light. "Why are you . . . ?"

"Shh," she hissed. "Not so loud. You'll wake Mom and Dad."

"What are you doing in here?" he said. "It's . . . midnight."

She handed him the first book. He reluctantly accepted it from her, rubbed his eyes open, and read the title.

"*Peter and the Shadow Thieves*," he said. "I already read this. As in like five years ago."

"I know that," she said. "But read this part." She was pointing to a paragraph on the bottom of page 475.

Aidan read it aloud quietly.

> **"First thing tomorrow," said Aster, "I will arrange to send you all back to London. But for tonight you must remain here. I'm going out for several hours with Mister Magill—the man who, ah, greeted you at the gate."**

Aidan looked up at Sarah. "So?" he said.

"Magill!" she said, holding up the document from the desk. "I *knew* I knew that name. He helped the Starcatchers!"

"Are you insane? You woke me up for this?"

"Magill!" she repeated.

"So it's the same name. Big deal. There's probably a million Magills. I can't believe you woke me up—"

"Do *you* know any Magills?"

"No, but that doesn't mean—"

"I'm not done," she said, holding up the second book. He read the title: *Peter and the Sword of Mercy*.

"Magill's mentioned in here, too," she said. "A lot."

"I still don't see why—"

"Just wait, okay?" she said, opening the book to a folded page. "Here. Leonard Aster is telling Peter and Wendy to go to a safe place. Look where he sends them." She presented the book to Aidan, this time pointing to the middle of page 312. He read:

> **"When you get out of here," he said, "go straight to a hotel in Sloane Square called the Scotland Landing."**

Aidan looked up. Sarah showed him the document again. "'In the Landing,'" she said. "It says 'In the Landing.' In the book, Magill lives there. In the Scotland Landing Hotel."

"That's just a coincidence," said Aidan. But he sounded less confident than before.

"Wait," said Sarah, now leafing furiously through the book. "Here!" She was pointing to the bottom of page 325. Again, Aidan read:

> **The taxicab rumbled through the dark streets for fifteen minutes, then stopped in front of a narrow three-story building on a quiet street near Sloane Square called Draycott Place.**

"Draycott Place," said Sarah. "In this book, Magill was in Scotland Landing, in Draycott Place." She waved the document. "Magill. In the Landing. In the Place."

Aidan looked at the book, then the paper, then back to the book again. "So are you, like, saying you think this Starcatchers stuff is for real? That's crazy."

"Then who wrote *this?*" she said, holding up the document.

Aidan thought about that.

"It could be a practical joke," he said. "Somebody read these books, and then they wrote that stuff on the paper, and then they hid it in the desk so somebody like you would fall for it."

"Really?" said Sarah. "You're saying somebody read the books, then found this ridiculously old-looking piece of paper and wrote this stuff on it, then hid the paper in the secret compartment of this really old desk, and it was all some kind of joke?"

"Well . . . yeah."

"But how would they expect anybody to ever find it? If you hadn't hidden under the desk and bumped your shoulder, we'd never have found it. Nobody would have ever found it. Ever, as in ever."

Aidan thought about that. "Okay," he said, pointing to the paper. "So what do you think it is?"

"What I think," said Sarah, "is that it's . . . a mystery."

"Wow. A mystery. Nice work, Sherlock Holmes."

"I'm not saying I have the answer to the mystery. I'm just saying it *is* one." She hesitated, then said, "And I'm going to solve it."

"You?"

"Yes."

"How, exactly?"

"I'm going to start at Draycott Place."

"Which is in London. We're in Pittsburgh, Pennsylvania."

"Right. And where are we going in two weeks?"

"Oh yeah," said Aidan, remembering that the Cooper family was taking their summer-vacation trip to England this year.

"So when we're in London, we'll go find this Draycott Place," said Sarah. "Meanwhile, we can do some research on the Internet. And I'm going to ask Dad what he knows about who used to own that desk."

"Are we going to tell Dad about this?" asked Aidan, pointing at the document.

"Not yet."

"Why not?"

"Because we found it, and I think we should have the first chance to figure out what it means. We'll tell him about it later, okay?"

"No," said Aidan. "It's Dad's desk, so he owns the documents in it. We have to tell him."

"No, we most certainly do not. That desk is in our house. That makes it just as much ours."

"Absolutely not," said Aidan. "We have to tell Dad. You are not going to change my mind about this."

"I'll introduce you to Amanda Flores," said Sarah.

"Deal," said Aidan immediately. He yawned. "Now please, can I go back to sleep?"

"Okay," said Sarah. "Just don't forget our deal."

"I won't. Don't you forget your part."

"I won't." Sarah turned off the light and opened the door.

"For the record," Aidan whispered in the darkness, "you are completely insane."

"Pleasant dreams." Sarah quietly shut the door. Holding the books and the document, she tiptoed back to her bedroom. It was well past midnight now, but she was too excited to sleep. She sat on her bed and looked at the covers of the books, which were illustrated with scenes of a flying boy and a heroic girl menaced by cruel pirates and hideous, evil creatures. Sarah knew these stories well; she had read and reread them over the years. But to her they had always been make-believe; there was no flying boy, she knew, and no magical island.

She set the books on her bed, then went to her window and looked out. The backyard, bathed in moonlight, was dominated by a massive oak. A gust of wind shifted its twisting branches; their shadows writhed on the ground. Sarah looked at them for a moment, then back at the books. A persistent thought kept bubbling up in her mind; she knew it was ridiculous, but somehow she could not completely dismiss it.

What if it's not make-believe?

CHAPTER 2

LETTERS IN STONE

ℐN LONDON THE COOPER FAMILY stayed at the Cadogan Hotel, a stately brick building on Sloane Street. Sarah and Aidan's father, Tom, had picked the Cadogan because, in his words, "it has some history." He loved history.

Aidan, whose idea of the ancient past was sixth grade, was less enthusiastic about the hotel, especially when he saw the television in the room he was sharing with his sister.

"It's not even high definition!" he complained. "What is this, the Middle Ages?"

His mother, Natalie Cooper, stood in the doorway; she had come from the room next door to check on her children. She was basically an older version of Sarah: tall, slender, and olive-skinned, with wide-set, dramatically dark eyes. And like her daughter, Natalie had a black belt in sarcasm.

"I know!" she said, gesturing at the children's elegantly

furnished room. "It's so primitive. We'll probably have to kill our own food."

Sarah, lying on her bed, snorted.

"Go ahead, laugh," said Aidan.

"Thanks, I will," said Sarah.

"Tom," Natalie called over her shoulder. "Did you bring the squirrel gun?"

Her husband appeared in the doorway behind her, a tall, rumpled, bespectacled man with a prominent chin and nose. He looked vaguely distracted, as he always did except when he was examining antiques.

"Did I bring the *what?*" he said.

"Never mind," said Natalie, exchanging eye rolls with her daughter. She turned to her son and said, "Aidan, we didn't come to London to watch television. We're here to do things."

"Not now, I hope," said Sarah, sitting up and looking at herself in a wall mirror. "I have airplane hair."

"Your hair does that," said Natalie, "because you—"

"I know, I know," interrupted Sarah. She imitated her mother's lecture voice: "'You use too much hair spray, young lady.'"

"Well, you do," said Natalie. Sarah had taken to wearing her hair in a retro style that she sprayed constantly from a can of intensive-hold hair spray she carried with her everywhere. Natalie hated the hairstyle; currently this was the topic of eighty percent of all conversations between mother and daughter.

"So what are we gonna do?" said Aidan, who was sick of the hair debate.

"Well," said Tom, "we're going to start this afternoon with a tour of London on a double-decker bus. Then we'll . . ."

He went on for several minutes, giving a detailed schedule of tours, museum visits, and excursions. When he finished, Natalie said, "So you see, there won't be time to watch television."

"There won't be time to go to the bathroom," said Aidan.

"Will we have *any* free time?" asked Sarah. She and her brother exchanged glances.

"Sure, you'll have some time on your own," her father answered.

"As long as we know where you are," added her mother.

"Of course," said Sarah, with another glance at her brother. Both of them made a point of not looking at Sarah's backpack, which contained the mysterious document they'd found in the desk.

"All right, then," said Tom. "We leave for the bus tour in a half hour."

"My hair!" said Sarah, heading for the bathroom.

Tom and Natalie returned to their room to continue unpacking. Aidan flopped on his bed and turned on the TV.

"Hey!" he said. "They have *Family Guy*!"

"Finally!" said his mother from the other room. "A sign of civilization!"

After three busy days filled with planned activities, Sarah and Aidan were finally able to get some time on their own. Telling their parents that they were going to explore the neighborhood—which was technically true, as Sarah pointed out to her brother—and promising to be back for dinner, they set out from the Cadogan in the late afternoon. It was a sunny and unusually warm day for June in England; the sidewalks were crowded with sightseeing tourists and Londoners trying to get home.

Sarah studied the Google map directions she'd printed out back in Pennsylvania.

"This way," she said, pointing south on Sloane Street. "Half a mile."

Less than fifteen minutes later they reached the north end of Draycott Place, a four-block street lined on both sides with red brick buildings.

"Okay," said Sarah. "In the book, the hotel was called the Scotland Landing. But according to Google there's no Scotland Landing here now."

"So why exactly are we here?"

"Because maybe one of these buildings used to be the Scotland Landing."

"How are we gonna find it?"

"We'll just walk down the street and see . . . whatever we see," said Sarah.

"Wow," said Aidan. "Clever."

Sarah rolled her eyes. "I'll take the left side of the street," she said. "You take the right."

They set off, one on each sidewalk, studying the buildings. They all looked pretty much alike; most appeared to be residences. After two blocks Sarah was starting to become discouraged. As they neared the end of the third block, her discouragement was turning to embarrassment.

What was I thinking? she wondered. *Getting all excited about a stupid story . . .*

"Sarah!"

Aidan's shout interrupted her thoughts. She looked across the street and saw him standing in front of a building with flags hanging from two poles jutting out over the entrance. A plaque on the wall to the left of the door identified the building as the Spanish consulate. Aidan, looking excited, was motioning for her to cross the street.

Sarah waited impatiently for a break in traffic and trotted across.

"What?" she said.

"Check this out," he said, pointing to the set of worn, white stone steps leading up to the consulate door.

"Steps," said Sarah. "Yeah, so?"

"Look at the top one."

Sarah moved nearer and studied the top step more closely. It had been worn down by countless footsteps, but Sarah could make out a faint design carved into the stone consisting of two interlocking letters.

"An *S* and an *L*," she whispered. She turned to Aidan. "Scotland Landing!"

"Could be," he said.

"You found it! How'd you even see this?"

"Keen powers of observation." He tapped his temple.

"Seriously," said Sarah.

"Okay," he said, "there was this really hot girl going in, and she had this ankle chain thingie, and I happened to be looking at her legs, and—"

"Okay, okay!" Sarah said. "Anyway, you found it." She started up the steps.

"Wait," said Aidan. "You can't just walk in there."

"Why not?" said Sarah. "Nobody's stopping me."

But somebody did stop her. In the consulate lobby, a uniformed guard manned a metal detector at a security-screening station. Beyond that was a counter where a dozen people waited in line.

"May I help you?" asked the guard, in accented English.

Sarah thought he was quite handsome, not at all like the security people at airports.

"Yes, I . . . that is, we . . ." Sarah stammered. "We'd like to, uh, come inside."

"Smooth," said Aidan, standing a few steps behind her.

"May I ask the nature of your business with the consulate?" said the guard.

"I . . . uh," said Sarah. "Just a moment please."

She turned and walked back to Aidan.

"Way to think on your feet," he said.

"Shut up," she snapped. "I'll think of something."

"Whatever it is, it's going to have to get you up to that counter in the next room."

"What are you talking about?"

"Take a look, Sherlock."

Sarah turned around, peering past the guard, who was watching them intently.

"I'm looking," she said. "So?"

"The archway. See it?"

"Yeah," said Sarah, looking at the stone archway above the counter.

"Look at the top of the arch."

Sarah looked. Then she gasped.

At the top of the arch, carved in stone, was the image of an eagle.

"'In the Place,'" said Sarah softly. "'In the Landing.'"

"'Beneath the eagle,'" said Aidan.

"We have to get in there," said Sarah. She stood for a moment, frowning in thought. Then she marched determinedly back to the guard.

"I'm studying Spanish in school," she said.

"*¿Sí? ¿Usted habla Español?*"

"What?"

Aidan snorted.

"Do you speak Spanish?"

"No . . . I mean, not yet. I just started."

"I see," said the guard, smiling slightly.

"And . . . I . . . I thought maybe I might get extra credit if I talked to a real Spanish person who works for the government. Of Spain."

"An interview," said the guard. He seemed quite amused.

"An interview! Exactly!" said Sarah.

"And do you have an appointment for this interview?"

"Ah, no."

"Unfortunately, you must have an appointment."

"But how do I make the appointment if I can't get inside?"

"You go there," he said, pointing to the line of people at the counter.

"Okay!" said Sarah. She glanced up toward the eagle. "We'll just get in line, then."

The guard held out a hand. "Your passports, please."

"What?"

"You must have passports to go inside."

Sarah, batting her eyes, smiled brightly at the guard and said, "Maybe you could let us in just to book the interview? And then we'll come back with our passports next time to actually do the interview."

"I am sorry," said the guard.

Sarah's shoulders slumped. "All right," she sighed. "We'll come back with the passports."

"I look forward to it, *señorita*," said the guard, with a slight bow.

In a moment they were back out on the sidewalk.

"Well, that went well," said Aidan. Mimicking Sarah's voice, he said: "Oh please let us in, Mister Handsome Spaniard!"

"Shut up," said Sarah. "We need to get our passports."

"How? Dad always has them in that stupid thing around his neck."

"I know," Sarah said. "But we only need them for, what, an hour or two? Technically, they're ours anyway, right?"

"Technically, I don't know."

Sarah turned to Aidan and put her hands on his shoulders. "Listen," she said. "We've come all this way, and now we're standing ten yards from the eagle. I am not going to leave without seeing what's beneath it."

"Also the guard is cute."

"That too."

"But how are we going to get the passports?"

"I don't know yet," said Sarah. She dropped her arms and started walking back toward the hotel. "But I'll think of something."

"That," said Aidan, mostly to himself, "is what I'm afraid of."

CHAPTER 3

BENEATH THE EAGLE

INSPIRATION STRUCK SARAH that night in the middle of a bite of hummus.

The Coopers were eating dinner at Dah Magreb, a Middle Eastern restaurant near their hotel with a sign outside advertising "Nightly Entertainment." There were no utensils; they ate with their hands, sitting on pillows on the floor. Halfway through their meal, to their dismay, the "entertainment" arrived: a somewhat overweight belly dancer emerged from behind a beaded curtain. She began gyrating, wiggling, and bouncing to unpleasant music blasting from a tinny sound system.

"Why is it so loud?" complained Sarah.

"*What?*" shouted both her mother and father.

"Never mind," said Sarah.

"Oh, no," said Aidan. "Don't look now, but jelly belly is heading our way." The belly dancer was indeed writhing toward their table. She was smiling at Tom Cooper in what she apparently thought was an inviting manner, but she looked more like a horse approaching the trough. Reaching their low table, she plucked at his sleeve, beckoning for him to stand up. He regarded her with a puzzled expression.

"What does she want?" he asked.

"I think," said Natalie, smiling, "she wants you to dance with her."

"Noooo," said Aidan, burying his face in his hands.

Sarah also frowned for a moment. Suddenly, her expression changed. "I think it's a great idea!" she said.

"You what?" said Aidan, jerking his head up. "Are you insane?" He looked around the restaurant; the other diners were watching all this with amusement.

"Shut up, Aidan," said Sarah, giving her brother a significant look. "C'mon, Dad! It'll make a great picture!" She pulled her father to his feet. "Mom, get the camera," she said. She shoved her father next to the belly dancer, who shook her hips violently at him. He stared at them with an expression of alarm. He was still holding his shish kebab.

"I'm going to kill myself," said Aidan.

Natalie, laughing, rummaged through her purse and pulled out the camera. She was aiming it at her husband when Sarah said, "Hold it! Let's take this off for the picture."

She grabbed the pouch that her father always wore suspended from a cord around his neck, much to the embarrassment of his children, who called it the Dork Sack. This was where he kept money and travel documents—including passports.

"Here, Aidan," she said, tossing it into her brother's lap. "Hold this for a sec, okay?" She gave him the look again.

"Uh . . . ah!" said Aidan, suddenly understanding. "Okay!"

Sarah moved in front of her brother, blocking sight of him from her parents, whose attention was fully focused on the belly dancer anyway. She took the shish kebab out of her father's hands, pinching its stick between her fingers.

"Say cheese, Tom," said Natalie.

"Feta cheese!" said Sarah, managing to win a grin from her mother.

But not from Tom. Nervously eyeing the writhing dancer, he attempted a smile, which came across as a wince.

The camera flashed, blinding Tom. "Got it," said Natalie.

"One more!" insisted Sarah. "For safety."

"Okay," said her mom. She raised the camera, held it steady, and it flashed again.

"How about one with Dad actually dancing?" urged Sarah.

"He *is* dancing," said Natalie. "That is your father dancing."

Tom had, in fact, begun to respond to the music by swaying back and forth. Realizing this, he stepped quickly away from the dancer.

33

"Yup, that will do it," said Aidan, now standing just behind Sarah. He handed the Dork Sack back to his father, then leaned closer to Sarah.

"Nice move," he whispered. "I got 'em."

The next morning, Sarah and Aidan left the hotel right after breakfast, having promised their parents that they would return by eleven A.M. when the family was due to leave for yet another historical tour. They walked directly to the consulate, reaching it shortly after the doors opened at nine. Manning the security station inside the entrance was the same guard they'd spoken with the day before. He smiled when he saw Sarah, and made a little bow.

"The Spanish student!" he said. "*Bienvenido, señorita.*"

"Likewise," she said, blushing.

"Likewise?" said Aidan.

Ignoring him, Sarah unzipped her backpack and took out the two passports Aidan had removed from the Dork Sack.

"Here you are," she said.

The guard studied the passports, then handed them back. He went through Sarah's backpack, then directed her and Aidan through the metal detector.

"That way," he said, pointing toward the counter. "The woman behind the counter will help you."

"Thank you," said Sarah, smiling brightly.

"*Con mucho gusto*," said the guard.

"Likewise!" said Aidan.

"Shut up," said Sarah.

The line at the counter was shorter this morning; there were only four people ahead of them. Behind the counter was a clerk, a serious-looking woman who wore her red-dyed hair in a tight bun. She was stamping some documents. The eagle in the archway was just in front of the counter, a few feet ahead of where Sarah and Aidan waited in line. Sarah looked up at it, then down, but all she saw beneath the eagle was a large man in a brown suit, now second in line.

"I don't get it," she said quietly to Aidan. "What's supposed to be beneath the eagle?"

Aidan was studying the floor.

"Beneath your feet," he said.

Sarah looked at the floor. It was made of marble tiles, each about two feet square, grayish-white with black veins running through them in random-looking patterns.

"Yeah? So what? It's a floor," she said. "Big deal."

"We're not under the eagle yet."

The line moved forward. Now the man in the brown suit was talking to the clerk; behind him was a young woman, and behind her stood Aidan and Sarah, last in line.

"Okay, *now* look," whispered Aidan, pointing at the tile directly under the young woman's sandals—and directly under the eagle.

35

Sarah looked, then frowned.

"What?" she whispered.

"That tile is different from the others," he said. "Don't you see? It's not as worn down, and the color's a little lighter. And the dark lines are . . . sharper."

Sarah studied the marble tile. "So one of the old tiles broke and they replaced it. So what?"

"Maybe," said Aidan. "Maybe not."

The clerk finished up with the man in the brown suit. The young woman ahead of them stepped up to the counter. Aidan and Sarah moved forward, now directly under the eagle. There still was nobody in line behind them.

"Quick," whispered Aidan. "Give me a piece of paper."

"Why?"

"Just give it to me."

Sarah unzipped the backpack, poked around inside for a moment, and withdrew a spiral notebook. She tore out a blank piece of paper and handed it to Aidan.

"Do you have a pencil?" he said.

"What are you doing?"

"Just give me a pencil," said Aidan, snapping his fingers.

"Okay, okay." Sarah rooted around in the backpack and produced a pencil. Aidan took it, then glanced back toward the guard station; the guard was talking with two people who'd just entered.

Perfect.

"May I help you?" said the clerk.

"Distract her," Aidan whispered to Sarah.

"But what should I—"

Aidan pushed her toward the clerk. "My sister has a question," he said.

"Right," said Sarah to the clerk. "I'm . . . I'm studying Spanish, and I need to interview a Spaniard. I mean a Spanish. I mean a Spanish person."

The clerk eyed Sarah doubtfully.

Aidan tugged on the backpack. Sarah clung to it, jerking it away from him.

"Let go," he hissed.

"Why should I?"

Aidan drew open the backpack's zipper farther, while at the same time he pulled on the backpack's strap. The clerk shook her head impatiently. *Americans.*

"Don't pull!" Sarah said to him. "You're going to—"

Aidan tore loose the backpack, but it tipped and dumped its contents.

"—spill it," said Sarah. "Nice move, moron."

"I'm sorry," said Aidan, not sounding at all sorry. "I'm going to pick it up now." He dropped into a crouch and cleared off the tile in the middle of the backpack's spilled contents: a Kleenex travel pack, three packs of gum, four tubes of mascara, some coins, hair ties, hair clips, a hair scrunchie, and the hair spray that Sarah carried everywhere. The counter prevented the clerk from seeing him. Aidan looked back; the guard remained occupied screening the two arrivals.

As Sarah stammered out a vague story about her needing an interview, Aidan placed the document onto the cleared section of tile. The dark lines on the tile showed clearly through the thin paper. Aidan moved the paper around, rotating it one way, then another. Suddenly, he stopped.

"Yes!" he exclaimed, a little too loudly.

"What?" said Sarah, looking down at her brother.

"Just getting this picked up!" Aidan said, still too loud. He stuffed a few items into the backpack.

Sarah turned back to the clerk, who was craning forward to peer over the counter. Sarah sidestepped to block her view of Aidan, who was now using the pencil to trace the lines in the stone.

"Sir!" Aidan jumped as the guard's stern voice called to him from the security area. "What are you doing?"

Aidan looked up; the guard was walking quickly toward him.

"What are you doing?" the guard repeated.

"Picking up what I spilled," said Aidan, now stuffing things into the backpack.

"With a pencil?"

"Oh, that," said Aidan, looking at the pencil in his hand

as though he'd just noticed it. "Ah . . . I'm tracing."

"You're tracing the floor?"

"The grain in the marble," said Aidan. "It's very . . . interesting." He continued tracing.

"Sir, this is not a museum or a cathedral," said the guard. "Please, no more tracing. Collect your things, please."

"But I'm almost done," said Aidan, working frantically.

The guard reached him and put his hand on Aidan's shoulder. "Sir," he said, "I'm afraid I must ask you to leave."

"Okay, okay," said Aidan, making a few last pencil strokes. "I'm done anyway." He gathered the remaining spilled items from around him and shot a look at Sarah as he stood, handing her the backpack.

"All right, then!" she said to the clerk. "You've been most helpful. Thank you."

"What about the interview?" asked the clerk.

"I . . . ah . . . I just remembered," said Sarah. "It's not Spanish I'm studying. It's Italian! I'm always getting those two languages mixed up. So sorry! Thank you! Bye!" She turned and followed Aidan, who was walking quickly toward the door. Once outside, Aidan burst out laughing.

"Italian?" he said. "*Italian?*"

"Hey, it was the best I could do. But what was with spilling everything? What were you doing there on the floor?"

"Tracing," said Aidan, grinning proudly. "And you won't believe what I got."

"What did you get? Tell me!"

Aidan held up the piece of paper. "I have no idea," he said.

CHAPTER 4

MAGILL'S MESSAGE

"LET ME SEE IT!" said Sarah, grabbing for the piece of paper.

"Not here," said Aidan, pulling it away. "He's watching."

Sarah looked back toward the consulate and saw the security officer standing at the top of the steps, regarding them curiously. They walked quickly away, not looking back until they had gone two blocks.

Aidan motioned her into a coffee shop. She ordered a decaf latte. Aidan bought something with a complicated Italian name that tasted like a vanilla milkshake.

"Okay," said Sarah. "Now let me see." Aidan handed her the tracing he'd made from the floor. It was covered with strange lines, very much like the document they'd found in the desk.

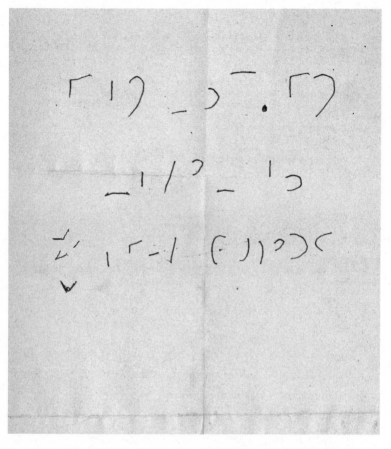

Sarah studied it for a moment, then said, "Great. Before we had one piece of paper with a bunch of random lines. Now we have two. We're really making progress."

"Okay," said Aidan, "but it has to mean something. I mean, this guy Magill went to all that trouble . . ."

Sarah dug into the backpack and pulled out the paper from the desk. She laid it down next to the tracing.

In the Place
In the Landing
Beneath the Eagle
Beneath your feet

Magill

"Same thing, right?" she said. "Random lines."

"But they're not the same," said Aidan.

"No," said Sarah.

"Maybe you have to fold them," said Aidan. "Let me . . ." He reached for the papers; in doing so, he bumped his drink, splashing some out of the cup. Sarah yanked the papers away from the spill.

"Watch it!" she said.

"Sorry," said Aidan. "I was just gonna—"

"Hey," said Sarah. "Look."

Aidan looked. Sarah, in pulling the papers away, had held them up to the window, one atop the other. The sunlight was streaming through them both.

The dark lines were now intermingled.

"Are you thinking what I'm thinking?" said Sarah.

"I have no idea what you're thinking," said Aidan, mopping up his spill.

Sarah, ignoring him, had pressed the two papers against the window and was now manipulating them—sliding them back and forth, flipping them over, rotating them, trying various combinations.

Suddenly, she stopped. She was now holding the papers still, pinned against the glass.

"Oh my god," she said. "Aidan, look."

Aidan looked—and gasped. The random-looking marks had aligned to form numbers and letters.

512257.52

21732.15

☆ FEED GUARDS
↓

In the Place
In the Landing
Beneath the Eagle
Beneath your feet.

Magill

"Whoa," said Aidan. "What is that? Are those numbers money? Because if they're money, we are rich."

"We don't know it's money," Sarah said. "What's this star supposed to mean? And the arrow? And what about 'Feed guards'? What guards?"

"I dunno," said Aidan. "Maybe they're guarding the money? I really hope it's money."

Sarah got out a pen and carefully traced the floor marks onto Magill's document, which now carried the full message. They both studied it some more.

"I don't think the numbers are money," said Sarah. "It seems like they're too exact."

"Maybe it's foreign money," said Aidan. "Like pounds, or kilograms."

"Kilogram is a weight, you moron."

"Oh yeah? Which moron figured out what was under the eagle?"

Sarah, not having a good answer to that, said, "We'll have to figure this out later. We need to get back or Mom and Dad'll kill us for making them miss the tour. And we don't want Dad realizing we took our passports."

"Good point."

They left the coffee shop, walking back toward the hotel.

"So what tour are we going on today?" said Aidan.

"Some boat tour. On the Thames."

"Great! We can ride past another batch of old buildings

and Dad can get all excited about how old they are."

"Yup," agreed Sarah. She was still looking at the document. "But while we're on the boat, we can try to figure out what this means."

"Yeah, right," scoffed Aidan. "Maybe the tour guide will give us a clue."

As it turned out, that was almost how it happened.

They'd been on the tour boat for about an hour, motoring past the Houses of Parliament, the London Eye, the Tower of London, Tower Bridge, and many other points of interest—at least of interest to Tom and Natalie Cooper, who were fascinated. Sarah and Aidan, sitting in the row behind them, were not so excited—Aidan was playing a video game on his phone, while Sarah was surreptitiously studying Magill's strange message.

As the winding Thames made a sweeping left turn, the guide, who'd been narrating the tour through the boat's public-address system, announced that they were approaching Greenwich, site of the Royal Observatory. The guide spoke in a rich baritone voice with the kind of British accent that makes even the simplest statement sound brilliant to Americans. Tom and Natalie were hanging on his every word.

"The observatory," intoned the guide, "is the location of

the prime meridian, zero degrees of longitude. All longitude on Earth is measured from here."

"How about that, kids?" said Tom Cooper, turning around to Sarah and Aidan. "Hey! No electronics, young man!"

"What?" said Aidan, looking up from his game. "Oh, yeah." He quickly pocketed the phone before his father confiscated it.

"We're at zero degrees!" Tom said.

Aidan's brow furrowed. "What are you talking about? It's got to be eighty degrees out."

Sarah snorted.

"Not temperature," said Tom. "Zero degrees longitude."

"Whatitude?"

"Longitude. You know, longitude and latitude? For navigation?"

Aidan stared at his father blankly.

"Doesn't your phone have a GPS?" said Tom.

That sparked Aidan's interest. "My phone? Yeah," said Aidan. "3-G, Wi-Fi, GPS."

"So turn it on," said Tom.

"I thought you said no electronics."

"I'm making an exception for your edification."

Aidan turned on the phone and GPS. It took a few moments to acquire the satellite signal; then a map of London appeared with a blue dot in the center indicating their location.

"There!" said Tom, leaning over to point out some numbers at the bottom of the small screen. "See? Zero degrees. That's our longitude."

Sarah's interest was piqued. She leaned over to look.

"So . . . what are those numbers after the zero?" she said.

"Those are minutes and seconds," said Tom.

"The what?" said Aidan. "It tells the time?"

"It's not time," said Tom, "not when you're talking about latitude and longitude. Each degree is divided into sixty minutes, and each minute is divided into sixty seconds. The seconds can be broken down into tenths or hundredths. That's how you can pinpoint exactly where you are."

"Where I am," said Aidan, "is confused."

Sarah took Aidan's phone. "So," she said, "right now our longitude is zero degrees, zero minutes, and fourteen point zero-five seconds, and the W means . . ."

"West," said Tom. "We're just a tiny bit west of the prime meridian, which is zero degrees longitude."

"And this other number," said Sarah. "Starting with fifty-one. That's the latitude?"

"Right," said Tom. "Fifty-one degrees, twenty-nine minutes, and nine point ninety-two seconds north of the equator."

"That's very interesting," said Sarah.

"It is?" said Aidan.

"Oh, yes," said Sarah, handing the phone back to Aidan. "Very."

Tom Cooper, thrilled to have his children actually listening to him, launched into a lecture on the history of navigation. Aidan took his phone back and returned to his video game. Sarah, out of politeness, pretended to be interested in her father, but all she was thinking about was getting back to the hotel and turning on her laptop.

⚓

"So what you're saying," said Aidan, studying the document, "is that these long numbers—"

"—are not money, but latitude and longitude," said Sarah, waiting for her laptop to come to life. "A location. A place. Didn't you notice? The latitude on the boat was fifty-one degrees. That's also the first number on the paper."

"Which means . . ."

"Which means it's the same distance north from the equator as we are. And the longitudes are close—it was zero degrees on the boat, and it's only two degrees on the paper. So I think whatever it is, it's around here."

"Where around here?"

"That's what we're about to find out."

"How?"

"Google Earth." The laptop finished booting up. Sarah

clicked on the blue-and-white orb that was the Google Earth icon; in a moment the screen was filled with an image of the Earth as seen from space. Sarah positioned the cursor over the box labeled "Fly to" and said, "Okay, read me those numbers."

It took Sarah several minutes of trial and error to figure out the right format—she needed a north latitude and a west longitude, with spaces between the degrees, minutes, and seconds. When she did that and pressed ENTER, the globe began to move.

"Okay," said Sarah. "Here we go."

The globe rotated, stopping when south-central England was at the center of the screen.

"I knew it!" exulted Sarah. "It's nearby."

She and her brother watched intently as the screen zoomed in, closer and closer, revealing, in ever-greater detail, satellite images of towns and fields. It stopped over what looked like a forest, partially surrounded by fields. The location that Sarah had entered was at the center, marked by a small four-by-four grid.

"There it is," said Sarah.

"There what is?" said Aidan.

"I don't know," admitted Sarah. She zoomed the view out, revealing more of the surrounding area, including nearby towns, their names appearing as labels.

"Monckton Farleigh?" read Aidan, chuckling. "Farleigh

Wick? What kind of names are those? They sound like rock stars."

"They're towns," said Sarah. She zoomed out a bit more. "Bath!" she said.

"What? All we have is a shower."

"Not that kind of bath. Bath," she said, pointing, "is a city. Right here. It's only . . ." She studied the scale at the bottom left of the screen. ". . . a couple of miles from Magill's location."

"So?"

"So there are historic tours to Bath. There are brochures downstairs. Historic tours, as in you-know-who." She nodded toward their parents' room.

"You think Mom and Dad'll actually want to go there?"

"I think they will after you and I tell them about all the fascinating history in Bath."

"I don't know about any fascinating history in Bath."

Sarah had opened Google and was typing in *historic sites bath england.*

"You will," she said.

CHAPTER 5

THE WOODS

"Who's up for one more tour?" said Tom, waving a brochure at his wife and children, who were sitting on a sofa in the living room of the bed-and-breakfast where they were staying in Bath. "It's a walking tour. Bath by Night."

"Wouldn't Bath by night be the same as Bath by day, only darker?" said Aidan.

Tom sighed, then looked toward Sarah.

"Dad, I'm really tired," she said, with a huge yawn. "All that pedaling today wore me out."

"Well," said Tom, "you were the ones who insisted on renting bicycles."

"I know, Dad," said Sarah. "And I can't wait to ride around some more tomorrow. But I think I'm going to bed early tonight."

"Me too," said Aidan, stretching dramatically.

Natalie frowned and said, "Are you two all right?" It was unlike her children to go to bed early.

"Really, Mom, I'm fine," said Sarah. She rose from the sofa. "G'night," she said, heading for the room she and Aidan shared.

"Me too," said Aidan, following his sister.

"We'll see you at breakfast, then," said Tom. He turned to his wife. "What about you, Nat? Up for a walking tour?"

"To be honest," said Natalie, "I'm pretty beat myself. What I'm up for is a nice cup of tea, a book, and bed."

"Okay, then," said Tom, a bit disappointed. "I guess it's going to be a quiet night."

⁂

Sarah and Aidan waited an hour and a half to be sure their parents had settled in for the night. As the minutes crawled by, Sarah verified, for the fifteenth time, that Aidan had entered the coordinates correctly into his phone's GPS. She also checked and rechecked her backpack to make sure it contained the supplies they'd bought earlier that day while their parents were antique-shopping—two flashlights, some cheese sandwiches, chocolate bars, four bottles of water, and, from a camping store next to the supermarket, a "Survival Kit in a Tin." This was a small, vacuum-sealed metal container, about the size of a coffee can, packed with supposedly useful items—a whistle, duct tape, a fishhook and line, a compass, first-aid supplies, and so on. Sarah thought it was stupid—"What, you think we're suddenly going to need a fish?"—but Aidan thought it was cool and insisted that they buy it.

At nine thirty P.M. Sarah, wearing the backpack, quietly opened the door to their room and stepped into the hall. She stood outside her parents' door for a moment, listening; hearing nothing, she gestured for Aidan to come out. They closed their door gently and tiptoed down the hall, through the empty living room, and outside. They went around the side of the building to the bike rack, unlocked the combination cable lock, and freed their rental bikes.

Sarah got out the Google map she'd had the concierge print out back at their London hotel. According to Google, they were three miles from the location indicated on Magill's document, although by road it was more like five miles. They wheeled their bikes to the street. At the moment there was no traffic. The night was cool and clear; a bright half moon was rising.

"This way," said Sarah, pointing up the street.

Aidan hesitated. "Are we really doing this?" he said.

"What do you mean?"

"I mean, are we crazy?" said Aidan. "Sneaking out in the middle of the night in the middle of England to go find something that . . . that we don't even know what it is? Because of some weird old piece of paper? I mean, it seemed like a fun idea, but now that we're actually doing it, it just seems a little . . . crazy."

"Maybe," said Sarah. "But after all this work, we're here, three miles away from the place that piece of paper is taking us to. You can chicken out if you want. But I'm gonna see what it is."

"I'm not chickening out," said Aidan.

"Then come on," said Sarah. She mounted her bike and began pedaling toward the end of the street.

Aidan, with less enthusiasm, mounted his bike and followed.

"Why couldn't I have a normal sister?" he said, mostly to himself.

They rode on wide, well-lit streets, sticking to the sidewalk. They came to London Road and followed it out of Bath. In two miles the road turned gently right, following the curve of the River Avon and becoming Bradford Road. Here the setting was more rural, the road passing through fields and woods; there was no sidewalk, so Sarah and Aidan had to dismount and stand by the roadside to avoid the occasional car speeding through the night. The road's name changed again, colorfully, to "Sally in the Wood"; it entered a forest, which closed in on both sides, blotting out the moon. Now, every hundred yards or so, Sarah stopped to check the GPS coordinates.

The fifth time she stopped, she said, "Okay, here."

Aidan looked around at the looming trees.

"What do you mean, here?" he said. "There's nothing here."

"We're at the right latitude," she said. "Now we just need to walk that way"—she pointed at the forest on the left—"about fifteen hundred feet."

"What about the bikes?"

"We'll hide them in the woods by the road. Nobody's going to be walking through here tonight."

"Yeah," said Aidan. "You'd have to be insane to be walking through here tonight."

Ignoring him, Sarah carried her bike a few yards into the woods and propped it against a tree. Aidan did the same. Sarah got the flashlights out of the backpack and handed one to Aidan. They turned them on and shone the beams into the woods. There was no path—only trees, underbrush, and shadows. To Aidan the flashlights somehow seemed to make the woods seem even darker.

"Okay," said Sarah, setting off. Aidan, with a glance back, followed quickly. They trudged forward on a course roughly perpendicular to the road, sometimes veering to avoid thicker patches of brush and bramble. Sarah checked the GPS constantly, making small corrections. After about fifteen minutes she slowed, then stopped, then began moving in a slow circle, her eyes riveted to the screen. Then she stopped again.

"It's somewhere around here," she said.

They swept their flashlight beams in circles.

"All I see is trees," said Aidan.

"It might not be this exact spot," said Sarah. "Look around."

They separated, but not by much; Aidan had no intention of getting out of sight of his sister in these woods. They wandered among the dark trees, sweeping their light beams left and right. Ten minutes passed.

"I think we should go," said Aidan. "There's nothing here but trees."

"There has to be something here," said Sarah. "There *has* to."

"Maybe there was something once, and it's gone now."

"I'm going to keep looking." Sarah started off in a new direction.

"Okay, you do that. I'm going to . . ." Aidan's light beam fell on a looming shape ahead. "Sarah! Come here!"

"What is it?" said Sarah, trotting through the brush toward Aidan.

"I'm not sure," said Aidan. "But it's not a tree."

Sarah reached him and saw that he was aiming his flashlight beam at an outcropping of massive boulders, some ten feet high. She moved closer. There was a narrow space between the nearest two boulders. She shone her light into it and saw that the space closed up after only a few feet. She started walking to her left around the outcropping, playing her light on the boulders. Between the fourth and fifth one she came to a bigger opening, three feet high and perhaps a foot wide at most. She crouched down and shone her light inside. She saw a space large enough to crawl in; after a few feet it turned to the right.

She took off her backpack and pushed it through the opening.

"What are you doing?" Aidan asked nervously.

"I'm going in."

"In there?"

"Yep," said Sarah, dropping to her hands and knees.

"I don't think that's a good idea," said Aidan.

But Sarah was already squeezing her shoulders through the opening. In a moment she was completely inside. Aidan watched nervously as she crawled forward, disappearing as the crawlway turned right. He glanced around nervously at the dark woods. He did not like being alone out there.

"Sarah?" he called into the opening. "What do you see?"

There was no answer.

"Sarah!" he repeated, frightened now. "Are you okay?"

Another pause, and then Sarah's voice, muffled, excited: "Aidan! Come here!"

"Why?"

"Just come here."

Reluctantly, Aidan dropped to his hands and knees and

pushed through the opening, feeling the cold, rough stone through his jacket. Shining his flashlight ahead, he worked his way around the narrow right turn. The space became wider there and the path slanted downward, giving Aidan enough headroom to rise to a crouch. He could see a slightly larger area ahead, lit by the light from Sarah's flashlight. He moved toward her, ducking to keep from hitting his head on the hard stone above him.

"What?" he said.

"Look!" Sarah said, moving aside so he could see where she was aiming her flashlight.

Aidan looked.

"Oh my god," he said.

Sarah's light was shining on a door.

It was made of dark-gray metal and it stood in a roughly rectangular space framed by massive boulders.

It had two symbols drawn on it: a star, and an arrow pointing down.

"Oh my god," said Aidan, again.

Without a word, Sarah found a stick on the ground and used it to brush away the cobwebs from the door. Scales of rust fell off as the stick scraped against them. Sarah then crouched and used the stick to push aside several inches of dirt accumulated at the bottom of the door.

"What exactly are you doing?" said Aidan.

"We're going inside."

"You think that's a good idea? There could be bats in there. With rabies. If you get rabies you have to get like six hundred shots. In the stomach."

"If you're chicken, you can stay here. I'll go in alone."

"Stop calling me chicken. I am not chicken."

"Good. Then you can go first."

Aidan frowned; this was not going as he'd planned. He stepped forward and pushed gently on the door. It didn't budge.

"It's locked," he said, relieved.

"Step aside," said Sarah. She raised her right foot and kicked the door hard. It eased open a few inches, still partially blocked by the dirt around the bottom. Sarah kicked again. And again. With each kick the door opened a little wider. On the fourth kick it swung fully open, its rusted hinges groaning. Sarah and Aidan peered inside at a narrow, low-ceilinged, pitch-black tunnel, sloping downward. They felt a slight movement of dank air wafting up toward them, stale and sour. There was another odor, vaguely familiar to both of them, although neither mentioned it.

Like a wet dog, thought Aidan.

"Go ahead," said Sarah.

Aidan shined his light down into the tunnel. He couldn't see where it ended—only cold, dark stone.

"I don't know about this," he said.

Sarah clucked like a chicken.

"Shut up," said Aidan. He dropped onto his belly and wriggled forward. The fit was tight; his shoulders scraped against the tunnel walls. He could not turn around now even if he'd wanted to—which he did. But he hated the thought of chickening out in front of his sister. So, fighting back his fear, he wriggled forward, aiming the flashlight ahead.

Sarah crouched at the entrance, watching her brother slowly move deeper into the tunnel; she almost felt sorry for him. After a minute all she could see of Aidan was a shadowy blob moving deep in the narrow tunnel, like a cork in the neck of a bottle.

Suddenly, the blob stopped. Aidan's silhouette flickered as he waved the flashlight around.

"Whoa!" he called. "You're not going to believe this!"

"What?" shouted Sarah.

But Aidan was gone; he'd apparently pulled himself into a larger space. Sarah could hear him clambering to his feet.

Sarah took a deep breath, dropped to her stomach, pushed the backpack into the tunnel, and began wriggling after it, pausing to brush spiderwebs from her face. From ahead she could hear Aidan shouting something, his words lost in a jumble of echoes. Finally, she came to the opening into which Aidan had disappeared. She poked her head through.

"No way!" she said. Aidan was standing proudly inside

a much larger tunnel; it looked big enough to drive a truck through.

"What do you think?" he said, shining his light around. The tunnel stretched so far in both directions that the flashlight beam simply faded into darkness.

"What is this?" she said, her voice echoing off the hard stone walls.

"Mister Magill's private dungeon," said Aidan.

Sarah pulled herself forward and got to her feet.

"Seriously," she said. "Why is this here?"

"It must be a mine," said Aidan. "Or it was a mine. It's old. No lights. No equipment. Who knows how long this has been here."

"Still think I'm crazy?"

"You don't really want me to answer that."

Sarah dragged her heel on the dusty floor, drawing a line from one side of the tunnel to the other.

"What are you doing?"

"Marking our entrance," she said, pointing to the small hole in the wall they'd crawled through. It would be easy to miss.

"Now what?" said Aidan.

"We look for clues," said Sarah.

"Clues?"

"There has to be something. Magill got us this far. Somehow he'll let us know what to do." She pointed to her right. "We'll start this way." Shouldering the backpack, Sarah started into the tunnel, swinging her flashlight back and forth, the beam painting bright lines across the dark stone. She'd gone no more than fifteen feet when she stopped suddenly, her flashlight aimed at the tunnel ceiling directly overhead.

"There it is," she said.

Aidan, joining her, looked up. Sarah's light was shining on the image of a star, drawn in faded white paint. Next to it was an arrow, pointing in the direction they'd been moving.

"Let's go," said Sarah.

"Wait," said Aidan.

His sister looked at him impatiently and snapped, "What?"

"I just . . . I'm wondering if this is a good idea. We're getting farther and farther from where we came in."

"We're also getting closer and closer to whatever Magill's leading us to."

"Yeah, but . . ."

"But what?"

"I just don't like this, that's what."

"So what do you want to do? Stay here?"

Aidan looked back into the blackness of the tunnel.

"No," he said. "Not alone."

"Then come on." She turned and started walking again, Aidan following unhappily. They walked for several minutes in silence, Sarah sweeping her flashlight beam continuously over the walls and ceiling, Aidan glancing back often, the only sound in the tunnel the echoes of their scuffling footsteps. After about fifty yards the tunnel was intersected by another, branching off to the left. On the ceiling they found another painted star and arrow, this time pointing to the left. With her heel, Sarah drew an arrow into the dusty floor, pointing back to where they'd come from.

The new tunnel was slightly smaller, but still cavernous.

"How far do you plan on going?" said Aidan.

"That's up to Mister Magill."

"But I mean, if we don't find something . . . at some point we're going to turn back, right?"

"Listen," she said, swinging her flashlight beam toward Aidan's face, "if you don't—"

Aidan screamed.

Sarah jerked violently, nearly dropping the flashlight.

"Do not do that!" she said. "What is wrong with—"

"I saw eyes!" interrupted Aidan, breathless, terrified. "We have to get out of here now."

"What are you talking about? What eyes?"

"Yellow eyes. Right when you moved your flashlight, I saw them. Over there!" He shined his flashlight ahead. They both looked, but the flashlight revealed only the empty tunnel, fading into blackness.

"There's nothing there," she said.

"There was. I'm telling you. A pair of yellow eyes, close to the ground."

"You imagined it, 'cause you're scared."

"Okay, listen," said Aidan. "We'll both turn off our lights."

"And that's going to accomplish what?"

"Then I'll turn mine back on. But this time we're both looking straight ahead."

"Aidan . . ."

"Just turn off your light, okay?"

Sarah sighed and switched off her flashlight, as did Aidan. They now stood in total blackness.

"I really don't see what—"

"Shh!" Aidan hissed. "Just wait."

Ten seconds passed. Twenty.

Aidan turned on his light, the beam filling the long tunnel.

Nothing. Cobwebs, some dust swirling in the air, but no yellow eyes.

"Satisfied?" she said.

"No. I saw something."

"Or not," said Sarah, starting into the branch tunnel. Aidan had no choice but to follow; the last thing he wanted now was to be alone. After a few minutes they came to another branch tunnel, and then another, but there were no star-and-arrow markers so they kept going straight. At the third tunnel, branching right, they found a marker directing them to the right; at the next branch they went left. Aidan glanced back constantly as they moved deeper and deeper into the dark labyrinth.

"Sarah," he whispered. "This is too far."

She didn't turn around. "We are not turning back now," she snapped. "Anyway, I think we're coming to some kind of room."

She was right; in a few yards they entered a high-ceilinged, roughly square chamber, its floor strewn with rocks large and small. Tunnels branched off in all four directions. Sarah drew her heel mark into the dirt to indicate how they'd entered.

Aidan was shining his light around. Suddenly, he froze.

"Oh, no," he whispered.

"What now?" said Sarah.

Aidan, his hand shaking, was aiming his flashlight at the floor. "Look," he said. "I told you I saw eyes!"

Sarah's eyes followed his flashlight beam. She swallowed. The dirt floor was covered in animal tracks. Large ones.

"Are those dog footprints?" she said, her voice low.

"If they are," said Aidan, "it's a big dog. Or many big dogs. We need to get out of here."

"These could be really old."

"I saw eyes, Sarah!"

Sarah flashed her light around the chamber. The beam swept across something in the corner. Sarah's eyes widened.

"Aidan! Look!" Her words echoed down all four tunnels. Her beam was fixed on a rock in the corner. On it was the star-and-arrow sign. The arrow pointed down.

"I really think we need to leave," said Aidan, his eyes still on the animal tracks.

Sarah paid no attention. She was walking to the sign.

"It's here," she said.

"What's here?"

"It's pointing straight down. There's no tunnel or anything. It has to be here."

"Sarah, there's big animals down—"

"Right here," she said, digging her heel into the dirt.

"We need to—"

"Dig," said Sarah, dropping to her knees.

"Sarah, we don't—"

"You start there," she said, pointing. "I'll start here. We work toward each other." She propped her flashlight on a rock, then found two flattish rocks. She handed one to Aidan and began digging, starting directly below where the arrow pointed. She dug down about six inches and continued toward Aidan, who was digging unhappily but rapidly, making a shallow trench perpendicular to hers.

When their trenches connected, he said, "What now?"

"Dig deeper," she said, attacking the dirt again. Aidan sighed and did the same. After a few minutes they paused for breath. Sarah was about to resume digging when Aidan put his hand on her arm.

"Did you hear that?" he whispered.

"What?"

"Like . . . breathing."

They both listened intently.

"Dig," she said. "Quickly!"

"You *did* hear it!" he said.

"Just dig!"

The dirt flew in all directions. They had now made a roughly circular hole about a yard across and more than a foot deep. Sarah glanced up to check the position of the arrow.

Clank!

Aidan's rock had hit metal. He pounded it twice more.

Clank! Clank!

Now they both dug furiously, scooping up loose dirt with their hands and hurling it aside. They uncovered a rectangular metal plate about the size of a sheet of paper, with words engraved on it. Sarah brushed off the dirt and shone her light on it. Together, she and Aidan read the words.

Use it wisely, or leave it be. Use it wrong, and death to thee.

"Maybe we shouldn't touch it," said Aidan.

"What are you talking about?"

"Death," said Aidan. "It says death." He started to rise. Sarah grabbed his wrist, stopping him.

"No," she said. "Listen to me, Aidan. We were meant for this. And this is meant for us. Look at what we've gone through to find this. He wanted us to find this."

"He wanted someone to. Not us."

"But it *is* us," she said, still holding his wrist. "We're going to find out what this is. And whatever it is, I promise: we're going to be wise about it."

Aidan looked at his sister. Then his gaze shifted slightly, over her shoulder. He slowly lifted his flashlight. Sarah watched as the color drained from his face.

"Aidan?" she whispered. "What is it?"

Then she heard the growl.

CHAPTER 6

THE GUARDS

$\mathcal{S}$ARAH FROZE, STARING INTO her brother's terrified face.

"What is it?" she whispered.

"It's not a dog."

Slowly, Sarah turned her head. Somehow she managed to suppress a scream when she saw what Aidan had been looking at.

A wolf.

A large wolf.

It was less than ten feet away, its eyes glowing bright in the beam of Aidan's flashlight. Its mouth hung open, revealing a pink tongue and jagged, glinting teeth.

There were more wolves behind it. Sarah counted seven in all. Their fur was matted and mangy. They looked skinny. Most of all, they looked . . . hungry. Their glowing eyes were fixed, unblinking, on the humans. Their black noses flexed, sampling the scent of the intruders.

"Oh my god," said Aidan, his voice on the edge of panic. "What are we gonna do?"

"Listen," said Sarah, forcing herself to speak calmly. "We are going to get out of here. We are going to move very, very slowly. But first we are going to get whatever this thing is we just found."

"Are you insane?"

"Just watch the wolves," said Sarah. With a deliberate movement she turned back to the hole she and Aidan had dug. She reached down, hooked a finger under the metal plate in the dirt, and gently pulled it aside. Beneath it was a cubical metal box, perhaps six inches on a side, its golden color glinting in the flashlight beam. She picked it up; it felt solid and seemed heavy for its size. She unzipped her backpack and put the box inside.

"They're coming closer," said Aidan.

Sarah turned slowly back. The alpha wolf, the leader, was now several steps nearer. The other wolves had moved forward behind it.

The wolves were blocking their exit from the chamber.

Sarah slowly raised her flashlight. She aimed it directly into the alpha wolf's eyes. He backed up a few feet, growling.

"They don't like the light," she said.

The alpha, still growling, moved a step closer.

"This isn't going to get us out of here," said Aidan. "We

have to get past them. I wish Magill had mentioned there'd be wolves in—"

"'Feed the guards,'" said Sarah suddenly.

"You mean . . ."

"The wolves are the guards," said Sarah. "I hope." Keeping her gaze, and her flashlight beam, on the growling alpha wolf, she slipped out of the backpack and handed it to Aidan. "Get the sandwiches," she said. "Hurry."

Aidan unzipped the backpack and found the bag of sandwiches. As he pulled it out, the survival tin fell at his feet. He picked it up and passed the bag to Sarah, who tore it open with her teeth, pulled out a cellophane-wrapped cheese sandwich, and tossed it toward the alpha wolf. He took one sniff, then snapped it up in a single bite, wrapping and all. Instantly, the other wolves surrounded him, looking for their share. He snarled at them, and they backed off—but not far. The wolves were still blocking the path to the exit tunnel. And Sarah and Aidan had one less sandwich. There were two left.

"We need to back them up," said Sarah. She shone the flashlight at the alpha. It growled, but this time it did not move.

"I think it's getting used to the light," she said. "We need something else to scare it."

Aidan looked at the survival tin. "Matches," he said.

"What?"

"I think there's matches in here." He yanked the metal tab on the survival kit and pulled off the lid. The tin was packed with survival items. He poked through them and found a metal cylinder labeled MATCHES and a small metal sleeve labeled RAZOR BLADE. He took these out and put the tin back into the backpack.

"I got matches," he said, opening the cylinder. "There're six of them. And there's a razor."

"I don't think a razor will do much good," said Sarah, eyeing the wolves. "I'm gonna try to move them so we can get past." She raised a sandwich over her head. Seven pairs of hungry wolf eyes followed her motion. She held the sandwich aloft for a few seconds, then threw it to her right. In an instant the wolves were on it, a snarling cyclone of mangy fur and snapping jaws. The alpha wolf and several others got pieces of sandwich; the rest got only bites and scratches, blood seeping through their fur.

The pack had moved a bit, but not enough for Sarah and Aidan to get past. The alpha stood still, watching them intently. Just behind him the other six paced restlessly, baring their teeth. The smell of food and blood was in the air.

Sarah had one sandwich left. She tore it in half.

"When I throw this," she said, "we head for the tunnel. If they come after us I'll shine my flashlight at them, and you light a match."

"Don't turn your back on them," said Aidan. "I saw this on TV. They go for your heels. That's how they drop you. They snap your tendons so you can't move. Then they eat you."

"I did not need to know that," said Sarah.

"They eat you alive."

"Shut up, okay? And get a match ready."

Aidan held a match head against the striking strip on the side of the cylinder. Sarah drew back her arm and threw a half sandwich across the chamber. The wolves were on it before it landed, their snarls echoing off the rock walls. Sarah and Aidan, walking sideways so they faced the wolves, moved quickly toward the tunnel.

In seconds the sandwich was gone, the battle over. The alpha wolf, licking his lips, turned back and spotted Aidan and Sarah on the move. He ran toward them, growling, the others right behind. Sarah's flashlight beam slowed him, but only for a second; he was coming this time.

"Now!" she said.

Aidan drew the match along the striking strip. The tip hissed and flared white. Instantly, the alpha stopped and retreated a few feet, whimpering. Sarah and Aidan moved a few steps closer to the tunnel. The match flame turned orange and began to wane. The alpha growled and began moving forward again. Sarah tore a piece off the remaining half sandwich.

"I don't have much sandwich left," she said.

"So make it count," said Aidan, preparing a second match.

All the wolves were coming now.

"One . . ." said Aidan. "Two . . ."

On "three" Sarah tossed the chunk of sandwich and Aidan struck the match. Again the wolves were both scared and distracted, but only for a few seconds. Sarah and Aidan had now reached the tunnel entrance. The alpha wolf was keeping his distance from the waning flame, but never took his eyes off them. The other wolves, having finished the sandwich scrap, were just behind their leader.

"One more piece of sandwich," said Sarah.

"Three more matches," said Aidan.

"That's not enough to get us out of here."

"I've got an idea," said Aidan. He quickly explained his plan. He shouldered the backpack by a single strap, readied a match, and said, "One . . . two . . . three."

Sarah threw the last piece of sandwich right into the midst of the wolves. At the same moment, Aidan lit the third match, crouched, and stood it up in the dirt floor.

Aidan and Sarah turned and took off running as a vicious fight erupted behind them. Aidan glanced back once and was relieved to see that the tunnel was empty; the match flame was holding back the alpha. For now.

Sprinting, panting, their flashlight beams waving wildly,

Sarah and Aidan reached the first heel mark and turned right. From behind they heard snarling; the wolves were in the first tunnel. They kept running, their breath coming in gasps. The snarls grew suddenly louder. Aidan and Sarah looked back. The wolves had entered the new tunnel and were coming fast.

"Hurry!" said Sarah, starting to run again. Aidan followed, but they were both thinking the same thing: *We can't outrun them.*

Aidan felt the backpack, the heavy golden box banging into him as he ran. He made a decision: he was going to throw the box at the wolves. He knew Sarah wouldn't agree with that decision, but he wasn't going to let himself get eaten to save a box. He jammed his flashlight into his pocket. Clutching the matches and razor in one hand, he used the other to unzip the backpack. He glanced back and nearly screamed; the wolves were only yards away. He reached into the backpack; his hand fell on something. He yanked it out. A candy bar.

Sarah had reached the next heel mark in the dirt and Aidan followed as she turned left. At the same time he bit off a chunk of the candy bar, wrapper and all, and spat it at the alpha wolf, which had just rounded the corner. The wolf stopped, startled; it bent to snap up the treat, snarling at the other wolves as they went for it also. Aidan quickly bit off and spat out three more chunks, then threw the last piece at the wolves. A vicious fight broke out. Aidan turned and ran after Sarah, the howls of the wolves echoing in the tunnel behind him. As he ran, he groped in the backpack and found another candy bar.

They reached the third heel mark and turned right, their lungs burning as they sprinted for the finish line. The wolves were coming again, gaining ground fast. Aidan spat out more pieces of candy bar. This seemed to slow the wolves, but not as much as the first time.

Sarah reached the last heel mark, indicating the small opening through which they'd entered the tunnel complex. She skidded to a stop and shone her light back at the oncoming wolves. She hesitated.

"Go!" shouted Aidan.

"But they'll get you!"

"Just go!"

As Sarah dropped to her belly and wiggled into the crawlway, Aidan lit the fourth match and turned to face the wolves. They stopped, but this time the alpha came much closer to the flame than he had before.

Aidan backed up, his foot finding the opening to the crawlway.

The match burned lower.

Aidan knew Sarah was right: by the time he turned and crawled into the hole the wolves would get him.

He decided his only chance was to throw the golden box

at the alpha wolf. Maybe he could injure it enough that the other wolves would attack their leader, giving Aidan time to escape. It didn't seem likely, but it was all Aidan could think of.

"I'm through!" Sarah's muffled voice came from the crawlway. "Aidan? You okay?"

"A little busy," he said, holding the very end of the almost-spent match toward the alpha wolf as he reached into the backpack and felt . . .

A metal cylinder.

Sarah's hair spray.

"Sarah, come back!" he shouted. "Hurry!"

For once she didn't argue; he heard her grunting as she wriggled back through the crawlway toward him. He could see the flicker of her flashlight.

The match was almost burned out.

The alpha wolf growled and took a step forward.

"When you see my feet," Aidan yelled, "pull!"

"What?" she called.

"My feet! Pull my feet. Hard!"

The match went out. The alpha took another step forward, his dagger teeth gleaming in the wavering beam of Sarah's flashlight coming from the crawlway entrance. The wolf tensed to lunge forward.

Aidan lit the fifth match and sent a stream of hair spray across it. A three-foot blowtorch flame shot out at the alpha wolf, which howled in rage and pain as it scrambled backward, its whiskers burned off. The pack was now cowering on the far side of the tunnel. Aidan released another burst of fire, and another, as he dropped to his knees, kicked the backpack behind him, and got onto his belly, using his elbows to crawl backward into the tunnel.

The match was dwindling.

He fired another blast. But he held the can too close and it blew out the flame. He could see nothing now, his eyes not yet readjusted to the blackness. But he could hear the wolves snarling and again coming closer.

"Pull my legs!" he shouted. He fumbled with the sixth—and last—match. He struck it against the cylinder . . . too hard. The match head broke off. Aidan was holding a useless splinter of wood.

As his eyes adjusted he saw, by the flicker of Sarah's flashlight in the cramped tunnel behind him, that the alpha wolf was coming for him. Aidan, on his stomach, felt helpless; the snarling wolf loomed over him.

"Pull my legs!" he shouted. Where was Sarah? Aidan raised the hair spray can and fired a blast into the wolf's eyes. The wolf howled and backed off a few feet, blinking furiously. Aidan wriggled backward, now almost fully into the crawlway. He felt Sarah's hands grip his ankles. Finally. She pulled, but Aidan barely moved.

"Harder!" he shouted.

"I know!"

The furious alpha lunged forward again; Aidan repelled it with another blast to the eyes. But this time the blast ended with a soft *pfffft*.

The hair spray can was empty.

Aidan felt Sarah heave on his ankles. The effort dragged him backward a foot or so. He did his best to help her. But their progress was much too slow. The big wolf was coming again, snarling, its snout probing the tunnel. Its jaws snapped a few inches from Aidan's face. Aidan threw the hair spray can; the wolf turned his head and the can bounced off his neck, clattering to the tunnel floor.

The wolf was coming again. Aidan had nothing left to fight with except . . .

The razor.

He still had the razor. As the wolf lunged forward Aidan tore open the cardboard envelope and, ducking to avoid the wolf's snapping jaws, lashed out desperately with the razor, once, twice. He felt something scrape his hand. He heard a deafening high-pitched yelp. He couldn't see anything. Another tug from Sarah moved him back another foot. In a flicker of the flashlight beam he caught a glimpse of his hand: blood. He thought the wolf had bitten him. Then he heard more yelping, and looked ahead to see the source of the blood—the wolf's snout was spurting dark liquid. The razor had found its target. The alpha wolf was now contending both with its own wound and the wolves behind it, excited by the scent of new blood.

Taking advantage of these distractions, Aidan and Sarah managed to wriggle backward the remaining few yards to the metal door. They scrambled out and Aidan yanked the door shut just as the alpha reached it. The wolf slammed into the door once, then again, but in the process he only closed it tighter. The tunnel rang with his muffled howls of pain and rage.

Sarah, shoving the backpack ahead of her, crawled into the last exit tunnel; Aidan was on her heels. In less than a minute they were standing outside the massive boulder outcropping. The dark woods, which two hours earlier had seemed so scary to Aidan, now looked safe and welcoming.

For a moment they stood still, exhausted, gasping for breath. Aidan found that he could not stop himself from trembling as he remembered the sight of the wolf's snapping jaws, just inches from his face.

Sarah held up the backpack.

"There!" she said. "That wasn't so hard!"

Despite himself, Aidan laughed.

"Remind me," he said, "when I get some strength back, to kill you."

It was Sarah's turn to laugh. Then, opening the backpack, she said, "I wonder what we almost got eaten for." She pulled out the heavy golden box and turned it over in her hands. Its smooth surface gleamed in the waning glow of Aidan's flashlight. There were no apparent latches or hinges.

"I wonder how you open it," she said.

"We can figure that out later," said Aidan. "The batteries are low. We gotta get out of these woods and back to Bath before Mom and Dad wake up."

For once Sarah didn't argue. She put the box back into the backpack as Aidan activated his phone GPS. In a few minutes they were trudging back through the woods toward their bikes and the road. They spoke little. But as the excitement of their triumph began to wear off, the same sobering words drifted through both of their minds, over and over:

Use it wrong, and death to thee.

CHAPTER 7

THE TOWER

AIDAN AND SARAH GOT VERY LITTLE REST that night; it was almost dawn by the time they sneaked back into the bed-and-breakfast and collapsed into their beds. They spent the next day sleepwalking through the busy schedule their father had set up, which included yet another bike ride around Bath, followed by a trip to an antique dealer, followed by a museum tour. Finally, when they could hardly keep their eyes open, they boarded a train for the trip back to London, falling asleep moments after they found their seats.

Through it all, even in slumber, Sarah never let go of the backpack, despite the heavy weight and awkward bulk of the golden box. Both she and Aidan were eager to find out more about their prize, but they had no time away from their parents until they reached their London hotel that evening. Declaring, truthfully, that they were very tired, they headed for their room immediately after dinner.

There, at last, they had the chance to examine the box. They were pretty sure it was made of gold, and quite a lot of it; the box felt dense and inflexible. There seemed to be no way to open it, and no place where it would open—not even the tiniest crack or seam. They tapped and prodded the box, pushed and pulled every side in every direction, but there was no hint of movement. At one point Aidan even stood on the box. It was like standing on a rock.

"Maybe," he said, "it's just a big square piece of gold. I bet it's worth a lot of money. We could sell it and each keep half."

"No way," said Sarah. "First of all, we're not selling it, not after all we did to get it. Second of all, it's not just a piece of gold."

"How do you know that?"

"If it was gold, Magill could have just put it in a bank or something. But he didn't. He went to a lot of trouble to hide it and to make sure only certain persons could find it."

"Not us, though."

"No, he wasn't thinking of us. But he was thinking of somebody in particular, and he warned them to use it wisely or die. He wouldn't say that about plain old gold."

"So what do you think it is?"

Sarah hesitated, then said, "Starstuff."

Aidan snorted. "Fairy dust?"

Sarah's face reddened. "It's not 'fairy dust,'" she said. "It's much more than that."

Aidan shook his head. "I'm sorry," he said, "but I don't believe that stuff is real."

"Do you believe *this* is real?" said Sarah, tapping the golden box.

"Of course."

"Do you believe Magill's paper was real?"

"Well, yeah, but . . ."

"Do you believe those were real wolves?"

Aidan shuddered. "Definitely."

"So why can't you believe starstuff is real?"

"Because that's magic, Sarah."

"Exactly," she said. "And it's real."

"You think there's magic in this box."

"I do."

Aidan stared at the box for a bit. "Okay," he said. "Say there is starstuff in there. So what? We can't get it out."

"There has to be a way," said Sarah. "Magill went to all that trouble to leave directions for finding the box—the paper in the desk, the lines in the floor under the eagle, the longitude and latitude . . . He wouldn't have done all that if there was no way to open the box once you found it."

"So why didn't he leave instructions for opening the box?"

"I've been thinking about that," said Sarah. "Magill didn't expect regular people like us to find the box. He left

86

the map for certain people—people who wouldn't need instructions to open the box."

"You mean Starcatchers."

"Yes."

"Then we're stuck," said Aidan. "Because we're not Starcatchers."

"Right. But maybe we can figure out how they would do it."

"How?"

"Okay, what made them different from regular people?"

"They talked to porpoises?"

Sarah waved her hand impatiently. "Yes, but what else?"

"They flew, sometimes."

"Right! And how did they fly?"

"They touched starstuff."

"Right again! And where did they get the starstuff?"

Aidan frowned. "I don't remember."

Sarah pointed at her throat.

"Oh yeah," said Aidan. "They wore whaddyacallems. Around their necks."

"Lockets," said Sarah. "They wore gold lockets, with a little bit of starstuff inside, for emergencies."

"So what does that have to do with the box?"

"Maybe," said Sarah, "the starstuff in their lockets would somehow let them open the box. It makes sense. That way, only a Starcatcher could get whatever's inside."

Aidan pondered that for a moment, then said, "Okay, so if you're right, the only way we can open the box is if we have some starstuff. But the only starstuff we have is inside the box, which we can't open."

"Right."

"So we're stuck."

"Unless," said Sarah, "we get some more starstuff."

"Are you serious? It was almost impossible to get this starstuff, which for the record we don't even know for sure is starstuff. How in the world are we going to find more?"

Sarah was staring at the box. "I don't know," she said. "But we're so close. It's right here. There has to be some way we can open it."

"Well," said Aidan, yawning, "you keep working on that. I'm going to bed."

In five minutes he was fast asleep and snoring. Sarah remained doggedly awake, sitting cross-legged on her bed staring at the box, forcing her tired brain to think but getting nowhere. The minutes ticked slowly by. Sarah dozed off, still sitting, her head slumped forward.

A gentle tapping sound snapped her awake. Sarah grabbed the golden box and shoved it into a dresser drawer, then went to the door and looked through the security peep-hole. Seeing her father, she opened the door.

"Hi, Dad," she said.

"Just checking on you two sleepyheads," said Tom.

"We're fine," she said, whispering. "Aidan's asleep."

"Oh, sorry," whispered Tom. "Listen, I was thinking that tomorrow we might go on a tour to—"

"Dad, do we have to talk about this now? I'm really tired."

"Okay," said Tom. He handed Sarah a brochure. "But take a look at this. It would be a shame for us to come all the way here and not visit the Tower of London."

Sarah sighed—not another tour—and said, "Good night, Dad." She closed the door gently and walked back to retrieve the golden box. She set the brochure down on the dresser and was about to open the drawer when three boldfaced words on the brochure cover caught her eye. She picked up the brochure and whispered the words: *The Crown Jewels*.

Quickly she turned and went back to her bed. Four books were stacked on the bedside table. She selected the bottom one and began paging through it. When she found what she was looking for, she read it, then read it again. Then she leaned over her sleeping brother's form and shook his shoulder.

"Aidan, wake up!"

"Go away," he mumbled.

"This is important," she said, still shaking him.

Reluctantly, he rolled over and opened his eyes, blinking. "You got the box open?"

"No, but I think maybe I know how we can."

Aidan was awake now. "How?" he said, sitting up.

"Read this," she said, handing him the book and pointing to a paragraph near the top of page 340.

As Mrs. Bumbrake climbed back up the stairs, Patrick said, "Lord Aster's words support the legend—that the sword was made from a strange metal rock that fell from the sky."

"Strange in what way?" said Neville.

"For one thing, it sometimes glows," said Patrick.

"It's starstuff!" said Peter.

"Not exactly," said Wendy. "A large lump of pure starstuff would kill whoever came near it. Grandfather Aster said the sword was made from metal that was *infused* with starstuff."

"What does that mean?" said Peter.

"It means the metal has some starstuff in it," said Wendy.

Aidan stopped reading and looked up at Sarah. "What sword is this talking about?" he said. "I never read this book."

"It's *Peter and the Sword of Mercy*," said Sarah. "It's what the whole book is about."

Aidan looked at the book cover. "Okay," he said, "so . . . what?"

"So it's a real sword," said Sarah. "It's part of the Crown

Jewels. It's here, Aidan. In London. In the Tower. And according to this"—she tapped the book—"it has starstuff in it."

Aidan nodded, getting it now. "So you think we could use it to open the box."

"Exactly!"

"Right. We'll go to the Tower of London and say, 'Hey, you mind if we borrow a Crown Jewel for a minute? We need it to unlock our fairy dust.' Yeah, there's no flaws in that plan."

Sarah took a deep breath, then exhaled slowly. "Just for once," she said, "could you try not to be such an idiot?"

"I'm not the one who wants to steal a Crown Jewel."

"I'm not saying we should steal it."

"Then how do we use it to open the box?"

"I'm not sure."

"Ah."

"Listen. Maybe you don't have to touch the box with starstuff. Maybe the box just has to be *near* starstuff."

"Okay, how do we get the box near this sword?"

"We go see the Crown Jewels, and we carry the box in the backpack, and we get it as close to the sword as we can."

"And then what?"

"Then we see what happens."

Aidan shook his head. "Sarah, there's gonna be a lot of guards and stuff there."

"So what? We're not stealing anything. What's the worst that can happen?"

"I don't know," said Aidan. "All I know is, the last time you had an idea, we almost got eaten by wolves."

"But we didn't, did we?"

"That's your argument? That we didn't get eaten?"

"Come on, Aidan. We have to try."

Aidan groaned, lay back down in bed, put his hands over his tired eyes, and asked the ceiling, "Why couldn't I have a normal sister?"

In the morning, Tom was thrilled to learn that his children not only wanted to tour the Tower, but wanted to do so as soon as possible. The family left the hotel right after breakfast, and shortly after ten A.M. emerged from the Tower Hill tube station, the walls and turrets of the Tower complex looming ahead of them. After waiting in line for tickets, they made their way across the moat and soon were inside the massive outer wall.

Tom was in heaven, stopping every few feet to lecture on points of interest. He had just finished discussing Traitor's Gate and was turning his attention to the Bloody Tower when Sarah, who was wearing the backpack, said, "Where are the Crown Jewels?"

"They're in the Jewel House," said Tom. "We'll get there soon enough."

Sarah was about to argue when she caught sight of two

large black birds perched above them on a high wall. She frowned. "Are those the ravens?" she said.

"They are indeed," said Tom, pleased. "The legendary Tower of London ravens. It's said that if they ever leave the Tower, the kingdom will fall. Their wings are clipped so they can't fly away. How'd you know about them, Sarah?"

"I read about them in a book," said Sarah.

"Excellent!" said Tom. "Now, the Bloody Tower has a fascinating history . . ."

He was off again, detailing the gory events that gave the Bloody Tower its name. But Sarah wasn't listening. She was trying to remember what she'd read about the ravens. She decided she'd have to look it up when she got back to the hotel.

Her father finished discussing the Bloody Tower and was leading them to the left, toward the White Tower, still talking. Sarah looked back at the ravens. They had not moved. Sarah turned away and followed her family.

Because of Tom's frequent stops to point things out, it took them more than an hour to reach the Waterloo Barracks, which houses the Jewel House. They joined the line of tourists waiting to enter, then shuffled forward for another forty-five minutes before finally reaching a series of dramatically lit rooms with exhibit cases containing the historic objects that are known, collectively, as the Crown Jewels. Tom was now in full guide mode, talking excitedly and constantly, but only Natalie was listening. Both Aidan and Sarah were darting quickly from case to case, reading the labels and then moving on.

Aidan was the one who found what they were looking for.

"Sarah!" he hissed, beckoning her toward a case in a corner. "Over here!"

Sarah walked toward her brother. He was pointing at a sword about three feet long, with a blade that looked like steel, gleaming in the exhibit lighting. The tip of the blade had been broken off, leaving the end shortened, the edge at a slight angle.

The Sword of Mercy.

Sarah looked around. There were Tower staff people keeping watch in every room, but in the horde of tourists milling around, nobody appeared to be paying attention to her. She shifted the backpack around so that she was carrying it in front of her, then unzipped the top so she could see the top of the golden box inside. She moved forward until the backpack was about a foot from the display case. Her eyes were on the box.

Nothing happened.

"Well?" said Aidan.

Sarah shook her head. She stepped closer to the case; the backpack was now just a few inches away. Still nothing. She lifted the backpack up and pressed it against the case.

She felt Aidan's hand on her arm. "There's a guy coming," he said.

Sarah glanced around and saw a uniformed Tower staff person walking toward her.

"Miss," he called. "Don't touch the case."

Sarah kept the backpack where it was. She was looking intently at the sword now.

"Miss!" said the man.

"C'mon, Sarah," Aidan pleaded.

"Aidan," she said. "Look at the sword."

Aidan followed her gaze.

"Whoa," he said.

The sword was glowing. It wasn't a bright glow, but it was unmistakable. And the blade now had a golden tint. Sarah felt warmth coming from her backpack. She looked down; the box was also glowing.

"Miss!" The man was next to Sarah now, gesturing at her to move away from the display case. "If you can't follow instructions, you'll have to leave."

"I'm sorry," she said, zipping the backpack closed. Her parents, seeing the commotion, were coming toward them.

"Sarah?" said her mother. "What's going on?"

"I got too close to the case," said Sarah. "I'm sorry." She looked at the sword; it was no longer glowing.

"Please move along," said the staff person.

They rejoined the shuffling throng moving past the

95

exhibits. Sarah paid little attention; all she wanted to do was look inside her backpack. She finally got a chance when they exited the Crown Jewels exhibit and found themselves in the inevitable gift shop. While her parents shopped for souvenirs, she found a relatively quiet corner and, with Aidan hovering close, unzipped the backpack and peered inside.

"Yes," she said.

"What?" said Aidan.

"Look," she said.

Aidan leaned over.

"It changed," he said.

It had indeed. Where the box had once been an unbroken block of metal, it now had a clearly visible seam running all the way around four sides.

"That's how you open it," said Sarah, a note of triumph in her voice.

"So are you gonna do it?" said Aidan.

"Not here," said Sarah. "Too many people around. When we get back to the hotel."

Tom and Natalie, having made their purchases, were coming; Sarah quickly zipped up the backpack and slid it onto her back.

"Ready?" said Tom.

The children nodded and the family exited the gift shop. The day was warm and sunny; the Tower grounds swarmed with tourists. Sarah was oblivious to the scene, walking a bit behind Aidan and her parents, her head down, her mind on the strange object she was carrying. She bumped into her father, not having noticed that he'd stopped walking.

"Look at that," he said, pointing ahead. Other tourists were pointing as well. Sarah looked. She inhaled sharply when she saw what was drawing the attention.

Ravens. Twelve of them, perched on a wall, evenly placed in a perfect line. All twelve struck the same pose; all twelve were looking in the same direction, with their heads cocked at precisely the same angle.

"I believe that's all of the Tower ravens, gathered in one place," said Tom. "I've never seen that before."

"What do you suppose they're looking at?" said Natalie.

Aidan and Sarah looked at each other, but said nothing.

"Strange," said Tom.

"What is?" said Natalie.

"Well," said Tom, "I know this is crazy, but . . . it's almost as if they're looking right at us."

CHAPTER 8

OUT THE WINDOW

"GOOD NIGHT, KIDS," SAID NATALIE.

"G'night, Mom," said Sarah and Aidan.

"Tomorrow," said Tom, standing behind his wife in the hotel hallway, "I was thinking we might visit the—"

"Good night, Dad." Gently closing the door, Sarah said to her brother, "Finally."

Since leaving the Tower, Sarah and Aidan had spent more than eight hours waiting impatiently for a chance to have a closer look at the golden box. But their father, as always, had crammed the rest of the day with sightseeing, so by the time they'd eaten dinner and returned to the hotel, it was past ten P.M.

Sarah unslung the backpack, set it on her bed, and unzipped it. She lifted out the heavy box and held it up in the light, examining the newly formed seam, which ran around what she assumed was the top of the box about an inch from the edge.

"So this is like a lid, maybe?" said Aidan, touching the seam.

"Looks like it," said Sarah.

"Are you gonna open it?" said Aidan.

"I guess so," said Sarah.

"You don't sound enthusiastic."

"I'm thinking about the 'death to thee' thing."

"Oh, *now* you're thinking about that."

"I just think we need to be careful, that's all."

"Meaning what?"

"I'm not sure."

"Now, there's a plan."

"Shut up. I'm thinking." Sarah studied the box. "The thing is, in the books, when they deal with starstuff, they wear gold suits."

"Okay, then! I'll just put on my gold suit."

Sarah rolled her eyes. "I'm just saying they're very careful."

"Maybe aluminum foil?" Aidan said. "We could wrap ourselves up."

"It's always gold."

"So if Starcatchers found the box, they'd have known to wear gold. Right? Otherwise, death to thee."

Sarah studied the box some more. "Okay," she said, heading toward the dresser. "I'll get a mirror. You get the curtain rod."

"What?"

"Just get it."

A minute later, the box was propped between two pillows on the bed. Aidan and Sarah were crouched on the floor. Sarah held the curtain rod; Aidan held the mirror up so she could see the box. Using the mirror, Sarah maneuvered the curtain rod so it was touching the lid.

"Get ready," she said.

"For what?"

"For whatever happens."

"I wish I had a gold suit," said Aidan.

Her eyes on the mirror, Sarah gently pushed the rod against the side of the lid. It came up easily, pivoting on two internally mounted hinges. As the box opened, Sarah and Aidan both instinctively turned away, wincing, fearful of . . .

Nothing.

No blinding light, no sound. Nothing.

After a few silent seconds, Sarah and Aidan opened their eyes, rose to their feet, and cautiously peered into the box. They saw what appeared to be a second lid. It was also made of gold, but at its center was a small, exquisitely crafted five-spoked wheel. Next to the wheel was a circular opening about a half inch in diameter and a half inch deep, closed at the bottom.

"What do you think?" said Sarah.

Aidan studied the box for a moment, then said, "I think if you turn the wheel, you open that hole."

"I think so, too. That way you can control how much comes out."

"And not kill yourself," said Aidan. "I hope."

Sarah set the box down on her bed. She put her hand on the wheel, took a deep breath, and exhaled.

"Here goes," she said.

She turned the wheel counterclockwise a quarter of a turn, then waited.

Nothing.

Sarah looked at Aidan. He nodded. She looked down and turned the wheel another quarter of a turn. Suddenly, the hole was glowing brightly, a warm golden color.

And the room was full of music.

Aidan jumped. "Do you hear that?" he said.

Sarah nodded. "Bells," she whispered.

"Like a million of them."

"Where's it coming from?"

Aidan waved an arm. "Everywhere," he said.

Sarah hugged herself. "Do you feel . . . different?" she said. "Like, kind of warm, but warm inside?"

"Yes!" said Aidan, smiling broadly. "I feel warm and . . . just good."

"Better than good," said Sarah, giggling. "Wonderful."

She put her hand on the tiny wheel again.

"Sarah . . ." cautioned Aidan.

"Just a little more." Sarah gave the wheel another quarter turn. Now the bells became a symphony, playing all around them and inside them.

"Oh my," she said.

"Yeah," said Aidan.

Sarah looked at the box.

"I want to touch it," she said.

"I don't know if that's a good idea," said Aidan. But his tone was unconvincing; he, too, wanted to touch the source of this glorious feeling.

Sarah reached out her right hand and gently tilted the box. She held her left hand cupped next to the glowing hole. She had barely moved the box when what looked like a tongue of light flowed from it, enveloping Sarah's hand as it flooded the room with a brilliant whiteness.

Aidan turned away, momentarily blinded. When the glare faded he turned back, blinking, waiting for his eyes to readjust. When they did, he froze.

Sarah was gone. The glowing box was still on the bed; the door was closed. But he saw no sign of his sister.

"Sarah!" he called, panic sweeping away the feeling of well-being. He dropped to his belly and looked under Sarah's bed, then his own. Nothing. He jumped up, his eyes sweeping the room frantically.

Then he heard the giggle.

From directly overhead.

Aidan looked up to see his sister suspended in air, her back gently bumping the ceiling, a huge smile on her face.

"It was true!" she said. "The stories were true!"

For a moment, Aidan could only stare.

"You're . . . flying," he said.

"Yes! Yes, I am!" she said. She angled her head down slightly; the movement caused her to drift across the room. She held her hands out to keep from bumping into the far wall.

"Wow," she said.

"What's it feel like?" said Aidan.

"Why don't you find out for yourself?"

Aidan went to the bed, hesitated, then gently tilted the box toward his cupped hand. Again, a brilliant light filled the room, and for a moment Aidan couldn't tell what was happening. He felt the top of his head brushing against something and realized it was the ceiling. He looked down. The movement sent him into a very slow 180-degree midair rotation that ended with him upside down and vertical, as though he were standing on the ceiling.

"Whoa," he said.

"Exactly," said Sarah.

They spent several giddy minutes getting the feel of flight, seeing how the angle of their bodies affected their direction and speed, occasionally bumping into walls and furniture.

Then Sarah opened the window.

"Wait a minute," said Aidan.

"If I'm going to fly," said Sarah. "I want to *fly*."

She swung her legs out and sat on the windowsill, looking down. Their room was on the fourth floor of the Cadogan; it looked down on a side street, which at the moment was deserted. The night air was cool and clear. A gentle breeze stirred Sarah's hair.

"Here goes," she said, slipping out of the window and into the night.

Aidan pushed off the far wall and flew to the window, grabbing the sill to stop himself from shooting through it. He stuck his head out and caught sight of Sarah as she swooped across the street, gaining speed, heading straight toward a parked car. Aidan was about to shout when she let out a little shriek and swooped upward, missing the car by inches and then gaining altitude rapidly until, seconds later, she was over the building on the other side of the street, making a soaring right turn and then swooping back toward Aidan.

"Come *on*," she called.

Aidan swallowed hard and pulled himself through the window, willing himself to keep his eyes on his sister, not the street below. He angled his body left and, after a few wobbles, got himself aimed toward Sarah, who was now flying about a hundred feet in the air, heading toward the busy traffic of Sloane Street. She shot across the street and into what appeared to be a private park, above which she made a series of swoops and turns, periodically emitting squeals of pure happiness.

As he followed her across Sloane Street, Aidan hazarded a glance down and was horrified to see pedestrians, although at the moment none appeared to be looking upward. He flew more cautiously than his sister and had trouble getting near her, but finally she drifted to a stop, reclining dramatically in midair as though relaxing on an invisible sofa. Her eyes shone with excitement.

"Isn't this fantastic?" she said.

"Yeah, fantastic," said Aidan. "But maybe we should go back."

"Why?"

"Because we're flying over London, Sarah. Somebody might see us."

"Nobody's looking up here."

"Um," said Aidan, pointing. "I think that guy is."

Sarah looked toward Sloane Street, where an elderly man had stopped on the sidewalk and was looking directly at them, shielding his eyes against the glare of a streetlight. As they watched he stopped a young couple and started gesturing insistently toward Aidan and Sarah.

"Uh-oh," said Sarah. "Follow me."

She swooped downward and in a few seconds flew the length of the little park. Aidan followed unsteadily, a little higher and slower. At the far end of the park he caught up with Sarah, now hovering behind a tree, peering through the foliage at the elderly man. He was still with the couple, who evidently had not seen Sarah and Aidan and wanted to move on. The man was arguing with them, still pointing toward the place where Sarah and Aidan had just been.

"Come on," said Sarah.

She rose straight up, Aidan trailing. They were now high above the park. The elderly man was arguing with the couple; they were edging away from him. Sarah leveled off and shot back across Sloane Street toward the Cadogan. Aidan followed. He heard a shout and looked down.

The man had seen them again. Aidan looked right into his eyes. The man was pointing and yelling; a small crowd was gathering, looking up. Aidan looked forward and flew as fast as he could after his sister, who had just swerved around the corner into the side street, now flying quite low. He heard more shouts from behind but did not look back. As he flew into the side street, he looked toward the hotel room window but didn't see Sarah. Assuming she was already inside, he flew toward the window.

"Aidan!"

His sister's voice came from below. He looked down and

saw her standing on the sidewalk. He heard yelling from Sloane Street.

"Come on!" he called to Sarah.

"I can't!" she called back. "It wore off!"

Figures appeared at the end of the street. Aidan hung suspended in the air for a moment, uncertain, then swooped toward the sidewalk. He landed next to Sarah a little too hard. He stumbled, his sister catching his arm to keep him upright.

"People are coming," he panted, pointing toward the end of the street.

"I see them," she said. A half dozen people were running toward them now.

"What do we do? Run?"

"No—we just act calm and walk toward them. They didn't get a good look at us, and they're looking for people going the other way."

Sarah started walking toward Sloane Street; Aidan joined her. The first of the runners—a young man—sprinted right past them, his eyes on the sky. Three more young men ran past, also looking upward, one of them holding up his cell phone, evidently shooting video. Next came the young couple, who hesitated when they saw Sarah and Aidan.

"Excuse me," said the woman. "Did you see anybody just go past in the, um, in the air?"

"In the air?" said Sarah.

"Yes," said the woman, embarrassed. "In the air."

"Like, flying?" said Sarah.

"Yes!" said the woman. "Did you see them?"

"Of course not," said Sarah.

The couple passed; Sarah and Aidan started walking again. On the sidewalk ahead another figure was approaching. Too late, Aidan saw who it was: the elderly man. Aidan turned his head away, but as bad luck would have it they were directly under a streetlight; the man had gotten a clear view of him. Blocking their path, he pointed a wavering finger at Aidan.

"You!" he said. "You were flying!" The man raised his voice to the others, now at the end of the block.

"Here they are!" he shouted. "I found them!"

"Come on," said Sarah, grabbing Aidan's arm. They sprinted past the man to the end of the street and turned left. They heard shouts but did not look back. Thirty seconds later, gasping for breath, they ducked into the Cadogan lobby. They strode briskly to the elevators and boarded one. As the doors closed they peered out anxiously, but there was nobody pursuing them.

"Man," said Aidan, slumping against the side of the elevator.

"Wasn't that great?" said Sarah, her eyes shining.

"Parts of it," said Aidan. He tried to rise off the elevator floor and found that he could not. "Mine wore off, too," he said.

"We'll have to keep that in mind next time."

"So we're going to fly again?"

"Of course. Don't you want to?"

"Yeah, but . . ."

"But what?"

"I'm not sure. I mean, the starstuff is amazing and everything, but I dunno if we should be messing with it."

Sarah was about to answer when the elevator doors opened. They tiptoed down the hallway past their parents' room. Sarah, grateful that she'd kept her key card in her jeans pocket, quietly opened the door to their room. Slipping inside, they immediately felt the warmth of the starstuff and heard the pleasant musical sound. Sarah went to the golden box on the bed and, somewhat reluctantly, turned the little wheel clockwise. The glowing hole went dark; the sound and the warmth went away. Both Sarah and Aidan suddenly noticed that the room was chilly. Cold air was pouring in through the open window.

Sarah walked toward the window to close it. As she reached it, she saw something just outside.

Then she screamed.

CHAPTER 9

THE BLACK WIND

SARAH TOOK A STEP BACK, her mouth open, her face frozen in fear.

"What?" said Aidan, moving up behind her.

Sarah, unable to speak, pointed out the window. Aidan looked, and suddenly stopped.

"What is that?" he said.

It was as if a curtain had fallen outside, blotting out the lights of the buildings across the street. But it was no curtain.

It was ravens.

There were hundreds of them, big ones, their bodies two feet long, their wings stretching as much as four feet from tip to tip. The roar of their beating wings filled the air as they whirled and fluttered like a black wind.

They were coming toward the hotel.

"Close the window!" shouted Aidan, startling Sarah out of her trance. They both lunged forward, Sarah grabbing the left windowpane as Aidan grabbed the right. They pushed them closed, but before they could latch them the mass of birds reached the panes and pushed against them with surprising force, opening a space between the two windows. Sarah and Aidan pushed back, closing the gap a bit, but not enough to prevent three of the birds from getting partway through the opening. Rather than try to free themselves, the birds lunged at Sarah's and Aidan's hands with their curved, sharp-pointed black beaks. The other ravens hurled their bodies against the windows, which shuddered with the impact. The hotel room echoed with the birds' harsh cries: *Caw! Caw! Caw!*

"Don't let go!" Sarah shouted, shifting her hands to avoid the savage pecks of the three wild-eyed ravens.

"Take my side!" Aidan said. "I'll try to push them out!"

Sarah knelt to avoid the trapped birds and put her right hand on the frame of the window Aidan had been holding, leaning with her full weight to hold both windows closed.

"Can you hold it?" Aidan asked.

"I think so."

Aidan tried letting go; Sarah was okay, at least for the moment. He turned and grabbed a pillow from the bed, then shoved it against the three pecking birds, covering them. One by one he shoved his fist against them, forcing them outside.

"Now!" he shouted as he pushed the last one through

the opening. Sarah slammed the window closed and Aidan quickly latched it. The birds were still swarming outside, their bodies thudding into the window. But the glass, and the latch, seemed to be holding.

Sarah looked at Aidan and said, "What was—"

Caw!

The sound came from behind them.

They turned to see a raven perched on the desk. It raised its huge wings and launched itself directly at them. Acting on reflex, Aidan swung the pillow hard, baseball-bat style, catching the raven just as it reached them. The raven slammed into the wall and bounced off onto the bed, stunned.

Aidan grabbed the bottom corner of the bedspread. "Get the other side!" he said.

Sarah took the other bottom corner and they pulled the bedspread toward the headrest, covering the raven. As it began to thrash around, they quickly folded the bedspread to trap it inside.

"Now what?" said Sarah.

"Out the window?"

"Are you kidding me? We are not opening the window."

"Well, we can't keep this thing as a pet." Aidan looked toward the window. "Anyway, I think they're gone."

Sarah looked out. Aidan was right: she didn't see the ravens.

"Okay," she said. "But really fast."

"Really, *really* fast," agreed Aidan. "You open the windows. I'll heave it."

Sarah put her hands on the window latch and looked out once again to make sure it was clear.

"Ready," said Aidan.

But Sarah, peering through the window, did not open it. "Oh, no," she said softly.

"What now?" said Aidan, moving to the window, holding the bedspread with the trapped raven struggling inside.

"They're still here," she said, pointing.

Aidan peered through the glass.

"What are they doing?"

The ravens were swirling over the middle of the street, but their movements no longer appeared random. They were flying in distinct, organized patterns now, forming an ever-more-compact mass.

"Birds don't do that," Aidan said.

"Apparently these birds do," said Sarah.

"Well, let's get rid of this one while they're away from the window," said Aidan, struggling to contain the trapped raven, which was moving more frantically, as if it sensed that the others were near.

Sarah quickly opened the window. Aidan held one edge of the bedspread and pushed the rest out. It unfolded like a flag, and with an angry *Caw! Caw!* the raven flew free. It headed directly to where the others were massing.

Aidan was hauling in the bedspread, but his attention, like Sarah's, was on the birds. "Oh my god," said Aidan. The ravens had formed a distinct shape. And it was moving their way. "Shut the window!" said Aidan, frantically hauling in the rest of the bedspread.

Sarah quickly closed the windows and fumbled with the latch, finally getting it secure. She and Aidan stared as the bird shape grew closer, now clearly illuminated by the lights of the hotel.

It appeared to be solid. Somehow the tightly packed ravens appeared to be almost floating, rather than flying; they moved in perfect synchronization, looking like one creature rather than many. It was huge—several stories tall, at least—and it was very clearly defined. It was the shape of a hooded figure, like a monk or priest, with stooped shoulders and wearing a long, black robe.

Sarah stared at it intently. "I know what that is," she said softly. "I know *who* that is."

"It's that guy from the books, isn't it?" whispered Aidan.

"Yes," said Sarah. "It's him."

The figure glided toward them. As it drew near the window it raised its head, and from under the hood appeared two red orbs, like huge glowing coals.

"Oh my god," said Aidan.

He and Sarah stood still, frozen in fear and fascination, as the hideous form came toward them. It was only a few yards from the window now, the red orbs at the level of their window.

"What does he want?" whispered Aidan.

"I don't know," Sarah answered. The shape stopped coming forward. There was movement to one side and an armlike form appeared, with long spindly fingers at the ends. The arm shape moved; now it was just outside the window, nearly touching it.

"Do you feel that?" whispered Aidan.

Sarah did feel it—a sickening chill seeping through her body. Suddenly, she knew what was happening. "Down!" she yelled, pushing her brother toward the floor and diving next to him.

"What are you—"

"It wants our shadows! We have to turn out the lights! Now!"

There were two lights—the overhead light and the lamp on the table between the beds. Aidan dove toward the lamp while Sarah scrambled across the floor to the light switch by the door. In seconds the lights were off; the room was dark.

Sarah and Aidan looked toward the window. The two red orbs were there, very close now, each nearly filling a window frame. Neither Sarah nor Aidan took a breath.

And then the orbs were gone.

For a moment the room was silent.

They jumped at a sound from the door. It was a key card being inserted into the lock. The door opened. It was their father.

"What's all the noise about?" he said. He stepped into the room and, by the light from the hallway, saw his children lying on the floor in the darkened room.

"What on earth?" he said.

"Excellent question," mumbled Aidan.

Tom reached for the light.

"No lights!" exclaimed Sarah, startling her father. "Sorry, Dad. We're, ah, we're playing a game."

"What game?" said Tom.

"It's, um, complicated," said Sarah.

"You wouldn't believe how complicated it is," said Aidan.

"Well, whatever it is, it's time to stop it and go to sleep," said Tom.

"Yes, Dad," said Sarah.

"I'm never gonna sleep again," said Aidan, mostly to himself.

"Early start tomorrow," said Tom, closing the door. The room was dark again.

Aidan and Sarah rose and went to the window. They could see the lights across the street again. The sky was empty; the ravens were gone.

They stood there for a few seconds, peering into the night. Aidan broke the silence.

"Didn't Ombra die?" he said.

"Apparently not," said Sarah. "He's very hard to kill. He keeps . . . coming back."

"As a bunch of birds?"

"You saw the same thing I saw."

Aidan shuddered. "I wish I hadn't," he said. "So how did he find us? *Why* did he find us?"

"The ravens at the Tower. Remember?"

"Yeah."

"We unlocked the gold box with the starstuff from the sword. They must've felt that—felt the starstuff. That's why they were waiting for us when we came out."

"But these weren't the same birds—the Tower ravens can't fly."

"Then they must be able to communicate. Somehow they told the other ravens."

"Talking birds?"

"Those aren't normal birds."

"No kidding."

Sarah looked hard at her brother. "They're him, Aidan," she said. "Lord Ombra."

"But how can that be? I mean, you saw . . . it's birds."

"Maybe each raven is a piece of him. Put the ravens together and . . ."

"That's crazy."

"It's not crazy. You saw it. They turned into him. And

he nearly got us. The light was coming from behind us, and he was touching our shadows. You felt it, right?"

Aidan nodded. "I don't ever want to feel that again," he said.

They were both quiet for a while; then Aidan said what they were both thinking.

"He doesn't want us, Sarah. He wants the box. He wants the starstuff. That's what brought him here."

Sarah nodded.

"Which means," Aidan continued, "that he'll come back. As long as we have the starstuff, he'll keep coming back."

Sarah nodded again.

"So maybe we should just let him . . ."

"No," said Sarah, shaking her head. "We can't give it to him."

"But he's—"

"He's evil, Aidan. He's evil, and if he gets the starstuff, he'll use it to do evil things. People died to protect that star-stuff from him. We can't let him have it."

"So what do we do?"

Sarah looked down. "I don't know," she whispered.

"Great," said Aidan.

They sat in silence for a minute. Again it was Aidan who spoke, and again he said what they were both thinking.

"I wish we'd never found that stupid piece of paper," he said. "Then we'd never have gone to the cave, and we'd never have opened the box. Then none of this would have . . ."

He stopped, realizing that Sarah was crying. Her face was buried in her hands; tears dripped through the cracks between her fingers.

"I'm sorry," she said, her voice muffled. "It's my fault."

"It's okay," he said, giving her shoulder a tentative pat.

Sarah raised her head and looked at him. Her cheeks were tear-streaked; her eyes were red and filled with despair.

"No it's not," she said. "It's not okay at all."

CHAPTER 10

"WE DON'T KNOW ANYTHING"

SARAH AND AIDAN WERE BEYOND TIRED, but sleep didn't come easily; they both kept glancing toward the window, although there was never anything there. Finally, exhaustion overcame fear, and they slept.

They awoke to the sound of their father's voice through the door, informing them they'd be eating breakfast in half an hour. It was just past eight o'clock; sunshine streamed through the window that, only hours earlier, had been a gateway for terror. Sarah sat on her bed staring at the golden box, which rested on the nightstand next to the stack of books. Aidan stumbled into the bathroom, emerging a few minutes later with a stream of toothpaste dribbling from the corner of his mouth. Sarah had not moved.

"I've been thinking about what we should do with it," he said.

"Me too," she said.

"I think we need to give it to the police."

Sarah turned to her brother. "No," she said.

"Why not?"

"I don't trust the police."

"Why not?"

"They could be in on it. They could be working for . . ." She nodded toward the window.

"Why would you think that?"

Sarah gestured toward the books. "Because the police were in on it before. Anybody could be in on it."

"Those are stories, Sarah."

"And so far they've turned out to be true."

"Good point. But we don't know the police are involved."

"We don't know anything," said Sarah. "Which is why we have to be very, very careful about what we do with the box."

"Maybe we should give it to Dad and Mom."

"I thought about that, too," said Sarah. "But two things. One, they'd be really mad at us for sneaking off to the caves and all—we'd be grounded for a minimum of forever. And two, they'd probably give the box to the police."

"But we could tell them about the birds, about . . . Ombra."

Sarah looked at her brother. "Do you think they'd believe it? Would *you* believe it? That some evil creature from a storybook has taken the form of a flock of birds?"

Aidan hesitated, then quietly said, "No."

"Exactly," said Sarah. "They'd send us to a shrink. And there's one more thing."

"Which is?"

"We have starstuff, Aidan. We can fly. It was amazing, wasn't it?"

"Yes."

"Well, I want to fly again. And who knows what else we can do with it?"

"If Ombra doesn't get us, you mean."

"Well, now we know he's out there," said Sarah. "So we'll be ready."

"Ready how?"

"I'm working on that part."

Aidan rolled his eyes and was about to say something when there was another tap on the door.

"Let's go, kids!" said Tom.

"Coming," said Sarah. She rose and picked up the golden box.

"What're you going to do with that?" whispered Aidan.

"Hide it," said Sarah, looking around the room. Her eyes fell on the cabinet that held the television. She went to it and pulled the TV out and sideways a few inches, making an opening just big enough for the box. She slid it into the cabinet and pushed the TV back into place.

"C'mon, kids!" said Tom.

"Okay, okay!" said Sarah, opening the door. She and Aidan followed Tom and Natalie down the hallway to the elevators, passing a man in a hotel uniform and overcoat carrying a room-service tray. As they boarded an elevator, Tom was enthusiastically discussing the day's sightseeing options; Aidan and Sarah were silent.

"What's wrong with you two?" Natalie asked.

"Nothing," said Sarah. "Tired, I guess."

"Me too," yawned Aidan.

"Really?" said Natalie. "You two went to bed plenty early last night."

"I had trouble sleeping," said Sarah. "Bad dreams."

"Me too," said Aidan. "Terrible dreams."

Natalie shook her head. "You kids have hyperactive imaginations," she said. "You're in London, on vacation, with your parents, in a nice hotel. What on earth is there to be afraid of?"

Aidan and Sarah looked at each other, but said nothing.

"I blame video games," said Tom.

"Right," said Aidan. "Video games."

CHAPTER 11

A COIL OF BLACK

THE ELEVATOR DOORS OPENED on the fourth floor. An older couple joined the Coopers as a waiter pushed a linen-covered room-service cart past in the corridor. As the doors shut, the old man looked down at his arm and scratched off a large scab, which drifted to the elevator floor.

"Did you see that?" Aidan asked Sarah.

"Aidan!" said Natalie, horrified, looking between Aidan and the man.

"Not that, Mom!" said Aidan. He cupped his hand and whispered in Sarah's ear, "That room-service waiter who just went by—he wasn't wearing a coat."

"So?" said Sarah.

"The guy carrying the tray on our floor had a big coat on. He was a doorman, not a waiter!"

Sarah frowned.

"He was heading toward our room," said Aidan.

The old man reached toward another scab; his wife slapped his wrist.

"Mom," said Sarah, pretending to search through her backpack, "do you have a hairbrush?"

"No," said Natalie. "You know I never carry one."

"Can I go back to the room and get one, please?"

"You can make it through breakfast without worrying about your hair," Tom said testily.

"Please, Mom?" Woman to woman. It usually worked.

"I don't see any harm," Natalie said. "Just hurry up, please."

The elevator doors opened; they had reached the lobby.

"I'll go with her and make sure she doesn't drag it out," Aidan said.

"Keep her moving," Tom said, as he and Natalie followed the old couple out of the elevator. "I'm starving."

Aidan punched the button for the fifth floor. As the doors closed, he said, "What do we do if he's in our room?"

"We make him leave," said Sarah. "We can't let him get the box." She drummed her fingers on the elevator door. "Come on," she muttered.

The elevator reached the fifth floor. They ran down the hall. There was a room-service tray on the carpet outside their room. The door was shut.

Aidan snatched a butter knife off the tray.

"As if you're going to use that," said Sarah.

"He doesn't know that."

Sarah removed the room card from her backpack, slipped it quietly into the slot, took a deep breath, and withdrew it. The door light turned green. She pulled down the handle and pushed the door open.

The doorman was bent over, searching a lower drawer in a dresser. He stood and turned toward them. His face was expressionless; his eyes were vacant, dominated by huge black pupils.

"What are you doing?" said Sarah. Aidan moved next to her.

The doorman said nothing.

The door closed behind them.

"This is our room," said Sarah. "You're not supposed to be in here."

The doorman took a step toward them.

Aidan gripped the butter knife. Sarah took a step back and opened the door. "Please leave right now," she said, gesturing toward the hallway.

Another step. The doorman was a yard away from them, next to the desk lamp. Aidan looked down and gasped.

"Sarah," he hissed. "He doesn't have a shadow."

Sarah would have screamed, but she never had a chance. The doorman, moving with impossible quickness, leaped forward and shoved her out into the hall. He then seized Aidan before he had time to react and shoved him out after her.

Aidan stabbed the butter knife into the closing crack and blocked the door from shutting completely. He leaned against the door, trying to force it open, but the doorman had his full weight against it.

"Help me!" Aidan shouted.

"We need to get somebody up here fast," said Sarah. She looked around frantically, then spotted a fire alarm a few yards away. She ran to it, opened the cover plate, and yanked the lever down. Instantly, a blinding white light flashed overhead and a very loud, very annoying alarm began sounding.

⚜

Downstairs, Tom was just raising his steaming coffee cup to his lips, anticipating the first sip, when he heard the alarm. All around the dining room, guests looked up from their breakfasts. A hotel employee trotted past the entrance, then another. A voice coming from the direction of the reception desk called out, "Fifth floor."

Tom and Natalie exchanged looks.

Oh, no . . .

⚜

"S . . . a . . . r . . . a . . . h!" Aidan shouted.

She ran for the door, leaped in the air, and kicked it hard with her karate-trained right foot. The doorman was thrown back onto the floor, banging his head hard on the corner of the desk as he went down. He lay on the floor, apparently stunned, moaning.

Aidan ran past him to the bed. "Grab it!" he shouted to Sarah, at the same time yanking the bedspread off the bed and onto the fallen doorman. The doorman, recovering, kicked at it to get it off, but was tangled just long enough for Sarah to reach for the box behind the television and make for the door, Aidan a step behind her. Sarah shoved the box into her backpack.

A few yards down the hallway they nearly ran into two men in gray suits, one with a walkie-talkie—hotel security.

"Excuse me!" Aidan said. "One of your doormen pulled the fire alarm and then barged into our room!"

At that moment, the doorman appeared at the doorway. His dead, coal-black eyes met Sarah's for a moment, then aimed at her backpack.

"There he is!" Sarah shouted, pointing. The doorman turned away and began walking quickly toward the stairs at the far end of the corridor.

"Hey, you! Stop!" shouted the man with the walkie-talkie.

The doorman, not looking back, started running. The two security men started after him, but the doorman had a big lead and his pursuers were slowed by hotel guests responding to the alarm, pouring from their rooms into the corridor.

"They're not gonna catch him," said Aidan.

"Come on," said Sarah. "We'll take the elevator."

They reached the elevators and joined a crowd of people pushing their way on. Although hotel guests were not supposed to use the elevators in case of a fire, no one was obeying the rule.

"What are we doing?" whispered Aidan.

"Following him," she whispered.

"Why?"

"To see where he goes. I want to know who's after us."

"I'm not sure I do," said Aidan. The doors opened in the lobby; Sarah pushed her way out, with Aidan behind.

"There!" she said.

The doorman, in a crowd, was walking briskly, purposefully, not looking back. Most of the hotel guests were outside now in a milling throng of hundreds on the sidewalk, with more streaming across the lobby and out the front entrance. But the doorman veered right, toward a side entrance. Sarah followed about twenty feet behind him with Aidan, reluctantly, on her heels.

The doorman started across a street, walking directly into the path of a taxi, which swerved to avoid him, its driver yelling something unpleasant. The doorman paid no attention, continuing across the street and into the park above which Sarah and Aidan had flown the night before. Sarah stopped on the sidewalk, watching.

"Where's he going?" said Aidan.

"I don't know," said Sarah. "It's like he didn't even hear that taxi . . ."

The doorman walked toward a huge oak, its branches lush with leaves. When he reached it, he stopped. For thirty seconds he stood motionless.

Then a raven landed in the tree.

Then another.

Then a dozen more.

And still more, and more, and more. Hundreds more. The tree was black now, its branches bending under the weight of the huge black birds.

Aidan put his hand on Sarah's arm.

"Let's get out of here," he said.

Sarah stayed where she was, her eyes fixed on the scene.

Suddenly, the tree came alive as the birds, moving as one fluid mass, rose from the upper canopy of the tree in a coil of black, like an enormous snake. With a roar of beating wings, the coil arched upward and then swiftly curved down, engulfing the doorman in a tornado of black feathers. The only sound was of beating wings. Then, as swiftly as they had descended, the mass of birds began to rise; the top of the mass again began to form a snakelike shape even as the bottom still covered the doorman.

The top arched and began to swivel, as if looking for something. And then it stopped.

It was pointing toward Sarah.

"Uh-oh," said Aidan.

"Run!" shouted Sarah.

Dodging traffic, she and Aidan sprinted back across the street toward the hotel. Behind them they heard the all-too-familiar roar of beating wings. Sarah glanced back and saw the dark mass swooping toward them. Behind the mass she caught a glimpse of a figure crumpled on the ground—the doorman, or what was left of him.

"Hurry!" she shouted to Aidan, who needed no encouragement. Moments later they reached the hotel, where the crowd was flowing back into the lobby; the alarm had apparently been declared false.

Sarah and Aidan plunged into the mob, then looked anxiously back; to their relief, they saw that the black mass of birds had veered away and was breaking apart, the ravens now flying separately, like ordinary birds. They flew off in all directions; in seconds they were gone. A few members of the crowd had noticed their odd behavior and were pointing upward, but most people were focused on getting back into the hotel. In the distance, Sarah and Aidan saw figures in the park gathered around the fallen form of the doorman.

They entered the lobby and spotted their parents on the far side, anxiously scanning the crowd. A moment later their parents saw them and started working their way toward them, their expressions a mixture of relief and anger.

"Sarah," said Aidan urgently, "we can't keep the box. You saw what happened to the doorman."

"Yes," said Sarah. "Ombra shadowized him. And then he . . . I don't know what he did to him in the park. I guess he was angry at him because he failed."

"Yes, but now he'll just shadowize somebody else. He's going to keep coming, Sarah. As long as we have the box, he's going to keep coming. Do you see that? *Do you see that?*"

Their parents had almost reached them. Sarah shifted the backpack, acutely aware of the heavy weight of the box. "Yes," she said. "I see."

CHAPTER 12

ONLY BIRDS

$\mathcal{T}$HEY WERE SURROUNDED BY CROWDS all that day as their parents took them out on one last round of sightseeing before their return to the United States. Sarah kept a tight grip on the backpack, and they both spent more time nervously scanning the sky than looking at whatever sight they were supposed to be seeing. But there was no sign of the ravens.

They took turns sleeping that night; Aidan stayed up until two A.M., then woke up Sarah, who kept watch until dawn. Both of them glanced a hundred times at the window; both of them tensed each time they heard footsteps in the hall. But as far as they could tell, the birds had not returned, and nobody came to their door.

They argued, sometimes heatedly, about what to do with the box. Aidan insisted that they had to get rid of it, either by turning it over to the police or simply leaving it behind. Sarah didn't trust the police and was utterly opposed to abandoning the box.

The argument resumed after breakfast as they packed for the trip home.

"If we keep it," said Aidan, jamming a pair of jeans into his suitcase, "he'll come after us again."

"If we leave it," she answered, "he'll get it."

"Sarah, you saw what happened to the doorman. Do you want that to happen to us?"

"No," Sarah answered, grunting as she zipped her bulging suitcase closed. "But it won't happen to us, because we're leaving England."

"What if he comes after us?"

"Aidan, we'll be an ocean away."

"How do you know he won't come?"

"It's too far, Aidan. He lives here. The birds live here."

Aidan was silent for a minute. Then he said, "You don't really know. You're just guessing. I'm going to tell Dad and Mom."

Sarah stared at him. "You wouldn't," she said softly.

Tears welled in Aidan's eyes. "I would," he said. "I'm not going to die for that stupid box. I hate that we ever found it. Leave it here, or I'm telling them. Do you understand me?"

Sarah held his gaze for a moment, then turned away.

"Yes," she said. "I understand."

Heathrow Airport was, as always, insane—its endless, dingy corridors a chaotic swarm of travelers arriving from and departing for points all over the world. It took the Coopers an hour to get boarding passes, check their luggage, and make their way to the security checkpoint. They shuffled along in line, finally reaching the screening area, where they placed their carry-on bags onto the belt for the X-ray machine—Tom first, followed by Natalie, Aidan, and Sarah.

"Whose bag is this?" said a security screener, pointing to Sarah's backpack as it emerged from the machine.

"Mine," said Sarah.

"I'm just going to have a look," said the screener. Sarah nodded. Aidan looked back at her; she avoided his gaze.

Ahead of them, their parents were gathering their carry-ons; Natalie was talking about doing some duty-free shopping.

"Sarah," said Aidan.

She shook her head.

The screener had opened the backpack and was poking around inside. He pointed to something and said, "What's this?"

"A jewelry box," said Sarah. Aidan started to say something; she held up a hand to stop him.

"Is this gold?" asked the screener.

"Yes," said Sarah. The screener studied it for a moment, then pushed the backpack across the table to Sarah with a look that said, *Unbelievable, these rich Americans.*

"Thank you," said Sarah, trying not to betray her relief as she picked up the backpack. She brushed past Aidan, not meeting his furious gaze, and started toward where their parents stood waiting in the huge, bustling lounge area.

Aidan grabbed her arm, stopping her. "You lied to me, Sarah," he hissed.

"No I didn't."

"Yes you did. You said you'd leave it."

"I didn't say that, Aidan. I said I understood you. And I do. You don't want to be part of this. Okay, I understand. You don't have to be part of it."

"But how can I—"

"Will you kids hurry it up?" called Tom, striding toward them, irritated.

Aidan looked toward their father.

"Aidan," Sarah whispered urgently. "Please don't tell him. Please."

For a few seconds they stared into each other's eyes. Then Aidan jerked his arm loose and began walking. When he reached Tom, he stopped and looked back.

Please, Sarah mouthed.

Without speaking to his father, Aidan turned and started walking again.

Outside on the airport ramp, about a hundred yards from the lounge, a baggage handler stood next to a jet being readied for departure to the United States. He was awaiting a baggage tug.

Had he turned around, he would have seen a large raven landing twenty feet from where he stood.

And then another, and another . . .

Had the baggage handler looked up, he would have seen many more of the birds, some on the edge of the terminal roof, others perched along the windows.

The ravens had started gathering two hours earlier, when the Coopers had emerged from the hotel. As they climbed into their taxi, a bird perched on the hotel roof had emitted a cry and taken wing. It was quickly joined by others from nearby trees and rooftops. By the time the taxi was passing Hyde Park, there were a dozen black birds flying above it through the light fog. As the taxi pulled onto the M5 motorway, the dozen had become fifty. Soon there were more than a hundred. Flights of birds were no strange sight in London. Geese and ducks sometimes flew in gigantic Vs, slicing across the London sky like arrows. The few people who saw the ravens thought nothing of it. It was only birds.

When the taxi reached Heathrow Airport and the Coopers went inside, the ravens had dispersed—some going to the roof, some perching near windows. As the Coopers made their way through the terminal, passing windows along the way, the birds shifted, getting ever closer to the U.S.-bound jet, where a growing mass of them now gathered behind the baggage handler.

Sensing their motion, the handler turned and almost jumped at the sight of so many birds. He thought they must have been feeding on something, as they were so concentrated. Birds posed a danger to jet engines, so he stepped closer to shoo them away. He expected them to flee at his approach.

They didn't flee. Instead they condensed into a tightly packed mass and, moving as one, rose into a shape that looked remarkably like a human silhouette. The baggage handler, more astonished than scared—they were only birds, after all—wished he had a camera. He was about to call out for his coworkers to come have a look.

That was when his shadow touched the edge of the mass of birds.

And that was the last thing he remembered.

Moments later, his eyes now pitch-black and expression-less, he opened one of the plane's rear cargo doors. Instantly, the mass of birds changed shape. Looking now like a snake, it streamed swiftly across the tarmac and into the cargo hold, where the birds dispersed and disappeared into the dark recesses. More swooped down from the terminal building and darted inside—a hundred.

Two hundred. Three hundred or more, vanishing in the gloom.

The baggage handler stood next to the baggage conveyor belt, his expression unchanging, his eyes staring at nothing. The tug arrived, pulling a train of carts full of luggage of every shape and size.

"Tim?" said the tug driver. "You okay, mate?" He waited, but got no response. "Up late, were you?"

Tim remained mute.

"You want inside or out?" the driver asked. One man would feed bags onto the conveyor belt from the bottom; the other would pull them into the hold and pack them tightly in netted bays inside.

Without a word, Tim climbed the conveyor belt and disappeared inside the plane.

The driver shrugged and started the conveyor belt. In ten minutes the baggage was loaded. As Tim, on his knees near the entrance to the hold, stowed the last bag, a dark shape swooped past, brushing against him. With a groan he fell over sideways. From the bottom of the conveyor belt, the driver shouted, "Tim! You all right, mate?"

Tim sat up, blinking, dazed. He looked down at the driver.

"How'd I get up here?" he said.

"What? You climbed up there! We just loaded the bags."

Tim looked around and saw the loaded bags. He shook

his head, confused. Gingerly, he climbed down the conveyor belt.

"Are you okay, Timmy?" said the driver.

"I dunno," said Tim, frowning. "I thought . . . did you see any birds around?"

"Birds? A few, maybe. Why?"

Tim thought for a moment, then shook his head. "Never mind," he said. "It was . . . only birds."

The driver climbed back onto the tug. As he started the engine, he called, "Get some rest, Timmy boy. You're looking like a zombie today."

✦

Sarah, having just taken her seat next to Aidan, looked out the window.

Toward the back of the plane she saw two airport workers talking. One of them drove away. The other stood for a moment, rubbing his head, then turned and looked at the plane. Sarah got a good look at his face; he looked troubled. After a few moments he shook his head, turned, and walked away.

The pilot announced that all the bags had been loaded and the preflight checks were complete. "We'll be on our way shortly," he said.

Sarah turned to Aidan, and he spoke for them both: "I am so glad to be getting out of here."

CHAPTER 13

MRS. TREMAINE

WHEN, FINALLY, THEY GOT HOME, Sarah and Aidan went straight to their rooms, enjoying the luxury of once again having their own space and their own stuff. They kept themselves busy—Sarah with Facebook, Aidan with video games—while the hot, humid summer afternoon turned to dusk. They ate a quick supper with their parents, then drifted back to their rooms as darkness fell.

Just after nine P.M. Sarah tapped on Aidan's door. "Come in," he said, not taking his eyes off the TV screen.

"Can I talk to you a second?" said Sarah, entering his room.

Reluctantly, Aidan paused *Call of Duty: Modern Warfare 2.* "What?" he said.

"You know what," she said.

"Oh. That. Where'd you put it?"

"In my closet, under a bunch of junk. But we need to figure out what to do with it."

"Which is why we should have left it in England."

Sarah sighed. "Let's not go over that again, okay? It's here now."

"Thanks to you."

Sarah moved a step closer and said, "I've been thinking."

"Uh-oh."

"Aidan, listen. I think we need to find the Starcatchers."

"What?"

"We have to find them and give them the box. They're the only ones who can protect it. That's what they do."

"What makes you think there even are Starcatchers?"

"There have to be. The starstuff's real. And Ombra's real."

"Definitely."

"So the Starcatchers must be, too."

"Sarah. The stories in those books, that was like a hundred years ago. Even if those Starcatcher people were real, they're all dead now."

"Unless they had children. They'd teach them to be Starcatchers. That's what they always did. They kept the Starcatchers going for hundreds of years. I bet they're out there, somewhere. We just have to find them."

"Okay, let's just say we did. The books were set in England. Where would their descendants live?"

"People move all over the place. Besides, we won't know until we find them."

"How come you keep saying *we*? You told me I didn't have to be part of this anymore."

"If you don't want to help," Sarah said quietly, "you don't have to."

Aidan looked away, toward his window. "I also thought you said we'd be safe once we left England."

"I think we *are* safe. But I also think we have to—"

"What was that?" Aidan was on his feet.

"What was what?"

Aidan moved quickly to the window. "I saw something," he said.

"What?" said Sarah, joining him.

"It was outside the window," said Aidan, his voice tight. "It was moving. And it was black."

Sarah peered out. The night sky was overcast; a light over the kitchen door provided what little illumination there was in the backyard, revealing only a ghostly outline of a big oak, its twisted branches perfectly still on this windless night.

"I don't see anything," she said.

"Well, I did."

"Okay, maybe you saw a bird."

"That's exactly what I'm afraid of."

"But there's always birds here, Aidan. Just because one goes by the window, that doesn't mean—"

She was interrupted by the doorbell chime echoing in the foyer. She and Aidan looked at each other, saying nothing.

143

From downstairs came the sound of the door opening, then their parents' voices, followed by another, unfamiliar voice. A minute later there were footsteps on the stairs.

"Sarah?" said Natalie's voice.

"In here," called Sarah.

Natalie opened the door. She looked worried.

"Mrs. Tremaine is here," she said to Sarah. "She wants to speak to you."

Mrs. Tremaine was their longtime next-door neighbor, a woman in her early eighties whose children were grown and whose husband had died two years earlier. She was friendly enough, but had little contact with the Coopers, and virtually none with Sarah.

"With me?" said Sarah.

"Yes, and I'm worried about her. She's acting a bit . . . strange."

"Strange how?" said Sarah.

"Well, for one thing, she's wearing sunglasses, and it's pitch-black out. I suppose she could be having eye problems. But her behavior is . . . it's just strange. And her voice sounds very odd."

Sarah and Aidan exchanged a look.

"Please come down," said Natalie. "She's quite insistent that she wants to talk to you. Let's find out what this is all about, okay?"

Sarah hesitated.

"Sarah, come on." Natalie turned and headed for the stairs. Sarah followed reluctantly, with Aidan behind. As they descended the stairs they saw their father first, standing at the edge of the foyer, looking uncomfortable.

Then they saw what he was looking at. Mrs. Tremaine was a tall, rail-thin woman with a narrow face, her hair dyed an unnaturally dark shade of brown, with gray peeking through on top. She wore a loose-fitting, light-blue house-dress and, as Natalie had said, sunglasses. She stood beneath the chandelier in the center of the foyer.

Aidan tapped Sarah's shoulder and pointed furtively to the floor. Sarah's eyes widened; Mrs. Tremaine cast no shadow.

They reached the bottom of the stairs. Mrs. Tremaine stood perfectly still as her head swiveled slowly to face Sarah. Her mouth came open, but the voice wasn't hers. It didn't sound like a voice at all. It sounded like the moan of a winter wind.

"Give it to me," the voice said.

Sarah took an involuntary step back; Natalie put her arm around her daughter.

"Give *what* to you, Mrs. Tremaine?" Natalie asked. "Are you all right?"

Without giving any indication that she had heard, Mrs. Tremaine took a step toward Natalie and Sarah. Her upper body remained rigid; she moved as though she were gliding.

The awful voice came again: "Give . . . it . . . to . . . me."

Aidan looked down. Mrs. Tremaine's shoe was only a few inches from Natalie's shadow.

"Mom!" he said. "Move!"

"What?" said Natalie. "Why are—*unnnhh!*" She stopped, mid-sentence, her eyes fluttering shut, as Mrs. Tremaine's right foot brushed against her shadow.

In a flash Aidan darted forward, hands out. He shoved his mother hard, knocking her shadow away from Mrs. Tremaine. Natalie, her eyes still closed, stumbled across the foyer. Tom leaped forward to grab her just as she fell.

"Aidan!" he shouted. "What are you doing?"

"Stay away from her!" said Aidan, pointing toward Mrs. Tremaine. Sarah jumped back. Mrs. Tremaine's head swiveled toward her, and she began to move. Sarah screamed.

Aidan dove for the light switches. There were four of them on the panel, and he slammed them all down with one swipe of his hand. The foyer was plunged into pitch-black darkness, as were the porch and living room.

"Aidan!" shouted Tom. "Turn the lights back on right now!"

"No, Dad, we can't," said Aidan.

"We most certainly can, and you will!" said Tom. "I want to see if your mother's okay. I want those lights on now!"

In the darkness Sarah felt Aidan brush past her as he whispered, "I'm gonna go turn off the circuit breaker." A moment later she heard him in the kitchen, opening then closing the door to the basement and flicking on the stairway light. His footsteps raced down the stairs.

"Aidan? Sarah?" said Tom. "The lights! Now!"

"I'm sorry, Dad," said Sarah.

"What is wrong with you kids?" shouted Tom. "Stay here, Nat. I'll find the lights." Sarah heard Tom fumbling along the wall.

"This is outrageous behavior," he muttered, reaching the switches.

The lights came on. Tom was by the light switches, blinking; Natalie sat slumped against the wall, dazed.

Mrs. Tremaine was directly in front of Sarah, facing her. The sunglasses were gone. Her eyes were two huge black voids.

Sarah screamed.

Mrs. Tremaine moved forward; Sarah felt the awful cold.

And then the lights went out again.

"What the—?" bellowed Tom. "Who did that?"

Sarah stumbled backward. The cold was gone, but she was disoriented and almost too weak to stand. She heard Aidan run up the stairs and open the basement door.

"Sarah?" he called.

"You turn those lights back on now!"

"Here!" Sarah answered her brother.

"All right," said Tom, his voice furious. "I'm going to

147

go turn the lights back on. And then you are both in major trouble."

She heard him bumping into things as he worked his way toward the kitchen in the darkness. A moment later she jumped as she felt a hand on her arm.

"It's me," said Aidan.

"Upstairs," said Sarah. "Now."

They felt their way to the stairs and began climbing.

From below came the awful sound, the grotesque cold moan.

"You will give it to me," it said.

The front door cried on its hinges. Aidan and Sarah looked back as street light seeped through the open doorway. In the dim light, they saw the silhouette of Mrs. Tremaine glide down their front walk, turn left, and disappear.

They ran the rest of the way up the stairs.

"We have to leave," said Sarah.

"I know."

"Right now, before Dad finds the circuit breaker."

"I know."

"Grab your phone and whatever money you have. I'll get the box and my phone and . . . money. We'll go out the back."

"What if that thing is out there?"

"We have no choice. We can't let it come back in here. It'll get Mom and Dad."

A pause, then Aidan said, "Yeah. Okay."

From the basement came sounds of a collision—possibly with the paint shelf. Their father cursed.

They were gone before the lights came back on.

CHAPTER 14

INTO THE DARKNESS

*T*HEY RAN THROUGH THE DARKNESS, ran until their lungs burned and their breath came in hoarse gasps, and still they ran. They stuck to side roads, avoiding illumination, keeping away from streetlights. From time to time they stopped to look back and listen, straining to hear over the ear-pounding sound of their own frantic heartbeats. But they heard nothing unusual and saw only blackness.

Their phones began ringing. The caller ID showed their home number; obviously their parents had discovered they were missing. They didn't answer, and eventually turned off their phones to stop the incessant ringtones.

After an hour on the move they ventured cautiously toward a main highway. They followed it for another mile until they came to a strip shopping center. It was largely deserted; most of the stores were closed for the night. At the far end glowed a familiar green sign.

"Let's go to the Starbucks," said Sarah.

"Do you think it's safe?" said Aidan.

"We won't stay long. I need to plug in my iPad. The battery's almost dead, and I want to do some stuff on the Internet."

"What stuff?"

"I'll tell you when we get there."

They made their way along the row of stores, heads swiveling; nobody appeared to be following them. Reaching the Starbucks, they peered through the window. There were two workers behind the counter; the only customers were two young men and a young woman sitting at a corner table, drinking coffee and talking. Sarah and Aidan went inside, Sarah heading for a table near an electrical outlet at the far corner from the other customers.

"Get me a grande skinny caramel macchiato," she said to Aidan.

"Get you a what?"

Sarah sighed. "Just get me a medium coffee," she said.

Aidan went to the counter; Sarah took the iPad out of her backpack, plugged it in, turned it on, and began tapping on the screen. A few minutes later Aidan returned with her coffee and a hot chocolate for himself.

"What are you doing?" he said.

"Writing an e-mail to Mom and Dad. Take a look."

She handed the iPad to Aidan, who read:

Mom and Dad—

Please don't be mad at us. We have to
do this, and we can't tell you why, at
least not now. Please don't try to find
us. We're totally safe, and we promise to
stay in touch. We're really really sorry,
and we love you.

xoxo

Sarah and Aidan

"I would never write 'xoxo,'" said Aidan, handing the iPad back. "I hate 'xoxo.'"

"Too bad," said Sarah, sending the e-mail.

"Why'd you say we're safe? We're not safe."

"I know. I'm just trying to keep them from worrying."

"They're going to worry anyway. A lot."

"I know. They're going to look for us. And call the police."

"Maybe we should go to the police."

Sarah shook her head. "We have the same problem here we had in London. We don't know where, or who, Ombra is. He can become anybody. If we go to the police, he can become the police. Then he's got the starstuff. And us."

"So what do we do?"

Sarah was tapping on the screen again. "We find the Starcatchers."

"But how? I mean, even if they're still around, how do we find them?"

Sarah turned the iPad screen toward Aidan. "This is how," she said.

Aidan looked at the screen and laughed.

"Facebook?" he said. "Are you serious?"

"If they're still around," she said, "they have the same technology we do."

"And you think they have a Facebook page. Like, 'Hi, there! We're the Starcatchers! Want to be our friend?'"

"No, idiot. They wouldn't do that. But they could be monitoring the Internet, looking for some situation like this, where there's starstuff that needs protecting. They could be looking for certain names or keywords."

"So what are you going to do?"

Sarah, tapping again, said, "I'm going to make a Facebook page for Molly Aster."

"I don't believe this."

"Do you have a better idea?"

That shut him up. For ten minutes they sat in silence, Aidan sipping his hot chocolate, Sarah leaving her coffee untouched as she tapped on the screen. When she was done she turned it toward Aidan again, showing him the simple Facebook page she'd created for "Molly Aster." In the profile, she had written, "I found Mister Magill's box. It's full of the stuff, but now I'm being shadowed. Can you help me?"

Aidan looked up at Sarah. "So this is it?" he said. "This is our plan?"

"No," said Sarah, taking the iPad back. "I'm also going on Twitter."

Aidan rolled his eyes; Sarah resumed tapping.

The young men and woman left. One of the workers told Sarah and Aidan that the Starbucks would close in ten minutes. Sarah was still tapping.

"What are you doing?" said Aidan.

"Craigslist."

Aidan sighed and slumped in his chair.

Then he sat upright and touched Sarah's arm. She looked up and he nodded toward the door. A dark figure stood outside, silhouetted by the bright outdoor lights.

"Oh, no," Sarah said softly.

"Maybe there's a back way out," said Aidan.

They stood quickly. Sarah unplugged the iPad and shoved it into her backpack. They walked toward the counter. One of the workers, a middle-aged woman, said, "Can I help you?"

"Is there a back way out?" said Aidan.

"What?"

"We're wondering if we can leave by the—" Aidan stopped at the sound of the door opening. He and Sarah turned. A tall man entered. He wore a long overcoat and a baseball cap pulled low, shielding his eyes.

The man started toward Sarah and Aidan. They stood

frozen; there was nowhere to go except toward the dark figure, now six feet away, now four, now . . .

"Hey, Bob," said the woman behind the counter. "Thought you weren't gonna make it tonight. We're about to close."

The tall man raised his head, revealing blue eyes in a broad, friendly face.

"Just got off work," he said. "Any coffee left?"

"Absolutely," said the woman, grabbing a cup.

Aidan nudged Sarah and pointed toward the floor; she looked and saw that the man was clearly casting a shadow. She looked back at her brother and they shared a moment of shoulder-sagging relief.

"Let's go," said Sarah, heading for the door.

"Where?" said Aidan, following.

"I don't know. We've got to find someplace to spend the night, and then we . . ."

"We what?"

"We hope somebody gets in touch with us."

She pulled the door open and they went out, their eyes scanning the shopping center and parking lot. Both were deserted. They crossed the parking lot, then the highway, and entered a poorly lit side street. Tired now, they trudged forward, every step taking them farther from home, deeper into the darkness.

CHAPTER 15

THE RESPONSE

$\mathcal{J}$UST WHEN THEY THOUGHT they'd be spending the night under a tree, Aidan realized that they were near the home of a friend of his, Matthew Langerham, whose family happened to have a bus-size camper parked alongside their house. Matthew had once shown Aidan the tricked-out camper's interior; Aidan had seen where the key was hidden, behind the rear license plate.

They slipped in quietly just after midnight, Aidan taking a bunk bed amidships, Sarah heading back to the master suite. Tired from miles of running and walking, they both fell asleep almost immediately.

Aidan awoke to see daylight streaming through the cracks between the camper curtains. He rose quickly and went back to the master suite. Sarah, too, had been awakened by the light; she was sitting up, rubbing her eyes.

"It's morning," he said. "We need to leave."

"In a minute," she said, pulling the iPad from her backpack and turning it on.

"Oh man," she said. "I'm almost out of battery." She frowned at the screen. "There's like ten e-mails from Mom. She's really mad."

"I bet," said Aidan, peering through the camper curtain.

"Oh my god!" said Sarah, leaning into the iPad.

"What?"

"Someone answered us!"

"From Facebook?"

"No. They responded to the Craigslist ad. Look."

Aidan took the iPad and read the e-mail: "If this is a joke, ha ha. If you're serious, I'd like to meet you."

Aidan looked at the sender's e-mail address: asterjd@ gmail.com.

"Asterjd," he said. "Aster."

"Yeah," said Sarah, taking back the iPad.

"Of course, anyone can create a Gmail account."

"I know that," said Sarah, tapping. "But whoever this is, they responded to us. This is all we have. So we'll work with it."

Aidan read over her shoulder as she typed a reply: "This is no joke. We need help. Who are you? Where are you?"

Sarah tapped SEND and the e-mail was gone.

"Can we go now?" said Aidan.

"Not yet. I need to answer Mom." She was tapping again.

"What are you telling her?"

"We're still sorry, still safe, please don't worry, blah blah . . . hey!"

"What?"

"Asterjd," she said. "He just answered."

"What'd he say?"

Sarah was reading, frowning. "Whoa," she said.

"What?"

"He's a professor. At Princeton!"

"Princeton. The college?"

"University. He's in the physics department."

"Where is Princeton, Connecticut?"

"No, idiot. New Jersey." She started tapping again, then stopped. "My stupid battery's dead," she said.

Aidan, peering out the window again, said, "We have a bigger problem than that."

"What?" said Sarah, joining him. "Oh, no."

Their father's car was pulling into the Langerhams' driveway. As they watched, the car stopped and their father got out. He disappeared from view, headed toward the front door.

"How'd he know we were here?" said Sarah.

"He must be checking our friends' houses," said Aidan.

"We have to go now," said Sarah, stuffing the iPad into her backpack.

They left the camper quickly, Aidan locking the door and returning the key to its hiding place. They ran across the backyard and through several neighboring yards onto a side street, then into a park where they hid for a while. Eventually they worked their way to a main road and followed it, Sarah in the lead.

"Do we have any idea where we're going?" said Aidan.

Sarah pointed ahead. "There," she said. "The bus stop."

"We're taking a bus?" said Aidan.

"Yes."

"Where?"

"Downtown. To the train station. We're going to Princeton."

"Wait . . . just like that, we're gonna get on a train for New Jersey? To see a guy we don't know anything about?"

"We also need disguises," she said.

"What?"

"I'm serious."

"That's what scares me," said Aidan.

They boarded the first bus that came along, which, as it turned out, was headed in the wrong direction. But after getting directions and changing buses twice, they finally made it to the train station, where, after consulting with the ticket agent, they bought tickets to Philadelphia, where they would change to a train to Princeton.

While they were waiting for the train they went next

door to a drugstore, where they bought a large quantity of non-nutritious food. At Sarah's insistence they also bought sunglasses, as well as a scarf for her and a ball cap for him. They tried to stay in well-lit areas of the station; whenever somebody approached, they looked at the floor, making sure the person cast a shadow.

When they boarded the train, Sarah plugged her iPad into a power outlet and turned it on. She found a new barrage of e-mails from their parents, but she was in no mood to read them, so she powered it back down and dozed off. Aidan did the same; neither had gotten much sleep in the camper.

When they reached Philadelphia they enjoyed a hearty meal of Krispy Kreme doughnuts and Coke before boarding the train to Princeton. Sarah again turned on her iPad and, with a sigh, began plowing through the mass of e-mails from her parents—some pleading, some threatening, some hurt, some angry, most of them a combination of all these things. She'd been reading these for forty-five minutes when suddenly she sat up straight.

"Wake up," she said, prodding Aidan, who'd fallen asleep.

"What?" he said, blinking.

"One of the earlier e-mails from Mom. I just read it. Get this: she mentions that we were at the Langerhams'."

"What?"

"Yeah. Dad got into a big fight with them because he thought they were hiding us, and he finally realized they weren't, and now the Langerhams are mad at Mom and Dad, and Mom is not happy. But why was Dad so sure we'd even been there?"

Adam frowned. "Wait a minute," he said.

"What?"

"That app," he said. "Whaddyacallit. That tells you where your iPad is."

"Find My iPad?"

"Yeah. Do you have it turned on?"

Sarah went pale. "Yes," she said.

"Turn it off."

Sarah turned it off, then said, "You think that's how they . . ."

"Yup," he said. "Dad has your password. They used Find My iPad to track us. That's how come Dad went to the Langerhams'. Think about it. He came pretty quick after you turned it on."

"So whenever I turned the iPad on . . ."

"They knew where you were. So where else did you turn it on?"

She frowned. "I turned it on for a few minutes this morning when the train was leaving Pittsburgh. And again when we were reaching Philly."

"Okay, so they'd know we were downtown, and then in Philly. The big problem is, now they also know we're moving north out of Philly. If they're using Google Maps, they might even know we're on a rail line. They could know we're on this train."

"You think they'd go to all that trouble?"

"Knowing Mom? The Marines are probably waiting at the next station. We need to stop leaving a trail. No iPad, no e-mails, no Skype. And we've got to turn off our cell phones. The cops can track those."

"Seriously?" said Sarah. "Do you think they'd call the New Jersey police?"

"This is Mom we're talking about. She'd call the White House."

"But even if she did call the police . . . there must be thousands of teens who run away every year. They can't wait at train stations for all of them."

"Have you ever heard of private detectives?"

"You think she'd do that?"

"I repeat: this is Mom we're talking about."

Sarah sighed. "You're right. What are we going to do?"

"I'm thinking," said Aidan.

"Well," said Sarah, "think fast."

Lester Armstrong, private investigator, was an imposing man—the size of a vending machine, and mostly muscle. But it was his brains, not his brawn, that got him into the P.I. business. He'd been working as an underpaid baggage handler for a discount airline at the Newark airport when he happened upon a commotion at the Lost Baggage department. A very angry passenger was pounding on the counter, demanding to know what had happened to his suitcase, which contained jewelry belonging to his wife. The man wanted his suitcase back so badly that he loudly offered $500 cash to the person who found it.

Lester's ears perked up at that; he had bills to pay. He also had a knack for computers that he had developed playing online poker, which is why he had bills to pay. Between flights, he logged into the baggage-tracking system; a half hour later he'd managed to track the bag down eight thousand miles away in Mutare, Zimbabwe.

The owner of the bag, whose name was Nestor Paolo, was so grateful that he not only gave Lester the reward, but also offered him a job. Paolo was a private investigator with a security company based in Chicago; he needed a computer-savvy investigator and figured Lester's size might also come in handy, as Nestor himself was diminutive in stature, though powerful of mind.

And so Lester left luggage to become Nestor's East Coast office, making more money than he'd ever made before. It turned out that his gift for finding things also worked with people. He became a master of the computer-aided search; nobody could find a runaway teenager or spouse faster than Lester Armstrong. He had a nationwide reputation, which is why when a frantic Natalie Cooper began calling various hotlines, looking for a way to track down her runaway children, Lester's name came up immediately.

The Coopers hired Lester over the phone; he questioned them and quickly found out about Sarah's iPad. Within minutes, using the password supplied by Tom, he had tracked her to the Langerhams' house and sent Tom in pursuit. That hadn't worked, but Lester had picked up the iPad's trail again—first at the Pittsburgh train station, and then in Philadelphia. He was soon speeding south in his Escalade, keeping one eye on the laptop computer in the passenger seat. He smiled when he picked up Sarah's iPad again, this time north of Philadelphia and moving.

"That's right," he said. "Come to Lester." He pulled off the road and, with some quick keyboard work, determined that the iPad was on a train. By noting where and when it stopped, and then making a quick call to an Amtrak dispatcher who owed him a favor, he figured out which train they were on. Its next stop was in eleven minutes; the station was thirteen miles from Lester. With a smile, he put the Escalade in gear.

***

"We've got to split up," Aidan said.

"Because?"

"Because they're looking for two of us. Together."

"Good point."

"You need to lose the hairdo."

"No way."

"Way. If they're looking for us, they'll have pictures, and in every picture ever of you your hair's piled up like some kind of freako sculpture."

"It's my trademark."

"Whatever. Lose it. You need to look a lot different, because you're staying on the train."

"Wait . . . what are you doing?"

"Getting off the train. We're splitting up, remember?"

"But how are we gonna—"

"Shh. Just listen. I'll stick near a family so I don't stand out. I'll hang around, and if the coast is clear, I'll get the next train and meet you in Princeton. We don't turn on our phones. We don't go online. Okay?"

Sarah looked unhappy. "I guess so," she said.

"The hair," he said.

"Do I really . . ."

He handed her his ball cap and pointed down the aisle.

A minute later, Sarah was staring into the mirror in a cramped and smelly bathroom, taking a last look at her beloved hairstyle. She sighed, then filled the tiny steel sink with water. Before she could think too much about it, she plunged her head in. The intricate edifice that had been her hairstyle collapsed. She tried to rinse out the stickiness, then emptied the sink and repeated the process. She blotted up as much of the water as she could with brown paper towels, then choked back tears as she saw herself.

"I look like a wet dog," she moaned.

She brushed her hair—she'd forgotten how long it was—then twisted it into a bun and stuffed it beneath the ball cap. Then she wiped off her mascara and lipstick.

She hated how she looked. But Aidan was right: she would be much harder to recognize. She barely recognized herself. She headed back to their seats.

"Much better," said Aidan.

"I hate you," she replied.

"That's the spirit," he said. "Okay, we're coming to the station."

"How're we going to meet in Princeton?"

"First of all, you don't use the iPad. Go to a library or an Internet café. Someplace with public computers. I'll do the same. We'll find each other that way."

"But can't they track our e-mails?"

Aidan grinned. "I have a Gmail account Dad doesn't know about."

Sarah laughed. "You, too?"

"Give me a pen and paper."

They exchanged e-mails. The train began to slow. A few passengers rose from their seats.

"You'll be careful?" she said.

"I'm touched."

"Shut up."

"Keep your head down," he said. "I'll see you there."

The brakes cried out as the train shuddered to a stop. He put on sunglasses and headed for the end of the car.

—※—

Aidan got off right behind a family with three kids, staying close, trying to look like the older brother. His eyes swept the platform. *No cops,* he thought. Then he corrected himself: *No uniformed cops.*

Then he saw the man on the bench—a large man. Very large. The man held a newspaper, but Aidan could tell he wasn't reading it; his eyes—eyes that looked like they missed nothing—were sweeping the platform. They swept over Aidan, stopping for just a heartbeat. In that instant Aidan was sure the man was coming after him. But then the eyes moved on.

He didn't recognize me, thought Aidan.

—※—

Why was the boy alone? Lester wondered. He'd spotted Aidan easily—the sunglasses were a pathetic disguise. But where was the girl? She definitely hadn't gotten off the train.

Lester had considered chasing the boy, but he was in no mood to test the boy's foot speed against his own endurance. He'd put on a few pounds, lost a step since his prime. He gave a casual glance at his watch, checked the platform to the left, and, convinced the boy was alone, stood, stretched, and moved toward the train.

His plan had been to board the train, find the kids, and haul them off at whatever stop came next—Princeton at the earliest, Newark if necessary. Rent a car. Call the parents. Do the paperwork. Collect the check.

But now the boy was off the train. And maybe the girl was still on it. Maybe they were smart enough to figure out they'd be harder to find if they split up. Maybe she got off at another station. Maybe she was still back in Pittsburgh.

Lester had a rule about kids: you bring in the girl first. The world was crueler to girls. But he had another rule: a bird in the hand. The boy was right here. It seemed stupid to board the train and let the boy go free. Maybe the boy would lead him to the girl. . . .

Lester stood by the gap between platform and train door, using the reflection in a train window to watch the boy following the family toward the platform stairs. At the top of the stairs, the boy looked back, then started down.

"All aboard!" called the conductor, leaning out of the next car, looking right at Lester.

Lester turned and headed for the stairs.

Sarah had thought the large man was staring at her; it was only when he turned that she realized he'd been using her window as a mirror to watch Aidan. As the man strode toward the stairs, she started to panic; the man was a cop.

She felt her phone in her pocket, but remembered her brother's warning. She started to get out of her seat, but the train lurched forward. Too late to get off now.

"Is there something wrong?" An older woman was leaning halfway across the center aisle.

"I . . . ah . . . my boyfriend got off at that station, and he forgot something. My phone's dead. I need to reach him somehow."

"You can have him paged."

"I can?"

"Yes. You may use my phone."

"Are you sure?"

"Of course." She rummaged in her purse and produced a cell phone.

"I can pay you for calling information."

"I think I can afford it," the woman said, smiling.

Directory assistance not only gave her the number, but dialed it for her.

"Hello," Sarah said, "I'd like to page a Mister Morgan

169

Chatterley. It's urgent." She smiled at the nice lady, then turned away and cupped the phone.

At first Aidan did not believe his mother's maiden name was being announced over the train-station PA system. But then he heard it again: "Mister Morgan Chatterly, please pick up the courtesy phone."

Morgan Chatterley was his mother's maiden name. It was a family joke: she hated the name Morgan and had insisted on being called Natalie since middle school. Aidan knew the page could not possibly be a coincidence. It had to be Sarah.

Or was it his parents? Some kind of trap?

He started toward the courtesy phone, stopped, turned away, stopped again. Finally, he went over and answered it.

He lowered his voice. "Hello?"

"Is that you?" said Sarah, whispering.

"I told you not to use your phone!"

"I'm not. I borrowed one."

"But what—"

"Just listen. There's a guy. Big guy. Looks a little like Hulk Hogan."

"I saw him. He got on the train. Keep your head down, like I told you."

"He didn't get on. He was watching you. He's following you."

"Are you sure?" Aidan felt his stomach tighten.

"Yes. Get out of there now."

The line went dead. Aidan hung up and quickly looked around. He'd planned to hang around the station until the next train; that wouldn't work now. He looked across the parking lot, where there was a busy street. A few blocks to the right was a village; he could make out a Radio Shack and a Starbucks.

He walked quickly across the parking lot and turned right. After a half a block, he glanced back.

The big man was behind him.

The man was about twenty yards back and didn't seem in any particular hurry. In fact, if Sarah hadn't warned him, Aidan wouldn't have been suspicious.

He walked a bit faster, then faster still. After a minute he glanced back. The man was the same distance behind him.

Aidan picked up his pace even more. *Stay calm*, he told himself. *Stay calm*. But he couldn't. He was afraid to turn around, and afraid to feel a big hand grab his shoulder.

He broke into a run.

He covered two blocks at a dead sprint, aiming for the Starbucks, hoping he'd be safe with people around. He burst through the door and almost fainted with relief when he saw the customer standing at the counter: a police officer.

His relief disappeared a second later when it occurred to him that if the big guy was a private investigator—which he surely was—then he would simply tell the policeman that Aidan was a runaway, and he'd be caught.

He looked out the window; the big man was getting close. He still appeared to be in no hurry.

Aidan looked back at the policeman, who was still at the counter adding sugar to his coffee. The big man was fifteen yards from the Starbucks. Aidan took a breath, then stepped outside. He stood on the sidewalk, waiting. The big man was five yards away.

"Hello, Aidan," he said, his voice a deep rumble.

"*Help! Police!*" shouted Aidan. "*He's hurting me!*"

The big man stopped, held up his hand.

"Hold it," he said.

"*Help!*" shouted Aidan, crumpling to the ground. "*Please!*"

The door behind him burst open. The policeman looked down at Aidan, then at the big man.

"*Ow!*" screamed Aidan. "Please make him stop!"

"I didn't do anything," said the big man.

The policeman drew his nightstick. "Sir, please turn around and put your hands against the wall."

"Officer, I didn't do anything. I'm a pri—"

"*I said turn around,*" bellowed the policeman, giving the big man a hard shove to the shoulder.

"This kid is a—"

"*Spread your legs!*" The cop started patting the big man down. It took him three seconds to find the gun.

The big man said, "Officer, this is a mis—"

"Keep quiet and don't move," said the policeman. He radioed for backup, then unclipped some handcuffs.

"You're making a big mistake," the big man said to the wall, through gritted teeth. "It's that kid you should be taking into custody."

"Oh, really?" said the officer. "Does he have a gun, too?"

"No, but he's . . ." The big man glanced back. "No! He got away!"

The policeman turned around. The big man was right. Aidan was gone.

CHAPTER 16

REUNION

$\mathcal{A}$IDAN, HAVING ROUNDED ONE CORNER and then another, was running hard on a side street, glancing back, pondering his next move. His plan had been to head back to the train station and catch the next train to Princeton. But things had changed. The police wouldn't be able to hold the big guy who'd been following him—after all, he hadn't done anything wrong. And if he was a P.I.—which Aidan was pretty sure he was—he'd tell the cop that Aidan was a runaway. Then the police would be after him, and they'd be watching the station.

He thought maybe he could take a bus to Princeton. The question was, which bus? And where to catch it? He was passing a Harley-Davidson shop. Glancing inside, he saw a wide, bearded man with many square feet of tattoos talking to a man dressed head to toe in black leather, wearing a red bandana.

Aidan went in. "Excuse me," he said. The men turned toward him. Aidan wondered if he was making a mistake.

The wide man, his voice a growl, said, "You look a little young for a Harley."

"I, um," said Aidan, his voice cracking, "I was just wondering, what's the best way to get to Princeton?"

The wide man tugged at his beard. "Well," he said, "there's the train."

"Right," said Aidan. "I was just looking for something . . ." —he paused, frantically trying to think of an excuse for not taking the train—". . . faster."

"Really," said the wide man, amused. "Faster than the train."

"Yeah."

"Well, then," said the wide man, "if you want fast, you could maybe hitch a ride with Tommy here. He's heading up that way right now, delivering a part. You up for a rider, Tommy?"

Tommy looked at Aidan. He had a lean, sun-baked face and a hard expression. But when he spoke, his voice was surprisingly soft.

"Happy to take you, kid, if we can find you a helmet."

"Seriously?" said Aidan. "On a real Harley?"

"I don't drive the imaginary ones," said Tommy.

In half an hour—one of the most exciting half hours of Aidan's life—he was climbing off the Harley at the doorstep of the Princeton town library. He thanked Tommy and went inside, where, after a few minutes, he found Sarah at one of the computer stations, typing away. He walked up quietly behind her and tapped her on the shoulder. She emitted a small scream—drawing disapproving stares from other library patrons—then, seeing who it was, jumped up and wrapped Aidan in the kind of warm embrace she normally reserved for dogs.

"Easy!" said Aidan, disentangling himself.

"Sorry!" she said. "I'm just . . ."

"Happy to see me?"

"Incredible as it seems, yes."

"Yeah, me too, with you. No more splitting up."

"Agreed." She attempted another hug, but he fended her off.

"Now what?" he said. "Where's our guy?"

"I've done some Google mapping," Sarah said, nodding toward the computer. "His office is on the Princeton campus. It's a little ways, but we can walk."

They set out from the library, Aidan filling Sarah in on his escape from the big man and his Harley ride. They reached the Princeton campus and, following Sarah's hand-written map, made their way along pathways, past well-manicured lawns and old brick buildings.

"I really, really hope this guy can help us," said Aidan.

CHAPTER 17

J.D.

$\mathcal{T}$HE PRINCETON PHYSICS DEPARTMENT was headquartered in Jadwin Hall, a massive, modern brick building next to the football stadium. The office Sarah and Aidan were looking for was on the second floor at the end of a long hallway. The door was closed. As they approached it, Sarah grabbed Aidan's arm.

"Look," she said, pointing to the nameplate next to the door, which read J.D. ASTER, ASSOCIATE PROFESSOR OF PHYSICS.

"His name is Aster!" she said. "J.D. Aster."

"I can read," said Aidan.

"So it's not just his e-mail address. It's his name. He's a Starcatcher!"

"Sarah, he's a guy named Aster."

"Who maybe can help us. I soooo hope he can help us." Sarah rapped her knuckles twice on the door.

"Come in," called a man's voice. Sarah opened the

door and stepped inside, followed by Aidan. The office was cluttered—papers were everywhere, occupying two chairs as well as a good section of the floor. Behind the desk, facing a computer screen, was a man in his twenties wearing faded jeans and a T-shirt that read DEATH TO SQUIRRELS. His tousled brown hair spilled over an angular face dominated by startlingly bright green eyes set above prominent cheekbones.

"Whoa," said Sarah, softly. Aidan rolled his eyes.

"Can I help you?" said the man.

"'Death to squirrels'?" said Aidan.

"A band," said the man. "I'm J.D. And you are . . ."

Sarah, wishing she'd checked her hair one last time before opening the door, stepped forward and, putting on her most winning smile, said, "I'm Sarah Cooper, and this is my brother, Aidan. I'm the one who sent you the . . . I mean, you sent it to me, but it was in answer to the thing I sent you, although of course I didn't know it was you, at the time."

"What?" said J.D.

"You answered our Craigslist ad," said Aidan.

J.D. frowned. "That was *you*?"

Sarah and Aidan nodded.

"But you're just . . . kids!"

Sarah reddened.

Aidan said, "Well, you don't look old enough to be a college professor."

178

"Associate professor," said J.D.

"Well, professor," said Sarah, "we're old enough to have found you, and to have come here to ask for your help."

"Help with . . ." He eyed them both curiously.

Sarah hesitated for a moment.

"Starstuff," she said.

"Excuse me?"

The words seemed to tumble out before she could stop them. "We have some starstuff."

"It's real," Aidan said. "Really real."

"We found a letter . . . and a map," Sarah said, "and we followed the map, and we found the starstuff in England."

"Hidden in a cave," Aidan said.

"And we took it," Sarah added. "We thought it would be fun, but now Ombra knows we have it, and he's after it."

J.D. smiled. "That would be Lord Ombra?"

"Yes!" said Aidan. "He's after us. He's a flock of birds, ravens, and he . . ."

He stopped, seeing the look on J.D.'s face.

"You don't believe us," Sarah said.

J.D. sighed. "I take it you're fans of the books."

"Yes," said Sarah, "but this is—"

"Listen," said J.D. "Those books, they're just stories. People get wrapped up in stories. But they're still just stories."

Aidan said, "You think we came all this way to tell you a fairy tale?"

"I'm afraid I do," said J.D.

"Well," Aidan said angrily, "maybe you'd like to see what's inside the—ow!" He yanked his arm away from Sarah's painfully pinching fingers. She gave him a *shut up* look, then turned to J.D.

"I have a question, Professor Aster," she said. "If you don't believe the starstuff stories are real, why did you answer our Craigslist ad? Why did you say you'd like to meet us? Why did you tell us to come here?"

"Because when I answered the ad, I didn't know you were children."

"We're not children. I'm seventeen."

J.D. snorted.

"Besides," Sarah went on, "what difference does it make how old we are? You answered the ad. You told us to meet with you. Why did you do that, if you don't believe us?"

J.D.'s face reddened. "I suppose I owe you an explanation."

"You think?" Aidan said.

J.D. sighed. "Okay, okay," he said. He took a deep breath. "What I'm going to tell you now is our big family secret, passed down through the generations. I shouldn't tell you this, but at this point I don't think it matters anymore. My great-grandfather, Henry, was an Englishman, and the nephew of a man named Leonard Aster—the same name that's in the books. Henry claimed he was a Starcatcher."

"Oh my god," said Sarah. "I knew it. You are one of them!"

"I am no such thing," said J.D. "I said my great-grandfather claimed he was a Starcatcher. It was a family legend, passed down through generations of Asters. But they're all gone now. I'm the last of the Asters, as far as I know. And I'm not passing it on, because I think it's a fairy tale."

"What did your parents think?" said Sarah.

"My mom thought the whole Starcatchers story was silly. My father wanted to believe. He loved and respected his father and grandfather. But he was a physicist, like me. He needed proof. The idea of starstuff, flying, shadow creatures . . . I don't think he really believed any of that. But he felt an obligation to his father, so he passed the instructions along to me."

"What instructions?" said Aidan.

"Basically, to keep an eye out. For what—that part was pretty vague. The story passed down in our family was that the bad guys were defeated back in England and all the starstuff was gone except for one batch, which they kept in case of an emergency, hidden in some secret safe place by this guy Magill. So the instructions, according to my dad, were that we Asters were to keep an eye out in case the bad guys reappeared, or the starstuff somehow got out, or somebody needed our help. It was all pretty vague, and I don't think my dad ever really bought it. I know I don't buy it. But I made my dad a promise that I would keep an eye out. So I did."

He pointed to his computer. "I use Web-search programs with keywords like 'starstuff,' 'Starcatchers,' 'Aster,' that sort of thing. Most of what I get is fans of the books blogging about them. But your Craigslist ad seemed different. It mentioned Magill, which was unusual. So I answered you. But now that you're here, to be honest, I feel pretty stupid for letting it get this far." He took a deep breath. "Listen, I'm really sorry I wasted your time. But I honestly don't want to waste any more of mine on this. So if you'll excuse me . . ."

"We're wasting your time?" Aidan said bitterly. "Do you have any idea—"

Sarah put a hand on her brother's arm, stopping him. "I have one more question for you, professor," she said.

"Yes?" he said.

"What about the books?" she said.

"What do you mean?"

"The Starcatchers books. You had this big family secret for all these years. Then all of a sudden, there's these books about exactly the same thing—starstuff, the Starcatchers, the Asters. Didn't that freak you out? How do you explain it?"

J.D. smiled. "Good question," he said. "Yes, it did freak me out—at first. But the more I thought about it, the more I realized that it made perfect sense."

"How?" said Sarah.

"It's obvious. The Starcatchers story must be an old legend. I don't know how it got into my family; maybe somebody told the story to one of my ancestors. Or maybe one of my ancestors made it all up and told it to his kids one night, and they believed it, and they've been passing it along ever since. But however it got started, it's obvious that other people, outside my family, have also heard basically the same story. And a few years ago somebody decided to turn it into a book for kids. But that just proves my point: it's a folk tale. It's all made up."

"You're sure?" said Sarah.

"Completely. I'm a scientist. I believe in what can be proven. There's no proof for any of this."

"Really," said Sarah. She unslung her backpack and set it on the desk. She looked at Aidan and said, "What do you think?"

"I think he's a jerk," muttered Aidan.

"I heard that," said J.D.

"Aidan," said Sarah, "we need his help."

"All right," Aidan said reluctantly. "Show him."

"Show me what?" said J.D.

"Proof," said Sarah. She unzipped the backpack and took out the golden box. She set it on the desk with a solid *thunk*. "There," she said.

"Nice box," said J.D.

"It's full of starstuff."

J.D. looked at the box, then at Sarah, and smiled. "Sure it is," he said.

"You don't believe me."

"I don't believe you."

"I told you he's a jerk," said Aidan.

"I'm a scientist," said J.D., glaring at Aidan.

Sarah touched the gold wheel on the box. "Stick out your hand," she said.

Aidan stepped forward. "Sarah," he said. "We showed it to him. That's enough. This is not a good idea."

"Just a little," she said.

Aidan shook his head. "It could bring them, Sarah. They can feel it."

Sarah hesitated. "From this far away?" she said.

"I don't know," said Aidan. "They could be anywhere."

Sarah took her hand off the wheel.

J.D.'s smile broadened. "Nicely done!" he said. "A fine performance. I gather that, because of the grave danger of the box's contents, you can't actually show me the starstuff."

Sarah's face turned deep red. She put her hand back on the wheel.

"Sarah . . ." said Aidan.

"Stick out your hand," she said to J.D.

"If you're videoing this . . ." said J.D.

"Stick out your hand!"

With a sigh, J.D. put his hand next to the golden box.

Sarah, one hand on the wheel, used the other to tilt the box.

"This better not be paint," J.D. said.

Sarah turned the wheel a tiny bit, then a tiny bit more. Nothing happened.

"Okay," said J.D., "this is getting old." He started to pull his hand away.

Sarah opened the wheel a quarter turn.

In an instant, the small office was flooded with golden light and a glorious sound.

Four hundred miles to the west, a massive oak suddenly came alive, its leaves and branches thrashing as though buffeted by a sudden storm. But it was no storm. It was the beating of hundreds of black wings.

Momentarily blinded, Sarah and Aidan couldn't see J.D.'s reaction. But they heard him—first a gasp, then a moan of pleasure. Then—"Whoa."

Sarah turned the wheel shut. As suddenly as it had appeared, the golden light was gone. J.D. was still behind his desk, a look of astonished delight on his face.

"What was that?" he said.

"That," said Sarah, "was starstuff."

"Which, according to you, doesn't exist," said Aidan.

"Well, I admit it was pretty . . . amazing," said J.D. "But I can think of various ways you could have done that . . . some kind of chemical mist with a fast-acting hallucinogenic—"

"Professor," said Sarah, cutting him off. "Look at your feet."

"What?"

"Your feet. Look at them."

J.D. looked down at his feet. They were a good six inches off the floor. "Oh my god," he said.

"Exactly," said Sarah.

"Try leaning forward," said Aidan. "Just a little."

J.D. leaned. He floated gently upward, his feet brushing his desktop, sending some papers fluttering to the floor. He drifted across the office, Sarah and Aidan stepping aside to make room. He put his hands out as he reached the door, stopping himself. He looked down, and his feet began to rise; in a few seconds he was upside down, facing Sarah and Aidan, his sneakers gently bumping against the ceiling.

"Oh my god," he repeated.

"It's not a chemical mist," said Aidan.

"No," agreed J.D.

"You might want to turn right-side up," said Sarah. "It wears off."

By waving his arms in a swimming motion, J.D. got himself roughly upright, two feet off the floor, smiling hugely.

"Okay," he said. "I believe you."

"Duh," said Aidan.

J.D. pointed at the golden box on his desk. "Now," he said, "I want to know everything."

"You're going to want to sit down," said Sarah. "If you can."

J.D. maneuvered himself to his desk chair, then took hold of its arms and positioned himself above it, hovering.

They told him the whole story, starting with finding the map in the desk. It took more than an hour; J.D. wanted every detail, and had many questions. When they were finally done, he sat utterly still in his chair—the starstuff had long since worn off—staring at the box. Finally, he spoke.

"So to sum it up—you found the last of the hidden starstuff, and now Ombra's after you, and you can't trust anybody because Ombra can get to anybody."

"Or *be* anybody," said Aidan.

"So you came to me for help," said J.D.

"Yes," said Sarah. "We need a Starcatcher."

"But I'm not a Starcatcher. My grandfather was . . . I guess," he said, looking at the box. "And maybe my dad, as well. But I'm not."

"You are now," said Aidan.

"You made a promise to your dad," said Sarah.

"I did, but I didn't realize—"

"—that you might actually have to *do* something?"

J.D. winced. "Guilty," he said.

"Well, are you a man of your word?"

J.D.'s smile was gone now. "I like to think I am," he said.

"All right, then. We have starstuff, and we need your help."

J.D. thought long and hard. "Trouble is, I don't know how I can help you. You know more about this than I do."

"Are you sure? Your family were Starcatchers!"

"Seriously, most of what I got from my dad was really vague."

"Good thing we just about killed ourselves getting here," said Aidan.

J.D. was drumming his fingers on his desk, frowning. "Okay," he said. "Listen, I've never believed it."

"Believed what?" said Sarah.

"I've always dismissed it as the ramblings of a Victorian woman who had nothing better to do than brood over some . . . some fairy tale she'd been told as a child," said J.D.

"Dismissed what?" Sarah pressed.

"There's this book, supposedly a diary."

Sarah was leaning forward now.

"My grandfather left it to my dad, who kept it in a safe-deposit box," said J.D. "When I was going through my parents' stuff, I flipped through it once. It made no sense to me. Of course, at the time I thought this starstuff business was ridiculous anyway. I almost threw it out."

"But you didn't," said Sarah.

"No. It's with some old stuff at my place."

"Can we see it?" said Sarah. "Like, now?"

"And get something to eat?" said Aidan.

"I don't see why not," said J.D., rising.

"One thing," said Sarah. "You call it a diary."

"Right."

"Whose diary?"

"Supposedly, a relative of mine from England, though I'm not exactly sure what the relationship is—something like great-great-great-aunt, if I have it right. I was told she sent the diary to my grandfather for safekeeping when she was getting old and frail."

Sarah stared at J.D. intently. "What was her name?" she asked softly.

"Mary Aster Darling," said J.D.

"Mary was her given name," said Sarah softly. "She was known as Molly."

CHAPTER 18

THE DIARY

$\mathcal{J}$.D. LIVED IN A BIG, OLD TWO-STORY wood house with a wide front porch facing a lawn that looked as if it were maintained by goats. The sprawling interior was a random jumble of worn furniture, books, laundry, cardboard boxes, magazines, CD cases, and musical paraphernalia.

"You live here alone?" said Sarah.

"Yup," said J.D.

"Are you, like, rich?" said Aidan.

"I am . . . comfortable," said J.D. "Thanks to an inheritance."

"How many guitars do you have?" said Aidan, surveying the living room, where at least three Fender Stratocasters poked their necks out of the clutter.

J.D. frowned. "Eleven," he said. "No, wait—twelve."

"Do you play?" said Sarah.

"Badly," said J.D. "But I love Strats. You guys hungry?"

"Yes," said Sarah and Aidan together.

"I'll order some pizzas," said J.D. "You don't want to know what's in the refrigerator. Pepperoni okay with everybody?"

"And extra cheese," said Aidan.

"Could you get the diary first?" said Sarah.

"In a hurry, are we?"

"We are."

"Okay, then." J.D. tromped up the stairs, returning two minutes later with a slim book bound in plain brown leather. He handed it to Sarah, who held it in both hands, looking at it reverently.

"I can't believe it," she said. "Molly's diary."

"So say you," said J.D. "Mary was the name I was given."

"She actually touched this," said Sarah. "She wrote in this."

"I have something else you might be interested in," said J.D. "I'd forgotten about it. It was in the same box as the diary."

"What is it?" Sarah said eagerly.

"This," said J.D., digging into his pocket. He pulled out a gold chain, which was threaded through a small golden sphere with a tiny hinge and clasp. He handed it to Sarah, who stared at it in disbelief.

"Her locket!" she exclaimed. "An actual Starcatcher locket!"

"You're awfully dramatic, you know that?" said J.D.

"Tell me about it," said Aidan.

"Is there anything inside?" said Sarah, fumbling with the clasp. "Because the Starcatchers used these to—"

"There's nothing inside," said J.D. "I checked."

Sarah had the locket open now; it was, indeed, empty. She closed it and said, "Do you mind if I wear it? While I read Molly's diary?"

J.D. waved it away. "Keep it," he said. "And good luck figuring out the diary. I'll go order pizza."

Sarah cleared a space on the ancient sofa, plopped down, took a breath, and opened the diary. The paper had yellowed with age, but the writing—a neat, compact cursive, in black ink—was quite legible:

Dear Reader:

I cannot know who you are. I can only hope that, because you have been entrusted with this diary, you understand the importance of our mission, and share our commitment to it.

These pages recount certain events that occurred in 1905 and subsequently. Our organization—what few of us remained—had agreed that it had become necessary to isolate the island permanently. Our concern was twofold. First, to protect the island and its denizens from outsiders, who were finding their way to its shores with increasing frequency; second, to guard against the danger that the material on the island—to our knowledge, the last large store of it left on Earth—would be discovered and fall into the wrong hands. We believe that we have defeated our enemy, but we have not exterminated him; he survives in the shadows, much weakened, but still a threat against which we must remain vigilant. As I write these words, our efforts concerning the island appear to have succeeded, thanks to the great generosity and unique genius of E. It is our belief that the island, and the material, are now permanently safe. However, we have decided to leave this record of our activities in the event that it might be useful for future members of our organization. I trust, Dear Reader, that your interest in this diary stems only from idle curiosity. If you have a more pressing reason for reading it—if, God forbid, a problem has arisen that we did not foresee—it is my fervent hope that these pages are helpful to you, and that you are able, as generations of us have before you, to meet the challenge you face.

Sincerely, and hopefully,
Mrs. Mary Aster Darling

"Wow," said Sarah.

"What?" said Aidan, who was attempting, so far without success, to tune a 1969 Stratocaster with a sunburst finish.

"This," said Sarah, holding up the diary. "Aidan, she's talking about the island!"

"What island?" said J.D., returning from the pizza-ordering mission.

"Never Land!" said Sarah. "It must be! Read this!"

She handed the diary, open to the first page, to J.D., who read it with Aidan reading over his shoulder.

"She's definitely right about the enemy not being exterminated," said Aidan. "We've seen that for ourselves. But who's this 'E'?"

"I don't know," said Sarah. "But I'm sure the island is Never Land."

"You actually think it exists?" said J.D.

"Yes."

"With a flying boy?" said Aidan. "And pirates?"

"And mermaids?" added J.D. "You really believe that, Sarah?"

"Do you really believe you were floating back in your office?"

J.D. grinned. "Touché," he said. "Okay, so let's say there really is a Never Land island. Where is it? We have satellites now, Sarah. They've mapped the entire world. We can see every speck of land. How come nobody knows about this island?"

"That's the point," said Sarah. "That's what the diary is saying. They didn't want people to find the island. So they did something. They isolated it."

"What does that even *mean*?" said Aidan. "How do you isolate an island?"

"I don't know," said Sarah, taking the diary back from J.D. "But it's in here, and I'm going to find out."

Lester Armstrong sped north on I-95, pushing the Escalade as fast as he dared.

It had taken him several frustrating hours to sort everything out with the Bensalem Township Police Department. Finally, after checking out his references and calling the Coopers in Pittsburgh, the police had agreed to release him without charges. Lester was free, but furious; he considered himself very good at what he did, yet a fifteen-year-old boy had gotten away from him easily and made him look like a fool.

Next time, kid, thought Lester. *Next time you're mine.*

The one good thing was that a police sergeant had agreed, after hearing a plea over the phone from a sobbing Natalie Cooper, to put out a missing-children bulletin, which had been broadcast, with photos of Aidan and Sarah, by a

Philadelphia TV station. The bulletin quickly produced a good lead: a motorcycle-shop owner called to say that Aidan had gotten a ride with one of his workers to the Princeton public library. The Princeton police had been alerted, and Lester was on his way there now, grimly determined to track down his quarry, especially the boy who'd made him look bad.

You're mine, kid.

❈

In a park near the town of Indiana, Pennsylvania, about fifty miles east of Pittsburgh, a three-year-old boy pointed at the late-afternoon sky.

"Birds!" he said.

The boy's parents looked up from their picnic meal of barbecued chicken and potato salad.

"My goodness," said the mother.

"Wow," said the father. "That's a lot of birds."

They were coming from the west, hundreds of them, flying in a densely packed group, looking almost like a fast-moving cloud. They flew low, so low that the family could hear their wings beating, so low that, as they approached, the mother felt the need to pull the little boy close to her.

The large black birds swarmed overhead in a rush of wind, their mass momentarily blocking the sun. The family watched silently as the swarm swept east, disappearing over a hill, leaving the park sunny and quiet again.

"What the heck was that?" said the father.

"I've never seen anything like it," said the mother.

"Birds!" said the boy.

"Yes," the mother said softly, her eyes still on the horizon. "Birds."

CHAPTER 19

ESCAPE

(D)USK CAME TO J.D.'S HOUSE, followed soon by pizzas. Sarah
chewed slowly through four slices, her eyes never leaving the
diary pages. Night fell. J.D. occupied himself on the Internet.
Aidan continued, without success, his efforts to cause the
Stratocaster to produce some sound that even vaguely resem-
bled music. Finally, he gave up and watched TV.

An hour passed, and a good part of a second. At last,
Sarah closed the diary and stood.

"Okay," she announced. Aidan and J.D. turned to her.

"Okay, what?" said J.D.

"Okay, I read it all."

"And?"

"A lot of it I don't understand. But I think I'm getting a
rough idea."

"And?"

"It's pretty weird."

"Weird how?" said Aidan.

"Okay," said Sarah. "Like Molly says in the letter in the front, the Starcatchers were looking for a way to protect the island. So one of the Starcatchers, a guy that Molly calls 'T,' who I think was some kind of professor, suggested that they should get in touch with this guy she calls 'E.' So in 1905, Molly went to see this E in"—Sarah paused to flip through some diary pages—"a place called Bern."

"Burn?" said Aidan.

"B-e-r-n," said Sarah. "Where is that, anyway?"

"I believe it's in Switzerland," said J.D. "You said 1905?"

"Yeah. Is that important?"

"Not sure," said J.D., frowning. "Go on."

"Okay. So this E guy worked on this for a long time. A couple of years. There was a lot of back and forth between him and the Starcatchers. But finally he came up with a solution to protect the island, which was . . . well, that's the part that's really weird."

"What was it?" said Aidan.

"A bridge," said Sarah.

J.D. nodded. "I remember reading that. I think that's exactly where I decided it was nonsense and gave up."

"A bridge to the island?" Aidan said. "I thought it's in the middle of the ocean somewhere? And how would building a bridge possibly isolate something?"

"I don't think it's a regular bridge," Sarah said. "This guy E was making it in his laboratory."

"What?" J.D. said.

"And he used starstuff to make it," Sarah said.

"Starstuff?" said Aidan. "To build a bridge?"

"To make it," said Sarah.

"How do you know it was starstuff?" said J.D.

"You should have kept reading," said Sarah. "Molly calls it 'material,' but it has to be starstuff. She says the Starcatchers gave E some material from the supply held by M, who has to be Magill."

"Okay," said Aidan. "They're isolating an island with a bridge, which they're making in a laboratory. Using starstuff."

"I think that's what the diary is saying," said Sarah.

"That makes no sense," said Aidan.

J.D. cleared his throat. Aidan and Sarah turned toward him. "I think . . . maybe, in a kind of incredible way . . . it *does* make sense," he said.

"How so?" said Aidan.

"I can't believe I'm saying this," said J.D. "And if I hadn't seen the starstuff for myself, I *wouldn't* be saying this."

Sarah and Aidan waited.

"I think I know what kind of bridge we're talking about," he said. "I also think I know who E is—who he *has* to be— although I admit I'm having a hard time wrapping my mind around it."

"Who? Who is it?" begged Sarah.

"If I'm right," said J.D., "E is Einstein."

"Albert Einstein?" said Aidan.

"No, Buddy Einstein," said J.D. "Of course Albert Einstein."

"But how?" said Sarah. "I mean, how could—"

J.D. held up his hand. "I'll explain," he said. "But if you're going to understand, I'm going to have to teach you a little theoretical physics."

Sarah sat on the sofa and patted the spot next to her for Aidan to sit down. "Teach away, professor," she said.

"Okay," said J.D. "To begin with, what we think of as—"

Bang!

Sarah screamed as the front door burst open, jagged pieces of the wood door frame flying across the room. A large man wearing padding and a plastic face shield hurtled into the room, others right behind him, all of them bellowing, their voices a jumble of harsh commands.

"Police! Police! On the floor, now! Down on the floor!"

Three of the policemen hit J.D., taking him down hard, face-first, paying no attention to his shouted pleas protesting his innocence. Others grabbed Aidan and Sarah, and in seconds they were being hustled out of the house.

A police van idled in the driveway. Sarah and Aidan were seated on one of the two facing bench seats inside. In the front seats were two officers, a male and a female, the female at the wheel. Between the cops and Aidan and Sarah was a metal mesh divider.

J.D., in handcuffs, was led to the van by two policemen, who opened the back door and pushed him inside. They sat him on the other bench and chained his handcuffs to the floor. One of the cops handed his weapon to a fellow officer and sat on the bench with J.D., nightstick in hand. The other cop slammed the rear door shut.

"You don't understand," Sarah pleaded. "This man is helping us. He didn't do anything!"

"Stockholm Syndrome," the male cop in the front seat said to the female, who nodded. He turned to Sarah and Aidan and said, "You're going to be all right, kids. You're safe now."

"But we were safe!" said Sarah. "He didn't—"

"We'll sort it out at the station," said the cop. "With your parents."

The van started moving.

"Our parents are coming?"

"On their way from Pittsburgh," said the female cop. "They're very worried."

"You had a lot of people worried," said the male cop, lecturing now. "Your pictures were all over TV."

"Oh, no," said Sarah.

"No, that was good," said the cop. "People saw you

leaving Jadwin Hall with the creep back there. That's how we tracked you down."

"He's not a creep!" said Aidan.

"Like I said, we'll sort it out at the station."

Sarah leaned closed to Aidan. "This is bad," she whispered.

"Tell me," he whispered back. "They're never gonna believe us." He nodded toward J.D. "And I don't know what they're gonna do to him."

She glanced back. J.D. was staring at the van floor, his face white with shock. A few hours ago, he didn't know Sarah and Aidan existed; now he was facing arrest, maybe jail. *Because he tried to help us*, she thought.

"It's not fair," whispered Aidan.

"I know."

"You two all right?" the female cop in front asked.

"No," said Sarah, softly. Tears burned her eyes. She looked down; she didn't want the police, or Aidan, to see her crying. A tear fell. It landed on Molly's diary. Sarah realized that she'd been gripping it all along, so tightly that her hand hurt.

Then she realized that her other hand was gripping the backpack. She looked at Aidan. He was looking at the backpack, too.

Lester Armstrong was following the van. He'd been just a step behind the police since he'd gotten to Princeton.

He'd reached the library just after dark. As he pulled up, a man and a woman hustled out of the building and climbed into an unmarked, illegally parked Chevy—so obviously a police car it might as well have had a light rack on top. *Detectives*, Armstrong figured. No way they were there by coincidence; they had to be on the trail of the Cooper kids.

The Chevy started rolling and was joined a few seconds later by a Princeton PD patrol car, siren blaring. Armstrong followed in the Escalade, keeping a safe distance. The cops were moving fast; they'd obviously found something out. Armstrong's plan was to stick close to them, looking for an opportunity—he was very good at this—to leapfrog their investigation and rescue the kids himself, thus earning a nice fee.

The police headed toward the Princeton campus, their destination a large brick building called Jadwin Hall. From the idling Escalade, Armstrong watched the detectives go inside. They emerged a few minutes later, without the two kids but in a hurry, and walked briskly to their car, cell phones glued to their ears. They roared off, again accompanied by the patrol car.

Armstrong followed them to a residential neighborhood not far from campus, where they stopped in front of a large, wood-framed house with an unkempt lawn. Armstrong killed his lights and pulled to the curb a half block away. A few seconds later a black panel van screeched to a stop in front of the house.

Uh-oh, thought Armstrong. *SWAT team.*

This was not good. If the kids were in the house, there was no way he'd get to them ahead of the SWAT team. By the look of it, he'd wasted his day.

The raid was efficient, professional; fifteen or twenty seconds, and it was all over. Armstrong felt slightly ill as he watched the cops bring out the two kids, including the boy who'd eluded him. They also brought out a man whom Armstrong didn't recognize. All three were loaded into a police van and driven away.

Armstrong saw his fee going with it. Unless . . .

He slammed the Escalade into gear, a plan forming in his mind. The Coopers wouldn't reach Princeton until the next day. What parents would want their kids held in a police station overnight? Wouldn't they be happier to have their kids released into his custody, and for him to put them up at a nice hotel until they arrived? If they hadn't left yet, they might even authorize him to escort the kids home, shortening the process and getting this whole miserable experience behind them. He'd have to charge them for this service, of course. But money was usually no object for parents who'd lost their kids.

He fished his cell phone out of his pocket and dialed. He

was counting on paperwork to slow the police down so that he would be the first to give the Coopers the good news—and the first to receive their gratitude.

He could practically smell the fee.

Aidan and Sarah were communicating with their eyes. He looked, with an exaggerated stare, at the backpack, then at her. She nodded, then arched her eyebrows. *Right, the star-stuff. But what do we do?*

Aidan's eyes tracked slowly back toward the steel grid separating them from J.D., then forward to the front seat. He touched his belt, then nodded toward the male cop in the shotgun seat. Sarah looked and saw a key ring clipped to the officer's wide police belt. One key was smaller than the others, silver in color. Sarah figured that must be a handcuff key.

She looked at Aidan and nodded. *Got it. The key. Then what?*

He pointed to the backpack again, then at his seatbelt, then at the seatbelts worn by the two officers in the front seat. Sarah looked puzzled. Aidan pointed at the cops and made a little floating motion with his hands. Suddenly, Sarah got it. She nodded.

Okay.

Aidan looked down at her backpack again, then at her. He mouthed one word.

Now.

Sarah, her hand trembling, slowly unzipped the back-pack. She slipped her hand inside, found the gold box. She nodded to Aidan.

Ready.

Aidan checked to make sure his seatbelt was fastened; Sarah did the same. She drew the golden box from inside the backpack and put her hand on the little wheel. The male cop looked back.

"What do you have there?" he said. "Is that gold?"

Sarah closed her eyes, gave the wheel a quarter turn, and tilted the box just slightly. The van filled with brilliant golden light and a musical sound that seemed to come from everywhere.

Aidan, his eyes also closed, leaned forward and felt around until he found the front seatbelt latches; he quickly released them both.

Sarah turned the wheel shut. The light was less brilliant now, but the interior of the van was still filled with a golden glow. The male cop was still in the shotgun seat, but now he was upside down. This did not appear to trouble him; he was humming happily. The female cop, who'd been driving, was floating with her back against the windshield, a rapturous smile on her face. "Hello back there!" she said, apparently to the officer guarding J.D., who was floating against the van's ceiling.

"I love you, Janine!" he responded. "I've always loved you!"

"I know, Tommy, I know," she replied. "But I'm driving!" She gestured vaguely toward the steering wheel, the motion causing her to somersault slowly in midair.

"Wait!" she giggled. "I'm not driving. Who's driving?"

Sarah and Aidan were also feeling giddy, but having been there before, they were a bit more aware of what was happening. They found the fact that nobody was driving the van somewhat troubling. Aidan looked out the side window. For a moment he saw nothing but night sky. Then a tree passed by. Underneath the van.

"Sarah," he said. "I think you used a little too much."

Armstrong was following the police van, three cars back, when he heard car horns blasting and brakes screeching. Then he saw the van.

Flying.

He stared, openmouthed, as the van rose gracefully above the traffic and soared over a tree. Armstrong lowered his window and stuck his head out to watch it. That was when he rear-ended the car in front of him, which had just rear-ended the patrol car following the van, which had smashed into another civilian car whose driver had also been mesmerized by the flying van.

The crash popped his hood open. Armstrong cursed, shut off the engine, and jumped out of the Escalade. He looked at the sky and picked out the van, still moving away but descending slowly.

In front of him, the cops were scrambling out of their wrecked patrol car. They were yelling at each other, shouting into their radios, pointing at the flying van. In the distance Armstrong heard sirens. His eyes again went to the van disappearing into the night sky. His brain struggled to process what he had just seen. He knew two things right away. One was that this was no longer an ordinary missing-kids case. The other was that he wasn't going away until he found out exactly what it was.

The police van was drifting slowly back to earth, but the three officers were not at all concerned. The female in front—Janine—was continuing her floating flirtation with Tommy in back. The third cop was still upside down; at the moment he was singing what sounded like "The Climb" by Miley Cyrus. He did not notice when Aidan leaned forward and unclipped the key ring from his belt.

The van was now about fifty feet off the ground, angling gently downward toward a park. Aidan and Sarah unfastened their seatbelts, slid open the van door, and eased themselves out. Floating now, they held onto the van and worked their way around to the back. Sarah opened the door; J.D., still inverted, was smiling at them.

"Hey!" he said, as if he were sitting in his office, as opposed to shackled in a flying police van. "Isn't this great?"

"Terrific," said Aidan, working the key into J.D.'s handcuffs. "Come on," he said, pulling J.D. out. "Sarah, get his other arm."

Holding J.D. on both sides, Aidan and Sarah pushed off from the back of the van. It continued its gentle downward path as the three of them soared upward.

"This is really great!" J.D. exclaimed. "Where are we going?"

Sarah and Aidan looked back. In the distance they saw flashing police lights as more patrol cars converged on the accident scene, sirens whooping.

Aidan looked at Sarah. "Where are we going?" he said.

"I have no idea," said Sarah.

"I love the way we always have a plan," said Aidan.

"Just look at that full moon!" said J.D.

In western Lancaster County, Pennsylvania, a farmer, having finished his nightly rounds, closed the barn door. He started back toward the house and had almost reached it when he stopped, listening. From the west he heard a deep whooshing sound, like a strong wind. But the night was still.

The sound was closer now, and louder. The farmer moved away from the house so he would have an unobstructed view to the west. He froze when he saw it clearly by the full moon—a black cloud, low to the ground, coming fast. But what kind of cloud moved like that, or made such a noise?

The farmer wanted to run—a reaction that embarrassed him, as he prided himself on being a tough man, and a man of common sense. He willed himself to hold still as the cloud came closer, closer . . .

Birds. He could see now that it was birds. Ravens, they looked like—huge ones. So many of them. They swept over him, blotting out the moon, the beat of their wings now a roar. In a minute they were at the far end of his land, and then they were gone. The farmer stood absolutely still.

The door to the house opened. The farmer's wife came outside and saw him standing motionless in the moonlight.

"Jake?" she said. "That noise . . . what was that?"

"Birds," he said.

"Birds? Birds made all that noise?"

"Yes."

He was still looking at the sky. She watched him for a few moments. "Is everything all right?" she asked.

"I don't know," he said.

CHAPTER 20

MAC

THEY FLEW AS FAR AND AS FAST as they could, Sarah and Aidan doing the steering, trying to avoid lights, J.D. between them, still feeling quite relaxed. They passed over what looked like a river, although J.D., acting as aerial tour guide, informed them that it was actually a long, narrow, winding lake called Lake Carnegie. About a mile later the starstuff began to wear off, and they gently descended into a dense stand of trees.

The landing was not a thing of beauty. They bumped into some branches on the way down, dislodging J.D., who turned a slow, midair cartwheel before tumbling to the ground.

"Are you okay?" said Sarah, alighting next to him.

"I think so," said J.D., sitting up.

Aidan landed next to Sarah. "Where are we?" he said.

"The Plainsboro Preserve," said J.D. "It's a nature reserve. There's a reservoir over that way."

"Great," said Aidan. "We have nature and water. Now all we need is food, shelter, and, oh yeah, some way to stop everybody in the world from looking for us. I mean, we made the police van fly. Then *we* flew. We're gonna be all over the news."

"In which case," said Sarah, "Ombra will definitely find out."

"Not to mention that the police will be very unhappy with us," said Aidan.

"Especially me," said J.D., who was feeling less euphoric now that he was on the ground. "The cops think I kidnapped you."

Sarah crouched next to him. "Listen," she said. "We can get you out of this. You go back, turn yourself in to the police. Then we call them from a pay phone and explain that you never did anything wrong, that it was all our idea. They'd have to believe us, because you surrendered and we're still running."

J.D. stared at the ground, then looked at Sarah.

"Nope," he said. "I'm . . . okay. I can't believe I'm saying this, but . . . I'm a Starcatcher. We can sort it out with the police when this is all over. But right now we need to figure out what to do about the starstuff so this Ombra dude doesn't get hold of it."

Sarah touched J.D.'s arm.

"If you saw him," said Aidan, "I don't think the word *dude* would come to mind."

213

There was no response from Sarah or J.D., who were looking into each other's eyes. Sarah realized that her hand was still on his arm. She quickly dropped it.

"Okay," she said. "We need to get away from here. The police are going to be looking for us."

"Not to mention Shadow Dude," said Aidan.

"Is there a train station around here?" said Sarah.

"Bad idea," said Aidan. "They'll be watching the train stations and airports."

"Then what?" said Sarah.

"We need a car," said Aidan. He looked around the woods. "Although I don't see any at the moment."

"I know somebody who might be able to help us," said J.D.

"Who?" said Sarah.

"A retired physics professor, Allen Macpherson, old family friend. He kind of mentored me when I joined the Princeton faculty. He lives in Monmouth Junction, not too far from here."

"You trust him?" said Aidan.

"Yup," said J.D. "He was really tight with my granddad and dad. Besides, we don't have a lot of choices."

"All right, then," said Sarah, getting to her feet.

"Which way?"

"North," said J.D., also rising.

"Which way is north?" said Aidan.

"That way," said J.D. "I hope."

An hour and a half later, after some meandering, they came to a modest house in an older subdivision. J.D. rang the bell; a minute later, the porch light came on, and the door was opened by a gaunt, elderly, white-haired man in pajamas.

"Hello, J.D.," he said, giving no indication that he was surprised by the visit.

"Hello, Mac," said J.D. "Sorry about the late hour."

Mac waved away the apology. "Since Eleanor died," he said, "I hardly sleep anyway. Come in."

Inside, J.D. introduced Aidan and Sarah to Mac. There was an uncomfortable pause, then J.D. said, "Mac, I need to ask a favor."

Mac looked at him, waiting.

"I was wondering if I could borrow a car."

"All right," said Mac.

"Really?" said J.D.

"Yes. I never use Eleanor's car anyway. I've been meaning to sell it. I barely use my own."

"But . . . I mean, aren't you curious about why I need it?"

"I assume you need it to get away from the police."

J.D.'s mouth fell open. "You know?"

Mac gestured toward the TV. "You were the top story on the eleven o'clock news. They've been showing photos of all three of you. And, of course, the flying police van."

"Oh, no," said Aidan.

"Oh, yes. There's video from somebody's cell phone. There are all kinds of theories about what happened. Some of them are quite entertaining, from a physics standpoint; one involves a giant magnet. The police are very interested in speaking with the three of you. I suspect others will be as well."

J.D. looked troubled. "Maybe you shouldn't get involved with this, Mac," he said. "I don't think you know what you're getting into."

"I know more than you might think," said Mac. "Over the years, your grandfather did me the honor of seeking my advice in certain matters, and I flatter myself in thinking that I may have been of some help to your . . . organization. I'm more than happy to help you now."

"So," said Sarah. "You know . . . you know about . . ."

"I know it wasn't a giant magnet," said Mac.

"Mac," said J.D. "I don't know what to say."

"No need to say anything," said Mac. "I'll get the keys to Eleanor's car." He left the room, returning a minute later with a set of car keys, which he handed to J.D. "I just hope it starts," he said. "Not that it's any of my business, but do you know where you're going?"

J.D., Sarah, and Aidan exchanged blank looks.

"We haven't thought that far ahead yet," said J.D. "Mainly we need to get somewhere safe, away from here, where we can figure out our next move."

"How about a cabin in North Carolina?" said Mac.

"What?"

"We bought it when I retired. Haven't been there in a while. Another thing I've been meaning to sell. I'll go get the keys."

Ten minutes later, with the help of jumper cables, Eleanor's car—an ancient green Volvo—was running. J.D. was at the wheel, with Sarah in the shotgun seat and Aidan in the back. J.D. rolled down the window.

"I don't know how to thank you," he said.

"Just stay safe," said Mac. "You need anything, get in touch. You remember my e-mail address?"

"Yes."

"Okay, then. Better get moving."

J.D. put the car in gear and eased it out of the driveway and onto the street. As they drove away, Aidan and Sarah looked back at the fading figure of Mac, watching them, looking frail and ghostly in his white pajamas.

"I can't believe that old guy has e-mail," said Aidan.

"That old guy," said J.D., "helped invent the Internet."

The sergeant had stepped outside the Princeton police station for a few minutes to stretch his legs. It had been a very long, very strange night—a flying police vehicle, for heaven's sake. And the night was not going to end any time soon, with calls coming in from all over, including Washington, D.C.

The FBI, he thought. *That's all we need.*

He walked a couple of blocks, then stopped under a streetlight to look at his watch. He sighed; time to get back.

A bird landed on the sidewalk next to him. The sergeant didn't know what kind it was, but it was black, and unusually large. It also seemed unusually bold, for a bird—it stood only a few feet away from him, apparently unafraid.

A second bird landed on the sidewalk. A third. The sergeant heard a rustling noise overhead. He looked up and gasped; the roof of the two-story building he stood next to was lined with birds, hundreds of them.

Feeling both nervous and foolish—*they're just birds*—he turned to walk back toward the station. He had taken only a couple of steps when he heard the furious beating of wings followed by a rushing sound. Suddenly, the sidewalk was covered with the black birds, swarming onto his shadow. He felt an awful chill creeping up through his body. He wanted to run, wanted to scream. But his legs would no longer move, and no sound came from his mouth. He fought to keep his wits about him—*don't panic*—but it was as if his very ability to think was being sucked out of him.

And then there was only one thought left: *Obey.*

Slowly, he trudged back toward the station.

Sam Cleavy worked a cash toll booth on the Pennsylvania Turnpike. It was a boring job, but it had become less boring thanks to the advent of live TV streamed onto smart phones. Sam basically spent his days watching TV while taking tolls. He was very good at both.

When the old green Volvo came through his booth, he had already seen the driver's face dozens of times on TV—it was the kidnapper, the one involved in the crazy story about the flying police van. Sam recognized the two kids, too; they didn't look like they were afraid of the kidnapper, but they were definitely the ones on TV.

Sam handed the kidnapper his change, then reached down to press a red button used to photograph the license plate of the car currently in his bay. As soon as the car pulled away, he picked up the phone and called his supervisor.

Then he went back to watching TV.

CHAPTER 21

THE BRIDGE

*T*HEY WERE IN MARYLAND NOW, southbound on I-81, J.D. carefully keeping their speed just under the limit. Aidan dozed in the backseat; Sarah, fighting fatigue, had been surfing the radio stations. As Mac had predicted, the strange story of the flying police van was attracting much attention. Finally, tired of listening to essentially the same report endlessly repeated, Sarah switched off the radio.

"We need a plan," she said.

"I agree," said J.D. "But right now I'm too tired to think. I need to focus on staying awake."

"Will it help to talk?"

"Sure."

"Okay, then maybe you can explain something. Remember when the police broke down your door?"

"And then knocked me down and dragged me out in handcuffs? I vaguely recall that, yes."

"Okay, just before that, you said you thought that E in Molly's diary was Albert Einstein."

"Right."

"And then you said you thought you knew what the bridge was."

"Yup," said J.D. "I don't know what good it'll do us, but I think I do. And if I'm right, I'm also pretty sure I know what the Starcatchers did with the island."

"You do? Seriously?"

"I do," said J.D. "But it's going to sound weird."

From the backseat, Aidan said, "We're being chased by a huge flock of birds inhabited by an evil being. We made a police van fly. Nothing you say is gonna sound weird."

"I thought you were asleep," said J.D.

"I was," said Aidan, sitting up, "but you guys started yakking."

"So what did they do with the island?" said Sarah.

"I think they moved it," said J.D.

"I take it back," said Aidan. "Maybe I am still asleep."

"What do you mean, *moved* it?" said Sarah.

"I mean they put it somewhere else," said J.D. "Which is why nobody has found it in modern times."

"They moved the whole island," said Sarah.

"Yes," said J.D. "And that's not even the weird part."

"It's not?" said Aidan.

"No," said J.D. "The weird part is where they moved it to."

"I'm afraid to ask," said Sarah.

J.D. took a breath, exhaled, and said, "I think they moved it to a parallel universe."

"What?" said Sarah. "*What?*"

"I saw that on *Star Trek*," said Aidan.

"I know, I know," said J.D. "It sounds like bad science fiction. But I think that's what they did."

"Okay, wait," said Sarah. "Let's say that's even possible. We're talking about, what, a hundred years ago. They didn't have anything like the technology scientists have today."

"True," said J.D. "But they had two things scientists don't have today. One was the most brilliant physicist, maybe the most brilliant scientific mind, in human history."

"Einstein," said Sarah.

"Him," said J.D.

"What's the other thing?" said Aidan.

"Starstuff," said J.D. "I haven't figured out what it is, but even in minute quantities it appears to contain vast amounts of energy, and it has some highly unusual properties—it counteracts gravity, it radically alters emotions; who knows what else? I believe Einstein harnessed that energy to create the bridge."

"The bridge in the diary," said Sarah.

"Yes. That's what I was trying to explain when the police broke down the door. In physics it's called an Einstein-Rosen bridge."

"Who's Rosen?" said Aidan.

"A guy who worked with Einstein," said J.D. "They came up with a theory that there was a way to pass from one universe to another. That became known as an Einstein-Rosen bridge."

"So there really is more than one universe?" said Sarah. "It's not just science fiction?"

"We're talking theory," said J.D. "But, yes, it's pretty much accepted that there are other universes, possibly an infinite number of them. And . . . hang on."

"What?" said Sarah.

J.D. pointed to the rearview mirror. Sarah looked back; overtaking them fast was a police cruiser, lights flashing. "No," she said.

J.D., his eyes flicking to the mirror, said, "Okay, I'm the one they really want. If he pulls us over, I'll get out and walk back toward him. You guys get out and run."

"Run where?" said Aidan, looking around. "We don't even know where we are."

"You'll have to figure it out," said J.D. "Get ready."

Sarah got her backpack off the car floor and held it in her lap. The speeding cruiser was fifty yards back . . . twenty-five . . . ten . . .

J.D. was gripping the wheel, his body tense. The cruiser pulled up next to them. Nobody dared to look over. And then the cruiser passed them. Not slowing at all, it hurtled along the empty highway ahead, quickly disappearing from view.

J.D. exhaled. "Guess he wasn't after us."

"I'm wide awake now," said Aidan.

Sarah eased her grip on the backpack and leaned back against the seat.

"Okay," she said, turning to J.D. "If there's more than one universe, where are all the other ones?"

"That part's a little tricky," said J.D. "It's not a question of physical distance. You can't get to them by flying in a spaceship. No matter how far you went, you'd still be in this universe. So what you need is a wormhole, which is another name for an Einstein-Rosen bridge. Theoretically, these wormholes are a path from one universe to another."

"You keep saying *theoretically*," said Sarah.

"Right, because nobody's been able to confirm their existence. Also, it's generally accepted that even if wormholes did exist, they wouldn't be stable enough for matter to pass through. Unless . . ." J.D. paused dramatically.

"Unless what?" said Sarah.

"Unless they were stabilized by some kind of highly exotic matter, currently unknown to science."

"Starstuff," said Aidan.

"Yes," said J.D. "Maybe Einstein figured out a way to use starstuff to create a stable bridge, then send the island through it."

"A whole island?" said Aidan. "I don't think so."

"Be quiet," Sarah told her brother. She turned to J.D. "How would that work, exactly?" she said. "I mean, is there, like, a tunnel somewhere? And wouldn't it have to be huge to fit an island through it?"

"It wouldn't be a tunnel, at least not what you think of as a physical tunnel," said J.D. "I'm guessing it would be some kind of device, which generated a . . . okay, let's call it a force field. I assume the device would have to be portable, so it could be transported to the island, presumably by ship."

"The *Sea Ghost*!" exclaimed Sarah.

"I beg your pardon?" said J.D.

"Hang on," said Sarah. She unzipped her backpack and dug out the diary. She opened the glove compartment and, using the light from its interior, began leafing through the pages. "Okay," she said. "About halfway through the diary, after all the stuff about E creating the bridge, Molly starts talking about . . . okay, here she starts talking about an expedition. That's where she mentions this *Sea Ghost*."

"That must be a ship," said J.D. "The expedition must have been to transport the bridge to the island."

"Okay," said Sarah, excited now, flipping pages quickly. "So then there are a bunch of entries about the expedition, and then . . . here, she says, 'Received a telegram today, via radio from the *Sea Ghost*. One wonderful word, SUCCESS. We are thrilled, especially E.'"

"So it actually worked?" said Aidan.

"Yeah," said J.D. "I think they bridged the island." He shook his head in wonderment. "Do you have any idea what this means? If this were published . . ."

The car was quiet for a moment, then Sarah said, "Does that mean the island's gone forever?"

J.D. thought about it. "I suppose it depends," he said.

"On what?"

"On what they did with the bridge. Does the diary say anything about that?"

"Yep," said Sarah, flipping more pages. "There's a bunch of stuff in here about keeping the bridge secure."

"So they didn't destroy it," J.D. said softly.

"No," said Sarah, still flipping. "For years they kept it in . . . Berlin."

"That's where Einstein lived," said J.D.

"Then . . . okay, listen to this. This is from 1933: 'The situation in Germany has become intolerable. E and his family will emigrate to the United States. We have arranged for the bridge to accompany him, as well as J, who will assist in maintaining it.'"

"Wait a minute," said J.D. "You're saying the bridge came to the United States, with Einstein?"

"That's what it sounds like," said Sarah.

"And he was accompanied by somebody named 'J'?"

"Yeah," said Sarah, looking at the diary. "Why?"

"Okay, listen," said J.D. "I'm named after my grandfather and my father. My grandfather was John; my father was Douglas. J.D. stands for John Douglas."

"Um . . . so?" said Aidan.

"So," said J.D., "my grandfather, John Aster, came to Princeton from England in 1933. The same year as the J in the diary."

"That's interesting," said Sarah, "but it doesn't mean that it's the same person."

"Do you know where Einstein settled when he came to the United States?" said J.D.

"No idea," said Sarah.

"Princeton," said J.D.

"Oh," said Sarah.

"So wait a minute," said Aidan. "Are you saying that this bridge thing is in Princeton?"

"I'm saying it's possible that it once was," said J.D.

"Do you think it could still be there?" said Sarah.

"What I think," said J.D., "is that we need to get back in touch with Mac."

CHAPTER 22

ROSEY

$\mathcal{M}$AC'S CABIN WAS AT THE END of a steep dirt road that snaked up a densely wooded hillside a few miles outside the North Carolina town of Highlands. They reached the cabin at mid-morning, bone-weary from the long drive. Sarah snagged the bedroom; J.D. and Aidan crashed in the living room. All three were asleep within minutes.

As morning turned to afternoon, J.D.'s growling stomach woke him. He rummaged through the pantry, dusted off a big can of ravioli, and heated it up in a pot on the stove. The aroma roused Sarah and Aidan, who trudged into the kitchen zombie-style.

"What's for lunch?" said Aidan.

"Ravioli from about 1987," said J.D.

"Any other choices?" said Aidan.

"Spam from 1971."

"I'll have the ravioli," said Aidan.

J.D. spooned the food into three bowls. They ate like wolves.

"Now what?" said Sarah, chewing her last forkful.

"Now I call Mac," said J.D., pulling out his cell phone.

"Can't the police trace your phone?" said Aidan.

"I'm just getting the number off my cell," said J.D. "There's no signal here anyway." He walked over to a wall-mounted phone. "I'm hoping Mac didn't disconnect this line." He lifted the receiver, heard a dial tone, and punched in the number. "You guys want to listen?"

Sarah and Aidan nodded. J.D. hit the speaker button. They heard the *brrrr* of the receiving phone ringing, then Mac's voice. "Hello."

"It's J.D., Mac. Sarah and Aidan are listening on speakerphone."

"Are you all right?"

"We're fine. We're at your place."

"Glad to hear it. From what I'm seeing on the news, you three are very much in demand up here."

"I bet. We really can't thank you enough for helping us out."

"Not at all."

"Mac, the reason I called is . . . okay. I'm just going to come right out and ask you. What can you tell us about my grandfather and the Einstein-Rosen bridge?"

There was a moment of silence, then, "Sounds as though you've been doing some sleuthing."

"So you know something about it?"

"Perhaps you can tell me what *you* know."

J.D. quickly summarized what they'd read in the diary, and his theory about what it meant. When he finished, there was a long pause on the other end.

"So," said Mac. "You've concluded that they created a stable Einstein-Rosen bridge, which they then used to transport an entire island to another universe. And they did all this without computers—essentially without modern technology."

J.D.'s face fell. "You're saying I'm insane," he said.

"I'm not saying that."

"Are you saying it's true?"

"I'm not saying that, either."

"Then what are you saying?"

Mac sighed. "I'm in a bit of an awkward position here. I gave my word to your grandfather that I wouldn't reveal anything about his organization or his work with Doctor Einstein."

J.D. was about to respond, but Sarah beat him to it.

"That's real noble, professor," she said. "Your word and all. But here's the thing: J.D.'s grandfather's organization was fighting against something evil. You knew that, right?"

"I was aware of it, yes."

"Well, that evil thing is still around, and it's after us. It's partly our fault—"

"*Our* fault?" said Aidan.

"Okay," said Sarah, "it's mainly *my* fault. I went poking around into something I probably should have left alone."

"Probably?" said Aidan.

Sarah ignored him. "The point is, we're in danger," she said. "And a whole lot more people are probably in danger too. And all we're doing about it is running away. We don't know what else we can do. But we can't keep running forever. We really, really need to find somebody who can help us. So if you can, or if you know somebody who can, or if you know anything, please . . ." Sarah stopped; she was determined not to cry.

The phone was silent for several seconds. Then Mac said, "You're right, Sarah. I apologize. The John Aster I knew would have wanted me to help."

"Thank you," whispered Sarah.

"I warn you," said Mac, "I don't know how much use this information will be," said Mac. "But here goes. J.D., did you ever hear the name Pete Carmoody?"

J.D. frowned, then said, "Yeah . . . my dad used to talk about him. He was a maintenance man, right? Kind of a legendary character, worked for the Physics Department?"

"He was more than a maintenance man," said Mac. "Much more."

"How so?"

"Pete Carmoody held degrees in physics, mathematics,

and electrical engineering. He forgot more about quantum mechanics than most professors will ever know."

"Then why on earth did he work as a maintenance m— oh. He wasn't a maintenance man."

"No. That was a cover, an excuse to be around the physics lab, so he could work on Rosey."

"Rosey?"

"That's what they called the device. I'm talking about Einstein, Pete, and your grandfather. They were working on modifying it, totally hush-hush, when I joined the faculty. After your grandfather got to know me, he swore me to secrecy and asked me to help them with some calculations. It was a great honor."

"Why were they modifying it?" said J.D.

"It had already served its original purpose, which was to relocate the island. But they no longer needed it for anything that massive. They wanted to make a smaller, more transportable version to be used purely as a portal to the island."

"How small?" said J.D.

"I never saw the finished version," said Mac. "After I'd done the calculations, they thanked me and told me, politely, that I was no longer needed. I'd gladly have done more—it was a fascinating project—but your grandfather wouldn't hear of it; he said the less I knew, the safer I'd be. But if I had to guess, based on the early plans, I'd say the new Rosey would be about the size of a household refrigerator.

It couldn't have been much bigger because of where they kept it."

"Where was that?" said J.D.

Mac chuckled. "I wasn't supposed to know," he said, "but I have good reason to believe that it spent the next few decades in Pete Carmoody's basement."

"What?"

"Yes. He had a room down there, very well secured, never let anybody in, not even his wife. I found that quite amusing, especially as time went on—the most astonishing technological achievement in human history, sitting in a basement that belonged to a guy who walked around in grease-stained overalls."

"Is it still there?" said Aidan.

"I don't believe so. Einstein died in 1955. The year after that, Pete quit and moved south. I'm pretty sure he took Rosey with him."

"Why do you think that?" said J.D.

"Because he drove the moving truck himself. I saw him off; he had a big rig, looked to me like a custom trailer—all reinforced steel, massive locks. Pete's wife, Fay, was most unhappy about it. She wanted professional movers. But he insisted. Gave me a wink as he pulled away. I think he knew I knew."

Sarah and J.D. asked the next question simultaneously: "Where did he move to?"

"Florida," said Mac. "Little town called Kissimmee."

J.D. said, "And that was in nineteen . . ."

". . .fifty-six," said Mac.

"And how old was he then?"

"Mid forties, I guess."

"So he's probably not still alive."

"I assume not, but I don't know. I don't even know if he stayed in Florida. I sent him a couple of letters. Never heard back."

"Professor," said Sarah. "Let's say the machine . . . Rosey . . . still exists. Would it still work?"

"I don't know," said Mac.

"But if it did work," persisted Sarah, "would a person be able to use it to get to the island?"

"I suppose so," said Mac. "Theoretically, at least. The problem would be the energy source. Rosey doesn't run on electricity. To establish a stable bridge, you need something far more powerful."

"An exotic substance," said J.D.

"Yes."

"The kind of substance that could, even in minute quantities, cause a police van to fly?"

The speaker emitted a chuckle. "Something like that, yes," said Mac.

J.D., Sarah, and Aidan were all looking at the backpack now.

"One more thing, professor," said Sarah.

"Yes?"

"How dangerous would it be? Using the bridge, I mean."

Mac paused, then answered, "I don't know. As I said, I was removed from the project before they finished the modification. I don't know whether they ever actually used it."

"So," said Sarah, "you don't know whether anybody ever got from here to the island alive."

"No," said Mac. "And there's something else you might want to consider."

"What's that?"

"Even if you could get to the island," Mac said, "I don't know if there's any mechanism there for getting you back."

"Yikes," said Aidan.

"Exactly," said Mac. "If you're even thinking about trying to use the bridge, you must . . . excuse me, I think there's somebody at the door." From the speaker came the sound of pounding and voices shouting.

"Mac?" said J.D. "What's happening? Are you all right?" There was no answer from the speaker; only a crashing sound, and more shouting.

"Mac!" said J.D. "Are you okay?"

Mac's voice was low, rushed: "I have to hang up now."

"Why?" said J.D. "What's going on?"

"The police are here. Don't call back."

CHAPTER 23

CLOSING IN

(*D*USK CAUGHT THEM IN CENTRAL GEORGIA, headed for
Kissimmee, Florida, where, according to directory assistance,
there was one listing for the name "Carmoody," first initial F.
They'd stopped at a public library in an Atlanta suburb and
used the Internet to look up the address. They decided, after
some discussion, not to call ahead, but to simply show up and
hope for the best.

They'd been using back roads, avoiding the interstate,
assuming that since the police knew about Mac, they also
knew about the Volvo. As darkness fell they stopped at a
gas station to buy gas, Cheez-Its, Ding Dongs, and Red Bull.
Back on the road, Aidan and Sarah resumed a debate they'd
been having, on and off, since they left Mac's cabin.

"I think it's crazy," said Aidan, not for the first time.

"Fine, then you don't have to do it," said Sarah, also not
for the first time.

"I'm not afraid, if that's what you're saying."

"I'm not saying that."

"But we could get killed," said Aidan. "Or stuck there. Right, J.D.?"

"That's what Mac said," said J.D.

"Fine," said Sarah. "So neither of you has to go. I'll go alone."

"But why?" said Aidan. "There has to be some other—"

"Listen," snapped Sarah. She turned to face Aidan in the backseat. "I'll make this as simple as I can." She lifted the backpack. "He wants this. It's my fault he found out about it. He won't stop until he gets it. If he gets it, he could do very bad things. So I'm going to put it in the one place where he can't get it. Understand?"

The car was silent for a few moments, then Aidan said, "I still think it's crazy."

"If you guys keep arguing about this," said J.D., "you can walk to Florida."

"All right," said Sarah. "But just tell me—do you think I'm crazy?"

"I think we need more information. We don't know if the bridge still exists, or if it does, what condition it's in. We have no idea how it works. We don't even know who this F. Carmoody is in Kissimmee."

"Mac said Pete's wife was named Fay," said Sarah. "It has to be her."

"Not necessarily," said J.D. "It could be a daughter or son who doesn't know anything about any of this. Or some random person who happens to be named Carmoody."

Sarah stared out the window and watched a mile marker, lit by the headlights, flash past.

"Whoever it is," she said, "I hope they can help us."

Despite the alertness and prompt action of TV-watching toll attendant Sam Cleavy, it had taken nearly three hours for his report to work its way through various turnpike and law-enforcement bureaucracies to the FBI, which was now handling the investigation because it involved interstate flight—not to mention a flying police van.

The owner of the green Volvo was quickly identified as a retired Princeton professor, who was brought in for questioning, but was not cooperating. The FBI had also put the license plate of the green Volvo onto a watch list; computers were screening tens of thousands of digitized license plates captured over a seven-state area by cameras like the one at the toll booth, looking for the Volvo plate.

They got one hit fairly quickly; the Volvo had been caught on camera heading southbound on I-81 in Maryland. But the photo was hours old; by the time it was discovered, the car was presumably long gone from the area.

The next day brought two more hits: one in South

Carolina, then another in Georgia, both times on less-traveled roads. Again, the timing was delayed too much to pinpoint the Volvo's current location. But it was clearly still headed south.

The fourth hit was taken just outside Daytona Beach, Florida. Then came a lucky break; an alert cashier at a Chipper Whipper gas station near Orlando recognized both J.D. and Sarah, and called the police quickly. The FBI notified its Orlando office and the local police; as a courtesy, the FBI also informed the police in Princeton. The trail was hot again. The investigation was closing in. Apprehension was imminent.

The sergeant, wearing dark sunglasses, stood in the back of the crowded briefing room of the Princeton police station house. He had not left the station—for that matter, had not slept—since the investigation began into the abduction of the two children. Some of the other officers, noticing his odd behavior, as well as the glasses, had asked him if he was okay; he had brushed them off with a grunt. But he was not known as a talkative man anyway; nobody paid much attention to him amid all the excitement.

The sergeant listened intently to the briefing. The green Volvo had been tracked to central Florida; the FBI was hot on the trail. An arrest was expected soon. At the end of the briefing he went outside and wandered, apparently aimlessly. It didn't occur to him to look down, but if he had he would have seen he didn't cast a shadow.

He turned a corner onto a deserted street. He came to a large oak and stopped beneath it, waiting—he wasn't sure why, or for what. There was a sound above him, and suddenly he was surrounded by a swirling storm of black birds, the beating wings forcing him to close his eyes, the sound deafening him. He wanted to run but could not move. He felt as if something was being sucked from inside him, as if his brains were being drawn out of his skull.

The birds were gone as quickly as they'd come, rising like a column of twisting smoke. The sergeant slumped to the sidewalk, moaning, unconscious.

He lay there for a minute, then moaned and opened his eyes. He looked around, blinking. He had no idea how he got there—in fact no memory of the past day, or more.

He rose unsteadily and began stumbling back toward the police station.

Lester Armstrong had been living in his Escalade, waiting for something to break. At the moment he was behind the wheel eating a cheeseburger, trying to keep the juice from dripping onto his lap.

His cell phone rang in mid-mouthful.

"Hrr-urr?" he said.

"It's me."

Armstrong recognized the whispering voice of his new pal, a Princeton police corporal he had befriended by means of a pair of excellent tickets to a Knicks-Heat game.

"Whaddya got?" said Armstrong, swallowing.

"They're in Florida. Orlando. This guy is baked. It's only a matter of time. My guess is sometime tonight, maybe tomorrow."

"The parents?" Armstrong asked.

"Being briefed now, as I understand it. Mother is pretty upset. Not so sure she could travel like that even if she wanted to."

"So they extradite back to New Jersey, or what?"

"That right there is for the lawyers. Listen, I gotta get off the phone."

"So do I."

Armstrong disconnected and hit the speed-dial number for the Coopers. He glanced at his watch as he listened to the phone ringing.

C'mon, answer, he thought. *I got a plane to catch.*

CHAPTER 24

FEED THE BIRD

AFTER STOPPING AT A CHIPPER WHIPPER for gas and junk food, they drove the rest of the way to Kissimmee, reaching it just before dawn. They pulled to the side of a rural road and dozed in the car, waiting for a decent hour to go calling on F. Carmoody.

The blazing sun awoke them. It was only mid-morning, but almost ninety degrees. Hot, sticky, and grumpy, they drove to the address they'd gotten from the Internet—a one-story brick house set amid a clump of trees in an older neighborhood along Old Dixie Highway. The mailbox said CARMOODY.

J.D. pulled to the curb, killed the engine, took a breath, let it out. "I'll talk first," he said.

Sarah and Aidan followed him up the walk. He rang the doorbell. They waited. Nothing. He rang the bell again, longer. Nothing. He was about to ring it again when they heard shuffling footsteps approaching and a frail voice calling, "Coming, coming."

The door was opened by a tiny old lady. She had paper-white hair and piercing blue eyes, and was wearing a prim, navy-blue dress. She regarded the sweaty trio doubtfully.

"Is this about magazines?" she said. "Because I have too many magazines already."

"No ma'am," said J.D. "This is about Pete Carmoody."

The woman frowned. "What about him?" she said. "Who are you?"

"I'm John Aster's grandson."

The suspicion disappeared from the woman's face, replaced by a radiant smile. "John Aster's grandson! My goodness, you do look like John." She looked at Sarah and winked. "He was a very handsome man."

"So you're . . . Mrs. Carmoody?" J.D. said.

"Pete was my husband, yes. He's passed on," she said, extending a frail hand. "Fay."

"J.D. Aster," he said. They clasped hands; he could feel the delicate bones beneath her skin.

"And these young people are . . ."

"These are, uh, family friends," said J.D. "Sarah and Aidan Cooper."

"Well, you just come right in," said Fay. "I'll make us some lemonade."

It took her a while; she did not move quickly, and she

used real lemons. But the lemonade was delicious; Aidan, Sarah, and J.D. quietly savored it and the welcome sanctuary of the cool and peaceful house while Mrs. Carmoody chatted happily about her memories of Princeton.

"But listen to me, going on and on," she said, finally. "Tell me, what brings you young people to Kissimmee?"

J.D. said, "We wanted to ask you about something your husband might have brought down here with him from Princeton." Something flickered in Mrs. Carmoody's eyes, and for a fraction of a second her smile faded. When it returned it looked just the slightest bit forced.

"What do you mean, something he brought?" she said.

"Um, the thing is, I don't really know what it looked like," said J.D. "But it would have been a machine of some sort. A special machine, very unusual."

Mrs. Carmoody shook her head. "I wouldn't know anything about that," she said. "Pete didn't talk to me about his work."

Sarah leaned forward and said, "But do you know if maybe he kept a . . . special machine, here? In this house?"

Mrs. Carmoody was looking down at her hands. "I'm afraid I can't help you," she said. The room fell into an uncomfortable silence.

J.D., Sarah, and Aidan exchanged *Now what?* looks.

Mrs. Carmoody looked up, her smile gone. "Well," she said. "It certainly was nice of you to stop by."

She stood and began shuffling toward the front door.

They had no choice but to follow. The visit was over.

Mrs. Carmoody opened the door. "Good-bye," she said.

"One more thing," said J.D., stalling.

"Yes?"

"Um, did Pete . . . I mean, Mister Carmoody, did he ever mention anything about a bridge?"

She shook her head.

"What about 'Rosey'?" said Aidan. "Did he say the name 'Rosey'?"

"No," said Mrs. Carmoody. "Now, if you'll excuse me . . ." She opened the door wider.

J.D. stepped out, followed by Aidan. Sarah started to follow, then stopped in front of Mrs. Carmoody, looking down into the old lady's eyes.

"Please," she said. "We've come a long way, and we really need to know . . ."

"I'm sorry," said Mrs. Carmoody. "I can't help you."

Sarah sighed. "All right," she said. "Thank you for the lemonade."

She stepped outside. Mrs. Carmoody started to close the door. As she did, Sarah caught a glimpse of something glinting just below the high neckline of Mrs. Carmoody's dress. She stuck her foot out, stopping the door. "Wait a minute," she said.

"Please remove your foot," said Mrs. Carmoody, anger creeping into her voice.

Sarah didn't answer; she was fumbling with her T-shirt collar.

"Young lady, if you don't remove your foot, I'm going to call . . ." She stopped, staring openmouthed at Sarah, who held, dangling from its chain, the golden locket J.D. had given her.

"Does this look familiar?" Sarah said.

Slowly, Mrs. Carmoody reached into her dress and pulled out a locket exactly like it.

"Please, come back in," she said.

When the Georgia State Patrol car arrived, two cars—a Toyota Camry and a Ford Fusion—were crunched together in the middle of the intersection. It looked to the trooper as though the Camry had T-boned the Fusion on the passenger side. The drivers, both young women, were standing outside of the vehicles; nobody appeared to be hurt.

That's good, thought the trooper. *Less paperwork.*

The trooper put on his flashers and got out to talk to the drivers. He was pretty sure he already knew what happened: the Camry driver was talking or texting on her cell phone, and she ran the red light. Happened all the time.

Except she swore that wasn't what happened. She admitted that she'd run the light, but not because of her phone. Instead, she blamed birds.

"Like, a million of them," she said. "Big black ones. I was, like, staring at them. I couldn't believe it."

The trooper looked at the other driver. She was nodding vigorously.

"I saw them," she said. "They were going that way." She pointed south.

The trooper sighed, and started filling out his accident-report form.

"Birds," he muttered.

They quickly resettled in the living room. Mrs. Carmoody, ever polite, offered more lemonade; the trio declined.

"Now," Mrs. Carmoody said to Sarah. "Why don't you tell me where you got that locket."

"It's J.D.'s," said Sarah. "I'm just wearing it."

"And how did you get it, J.D.?"

"My father left it to me when he died," said J.D.

"He specifically bequeathed it to you?"

"Yes."

"All right, then," said Mrs. Carmoody. "Then I'm supposed to give you this." She reached behind her neck and, with shaking hands, unclasped her locket. She handed it to J.D.

"Pete gave this to me when he got sick and the doctor said he didn't have long," she said. "Pete told me never to open it or take it off, and never to give it to anybody unless that person had a locket exactly like it."

J.D. was staring at the locket. "Did he say what that person should do with it?"

"No, he didn't."

"And you never peeked inside?"

"Never."

J.D. looked at Sarah and Aidan. "What do you think?" he said.

"I think you should open it," said Sarah.

"Wait!" said Aidan. "What if it's full of . . ."—he glanced at Mrs. Carmoody—". . . you know . . ."

"Aidan," said Sarah, "he left that locket for a reason. He must have wanted the person who got it to open it."

"I think you're right," said J.D. He turned the locket in his hands, finding the clasp. "Here goes." He carefully undid the clasp, then opened the locket a tiny crack.

There was a burst of golden light, a rush of soaring sound. But as quickly as it came, it was gone. "My goodness," said Mrs. Carmoody, smiling. "If I'd known it could do that, I might have opened it myself, no matter what I promised Pete."

J.D. shook the open locket, frowning. "I guess that's all that was in there," he said. "Just a tiny, tiny amount. I wonder why."

"Can I see it?" said Sarah.

J.D. handed her the locket. She held it open, peered inside. "There's something written in here," she said.

"What's it say?" said Aidan.

"It's really small," said Sarah, squinting at the tiny engraved letters. "It says . . . okay, that's weird."

"What?" said Aidan.

"It says 'Feed the bird . . . when Ben says.'"

"What?"

"That's what it says," said Sarah, handing the locket to Aidan, who read the lettering.

"What does that mean?" he said. "Feed what bird? And who's Ben?"

J.D. looked at Mrs. Carmoody. "Does that mean anything to you?" he asked.

"I'm afraid it doesn't," she said. "I didn't even know there was writing inside."

"Was your husband friends with someone named Ben?" Sarah asked. "Maybe someone he worked with?"

She shook her head.

J.D. frowned. "Okay," he said. "What about the machine?"

"Machine?"

"I asked you before if your husband brought a machine down from Princeton. That's when you decided to kick us out."

Mrs. Carmoody blushed. "I apologize for my rudeness. But I didn't know I could trust you."

"So there was a machine?" said Sarah.

"There was something," said Mrs. Carmoody. "Something

large that Pete brought down with us. He insisted on driving the truck himself. I could have wrung his neck for that." She chuckled at the memory, then went on. "But I never saw it. He told me it was best if I didn't know anything about it—he'd always had his secrets, with Doctor Einstein and the others. I always assumed it had something to do with national defense."

"So he brought the machine here?" said J.D. "To this house?"

"Yes. There was a special room in the basement, same as we had in Princeton. Lots of locks. It was like Fort Knox."

"Was?" said Sarah. "You mean it's not still here?"

"No," said Mrs. Carmoody. "He moved it out in . . . let's see . . . it would have been 1971. I remember because that's when I was finally allowed to remodel the basement."

"When he moved it," said Aidan, "did you see anything?"

"No, he did it in the dead of night. Some fellows from his work helped him. He made me stay in the bedroom. Wouldn't even let me offer them coffee!"

J.D. leaned forward. "Do you know where he moved it to?"

She shook her head. "No. As I say, everything about it was a big secret."

"You said 'fellows from his work,'" said J.D. "Where did he work?"

"Oh, he worked many places," said Mrs. Carmoody.

"Consulting work, he called it. He was very smart, you know. And he could build or fix anything."

"Do you remember which work these fellows were from?" said Sarah.

"I'm sorry, I don't," said Mrs. Carmoody. "As I say, I didn't even see them. And it was so long ago. I wish I could be more helpful."

"No, you've been great," said J.D. "Thanks for your time."

"Not at all," said Mrs. Carmoody.

She saw them to the door a second time. They said goodbye and trudged back to the Volvo, which was now an oven.

"Now what?" said Aidan, as J.D. started the engine.

"First off, we need to find someplace safe," said J.D. "The cops have to be looking for this car, so the longer we're driving around, the more danger we're in."

"And we need to figure out what *this* means," said Sarah, holding up the locket. "'Feed the bird when Ben says.'"

"How do you know it means anything?" said Aidan.

"Because he left it for us," said Sarah. "It's a message from Pete. He's trying to tell us something."

"Like what?" said Aidan.

Sarah was staring at the locket. "Like where he put the bridge," she said.

CHAPTER 25

JAWS

$\mathcal{A}$ TRAFFIC CAMERA PHOTOGRAPHED the license plate of the green Volvo southbound on the Orange Blossom Trail near Kissimmee, but it was two hours before the hit was identified and reported to the FBI. The FBI then asked area police departments to check the other cameras in their traffic-monitoring systems. This search produced another hit, also on the Trail, a mile south of the first hit. But that was it.

The FBI also requested police dispatchers for Kissimmee and surrounding areas to issue a BOLO—be on the look-out—alert for the green Volvo. The problem was, there was no way to know whether the car had continued south, or changed direction, or stopped at one of the many stores, malls, restaurants, hotels, and attractions in the heavily touristed area. And the local police were too busy dealing with the traffic and the usual tourism-related crimes to devote full attention to the search. Nevertheless, the

FBI investigators were encouraged; they were close.

Also feeling encouraged was Lester Armstrong, who had arrived at the Orlando airport on a flight from Newark. The first thing he did when he got into his rental car was plug in and turn on his portable police-radio scanner. He heard the BOLO on his way out of the airport and smiled; the kids were in the area, and the police had not found them yet.

Armstrong headed for the Orange Blossom Trail, joining it near where the Volvo had first been photographed. He drove slowly south, passing strip malls, fast-food joints, and souvenir shops, his eyes flicking left and right. He came to a less-congested area, and on the left-hand side saw a sign that said GATORLAND standing in front of a building whose front doors were guarded by a gigantic set of green fiberglass jaws sporting enormous sharp fiberglass teeth. A tourist was standing in the jaws pretending to be terrified while another tourist took his picture.

Armstrong looked at the snout and shook his head. *They're on the run*, he thought. *They're not going to Gatorland.* He aimed his gaze ahead and continued south on the Trail, searching for the green Volvo, and the Cooper kids, and his paycheck.

CHAPTER 26

TWO CALLS

"CHECK OUT THE FIRST ITEM," said J.D., pointing to the menu board in the Gatorland snack bar.

"I don't believe it," said Aidan. "They sell gator nuggets?"

"That's disgusting," said Sarah.

"You don't even want to try the gator sampler?" said J.D.

"What I want," said Sarah, "is a nice, normal, nonreptile hamburger."

"You get those at Cowland," said Aidan.

The three shared their first laugh in a while, feeling safe for the moment. It had been J.D.'s idea to go into Gatorland—to get the car off the highway, put them in a place where they could blend in with a crowd. They parked in a far corner of the lot, away from the street, paid their admission, and, with barely a glance at the various gator attractions, headed for the snack bar. When they got their food—nobody ordered gator—they settled at a table and ate hungrily.

It was Sarah, as usual, who got them down to business.

"Okay," she said, sticking a french fry into her mouth. "'Feed the bird when Ben says.' We need to figure out who Ben is. So who are some famous Bens?"

"Ben Franklin," said J.D.

"What time would he say?" said Aidan.

"Dunno," said J.D. "I do know he said a penny saved is a penny earned."

"What does that even mean, anyway?" said Aidan.

"Dunno that either."

"Ben Affleck," said Sarah.

"Does he say a time?" said Aidan.

"Not that I know of," said Sarah. "But he's cute."

"Helpful," said Aidan.

"Ben Stiller," said Sarah.

"Can't be a modern Ben," said J.D. "Has to be a Ben from back when Pete gave Fay the locket. It could have been a friend of his, or an associate of the Starcatchers, in which case the odds against our figuring out who he is are pretty huge."

They sat silent for a minute.

"Okay," said Sarah, "let's try it another way. What could 'Feed the bird' possibly mean?"

"The ravens?" said Aidan. "That seems pretty obvious."

Sarah said, "But then why does it say bird, not birds? Plus, the ravens are only here because they followed us. Back when Pete gave Fay the locket, they were in England."

"I wish they still were," said Aidan.

"Wait a minute," said Sarah, snapping her fingers.

The other two looked at her.

"England," she said.

"Maybe you could explain that a little more," said Aidan.

"There's a famous Ben there," said Sarah. "Maybe the most famous Ben of all. Aidan, we walked past it like fifteen times."

Aidan frowned. "Big Ben?"

"Bingo. And what's Big Ben?"

"A clock," said Aidan.

"Exactly," said Sarah. "And clocks do what?"

"Tell time."

"Yes!" said Sarah. "They say what time it is! You feed the bird when Ben says."

J.D. shook his head. "You have the same problem you had with the ravens. Big Ben's in London, not here."

"Yeah, I know," said Sarah. "But it just seems . . . right."

"Except for the part about Big Ben being in London," said Aidan. "You'd have to fly over there, which doesn't make sense if the bridge is over here."

"Wait a minute," said Sarah, snapping her fingers again.

"What?" said Aidan.

"Fly over," said Sarah. "You said 'fly over.'"

"Yeah. So?"

"So you don't have to fly to England to fly over Big

Ben. We've both done it dozens of times."

"What are you talking about?" said Aidan. "It's in London."

"The original Big Ben is, yeah. I'm talking about a miniature Big Ben, in a whole miniature London. Which happens to be right here."

"In Gatorland?" said Aidan.

"No, moron! Disney World!"

Aidan's mouth fell open. "You mean . . . the Peter Pan ride? Are you serious?"

"I'm dead serious," said Sarah. "That's my favorite ride. You get in a little ship and fly over London at night, and there's Big Ben, right below you."

"Wait," said J.D. "Are you saying you actually think the bridge could be in Disney World?"

"What I'm saying," said Sarah, "is that Pete Carmoody brought the bridge here. Disney World is here. Pete left the locket here. The locket says 'when Ben says.' There's a model of the world's most famous Ben in Disney World."

"But," said Aidan, "how . . . I mean, to put this machine in a Disney ride . . . how in the world would he do that?"

"I don't know," said Sarah. "But word is that he was a really, really smart guy."

"That's your argument?" said Aidan.

J.D. was drumming his fingers on the table. "Okay," he said. "I think Sarah's probably crazy."

"Thank you," said Aidan.

"But," continued J.D., "we don't have much else to work with. Is there a pay phone here?"

"Over there, near the snack counter," said Sarah, pointing. "Who're you going to call?"

"You're going to call them, actually," said J.D., rising.

"Call who?"

"Disney. You're a high-school student working on a research project. And you need to know what year they built the Peter Pan ride."

"Ah," said Sarah. "Because Mrs. Carmoody said Peter moved the machine out of the basement in . . ."

". . . in 1971," said J.D., heading toward the phone. "C'mon."

It took Sarah several calls, followed by twenty minutes of being transferred, but finally she reached a helpful man at Imagineering by the name of Alex Wright.

"Right," she was saying, as Aidan and J.D. stood by, listening. "The Peter Pan ride. No, the one at the Magic Kingdom. Yeah. Oh, really? Okay, I didn't know that. Anyway, so the year it was built was . . . uh-huh . . . right . . . uh-huh . . . okay, thanks very much."

She hung up.

"Well?" said Aidan. "What'd they say?"

"He said the correct name of the ride is 'Peter Pan's Flight,'" Sarah answered. "He was really strict about that."

"But what did he say about the year it was built?" said J.D.

Sarah smiled. "1971," she said.

"Whoa," said Aidan.

J.D. picked up the phone handset. "One more call," he said, punching in a number.

"Who?" said Sarah.

J.D. held up his hand to indicate *hang on*.

"Hello," he said into the phone. "Mrs. Carmoody? This is J.D. Aster again . . . Fine, thanks . . . We did, too, thanks. Listen, I'm sorry to bother you again, but I had one more question. You mentioned that Pete worked as a consultant . . . right . . . right. So I was just wondering if you happen to remember any of the specific places he worked around 1971? When you finally got your basement back? Uh-huh . . . right . . . right . . . right. Oh really? He took you? Right . . . uh-huh. Well, that's great, Mrs. Carmoody. Thanks for your time. Okay, I will. Thanks again. Bye."

J.D. hung up and turned to Sarah and Aidan.

"What'd she say?" said Sarah.

"She said to be sure to say hello to both of you nice young people."

"J.D.! What'd she *say*?"

"She said Pete consulted for Disney."

"I knew it!" said Sarah.

"It gets better. He consulted for a couple of years, impressed them with his management skills, and ended up pretty much running one major project. Guess which one."

"No!"

"Yes. He took Fay to the grand opening of Peter Pan's Flight. Their last real date, she said."

"Aw," said Sarah.

"Okay," said Aidan. "I guess we know who Ben is. Or what Ben is. What about the bird we're supposed to feed? Where's that?"

J.D. arched his eyebrows at Sarah. "Any ideas about the bird?" he said.

She shook her head. "Not at the moment."

"So what do we do?" said Aidan.

"I don't know about you," said J.D. "But I'm going to Disney World."

Fay Carmoody hung up the phone and headed for the living-room sofa. She found herself drawn to that particular place—the place where J.D. had opened the locket, and where for a moment that wonderful golden light had filled the room. It had made Fay feel wonderful—as if she were young again, as if in that instant all the pain and weariness of all the years were gone. Whatever had been in the locket, it was still there, in her house, in the air, just a little. She could feel it. And in some strange way it made her feel as though Pete were near.

She sat on the sofa, eyes closed, smiling, lost in memories.

She opened her eyes. She'd heard a sound outside, from the front of the house, a sound like rushing wind.

She rose and turned toward the door. There was a window to the right; on the sill sat a large black bird.

Odd, she thought. In all the years she'd lived here, she'd never seen a bird like that. She walked toward the door, and stopped again; through the window she could see more of the birds. Many more.

What on earth? she thought. She decided to go outside and have a look.

CHAPTER 27

ONE AT A TIME

RAY HOLLISTER WORKED SECURITY in the Downtown Disney parking lot, but what he wanted to be—what he *dreamed* of being—was a real law-enforcement professional.

When he saw the old green Volvo, he nearly wet his pants. He'd memorized the license plate that morning when he saw the police flyer posted on the break-room bulletin board. Besides a description of the car, the flyer had photos of two teenagers and their suspected kidnapper, who was wanted by the FBI.

And the car was right there, right in front of Ray. In Downtown Disney!

His heart was beating so hard he nearly dropped his radio when he unclipped it from his belt to call in his discovery. Minutes later, a dozen police cars converged on the Volvo, sirens whooping. The police hustled Ray to the break room, where they asked him a bunch of questions, most of them about whether he'd seen the kids or the kidnapper. Ray was sorry he hadn't; he felt he was disappointing them. But his spirits rose when a man and woman in business clothes came into the break room and identified themselves as agents Hector Gomez and Wanda Blight of the FBI.

The FBI!

They questioned Ray briefly, but quickly lost interest when he said he hadn't seen the occupants of the car. The agents then went to the surveillance room, where Ray's boss, Earl Specter, was pulling up video shot by the various security cameras around Downtown Disney. Ray, eager to watch the pros at work, followed the agents.

Specter quickly found video showing the Volvo entering the lot and parking.

"Here we go," he said.

On the screen, a male driver got out of the car, then a teenage girl and boy.

"That's them," said Gomez. He pointed to the time stamp in the corner of the screen. "So this was . . . what? Twenty minutes ago?"

"Right," said Specter. "This was shot twenty-two minutes ago."

Specter switched to another camera. The trio on the screen crossed the parking lot and joined other visitors on the sidewalk.

"Doesn't exactly look like they're being held against their will," Agent Gomez said.

"Can't trust that," said Agent Blight. "You never know what kind of psychological damage results from captivity. Those kids could be zombies."

"They don't look like zombies, is all I'm saying."

"They do look awfully cooperative, if you ask me," said Ray, from behind them.

"I didn't ask you," snapped Gomez and Blight in unison.

Specter worked the controls, picking up video from a series of cameras that showed the fugitive trio moving across the Downtown Disney Marketplace then out to the bus-stop area. They walked down a row of buses, then boarded one, which pulled out thirty seconds later.

"Where does that bus go?" said Blight.

"To the parks," said Specter.

"They're going to Disneyland?" said Gomez.

"It's actually Disney World," said Ray. "Disneyland is the one in—"

"Shut up," snapped Gomez and Blight.

"Technically," said Specter, "the bus goes to the Transportation and Ticket Center. From there you get transportation to the parks."

"Show me the cameras from the Transportation and Ticket Center," said Gomez.

"Can't do that from here," said Specter.

264

"I need to find that bus," said Gomez. "Now."

Ray, who'd been listening to his radio, said, "Excuse me?"

"Shut up," snapped Gomez and Blight.

"But this is about the bus," said Ray.

Gomez whirled to face him. "What about the bus?" he said.

Ray pointed to his radio and said, "There's an accident, a traffic jam, on the on-ramp between Bonnet Creek Parkway and Epcot Center Drive. It's backed everything up. A bunch of buses have been delayed. If you take Bonnet Creek north to Vista and go west on Vista, you can avoid it."

"Come on," said Gomez, heading for the door. Blight was right behind.

"You want me to ride along?" said Ray. "I know all the—"

"No," snapped Gomez and Blight, exiting.

Ray shook his head. He was beginning to have doubts about a career in law enforcement. It seemed to make people awfully irritable.

***

Armstrong was still patrolling the Orange Blossom Trail when the police scanner crackled and the dispatcher broadcast that federal officers needed backup at Disney's Transportation and Ticket Center.

Armstrong hung an illegal U-turn and stomped the gas pedal down. He couldn't imagine why the runaways would go to Disney World. It seemed stupid; once inside a theme park, they could easily be trapped.

And Armstrong planned to be the trapper.

The Disney bus apparently had a nuclear-powered air conditioner; the interior was the temperature of a meat locker, and it seemed to grow steadily colder as it inched forward in the traffic jam. The passengers, including Aidan, Sarah, and J.D., were shivering. Those who had brought sweatshirts put them on.

The good news was that, by looking over the tops of the cars ahead, they could see that the accident was finally clearing and traffic was beginning to move. A few minutes later they approached the Transportation and Ticket Center, passing an ocean of parked cars. Finally, they reached the bus stop, where the driver apologized for the delay and told them to have a Magical Day.

The passengers quickly exited the frigid bus, happy, for the moment, to feel the humid Florida heat. Aidan, Sarah, and J.D. stood on the sidewalk as a river of tourists flowed past them.

"Is it just me," said Aidan, "or do these people look really large to you?"

"They're the size of buffalo," said Sarah. "And those are the children."

"That's good," said J.D., "because we need something to hide behind."

"Hide from who?" said Aidan.

J.D. pointed. Walking toward the buses, their eyes scanning the crowd, was a group of security guards. With them were several uniformed police officers and a man and woman in business suits—clearly not tourists.

"What do we do?" said Sarah.

"We can't stay here," said Aidan.

"We need to get into the Magic Kingdom," said J.D. "There's way more people there. Much easier for us to disappear."

"The monorail?" said Aidan.

J.D. squinted into the distance. "Bad idea. There's a long line. We'd be sitting ducks waiting there."

Sarah pointed to a sign by the parking area. "How about the ferryboat?"

"Bingo," said J.D. "There's basically no line."

"But how do we get past them?" said Aidan, pointing to the oncoming security guards.

"We split up," said J.D. "They're looking for three of us, so we go one at a time. Put on your sunglasses, get with a group of people, and keep your head down. We meet on the ferryboat. I'll go first. If they catch me, try another way."

Agent Blight spotted Sarah first. The girl was alone, moving through the thick crowds away from the ticket center and away from the monorail. Even stranger, she was making no apparent attempt to make herself known to anyone around her, no attempt to be rescued.

"I've got a twenty on the girl," she told Gomez, who spun around sharply. Blight pointed across the bus area. "You can't see her now, but it's her. Moving away from us."

"Go!" said Gomez, waving the security people forward. Blight was already running through the mob, jumping up every so often to try to catch sight of Sarah.

What are you doing, Sarah Cooper? she wondered. *Where are you going? And where are the other two?*

Head down, J.D. worked through the crowd. He knew better than to look back toward the security people; the back of a head was far more difficult to identify than a face. He made no attempt to track Sarah or Aidan. For now they were all on their own.

The thought struck him suddenly: *Maybe I should turn myself in.* His life had become a disaster since the kids had shown up at his office. As intriguing as the Einstein bridge was, it wasn't worth going to jail for. What had he gotten himself into? What if he just let the kids board the ferry, and he surrendered? Wouldn't that help prove he was innocent?

He could even tell the police that the kids were heading to Peter Pan's Flight. This was his chance—probably his last chance—to make this right.

He stopped. The crowd moved past him, like water around a stone. All he had to do was turn around and walk back with his hands in the air. It would be bad—cops, lawyers, courtrooms, press—but not as bad as if they hunted him down.

He turned around. All he had to do was take that first step. Off to his right he saw Sarah heading toward the ferry. His eyes swung left, and he froze. About twenty-five yards behind Sarah, trotting in the same direction, was the woman in the dark suit who'd been talking to the security people. A detective? An FBI agent? Whoever she was, she was heading in Sarah's direction, her eyes searching the crowd.

She was on Sarah's trail.

J.D. found Aidan to be something of a pain. But he liked Sarah—liked the way she thought, liked the way she overcame her fears, liked the way she never gave up. She was so close now to her goal, or at least she believed she was.

And she had put her trust in J.D.

He took a step toward the woman in the dark suit. For just an instant, he considered putting his hands in the air.

Instead, he cupped them around his mouth and yelled, "Hey! Lady cop!"

She looked his way; he could tell she recognized him.

He turned and started running into the dense crowd headed toward the monorail. He glanced back. The lady cop was now running after him, with some security people right behind her.

J.D. ducked his head and plunged deeper into the crowd.

What is he doing? Sarah wondered as she heard J.D. shout. Then she saw him take off running, away from the ferry, with quite a few people chasing him.

She wanted to help but knew there was nothing she could do. Reluctantly, she turned and made for the ferry. Ahead she saw Aidan, nearly to the dock, looking back at her. He waved at her to hurry; the ferry was about to leave.

Sarah picked up her pace, reaching Aidan as he boarded. "Where's J.D.?" he said.

"He took off toward the monorail. He was leading the police away from us."

"That's nice of him. But what if they catch him?"

"Then we have to do this alone."

A recorded voice over the ferry loudspeakers announced that the boat was about to depart for the Magic Kingdom. The deckhands were getting ready to take in the gangway. Sarah's eyes anxiously scanned the throng onshore. Then she saw him—a lone figure sprinting toward the ferry.

"There's J.D!" she said.

"Is anybody following him?" said Aidan.

"I don't see anybody. He must have lost them." Sarah ran to one of the deckhands. "Could you hold it just one second, for my friend there?"

The deckhand looked at J.D.'s sprinting figure. "One second," he said.

"Thank you!" said Sarah. It was more like thirty seconds, but J.D. made the boat. He ran up the gangplank and collapsed on a bench, sweating and gasping.

"That was exciting," he said.

"How'd you lose them?" said Aidan.

"It's a big crowd," said J.D. "I hid behind a guy selling balloons, then when they went past me, I circled back."

"You know," said Sarah, "when I saw you take off . . . for just a second there I was afraid you were leaving us."

J.D. looked up at her and smiled. "Wouldn't dream of it," he said.

"Still," said Sarah. "That was close."

"Tell me about it," said J.D.

CHAPTER 28

FINDING BEN

*T*HEY MADE THEIR WAY TO FANTASYLAND, walking separately, staying just close enough that they could keep track of each other in the dense crowd. When they reached Peter Pan's Flight, they remained apart for a minute, scanning the area. Seeing no security people, they joined up and entered the Peter Pan building arcade, joining a line that snaked back and forth in the crowd-control maze.

"The sign said it's a forty-five-minute wait," said Aidan.

"This is not a bad place for us to be," said J.D., keeping his voice low. "We're out of the sun, and out of sight of anybody walking past out there."

"So what do we do when we get on the ride?" said Sarah.

"Well, obviously we look at Big Ben," said J.D. "And we look for a bird. Beyond that, I guess we mainly just try to observe as much as we can."

"What about the . . . the secret ingredient?" said Sarah, pointing to her backpack. "When do we use that?"

"We'll have to figure that out once we get inside," said J.D.

They inched forward, speaking little, wondering what lay ahead, barely aware of the horde of chattering tourists around them. Finally, they reached the front of the line, where a costumed ride attendant guided them onto a moving walkway running parallel to the line of "sailing ships" suspended from an overhead track.

It was a tight fit, but the three of them squeezed into one ship together, with Sarah in the middle, holding the backpack on her lap. The safety bar came down and the ship made a left turn into the ride, then angled upward.

Suddenly, they were in the nursery of the Darling house in London, looking down on Wendy, Michael, and John Darling. They heard music, an orchestra playing "You Can Fly!" They flew out the window and passed over Nana, the dog, who barked forlornly up at them. Now the ship was flying through the darkness above an elaborately detailed miniature replica of nighttime London—the Thames, the Houses of Parliament, Tower Bridge, buildings, even streets with moving cars, their headlights lit.

"There's Big Ben," said Sarah, pointing ahead. All three of them leaned forward, eyes focused on the approaching clock tower.

Aidan made it out first. "It says 9:07," he said.

"Do the clock hands move?" said J.D., squinting.

"Doesn't look like it," said Aidan.

"I think they're painted on," agreed Sarah.

"Do you see a bird?" said J.D.

Aidan and Sarah leaned out, looking down as their ship swept over Big Ben.

"I don't see a bird," said Sarah.

"Me either," said Aidan. "But it's pretty dark."

"Okay, keep looking."

They flew past the moon, upon which were silhouettes of Peter Pan flying with Wendy, John, and Michael Darling. Then the ship rounded a turn and they were flying over Never Land island, being fired at by a cannon on Captain Hook's ship far below. They flew over a volcano, then mermaids, then Indians. Colorful illumination came from the scenes passing below; the ship was flying through darkness.

"I still haven't seen a bird," said Aidan.

"Yeah," said Sarah. "It's so dark in here."

Ahead they could see a much larger version of the pirate ship, with Wendy, prodded by a gang of nasty-looking pirates, about to walk the plank.

They heard a harsh noise over the music.

"Did you hear that?" said Sarah.

They heard it again, a high-pitched *Caw! Caw!*

Suddenly, there it was, appearing out of the gloom just

before the pirate ship: Skull Rock, a ghostly, pale skeleton face of stone with gaping empty holes for its eyes and nose. But one of the holes wasn't completely empty. "There!" cried Aidan, pointing at the skull's right eye socket. Perched in the opening, staring at them, was a bird.

It was a Disney Audio-Animatronic creature with bugged-out eyeballs behind a bright yellow beak and a wide wingspan. It cawed again; the ship veered sharply left. The skull was gone.

They were passing the pirate ship now, but all three of them were looking back.

"Okay," said Sarah. "That was definitely a bird."

"Aidan," said J.D. "Would you have been able to reach the bird from where you're sitting?"

"I don't think so," said Aidan. "It was too far away."

Now they were flying over Captain Hook, who was trying desperately—as he had been since the ride opened decades earlier—to escape from the jaws of the hungry crocodile, while Smee perpetually rowed to his captain's rescue. Then the ship rounded another corner, and daylight appeared ahead; the ride was over.

"We need to ride again," said J.D., as the safety bar lifted and they stepped onto the moving walkway.

"Right now?" said Aidan.

"Yup," said J.D. "We know the time Ben says, and we found the bird. We can assume that what we're supposed to feed the bird is starstuff; that's what powers the bridge. But how do we feed the bird if we can't reach it?"

"Could we hide somewhere and wait until the Magic Kingdom closes?" said Sarah. "Then we could sneak in and feed it."

J.D. shook his head. "Won't work. We have to feed it when Ben says—that's 9:07 P.M. I'm pretty sure the park is still open then."

"So we have to feed it while the ride is moving?" said Sarah. "How're we supposed to do that?"

"Okay," said J.D., "we need to look at the bird really carefully this time. We also need to time the ride exactly, down to the second."

"Why?" said Aidan.

"So we can know exactly how long it takes to get to the bird. We also need to know the exact time of day. That way we can get on the ride at the right time to reach the bird at exactly 9:07 P.M."

"How do you know it's P.M.?" said Sarah. "Couldn't it be A.M.?"

"Nope," said J.D. "It's nighttime in the London scene. The time Ben says has to be P.M."

They were walking back to the line again. J.D. pointed to the waiting-time sign, which now said fifty minutes. "That's another thing we have to factor in," he said. "The wait time."

"This is getting really complicated," said Aidan.

"And we still don't know how we're gonna feed the bird," said Sarah.

"Well, we'd better figure it out fast," said J.D., looking at his watch. "It's 6:30 P.M., which means we have less than three hours left."

"And we're going to use up nearly an hour of that taking the ride again," said Sarah, looking at the line snaking ahead.

"Other than that," said Aidan. "We're doing great."

Armstrong knew Disney was very good at finding missing children in the parks; the company was famed for its efficiency and professionalism in such matters. So rather than try to compete with the experts, Armstrong chose a different tactic: cheating.

He walked slowly along the Magic Kingdom's Main Street, looking for a Disney security guard. He'd seen the Disney security team at the main entrance, searching handbags; their uniforms consisted of a white, neatly-pressed, collared shirt, dark pants, and black shoes. They wouldn't be hard to spot amid all the T-shirts and tank tops.

Cinderella Castle loomed into the sky in front of him. He passed a crowd gathered to hear a brass band play Dixieland music. Just ahead, outside the Plaza Ice Cream Parlor, he spotted a security man old enough to be his grandfather.

He was eating an ice-cream cone and listening to the band, his foot tapping to the music.

Armstrong moved in. He came from slightly behind and to the side, bumping hard into the guard's left shoulder. The top scoop of ice cream—mint chip, Armstrong noted—went airborne, and the security guard instinctively threw out his right hand to catch it.

In that instant Armstrong expertly slipped the black radio off the man's belt, apologizing profusely at the same time.

"I'm so, so sorry! I'll buy you another!" Armstrong said, slipping the radio into his back pocket.

"Don't be silly! Just an accident."

"You sure?" Armstrong said.

"Absolutely! Forget it! Really!" said the guard. Armstrong suspected that the reason the guard was being so insistent was that he was not supposed to be eating on duty.

Mumbling one more apology, Armstrong backed into the crowd and disappeared.

After walking twenty yards, he fished the radio out of his pocket and pressed it to his ear—security dispatch was directing guards around the park; other guards were checking in and reporting their positions.

Armstrong was hearing it all.

CHAPTER 29

FAIRY TREASURES

$\mathcal{A}$S THE WAITING-TIME SIGN HAD PREDICTED, it took them fifty minutes to get to the front of the line for Peter Pan's Flight. They squeezed into the flying ship and J.D. pressed a button on his watch, which was in stopwatch mode. The safety bar came down; the ship rounded the corner and flew into the nursery, then out over nighttime London. All of them leaned forward as they approached Big Ben.

"It still says 9:07," said Aidan.

"Fifty seconds to Ben," said J.D., looking at the glowing dial of his watch. They flew past the moon into Never Land—the volcano, the mermaids, the Indians. In the distance they saw the form of Wendy on the plank.

"Coming up," said Sarah, softly. They stared intently ahead.

Caw! Caw!

Skull Rock loomed out of the darkness.

"Two minutes, fifteen seconds," said J.D. Aidan reached his arm toward the bird; it was well out of reach. The ship turned left; the skull disappeared.

J.D. looked up from his watch. "We're going to have about five seconds, max, near the bird," he said. "That doesn't leave us much margin for error."

"Assuming we even figure out what we're supposed to do," said Aidan.

"We'd better figure it out soon," said J.D. "It's almost 7:30. We're under two hours now."

They exited the ride; it was still light out, but the sun was waning. The Disney crowd, if anything, had grown. It swirled around Aidan, Sarah, and J.D. as they stood by the stroller-parking area outside Peter Pan's Flight. The waiting-time sign for the ride now showed fifty-five minutes.

"Okay," said J.D. "It's two minutes, fifteen seconds to the bird, so to reach it at 9:07, we need to board the ship at 9:04 and forty-five seconds. Assuming the waiting time is still fifty-five minutes, we'd want to get in line at . . . 8:09 P.M. and forty-five seconds."

"How do you do that in your head?" said Aidan.

"It's called subtraction," said J.D. "They used to teach it in school. Anyway, we'd want to give ourselves a cushion, so let's say we'll get in line at eight P.M. That gives us a half hour now to figure out the bridge."

"I don't think we should stay out here in the open," said Sarah. "Let's go into that gift shop."

"Tinker Bell's Fairy Treasures?" said Aidan. "Seriously?"

"You have a better idea?" said Sarah.

"Of course not," said Aidan, reluctantly following Sarah and J.D. into the shop. "I don't even know how to subtract."

Agents Gomez and Blight had split up at Cinderella Castle, Gomez going left into Frontierland, Blight straight ahead into Fantasyland. Like Gomez, she was accompanied by a senior security guard listening to dispatch over a radio earpiece.

The code had been transmitted only minutes earlier—"Christopher Robin." Missing child! A description of both Sarah and Aidan had then been read over the secure radio. Over five thousand Cast Members in the Magic Kingdom heard the alert. On average, a Christopher Robin would result in thirty-seven false alarms—the wrong child matching the description. But despite that number, on any given day, a missing child was found within the first eleven minutes of the issue of such an alert.

So far there had been sixteen reported matches. The security man had relayed these to Blight, but they had all been in other areas of the park, and had all turned out to be false alarms.

Now dispatch was reporting a seventeenth match—this one nearby.

"Copy that, Crow's Nest," the security man said into his radio. "This is one-nine, en route to DC. Stand by." He said to Blight, "This one's ours."

"Review in progress, one-nine," came the dispatcher's voice. This meant they were reviewing video footage, looking for Sarah's likeness.

Blight and the guard broke into a jog, quickly reaching the carousel. They spun in circles, trying to separate one face from another in a moving sea of thousands of park guests. One minute passed . . . two . . .

The dispatcher reported. "All units, we have a twenty on Christopher Robin. Last seen passing DC headed in the direction of PPF. Units one-seven and one-three converge. All other units, stand by."

"We've got confirmation," the guard told Agent Blight. "Your colleague is on his way."

"That was fast," said Blight.

"This is Disney," said the guard.

"Where to?"

"Straight ahead."

The two hurried to Peter Pan's Flight. They walked the length of the arcade, studying each face in the long line. They then observed the loading and unloading area, waiting until a group they watched enter the ride came out the exit. They watched each ship intently but saw no sign of the runaways.

"Nothing," Blight said. "What's next?"

"Small World," said the guard, leading her across the concourse. Their attention was focused ahead, on the crowd surging into the hugely popular ride. Neither even glanced at another building close by, though they passed within fifteen yards of it: Tinker Bell's Fairy Treasures.

Sarah, J.D., and Aidan huddled in a corner of the gift shop, next to a display of Tinker Bell jewelry. They kept their voices low to avoid being overheard by the steady flow of souvenir shoppers grazing around them.

J.D. glanced at his watch. "We have twenty-six minutes to get back in line," he said.

"No pressure or anything," said Aidan.

"Okay," said Sarah, "to feed the bird, we have to get star-stuff to it, but we can't reach it from the ship. Could maybe one of us jump out of the ship?"

"I'm not sure, but I think it's too high up," said J.D. "You might not be able to reach the bird from the floor even if you managed to jump out without breaking your ankles."

"Could we throw some starstuff at the bird?" said Aidan.

"Hmm," said Sarah. "I've only handled a little, but I don't

see how you could throw it. It doesn't seem to have any, I dunno, *weight* to it. It seems to just . . . flow, almost like it has its own mind."

J.D. said, "But you can transport it. You've been transporting it, in the gold box."

Sarah's glance fell on the Tinker Bell jewelry. Suddenly, her eyes went wide.

"The locket!" she exclaimed.

One of the shop clerks looked over and said, "Can I help you with some jewelry?"

"No, sorry," said Sarah. Lowering her voice again, she said, "We use the locket Pete's wife gave us!"

"Of course," said J.D., pulling the locket out of his pocket. "Why didn't I think of that? That's why he put the message in there!"

"Along with a little starstuff," said Sarah. "He was showing us how to use it!"

"What are we talking about?" said Aidan.

Sarah rolled her eyes. "We're going to put some starstuff in Pete's locket and throw it to the bird," she said. "It's your idea, moron."

"It is?" said Aidan.

J.D. was looking at his watch. "Okay," he said, "we have to be in line in twenty minutes. I need to find a pay phone so I can get the exact time and set my watch to it. I'll go alone so we're not all together. You guys stay out of sight. Meet me at the line in fifteen minutes, okay?"

"When do we put the starstuff into the locket?" said Sarah.

J.D. frowned. "Not here, obviously. I guess we'll have to do it when we're in the line. Aidan and I can huddle around you—do you think you could pour some in quickly?"

"I guess I'll have to," said Sarah.

"Okay," said J.D. "Meet you at the line in fifteen. We're going to have one chance at this, and that's it." Then he was out the door, disappearing into the crowd.

They perched atop the wrought-iron work mounted on the peak of the Haunted Mansion—a decoration with the dual purpose of keeping birds off the roof. They also perched on the stone cap of every gable and the edge of every gutter— hundreds of ravens, in regimented lines. Not a beak turned, not an eye flinched, not a wing stirred.

"Look, Daddy!" a girl cried out from the waiting line. "Look at all the black birds!"

"Amazingly real-looking, aren't they, sweetheart?"

"But they *are* real, Daddy."

"Of course they are!"

"I don't like them, Daddy."

"Why not?"

"I can feel them."

"Here, hold my hand."

She reached for his hand but kept her worried eyes on the birds.

The father grinned, marveling at Disney's attention to detail.

CHAPTER 30

THE CLOUD

$\mathcal{T}$HEY JOINED THE LINE for Peter Pan's Flight at 8:01 P.M. The ride was even more crowded than it had been earlier, but the waiting-time sign still said fifty-five minutes.

"I hope I figured this right," said J.D., eyeing the long, shuffling line ahead, then glancing anxiously at his watch.

They inched forward, keeping their faces turned away from the hordes of people flowing past on the concourse outside the arcade. Each minute felt like an hour.

"Could this line move any slower?" said Aidan. "We're never gonna make it."

"If we have to," said Sarah, "we'll cut ahead in line."

Aidan gestured at the crowd in front of them, an army of exhausted parents, cranky kids, and wailing toddlers. "You actually think they'll let us in front of them?" he said. "Like, we'll tell them we have an urgent appointment with a bird in a skull and they'll just step aside?"

"Shut up," said Sarah.

"Maybe you could both shut up, okay?" said J.D.

"The Happiest Place on Earth," said Aidan.

A tense and silent half hour later, they were past the midway point—Sarah gripping the backpack straps, J.D. checking his watch for the hundredth time, Aidan staring ahead at nothing. The line was still moving agonizingly slowly, but it was moving. Another ten minutes passed, and J.D. whispered, "I think we're going to be okay. We might have to let a couple of groups go past us to get it exactly right."

Sarah said, "When do we transfer the . . ." She nodded at the backpack.

"Soon," said J.D., pointing. "Where the line runs next to that wall. We'll use the wall as a shield on one side."

"How much?" said Sarah. "If I pour a lot, we're all going to be flying."

"I'm figuring you should try to use the same amount as Pete did in the locket Mrs. Carmoody gave us," said J.D. "Just the tiniest amount, a quick flash. Not like in the van."

"Okay," said Sarah.

"Don't spill it," said Aidan.

"Shut up," said Sarah.

***

Armstrong hadn't heard much useful on the radio he'd lifted from the security guard. There'd been something about

Christopher Robin at one point—typical Disney World problems. Minnie Mouse would be next, he thought.

The searchers were going ride by ride, but so far hadn't found the Cooper kids or J.D. Aster. Armstrong had shadowed them for a while but recently had decided to strike out on his own. He had gone through Tomorrowland and, as darkness fell over the Magic Kingdom, was making his way through Fantasyland, scanning the crowd with practiced eyes. His plan, if he saw either runaway Cooper kid, was to move quickly and to be as physical as necessary. The boy had slipped through his fingers once; Armstrong wasn't going to let that happen again.

"All right," said J.D. "We need to be on the ship in five minutes. Let's do this."

He and Aidan took their positions next to Sarah, shielding her as much as they could from the people in line around them. He handed Pete's locket to Sarah. She faced the wall and set her backpack down, then quickly knelt next to it and unzipped the top. She reached inside and found the golden box. With trembling hands she positioned the locket next to it and thumbed open the catch. She tilted the box slightly and, holding the locket next to the hole, gave the golden wheel just the tiniest counterclockwise turn. The instant she saw the beginnings of a glow she closed her eyes tightly.

Even through her eyelids she saw the brilliant flash of light that followed, accompanied by a melodic humming sound. She quickly twisted the wheel closed and shut the locket, then opened her eyes.

The brilliant light was dying rapidly, but it still filled the area of the arcade where they were standing. All around them people were blinking, pointing, shouting; voices young and old were asking, "What was that?"

✳

With a roar of wing beats, the ravens exploded into the night sky over the Haunted Mansion. The birds swirled, a tornado of ebony feathers, then formed into what looked like a gigantic airborne spear, its tip aimed at Fantasyland.

Seconds later they were gone, the sound of their wings replaced by the oohs and aahs of the crowd below, marveling at this latest brilliant display of Disney Imagineering. How on earth did they do it?

✳

"Sorry!" J.D. shouted to the crowd as Sarah zipped up the backpack and scrambled to her feet. "Stupid camera flash went off! Sorry!"

"That was a camera flash?" said a man directly behind them. "Making all that light?"

"It's a new camera technology," said J.D. "It uses

deuterium-tritium fusion. Very efficient, and it's environmentally friendly."

"Huh," said the man.

"I heard a weird sound," said a woman who was with the man.

"That's the energy release from the free neutron," said J.D.

"Huh," said the woman. "Sounded like . . . bells!"

The bystanders didn't pursue the matter any further, partly because they were almost to the flying ships and partly because everybody was suddenly feeling surprisingly mellow and happy, especially for people who'd been on their feet in the heat all day. Even the babies had stopped crying.

J.D. whispered to Sarah, "Did you make the transfer?"

"I think so," said Sarah.

"Good," said J.D., looking at his watch. "Because we have to be on the ship in exactly two minutes and thirty seconds."

Armstrong was at Prince Charming Regal Carrousel when he saw the flash of light. He wondered what would make a flash that bright; he half expected to hear an explosion. He decided to trot over and take a closer look.

"Two minutes," said J.D., his eyes on his watch. They were almost at the front of the line—only four groups were ahead of them. Making a quick calculation, J.D. turned to the couple behind—the ones who'd asked about the flash—and said, "You guys can go ahead of us."

The couple went past. J.D. eyed the line ahead, then his watch. "One minute forty-five," he said.

Armstrong was fifty feet away when he saw them, all three together, waiting in line for Peter Pan's Flight. He had a decision to make: should he wait for them as they exited the ride, or grab them now? Remembering how the boy had gotten away from him last time, he decided to take no chances. He'd grab them now, and he'd make sure he grabbed the boy.

He started toward the trio.

They had reached the moving walkway. The group ahead was boarding a ship; they were next.

"Ninety seconds," said J.D. "We have to stall a little."

Aidan looked out at the concourse and froze. "We got trouble," he said.

"What?" said Sarah.

"That big guy," said Aidan, pointing. "He's the one who tried to grab me at the train station."

"Are you sure?"

"Yes, and he sees us."

Armstrong was, indeed, coming their way. One of the Peter Pan Cast Members moved to block his path, apparently telling him he couldn't enter the ride that way. Armstrong pushed past the Cast Member, pointing at Sarah, Aidan, and J.D., who were now at the head of the line to board the ships.

"Stop the ride!" Armstrong shouted. "Police emergency! Stop the ride!"

"If he stops the ride," said J.D., "it's over."

"You guys go ahead," said Aidan. "I'll slow him down."

"Wait!" said Sarah. But Aidan had already vaulted a divider and was running toward Armstrong.

"Aidan!" shouted Sarah. She turned to J.D. "I have to go help him."

"Sarah," said J.D., "this is our only chance. We have to be on the ship in seventy-five seconds."

"But I can't just . . ."

Sarah was interrupted by a shout from Aidan as he ran directly into the midsection of the oncoming Armstrong. The big man, surprised by the assault, staggered backward into the concourse. But he had his powerful arms around Aidan and clearly did not intend to let go.

"Aidan!" shouted Sarah. She went toward the divider.

"Wait!" said J.D., grabbing her arm.

And then they both froze, watching in horror as the struggling figures of Armstrong and Aidan were suddenly engulfed by black shapes falling like living stones from the sky.

"No!" screamed Sarah, her voice matched by screams from people on the concourse as the raven swarm swirled around the now-fallen pair. Both J.D. and Sarah were now climbing the divider to go to Aidan's rescue.

And then, incredibly, Aidan emerged from the swirling black mass, on his feet again, walking toward them. Behind him the birds were darting back upward, leaving the form of Armstrong lying face-down on the concourse, apparently unconscious. A crowd was gathering around him. Some were applauding, believing this to be a show.

"Aidan!" shouted Sarah, relief flooding her face.

J.D. looked ahead. The ride was still moving; the Peter Pan Cast Members, like the people in line, were distracted by the drama surrounding Armstrong on the concourse. J.D. looked at his watch. "Fifteen seconds!" he said. "We can do this! Come on!"

He tugged Sarah's arm, pulling her toward the walkway. She resisted, looking back toward her brother.

"Come on, Aidan!" she shouted. "Run! Why don't you . . ." Then she screamed.

J.D. looked back; Sarah's face was a mask of horror. No longer resisting, she stumbled after J.D. onto the walkway. He looked at his watch; they had five seconds. No time to wait for Aidan.

He stepped quickly forward and got into the closest sailing ship; he pulled Sarah onto the seat beside him. Another glance at his watch: it read 9:05:46. Only one second off. He turned to Sarah, who was staring straight ahead, her backpack on her lap.

"What happened to Aidan?" he said.

Sarah turned to him. Her face was paper-white. "That's . . . not . . . Aidan," she said.

"What are you talking about?" J.D. turned his head, looking back along the walkway. The ship behind them, and the one behind it, were both empty. Getting onto the walkway now and approaching the third ship back was Aidan. As he reached the ship and started to climb in, he looked directly at J.D. Where his eyes should have been were two black voids.

"Oh my god," said J.D.

"Ombra," said Sarah. The safety bar closed. Their ship was turning left and rising, entering the Darling nursery.

"Is he following us?" said Sarah.

"Yes," said J.D. "But he's three ships back. Do you still want to try the bridge?"

Sarah looked down at the backpack, then at J.D.

"Yes," she said. "We have to get the starstuff away from him, away from us, forever. He's only using Aidan to find out what our plan is. If we get the starstuff to the island, he'll know he can never have it, and he'll leave us alone."

They were passing over the ever-barking Nana. "All right, then," said J.D. "Get the locket ready."

"Okay," said Sarah, digging into the pocket of her jeans.

Now they were over London. Ahead and below was Big Ben, still indicating 9:07. The overhead track curved, turning their ship so they could see clearly behind them.

Sarah fought back a scream.

By the dim light of the artificial moon, they saw that Aidan had left the seat of his ship and was crouching on the bow, in front of the sail. It looked like a precarious position, but he seemed to balance there without effort. As they watched, he leaped forward, traveling what seemed like an impossible distance through the air and landing with astonishing agility on the stern of the ship in front.

"He's coming after us!" said Sarah.

"There's still a ship between him and us," said J.D. "And we're less than a minute away."

They were over Never Land now; the volcano was passing below. J.D. looked back. Aidan was now perched on the bow of the second ship behind them. With a movement too quick to be human, he again leaped forward, landing easily one ship back.

"Where is he?" said Sarah, not looking.

"He's right behind us," said J.D.

Below them now was the mermaid lagoon. Just ahead was the Indian village.

After that was the bird.

J.D. looked back. Aidan was moving toward the bow of the ship behind them. In the ghostly, dim light of the ride his gray, eyeless face looked like a skull. J.D. looked down; there were the Indians. He looked ahead and saw Wendy, about to walk the plank.

"Get ready," he said. "Toss it right at the bird, okay?" Sarah nodded and gripped the locket.

J.D. looked back. Aidan had reached the bow of the ship. He looked forward. Skull Rock—finally—loomed out of the darkness. He looked back. Aidan was crouched to spring.

Caw! Caw!

"Now!" shouted J.D.

Sarah's arm flicked out. The golden locket glinted as it sailed through the gloom toward the bird perched in the gaping eye socket of the skull.

From behind them came a hideous, unearthly groan.

J.D. turned and saw Aidan flying through the air like some ungodly bat.

And then the world went utterly white, its features obliterated by a light of blinding intensity. J.D. closed his eyes, or at least thought he did, but the light was still there, as if coming from inside his eyes, inside his mind. He heard a scream, and realized it was his own voice, but somehow it seemed to be coming from him, and from somewhere else, at the same time. Then he heard another voice screaming, Sarah's voice, but he couldn't see her, nor could he touch her, though he knew she had to be right next to him.

Then he felt that he was falling. Not fast—more of a

gentle downward drift, falling through the all-consuming whiteness, falling through a cloud made of pure light.

And then as suddenly as it had come, the whiteness was gone, the world came back, and J.D. saw that he was still in the little Peter Pan's Flight ship, and he was still sitting next to Sarah, and . . .

And they were flying. Not suspended from a pole in a building in Florida, but really flying, over blue-green water sparkling with a billion flashes of sunlight. Flying, but also descending; the little ship was drifting downward.

"Sarah," he said, as the water drew closer. "We have to . . ."

"Look," she said.

He looked where she was pointing and saw it rising from the water beside them, in all its malevolent massiveness.

Skull Rock.

"Oh my god," he said. "It's real."

"That's not all that's real," said Sarah. Now she was pointing directly behind them.

J.D. turned and gasped. Bearing down on them, under full sail, was a large wooden ship flying the Jolly Roger. Standing in the bow, pointing at them and shouting, was a man with long, greasy black hair and an enormous black moustache. He was pointing with a hook.

CHAPTER 31

THE POWER

"PADDLE!" J.D. SHOUTED, reaching over the side and scooping seawater. The tiny Peter Pan's Flight boat had settled into the azure sea directly in front of the pirate ship, which was closing in quickly, foam surging along both sides of its bow. J.D.'s frantic efforts to move them out of the way were having little effect, and Sarah was not helping; she was still staring at the shouting man in the front of the pirate ship.

"That's him!" she said. "That's Captain Hook!"

"Yes, and we're going to be fish food if we don't get out of the way. *Paddle!*"

Suddenly aware of the danger, Sarah leaned over to help J.D. move the little boat. But their efforts had little effect; the hull of the big ship loomed closer, about to crush them. At the last second, Hook bellowed a command, and the ship turned sharply left, its sails suddenly slack. The ship slowed and settled gently next to the little ride boat.

More commands from Hook, and a sailor swung down to J.D. and Sarah on a rope. Agile as a monkey, he tied the rope to their little craft—a good thing, since the starstuff had almost worn off and it was about to sink. A minute later it was being hauled upward, with J.D. and Sarah still in it. As they rose, Sarah nudged J.D. and pointed; in the distance, rising majestically from the water, was a green and mountainous island.

"That's it!" she said. "That's Never Land! J.D., we're here!"

"Not to be a wet blanket or anything," said J.D., "but we're also being captured by pirates."

They had reached the big ship's rail; their little vessel lurched sideways, spilling them both onto the deck, Sarah clutching her backpack in front of her.

"Well, well," said an unpleasant rasp of a voice. "What have we here?"

They looked up to see Hook, tall, gaunt, and sun-baked, regarding them with a sneering smile that revealed a random collection of jagged, yellow teeth. Enjoying the drama of the moment, Hook slapped back the ragged hem of his faded red coat and prepared to stride manfully toward them, only to catch the toe of his worn boot on an uneven deck plank and stumble forward, saved from falling onto his hatchet face only by landing on Smee, his barefoot, rotund, and balding first mate.

"Out of my way, you clumsy idjit!" bellowed Hook, belting Smee on the ear, fortunately with his non-hook hand.

"Sorry, Cap'n!" whimpered the little man, scurrying aside to join the rest of the ragtag pirate crew, who were staring, mouths agape, at the new arrivals.

Hook resumed his manful striding, managing to reach Sarah and J.D. without further mishap. For a moment he stood there stroking his matted beard, which was festooned with food scraps. Sarah and J.D. looked up with expressions that were equal parts fear and disgust; Hook smelled like the wrong end of a goat.

Hook turned to look at their little boat, lying sideways on the deck. "What kind of craft have we here?" he said. He tapped it with his hook, then dragged the sharp tip, peeling off a curl of paint with a screech that made the pirates wince. "Seems a tad . . . puny for the open sea, don't it, boys?"

The pirates nodded vigorously. No matter what Hook said, they either nodded or shook their heads in unison. Hook appreciated his crew's unflagging loyalty.

"No, you couldn't go far on this ship, not in the water," said Hook. He turned toward Sarah and J.D. "Of course, you two wasn't in the water, now was you? No, you was flying when we spied you. That's mighty curious, ain't it, men?"

The men nodded vigorously.

"Yes," said Hook, a hardness coming into his dark eyes. "Around here we're very interested in things that fly. *Very* interested." He spat onto the deck, then glared at his men. They all spat onto the deck.

Hook moved closer to Sarah. She stiffened as his hook found its way to her trembling chin. "And who might you be? Hmm? Such a fine lass these eyes have not seen for . . ." He looked at Smee.

"One hundred four years, three months, and twenty-two days, Cap'n."

"A long time," said Hook, catching some of Sarah's hair in his hook and letting it slide off the metal slowly back onto her shoulder. "A very long time. So who are you, girl?"

Sarah pulled her head away from the hook. "My name is Sarah Cooper," she said.

"Cooper, is it? I knew me a cooper once, and a fine cooper he was, too. Made a fine barrel, never leaked a drop of rum. Eh, Smee?"

"Kaden Cooper, I believe it were, Cap'n. Off St. Bartholomew's, it was. Though it might have been Kaleb."

"Expensive place, St. Bart's," the captain said to Sarah. "Ever been?"

She shook her head. "No."

"If you ever get there," said Hook, "take money."

J.D. cleared his throat.

Hook glared down at him. "Are you clearing your throat at me, boy?" he said.

"Yes sir," said J.D. "I . . ."

"Stand up when you speak to me, boy!" roared Hook.

J.D. scrambled to his feet.

"What's your name, boy?" said Hook.

"J.D."

"What kind of name is that?"

"It's initials," said J.D. "It stands for . . ."

"I know what initials is!" roared Hook, who had no idea what initials were.

"I'm sorry," said J.D. "I was just going to say, we, that is Sarah and I, we don't want to cause any trouble. We're very grateful to you for rescuing us, and we're just wondering if you could take us to that island?"

Hook put his hand to his chin and frowned thoughtfully, as if he were seriously considering this request.

"No," he said.

"But—"

"Shut yer hole, boy, before I fill it with hot tar for you!"

J.D. shut his hole.

Hook stepped closer to J.D., who struggled not to gag from the stench of the pirate captain's breath. With a delicate motion, Hook raised his hook, then lowered it slowly until it touched J.D.'s plastic digital watch.

"What manner of bracelet is that?" he said.

"It's a watch," said J.D. He held it up so Hook could see the display. "It has a lot of functions; like, here's the stopwatch." J.D. pressed a button and the watch beeped. The pirates gasped. Hook stared at the flashing numbers on the watch display.

"It's digital," said J.D. Seeing Hook's frown, he said, "That means it—"

"I know what digitile is!" roared Hook.

"Sorry," said J.D.

"Give it to me," said Hook.

J.D. quickly removed the watch from his wrist and handed it to Hook, who held it awkwardly.

"Do you want me to put it on for you?" said J.D.

"Do you think I don't know how to put it on?" bellowed Hook.

"No, sir," said J.D.

"Of course I know how to put it on, boy. But I choose to have you put it on me." Hook held out his hook; with shaking hands, J.D. fastened the watch to the pirate's bony wrist. Hook admired it for a moment, then turned to Sarah.

"Now," he said. "Let's see what gifts the lady Cooper brought me." He grabbed hold of her backpack. She tightened her grip.

"Let go, girl," he snarled.

"No," she said.

"No?" said Hook, shocked. Nobody said no to Hook. He yanked on the backpack. Sarah yanked back. With a roar, he raised his hook hand.

"Sarah!" shouted J.D. "Let go!"

Sarah let go of the backpack. Hook staggered backward, and would have fallen if Smee had not caught him from behind.

"Let *go*, you idjit!" bellowed Hook, giving his first mate a bony elbow to the head.

"Aye, Cap'n," said Smee, scuttling away.

Hook now examined the backpack, turning it around, upside down, and backward, clearly confused by it.

"Smee!" he yelled.

Smee scuttled forward again.

"Aye, Cap'n?"

"Open this," said Hook, handing over the backpack.

The little man turned the backpack in his hands, his face knotted in puzzlement.

"But there ain't no hasp, Cap'n," he said. "No buttons. No laces nor strings."

Hook stepped toward Sarah, hoisting a hairy eyebrow.

"Tell me how it opens," he growled.

"No," said Sarah.

Hook stepped toward her and raised his hook again.

"Tell him!" said J.D.

Sarah remained silent. Hook took another step.

"Zippers!" said J.D.

All the pirates laughed at this strange new word.

"Silence!" Hook cried. He turned to J.D. "What'd you say, boy?"

"Zippers. It opens with zippers."

The pirates, eyes on Hook, stifled their snickers.

"Zipplers," said Hook.

"*Zippers*," said J.D. "They're a kind of . . ."

"I *know* what zipplers is," said Hook. He snatched the backpack from Smee and thrust it at J.D. "Open it!" he barked.

J.D., with a glance at Sarah, unzipped the backpack's small front compartment, avoiding the larger compartment that held the golden box.

"See?" he said. "That's a zipper."

Hook's eyes were wide. "Do that again," he ordered. Smee and the others gathered around to watch as J.D. worked the zipper back and forth. The pirates oohed and aahed. Convinced that there was no danger, Hook grabbed the backpack away from J.D. and played with the zipper himself. "Looks like a saw blade," he muttered. He touched the plastic zipper. "But it don't cut your finger."

"It's a very useful invention," said J.D., hoping to distract Hook from the backpack. "Zippers can be used in all kinds of ways. Clothing, for example." He pointed to the zipper on his jeans. This created an uproar among the pirates.

"What are you doing?" Sarah said.

Ignoring her, J.D. worked the zipper. Hook's eyes were now as big as saucers.

"Get me them trousers!" he bellowed.

Immediately, two sailors grabbed J.D. and turned him

upside down; two others yanked his jeans off. He was returned to his feet in his boxer shorts.

Hook turned his back and, shielded by his coat, exchanged his torn leggings for J.D.'s blue jeans. He played with the zipper repeatedly, then shouted *"Owww!"* and bent over.

"What happened, Cap'n?" said Smee.

"Never mind what happened!" roared Hook, turning back around, his face beet-red. He pointed at the backpack and snarled. "Open it!"

Sarah and J.D. exchanged helpless looks as Smee gingerly opened all the zippers, then tipped over the backpack. Sarah's iPad and cell phone tumbled onto the deck, followed by the golden box. The pirates were in an uproar now, gathered around these strange objects.

"Stand back!" bellowed Hook.

The men parted. Hook leaned down and picked up the iPad. He studied the black glass screen. "It's a mirror," he declared. He held up the iPad and, using the reflection, combed some debris from his beard with his hook. Shifting his grip on the iPad, he pressed the power button. He jerked his head back in alarm as the screen came to life, displaying Sarah's wallpaper: a pristine, white-sand, Caribbean island in a sea of turquoise water. Hook nearly dropped the device.

"Smee!"

Smee waddled over, looked at the screen, and gasped. "As fine a painting as I've seen, Cap'n!"

"It wasn't there a second ago," said Hook. He glared at J.D. "Where did this painting come from?" he demanded.

"It's, um . . ." J.D. hesitated, not sure where to begin.

"It's magic," said Sarah.

The pirates muttered nervously.

"What did you say, girl?" said Hook.

"It's a magic . . . picture thing," said Sarah.

Hook frowned. On the one hand, he could not appear to be afraid of this girl, especially in front of his men. On the other hand, he was a bit afraid of this girl, and this thing he was holding did appear to be magical. Perhaps even dangerous.

"Hold this, Smee," he said, handing the iPad to his first mate, who took it nervously.

"You can have the magic picture thing," said Sarah. She pointed toward the cell phone. "You can also have that. It's a magic, um, talking thing. Very magical. You can talk to people far away. And send magical texts. I'll show you how to use these things. All I ask is that you let us go, and let us keep this." She pointed to the golden box. "It's just an old family . . . thing."

She bent to pick up the box. She was stopped by the hook on her arm, its point pressing painfully into her skin.

"And old family thing, eh?" said Hook, his dark eyes glittering.

"Yes."

Hook bent and picked up the box. He found the little golden wheel, and touched it with his hook.

"Don't!" said Sarah.

"Why not?" said Hook.

"It's dangerous," she said.

"Very dangerous," said J.D.

Hook looked at Sarah, then J.D., then the box.

"Smee," he said.

"Aye, Cap'n."

"Take this box."

"What do I do with the magical picture thing?" said Smee.

"Put it down, you sponge-brained idjit," said Hook, "and take the box."

"Aye, Cap'n," said Smee, putting down the iPad and taking the box from Hook.

"Now," said Hook, "turn the wheel."

"But they said it was dang—"

"I *know* what they said, you idjit. They're lying."

"They are?"

"Of course they are," said Hook, taking a step back. "Turn the wheel."

"You're making a big mistake," said Sarah.

"Silence, girl!" said Hook. "Turn the wheel, Smee."

With great reluctance, Smee put his hand on the wheel. Beads of sweat appeared on his broad forehead. He looked at

J.D. and Sarah, who both shook their heads. Then he looked pleadingly at Hook.

"Turn the wheel!" Hook roared.

His whole body trembling, Smee turned the wheel. The deck instantly filled with sound and a light far brighter than the sun overhead.

"Shut it off now!" yelled Sarah. "Right now!"

Somehow, through the blaze of light and sound, Smee heard her, and obeyed. The light began to dim immediately, but it was thirty seconds or so before the pirates could see anything. What they saw, as their vision returned, was that they were no longer on the deck; they were floating, every one of them, up into the ship's rigging. And yet they were not afraid—in fact, they were delighted, even Hook, who smiled hugely beneath his flamboyant moustache, revealing his foul teeth in all their mismatched hideousness. Floating above the rest of the pirates, like an overinflated balloon, was Smee, grinning blissfully, still clutching the golden box.

Sarah and J.D. were also floating, but being starstuff veterans, they were not surprised. They had both closed their eyes when Smee turned the wheel, so their vision came back more quickly than the pirates'. J.D. spotted Sarah in the midst of the floating pirates, angling her body upward, trying to get to Smee. But she was having trouble gaining altitude, as was J.D.; they both could sense that the small amount of starstuff Smee had released was already wearing off.

J.D. grabbed a mainmast stay and used it to propel himself toward Sarah. "We need to get out of here," he said, catching hold of her arm.

"We need to get the box," she answered, still struggling to rise.

"We can't reach it," he said, looking up at the giggling Smee, now floating near the crow's nest, with Hook about ten feet below him. "And when Hook comes down, we need to be gone."

Sarah continued to strain, but she and J.D. were both starting to sink. Around them, the other pirates were also slowly descending.

"Sarah, come on," said J.D.

Seeing that her efforts were hopeless, Sarah reluctantly gave up. She followed J.D. as he veered away from the ship and out over the open water, pointing toward the mountainous island in the distance.

From above, Hook saw them leaving, but he was untroubled. In part, this was because of the unaccustomed mellowness he was feeling. But mostly it was because of the golden box. Hook knew what was in that box; he'd had dealings with it long ago. He knew it was, indeed, magical—and very powerful.

And now, he thought, as he drifted back toward the deck, with Smee and the box descending lazily after him, *that power is mine.*

CHAPTER 32

THE WELCOMING PARTY

"WE'RE NOT GOING TO MAKE IT!" Sarah called over her shoulder.

J.D., flying just behind and below her, knew she was right; the island was still well in the distance, and they were almost in the water.

"We'll have to swim for it," he shouted. "Keep flying as long as you can. I'll catch up. I'm a good swimmer."

Seconds later, his toes brushed the water; seconds after that, his legs were dragging, and the rest of him was dragged in. Sarah heard the splash and glanced back to see J.D. waving at her to keep going. She did; she was not a strong swimmer, and wanted to fly every foot she could. She made herself as horizontal as possible as the water came closer and closer until she was skimming along hardly a foot above the surface.

When the plunge came, it happened more suddenly than she expected, and caught her with her mouth open, her velocity forcing salt water into her throat as it drove her body underwater. She panicked, twisting her body frantically, looking for the surface, thrashing her arms and legs. She realized to her horror that she wasn't rising; she was sinking deeper into the blue-green water. She redoubled her efforts to swim but found she had no strength left in her limbs. Her vision was dimming, her lungs were on fire, and the air she craved so desperately was receding above her, farther and farther . . .

And then, suddenly, somehow, she was rising—gripped from behind by powerful arms, the water rushing past her face as she shot upward. Her head broke the surface and she gasped and coughed and heaved, trying to simultaneously take air in and vomit seawater out. It was more than a minute before she had regained some control, her breath coming in harsh rasps.

"Th—thank you," she said, turning her head, expecting to see J.D. She jerked in surprise when she saw that the face only inches from hers was that of a woman—a stunningly beautiful woman, with long blond hair and huge, brilliant green eyes.

"Who are you?" said Sarah.

The woman smiled at her, but said nothing. Her teeth were small and very white, ending in sharp points. Her breath smelled like seaweed.

"There was someone with me," Sarah said. "He must be in the water somewhere. I have to find him." Sarah twisted her head around, looking for J.D., but saw only empty water. She turned back to her rescuer. "Please," she said. "I need to find him. He could be drowning." She struggled, trying to break free of the woman's grasp, but could not; the woman was incredibly strong.

"Please," said Sarah again. "I . . . hey!"

She was suddenly being propelled through the water toward the island with impossible speed, still in the grip of the woman. No human could swim that fast, Sarah realized, and in that moment she also realized what her rescuer was. She looked back and saw, in the foaming wake behind them, a flash of glistening green, sun reflecting from a long, graceful, and very powerful tail.

"You're a mermaid," she said, over the rush of the water. Her rescuer flashed her a quick sideways smile. Sarah frowned, trying to remember the name of the head mermaid in the stories she'd read. "Are you Teacher?" she said. This got a bigger smile.

"Teacher," said Sarah, "I need to find my friend."

The mermaid nodded ahead. Sarah looked, squinting against the sun and sea spray, and saw a long, curved beach, its bright, white sand ringed with palms. Beyond that rose a steep mountainside covered with dense vegetation in a thousand shades of green. As they drew nearer she saw figures in the shallow water next to the beach. One was standing.

"J.D.!" she shouted, her voice breaking with relief.

J.D. spotted her and waved. She could see now that the figures in the water around him were mermaids, a half dozen of them, smiling radiantly.

"I see you got a ride, too," J.D. called, as Teacher, with a few more sweeps of her powerful tail, brought Sarah to him. Sarah stood and waded to him on shaky legs.

Seeing the look on her face, he said, "You okay?"

She intended to answer, but what came out was a sob. J.D. stepped forward and gave her an awkward hug, patting her back. She held him tightly for a moment. This displeased the mermaids who'd been surrounding J.D.; several of them snarled and hissed until a look from Teacher quieted them.

"I'm sorry," said Sarah, wiping her eyes. "I had a little trouble out there."

"I'm sorry," said J.D. "I shouldn't have told you to go ahead. But you're okay now."

"Except for losing the starstuff to Hook and Ombra getting Aidan."

"Except for that," agreed J.D. "On the other hand, we're here," he said, looking around at the beach and the jungle-covered mountainside beyond. "So this is Never Land."

"Yes," said Sarah. "Where nobody ever grows old."

"Do you really believe that?"

"Do you believe in Captain Hook? Mermaids?"

J.D. smiled. "Good point. So remind me how that works, the whole never-grow-old thing."

"According to the books," said Sarah, "there's starstuff in the water supply, way underground somewhere."

"And it's still working, after all these years?"

"I guess so. A little seems to go a long way. And there was a lot here."

J.D. was about to ask another question when he saw movement up the beach at the edge of the jungle.

"Looks like we have a welcoming party," he said.

Five muscular men were walking down the beach toward them. They were barefoot, wearing only loincloths and necklaces made of shells. All five carried spears. "I think those are the Mollusks," said Sarah.

There was a splashing sound. J.D. and Sarah looked around to find that the mermaids had disappeared.

"Are the Mollusks friendly?" said J.D.

"Sort of," said Sarah.

"What does that mean?"

"I don't think they're crazy about visitors."

"Swell."

The five men stopped at the water's edge and spread out, watching J.D. and Sarah with unreadable expressions.

"Hello," said J.D., raising his hand in what he hoped was a peaceful gesture, then feeling stupid and putting it back down.

The Mollusk in the middle, the tallest one, stepped forward, his eyes on J.D. "Who are you," he said, "and how

316

did you come here?" He spoke in British-accented English.

"I'm J.D. Aster."

"An Aster," said the Mollusk.

"Yes."

"I see. And the way you came here?"

"It's . . . complicated," said J.D.

"Too complicated for a savage such as myself to comprehend?"

Sarah smirked. J.D. reddened.

"I didn't mean that," he said. "It's just that the way we got here, it's a very—"

"We came on the bridge," said Sarah.

The Mollusk smiled at her. "Thank you," he said. "I suspected as much. It's been quite a while since anyone used the bridge."

Sarah was studying him. "Are you the chief's son . . . Bold Abalone?" she said.

The Mollusk smiled again. "I am. And you are . . ."

"Sarah. Sarah Cooper."

"You're not an Aster."

"No. But I'm . . . I'm sort of working with the Starcatchers."

Bold Abalone nodded. "Perhaps, Sarah Cooper, you can explain to me why you and Mister Aster came to our island."

"Okay," said Sarah. "But that part really is complicated."

"In that case," said Bold Abalone, "it would be best if you explained it to my father."

CHAPTER 33

ANOTHER PROBLEM

$\mathcal{T}$HEY TOOK A PACKED-DIRT PATH through the jungle, Bold Abalone leading, followed by two Mollusk warriors, then Sarah and J.D., then two more Mollusks bringing up the rear. The jungle crowded close on both sides, the vegetation overhead so thick that the sunlight was reduced to a dim green glow. From all around came the buzzing of insects and the cries of exotic birds flitting through the trees. Occasionally, from the mountainside, came a deeper, muffled sound, apparently emitted by a larger animal—though what kind it was, Sarah and J.D. couldn't tell.

They followed the coastline, the water somewhere through the jungle off to their left, the mountainside rising steeply to their right. In about a half hour they came to a large clearing, at the far side of which was a tall log fence with a gate standing open. From inside the fence rose plumes of gray smoke. The air now carried the aroma of something cooking; Sarah and J.D. both became aware of how hungry they were.

As they approached the gate, children's heads appeared, poking out from both sides of the opening, staring at them. Passing through the gate, they found themselves in a large compound with several dozen thatch-roofed huts arranged around cooking fires. There were at least a hundred Mollusks inside, adults and children, every one of them staring at the new arrivals.

Bold Abalone led them through the crowd to the middle of the compound, where a group of warriors was gathered in front of a large hut. Emerging from the hut was a tall, gray-haired man, older than the others, but still lean and muscular. He studied Sarah and J.D. with dark, intense eyes.

"Fighting Prawn," whispered Sarah to J.D.

"What?" said J.D.

"He's the chief. Bold Abalone's father."

"He doesn't look thrilled to see us."

Bold Abalone stopped in front of his father and spoke to him in a language consisting of odd-sounding grunts and clicks; the only word Sarah and J.D. understood was "Aster." When he was done, Fighting Prawn nodded and looked at J.D.

"You are an Aster?" he said. He spoke with the same accent as his son.

"I am," said J.D.

"A relative of Leonard Aster?"

"He was the uncle of my great-grandfather."

"So you are a Starcatcher?"

"Um . . . sort of."

"What does that mean?"

"It's, uh . . . it's kind of complicated."

"But it is the reason you have come."

"Yes."

"And you," said Fighting Prawn, turning to Sarah. "Are you a Starcatcher?"

"Not by birth," said Sarah. "But I've become, um, involved with them. I'm really the reason we're here. I did something really, really stupid."

Fighting Prawn's expression softened just a bit.

"You can explain it to me after dinner," he said. "Would you like to join us?"

J.D. and Sarah accepted eagerly. The Mollusks ate in circles, sitting cross-legged on the ground. Sarah and J.D. sat with the chief and his family. They were given bowls made from what appeared to be large clamshells, filled with grain and chunks of a cooked meat neither recognized, but both ate ravenously. They drank water from coconut shells; both were struck by how sweet and pure it tasted and how energized it made them feel.

When the meal was finished, they thanked Fighting Prawn for his hospitality.

"That was delicious," said J.D. "What kind of meat is that?"

"The Mollusk word for it," said Fighting Prawn, "is . . ." Here he made a low-pitched nasal sound.

"What does that mean in English?" asked Sarah.

"Giant tree spider," said Fighting Prawn.

"I need some more water," said Sarah.

The Mollusks smiled with amusement as she and J.D. gulped from their coconuts.

"Now," said Fighting Prawn when they were done. "Please explain your presence here."

Sarah started at the beginning, leaving out nothing. She spoke for nearly a half hour uninterrupted. At that point J.D. picked up the story—the locket, Molly Aster's diary, and the realization that Einstein had built the bridge. At the mention of the scientist's name, Fighting Prawn smiled for the first time.

"Doctor Einstein was a great man," he said.

"You met him?" said J.D.

"Yes," said Fighting Prawn. "He came on the ship that brought the machine. Doctor Einstein met with us and explained what the machine would do, or at least what he *believed* it would do. He said there was no way to be certain it would work other than to try it. He said that if we did not want them to use the machine, they would not. We decided that it was worth the risk; more and more ships were coming to the island, and if we had done nothing, in time we would have lost everything, forever. Fortunately, it worked."

"What was that like, when the island was moved?" said J.D.

"It was like a storm, a hurricane," said Fighting Prawn. "But instead of wind, it was a storm of light—as if the island itself, and the sky and the sea, had all turned into light. Then it felt as if we were falling. We were all afraid, even the warriors. But when it was over, it was as if nothing had changed—except now we are free from outside threats. For that, we will be forever grateful to Doctor Einstein. I regret that I was never able to thank him. He never returned."

"Did others return?" said J.D.

"Yes. One day, some years after the island was moved, we had two visitors. They came to tell us that they created a permanent bridge between our island and the world we once lived in, but that it would be carefully guarded and used only if absolutely necessary. One was an older gentleman named John Aster."

"My grandfather," said J.D.

"The other was a younger man, named . . ." Fighting Prawn frowned, trying to remember.

"Pete Carmoody?" said Sarah.

"Yes," said Fighting Prawn, smiling. "A very capable man. Is he still . . ." Fighting Prawn's voice trailed off.

"No," said J.D. "He passed away. We were with his widow recently; that's how we found the bridge."

Sarah, with J.D.'s help, then resumed their story—getting the second locket from Mrs. Carmoody; realizing where the bridge had been hidden and how to activate it; Ombra's capture of Aidan; and Sarah and J.D.'s frantic effort to use the bridge before Ombra/Aidan got to them. Fighting Prawn was confused by some of it—the concept of Disney World especially—but eventually he seemed satisfied that he understood the strange journey that had brought Sarah and J.D. to his island.

"To summarize," he said, "you brought the starstuff here, to this world, so that Ombra can never have it."

"Yes," said Sarah.

"Where is it, then?"

Sarah looked down. "Captain Hook got it."

Fighting Prawn's eyebrows arched.

"Hook?" he said. "How did that happen?"

"He was there when we came across the bridge," said J.D. "He grabbed us and took the golden box."

"And he knows what it contains?"

"I'm afraid he does," said Sarah. "They figured out how to open it. We escaped while they were floating around."

Fighting Prawn shook his head. "That is very unfortunate," he said. "Hook is a villain. We allow him to exist on his side of the island because he is an incompetent villain;

he actually provides the rest of us with a measure of entertainment. But with starstuff in his possession, he is far more dangerous."

"There's another problem," said J.D.

Fighting Prawn looked at him, waiting.

"We need some of that starstuff to get back to our world," he said. "We have one locket left. But without starstuff, we can't activate the bridge."

Sarah put her hand to her mouth. "I didn't think of that," she said. "We have to get the box back!"

"I agree," said Fighting Prawn. "For your sake as well as ours." He turned to Bold Abalone and said something in the Mollusk language. His son responded, then left at a run, followed by most of the warriors. Fighting Prawn turned back to J.D. and Sarah. "My men will ready the war canoes. We will go after Hook at sundown."

"Do you know where he is?" said J.D.

"At the moment, no. But Peter can find him quickly."

Sarah's eyes grew wide. "Peter?" she said. "He's here?"

"He is indeed."

"Where?"

Fighting Prawn smiled.

"Directly over your head."

CHAPTER 34

PETER

SARAH AND J.D. LOOKED UP AND GASPED. Suspended ten feet over their heads, his legs crisscross, looking down at them with a mixture of curiosity and suspicion, was Peter Pan.

Sarah stared at him, fascinated. In some ways, he looked as she expected—a wild tousle of red hair, a thin, extravagantly freckled face with a pointed chin and upturned nose. But in other ways he differed from her mental image. He was filthy and disheveled, clad in ragged, short pants and a sleeveless shirt made of cloth that seemed to be mostly holes, held together by a belt made of vine, into which was tucked a dagger. The soles of his feet were black with dirt; the rest of him was not much cleaner.

But what struck Sarah most was how young he looked. She knew, of course, that he never aged, but his appearance in the flesh drove the point home emphatically: he's just a boy.

For several seconds, she and J.D. gaped up at Peter as he looked down at them. The silence was broken by the sound of bells—high-pitched, melodic, heavenly.

Peter snorted.

"They do, don't they, Tink?" he said. "A pair of cows."

Sarah realized something else about him she hadn't considered previously; he had a British accent.

The bells sounded again, and now Sarah saw their source—a tiny face peeking out from Peter's mass of curls, exquisitely beautiful despite the contemptuous sneer she was aiming at the people below.

"Tinker Bell!" exclaimed Sarah.

More bells, and a laugh from Peter.

"What's so funny?" asked Sarah.

"You wouldn't understand," Peter said.

"Why don't you try explaining it?" said Sarah, irritation creeping into her voice.

He ignored her question. "Who are you?" he said. "And who's he?"

"My name is Sarah Cooper," said Sarah. "That's J.D. Aster."

The name brought on another burst of bells. Peter focused on J.D. "You're an Aster?" he said.

J.D. nodded.

"Do you know . . . that is, *did* you know Molly? Or Wendy?" Peter asked.

J.D. shook his head.

Peter nodded, looking into the distance, his mind momentarily elsewhere. Then his gaze returned to the visitors and his unwelcoming tone returned. "What are you doing here?"

"We brought some starstuff, in a gold box," said Sarah. "We were trying to keep it away from Ombra."

This produced the loudest outburst of bells yet.

"Ombra?" said Peter. "Is he after you?"

"He was," said Sarah. "But we left him back on . . . the other side of the bridge."

"So he's not here on the island," said Peter.

"No," said Sarah. "But he's got my brother. We need to go back." She paused, her eyes downcast. "My brother needs us."

"So why don't you go?" said Peter.

His callousness irritated Sarah further. He didn't seem at all concerned about her brother.

"We can't. Not yet, anyway," said Sarah. "We need starstuff to use the bridge. And Captain Hook has the box."

"Hook?" exclaimed Peter. "How did that happen?"

"He captured us," said J.D. "The minute we got here."

"And you let him take the starstuff?" said Peter.

"We didn't *let* him," said J.D. "As I said, he captured us."

Peter gave J.D. a scornful look. J.D. glared back. They were not hitting it off.

Fighting Prawn interrupted the standoff. "Peter, Bold Abalone is readying the war canoes. We will attack him at sundown and retrieve the starstuff. Then we can see about getting our visitors on their way home."

"Call me crazy," said J.D., "but I'm getting the feeling we're not welcome here."

Fighting Prawn and Peter exchanged a look, then Fighting Prawn said, "We don't mean to be rude. But we have all been together a long time on this island. We are accustomed to each other, comfortable in our way of life."

"And we're messing it up," said Sarah.

"You're a . . . disruption," said Fighting Prawn.

"You don't belong here," said Peter, coldly.

Tink chimed something. Peter snickered.

Sarah's faced darkened. "Well, we're really sorry that we disturbed your little paradise," she snapped. "We'll leave as soon as we can. We'll go back to face Ombra, and you"—she paused to glare at Peter—"*you* can go back to playing your little flying games with your little fairy friend."

This brought a furious burst from Tink. Peter's face was now beet-red. He turned to Fighting Prawn and said, "You won't need the war canoes. I'll get the starstuff box myself."

"Peter," said Fighting Prawn, "I don't think that's wise."

"I'm not afraid of Hook," said Peter. "I've dealt with him many times, and he's never beaten me."

"I know," said Fighting Prawn. "But now he has starstuff."

"That doesn't worry me," said Peter. "I'll get it back." He glared at Sarah and J.D. "And then they can leave, and we can have things the way they were again."

"Peter . . ." began Fighting Prawn. But it was too late. With one last baleful look at Sarah and J.D., Peter was gone, disappearing at astonishing speed over the fence surrounding the Mollusk compound, heading for the water—and Captain Hook.

CHAPTER 35

AN UGLY SOUND

FROM THE BEACH, BOLD ABALONE saw Peter flying just above the tree line, coming toward the fleet of war canoes waiting to push off from the shore. Bold Abalone waved, expecting Peter to land next to him so they could coordinate the attack on Hook.

Instead, Peter kept going, sailing over the Mollusk warriors without even looking down, heading out over the water and making a graceful, banking turn to the left toward a rocky point at the far edge of the beach. In a few seconds, he was around the point and gone, leaving Bold Abalone wondering what was happening. The plan had been to attack at sunset.

He got an answer a minute later when a warrior came running down the beach with an urgent message from Fighting Prawn: Peter intended to take Hook on by himself. The warriors were to follow Peter as best they could, finding the pirate ship and helping Peter if needed.

Bold Abalone ran to the lead canoe, shouting a command as he jumped in. The warriors, in perfect unison, dug their paddles into the water. The canoes surged out to sea, quickly gaining speed, aimed like arrows at the rocky point. The Mollusks were masterful canoeists; Bold Abalone knew that if Hook was anywhere near this side of the island, they would reach him quickly.

But he also knew that Peter would get there well ahead of them. He hoped Peter would not do anything foolish. Peter was his friend—they'd been friends for more than a century. But Peter could be hotheaded.

Very hotheaded.

Bold Abalone signaled his men to paddle harder.

Peter soared upward, letting the cooler air blast against his face, still flushed with anger. The girl's words echoed in his mind . . . *playing your little flying games with your little fairy friend.* She'd been mocking him. And yet it was this same stupid girl, and her stupid friend, who had let Hook take the starstuff!

As he gained altitude, he scanned the horizon. He would show them what kinds of games he could play . . .

"I don't believe it," Sarah said to J.D. "I finally meet Peter Pan. *The* Peter Pan. And he's . . . obnoxious! He's worse than my brother!"

"He did have something of an attitude," said J.D. "I hope he can back it up, because we need to get that box back or we're stuck here. And I really don't want to be stuck here."

"Me neither. J.D., I'm so worried about Aidan . . ."

J.D. pointed across the compound. "There's some kids coming."

Sarah looked and saw a ragtag group of boys passing through the gate. There were six of them, of varying sizes; they were dressed like Peter, more or less, and every bit as filthy, if not filthier.

"The Lost Boys," said Sarah. "Peter's crew."

They stopped about ten feet from J.D. and Sarah, staring at them for several seconds. Then one of the older ones spoke. "Who are you?" he said.

"I'm J.D."

"Who's she?"

"I'm Sarah."

"Is she your wife?" the boy asked J.D.

"No!" said Sarah. "And I can talk for myself."

"You talk funny," said the boy.

Sarah turned to J.D. and said, "What is it with the boys on this island?"

J.D. laughed. "Who're you?" he asked the boy.

"I'm Nibs," said the boy. He pointed to the others and said, "Them is Tootles, Curly, Slightly, and the Twins."

"Do the Twins have names?" said J.D.

"Yes," said Nibs. "Their names is the Twins. Have you seen Peter?"

"He was here a couple of minutes ago," said J.D. "He's gone after Captain Hook."

"Without us?" said Slightly.

"Why'd he go without us?" said the Twins, simultaneously.

"Which way did he go?" said Tootles.

"That way," said J.D., pointing.

"We'll go that way, too, then," said Nibs. "Maybe we can see the fight." He turned to go, then turned back. "D'you want to come?" he said.

"It's fun to watch Peter fight Hook," said Tootles.

"Peter always wins," said Slightly.

"Always," said the Twins.

J.D. looked at Sarah. Fighting Prawn had left the compound, apparently to be closer to the Hook situation; there seemed to be nothing keeping them here.

"Why not?" said Sarah, shrugging. They followed the boys out through the gate, their eyes searching the clear blue sky.

Peter spotted Hook's ship a mile off Skull Rock. He flew in a wide semicircle around it so he could approach with the sun directly behind him, making himself more difficult to see. When he was in the right position, he began his downward swoop. He saw a dozen pirates at various places on the deck, a half dozen more in the rigging, but apparently they had not seen him. There was no warning shout as he approached, no unusual activity. He spotted Hook now; the pirate captain was lying near the stern, apparently asleep.

From Peter's hair came a chime—Tink always saw everything first—and then Peter spotted it: a golden box, set on the foredeck, with nobody around it. Peter slowed a bit, looking for pirates hiding near the box, but not seeing any.

Could it really be this easy? he wondered.

Tink emitted a warning chime.

"I know," said Peter. "But what can they do? I'll snatch it and be gone before they know it."

He dropped lower, increasing his speed, calculating the angle. He was a hundred feet from the ship now . . . fifty . . . He didn't understand why the pirates hadn't seen him, but at this point it didn't matter—he would reach the box before any of them could stop him.

He crossed over the ship's rail at full speed, arms extended. He snatched the gold box in both hands and at the same instant angled his body upward. The box was heavier than he expected, but he cleared the ship's rail easily. He'd done it!

Over the water now, he angled his body into a sharp right turn, planning to make a triumphant pass over the hapless Hook at the stern.

But Hook wasn't there.

He heard the burst of bells from Tink at the same moment he sensed something above him.

How could there be something up there?

As he looked up, the net came down. He dove to escape it, but one of his feet was tangled in the rope. And now the net was all around him, imprisoning him, its edges held firmly by the pirates who had only moments earlier been in the ship's rigging.

The pirates were in midair.

The pirates were flying.

Peter struggled furiously, but he was no match for their muscle and the rough rope. With one last burst of bells in his ear, Tink wriggled through the net and, in a flash of light, was gone.

Peter felt himself being dragged down, back to the pirate ship. From above, he heard a laugh he knew all too well—an ugly, rasping sound.

As he and the gold box were slammed onto the rough wood deck, he looked up to see Hook above him, glowering triumphantly, ten feet in the air.

CHAPTER 36

VERY BAD DANGER

"THERE IT IS!" CALLED NIBS, from the front of the line. "Hook's ship!"

They had been following a path through the jungle, angling up the mountainside; now they were emerging onto a lava outcropping, from which they could see the entire side of the island and far out to sea.

Sarah and J.D. followed the Lost Boys onto the ledge and looked out. To the far left they could see Skull Rock, where they'd landed in their little ship. To the right of that, farther out, was Hook's ship, moving slowly from left to right, under little sail. And to the far right, coming around a rocky point and aiming toward the ship, was the fleet of Mollusk war canoes.

"I don't see Peter," said Tootles.

"I bet he's beat Hook already," said Slightly.

"Peter always wins," said the Twins.

Nibs was frowning. "That's odd," he said.

"What's odd?" said Sarah.

"Hook's ship," said Nibs. "He's sailing toward the canoes. He should be sailing away from them to his side of the island. He can't possibly want to fight the Mollusks, can he? They'll destroy him!"

"They will," said Tootles. "Again!"

"The Mollusks always win," the Twins told J.D. and Sarah.

Slightly pointed down the mountainside. "Here comes Tink!" he said.

They all looked down to see a flash of light zooming toward them across the dark-green jungle canopy.

"Where's Peter?" said Tootles.

"That's odd," said Nibs.

"Tink is always with Peter," said the Twins.

Tink had reached them now; she went straight to Nibs and began chiming furiously.

"Slower!" he said. "I can't understand you!" Aside from Peter, very few people could decode Tink's bells; of the Lost Boys, Nibs was the best at it, after decades of listening to her. But even he could understand only a word here and there.

Tink, with a look of angry impatience, began again, making slow, exaggerated chiming sounds. Nibs listened to the first few, then said, "Peter."

Tink nodded. More chimes.

"Pirates," said Nibs.

Another nod, more chimes.

Nibs frowned. "I don't know that word," he said.

Tink rolled her tiny eyes, then flew up and down rapidly, still chiming.

"I don't understand," said Nibs.

Tink was beside herself now, flying up and down frantically.

"What's she saying?" said Nibs.

"Maybe she's showing you the word," said Sarah.

Tink pointed to Sarah and nodded, reluctantly. She flew up and down again.

"Flying!" said Sarah. "Is that the word?"

Another nod.

"Peter was flying?" said Nibs.

Tink shook her head and repeated an earlier sound.

"Pirates," said Nibs.

Tink nodded, then flew up and down.

"The pirates are flying?" said Nibs.

Tink nodded.

"Pirates don't fly," said the Twins.

"Tink's saying they do," said Nibs.

Tink was directly in front of Nibs's face now, chiming urgently.

"Are you sure?" said Nibs.

Tink nodded rapidly.

"What's she saying?" said Slightly.

"I think she's saying Peter's in danger," said Nibs. "Very bad danger."

Tink chimed again, pointed at Nibs, and nodded vigorously.

"I think she wants us to help," said Nibs.

"But what can we do?" asked Slightly. "We can't fly!"

"The Mollusks are coming," Nibs told Tink, pointing out to sea and the canoes. "They'll save Peter."

Tink shook her head no, suddenly frantic again.

"Of course they will!" Nibs said.

But Tink continued to emit the high-pitched chimes while shaking her little head. Then she reached up and wrapped her hand around her neck.

And that needed no translation.

CHAPTER 37

MUCH, MUCH WORSE

*B*OLD ABALONE PADDLED FROM THE STERN of the lead canoe, his weapons—bow and arrows, spear, and a long knife carved from sea-turtle shell—leaning against the thwart. In the Mollusk language, he called to the warrior in the bow of the canoe, Stalwart Barnacle. "The pirate must be mad. He is headed right for us."

"Strange. The hairy-faced coward always runs away."

"Strange, indeed," agreed Bold Abalone, frowning. He wondered if Hook was planning a surprise, but could think of nothing that would threaten his fleet. He raised his left hand and pointed forward, the signal for attack.

The canoes picked up speed and fanned out, forming a V.

"Look!" called Stalwart Barnacle. "They are stern-heavy! They must be leaking badly!"

Indeed, the bow of the pirate ship seemed to be rising, revealing more and more of the slimy hull, covered with seaweed and barnacles. Bold Abalone tried to make sense of the ship's odd angle, wondering if the ballast had shifted. Wary of a trap, he raised his hand. At once, all the warriors stopped paddling, the canoes gliding to a stop.

The pirate ship kept coming—and rising. The warriors began to mutter nervously. Then several shouted with alarm as the ship, its hull dripping, rose completely out of the water.

It was flying!

Only once before had Bold Abalone seen such a sight— more than a century ago, when this same ship had flown to the island and released the huge cascade of starstuff—brighter than the noonday sun—that had transformed Mollusk Island forever. Now, watching Hook's ship, Bold Abalone knew his father's worst fear had been realized: Hook had found out what was in the gold box brought by Sarah and J.D. The pirate now had the power of starstuff.

Bold Abalone threw down his paddle and waved both arms out to the side, frantically signaling for the canoes to separate.

Hook had lured him into a trap.

"Steady! Steady now!" Hook called out to his helmsman, his eyes on the canoes below.

Hook was far from brilliant. But he was ruthless and cunning, and he had learned the hard way, from his time on this cursed island, that the advantage went to the man with the higher ground. He was also an excellent sailor, and had once flown this very ship many miles with the help of a considerable amount of starstuff.

Now he was flying it again. He'd gotten it aloft himself, carefully pouring starstuff onto the hull. It had taken a large amount—far more than it took to enable Hook and his men to fly—but finally the ship had lifted free of the water.

From the bow, Hook watched the Mollusk canoes below, the warriors paddling furiously to get away. He smiled. After all these years of humiliating defeats, he was chasing the savages. They were fleeing from him.

He glanced behind him. "Keep the ballast coming!" he shouted.

Every ship carries heavy weight in its keel to keep it stable. In the *Jolly Roger*, this weight was in the form of large rocks loaded by Hook's men when they had repaired and refloated the partially sunken ship on Mollusk Island. The men were now carrying some of these rocks topside, making a pile in the bow.

Hook looked down again. The ship was almost directly over the closest of the Mollusk canoes.

"Ready, men!" roared Hook.

The pirates grabbed rocks, some so heavy it took two men to lift them.

They carried them to the ship's rail.

"On my command!" yelled Hook. He peered downward. "Now!"

The men let loose a rain of heavy rocks. There were cries of alarm from the Mollusks below. Hook felt joy in his heart as the warriors leaped from the canoe. Most of the rocks missed, but two of them slammed into the now-empty canoe, breaking it into pieces. From the other canoes, some warriors shot arrows at the ship. A few stuck into the hull, but none posed a threat to the pirates.

"Reload!" bellowed Hook, and his men scurried for more rocks. "Starboard," he yelled to the helmsman, positioning the ship over the next canoe.

"Now!"

More rocks went over the side and another canoe was shattered. The pirates, roaring with delight, grabbed still more rocks. Below, the terrified Mollusks paddled frantically, but they could not outrace the flying ship. In a few minutes, half of the fleet of twenty had been destroyed, but Hook was relentless. He intended to destroy them all.

Soon there was just one canoe left, the one Hook had saved for last: the canoe under the command of Fighting Prawn's son, Bold Abalone. Hook was going to use this canoe to deliver a message that the Mollusks would remember.

"Ready the toy ship!" hollered Hook. He smiled, savoring the cleverness of it—smashing this canoe with the very vessel that had brought the new starstuff to the island.

It took four men to hoist the little ship onto the rail.

"Steady!" Hook called, calculating the precise moment to release it.

"*Now!*" he shouted. He watched the ship drop toward its target, then roared in triumph as it smashed, perfectly aimed, into the center of the canoe. All the Mollusks were swimming now; their fleet was destroyed.

Hook's heart swelled with pride. The rout was complete. Finally, after all these years, he had won a decisive victory.

He ordered the helmsman to turn the ship, putting it on a course back to the pirate side of the island. Hook sensed that the ship was descending gently now that the men were no longer heaving weight over the side. He thought he might have to pour some more starstuff into the hull. He wondered how much was left in the gold box. He hoped it was a great deal. He had plans for it.

He strode back amidships. Peter was there, still wrapped in the net, which in turn had been tied with rope, binding Peter to the mainmast so tightly that he could barely move a muscle.

Hook stood with his face only a few inches from Peter's.

"Your savage friends are swimming for their lives," he said. "They didn't care for having rocks dropped on them." Hook smiled an ugly smile. "I got that idea from you, boy— from the time long ago when you dropped mangoes on my head. Remember? Thought you were clever, you did, because you could fly. But your flying days are over, boy. I'm the one who's flying now."

Hook leaned closer. "Things have changed on this island," he said. "For me, it's going to be much better. But for you . . ."

He lifted his hook, holding the needle-sharp point an inch from Peter's right eye.

"For you, it's going to be much, much worse."

CHAPTER 38

NOT SO SAFE

𝔉ROM THE MOUNTAINSIDE LEDGE overlooking the water, Sarah and J.D. watched the rout with the Lost Boys and Tink. When the pirates dropped the little ship from Peter Pan's Flight, smashing the last Mollusk canoe still afloat, the group stood in stunned silence for several seconds.

"I can't believe it," said Nibs. "Hook won."

"Hook never wins," said the Twins.

"He did this time," said Nibs. "And he's got Peter." This drew a burst of bells from Tink.

"He's also got the starstuff," said Sarah, dejectedly. "And he's figured out how to use it, obviously."

"Where's he going now?" said J.D., pointing at the pirate ship. It had executed a graceful turn in the sky, its course now taking it past Skull Rock and around the island coast curving away to the left.

"Looks like he's going back to his side," said Slightly.

Tink was in Nibs's face now, chiming urgently.

"Slower," said Nibs.

More chimes.

"What's she saying?" said Curly.

"I think she's saying we need to go rescue Peter."

"From the pirates?" said Tootles. "Shouldn't we ask the Mollusks to do that?"

"I don't think the Mollusks are in any position to go after Hook," said J.D., looking at the battle scene below. "Their canoes are wrecked and half their guys are still swimming."

"Maybe we should wait until they can help," said Tootles. "Or at least until morning. It'll be dark soon."

This produced a furious, head-shaking eruption from Tink.

"Tink's right," said Nibs. "We don't have time to wait. Hook hates Peter, you all know that. No telling what he'll do."

"Besides . . ." added Slightly, ". . . if Hook captured us, Peter wouldn't wait. He'd come rescue us."

The others nodded. Peter had his flaws, but he always stood by his friends.

"All right, then," said Nibs. "It's settled. We head for the pirate side." He turned to Sarah and J.D. "You can go back to the Mollusk village by the path we took to get up here."

Sarah shook her head. "We're going with you." J.D. gave her a look, but said nothing.

"Are you sure?" said Nibs. "It's a rough hike over the mountain. And not so safe on the pirate side."

"Especially at night," said Curly.

"There's snakes," said the Twins.

"I'm sure," said Sarah. "If we don't get the starstuff, J.D. and I can't get back across the bridge. Besides, this whole mess is my fault. Peter would never have been captured if I hadn't shown up here."

Tink glared at Sarah and chimed something that needed no translation.

"All right, then," said Nibs. "Let's get going."

They started up the mountainside, following a steep, little-used, zigzagging path that at times disappeared altogether. The sun soon dropped low in the sky, producing a spectacular sunset followed by darkness, but a bright half moon gave them enough light to make their way. Sarah, who was not a big fan of snakes, walked close behind J.D.

After they'd been trudging upward for almost three hours, they came to the ridge that divided the island roughly in half. There was a clearing there from which they could see the water far below on both sides, the surf forming pale, shifting lines in the moonlight. Nibs announced that they would rest for a few minutes. Tink objected, but everyone ignored her, the Lost Boys plopping to the ground.

Sarah and J.D. sat down next to each other a few yards away.

"What if we don't get the box back?" she whispered.

"We *have* to get the box back," he said. "I really, really don't want to spend eternity here."

"Me neither," she said. "I just want to go home." She put her face in her hands for a moment, on the verge of tears, then took a deep breath and exhaled. "We'll get the box," she said. "We have to, so we will."

"That's not all we have to get," said J.D.

"What do you mean?"

"I've been thinking about it; how we're going to use the bridge at this end. First of all, we need to locate it. Fighting Prawn said Einstein and Pete Carmoody used it, so I'm hoping he'll know where it is. Second, of course, we need to get enough starstuff to activate it. But then there's the question of when we activate it. That gets a little tricky."

"Why?" asked Sarah.

"Okay, if I have this figured right, we need to cross the bridge back to our universe when it's operable at the Magic Kingdom end. That means at exactly the same time that we came here."

"At 9:07 P.M.," said Sarah.

"Yup. And how do we know when it's 9:07 P.M. in Disney World? We look at my watch. I set the time exactly before we crossed in this direction. So it ought to work going the other way."

"So why is that tricky?"

J.D. held up his left wrist. "I don't have my watch."

"Oh my god," said Sarah. "I forgot. Hook took it!"

"Right. So we have to get the starstuff and my watch."

Sarah's shoulders slumped. "How are we going to do that?" she said.

"I don't know," said J.D. They sat in subdued silence for another minute.

Then Nibs, prodded by Tinker Bell, started the group moving again, heading down the mountainside into pirate territory. Every now and then, Tink would dart ahead, flying above the treetops, then return to chime something in Nibs's ear. Sarah noticed that the Lost Boys were acting more nervous than they had earlier, saying little, walking closer together, jumping at jungle sounds. She turned to Tootles, who was walking behind her.

"Is there something we should be worried about?" she whispered. "Aside from Hook, I mean. And the snakes."

"Yes," said Tootles.

"What?"

"You see those droppings on the trail?"

"No. I can barely see the trail."

"Oh. That explains why you keep stepping in them."

"What?"

"The droppings. You keep stepping in them."

"What kind of droppings?" said Sarah, scraping her shoes against a bush.

"Boars. Wild boars. There's a lot of them on this side of the island."

"And they're dangerous?"

"They can be. But that's not what we're worried about."

Sarah was getting exasperated. "So what are we worried about?"

"Mister Grin," said Tootles.

"Oh," said Sarah, looking around nervously. "You mean he's real, too?"

"Real?" said Tootles.

"Forget it," said Sarah.

"We never forget about Mister Grin," said Tootles.

They walked on in silence for another hour, making their way slowly down the steep mountainside. Tink returned from another one of her scouting missions and chimed something to Nibs. He halted the line.

"Quiet, everyone," he whispered. "Listen."

They listened. From somewhere in the dark distance below, drifting over the treetops, came the sound of men shouting and singing. There was an explosion of some kind.

"The pirate fort," said Nibs. "They're celebrating."

"I guess they don't think the Mollusks will attack tonight," said Slightly.

"I suspect they're right about that," said Nibs. "I suspect the Mollusks won't be attacking for a while."

"So what's our plan?" said J.D.

"We get closer to the fort," said Nibs. "Then we wait for dawn. The pirates will fall asleep. Then we attack."

"We what?" said J.D.

"Attack."

"Wait a minute," said J.D. "There's eight of us, and we have no weapons. How do we attack a fort full of pirates?"

Tink chimed something.

"We have a weapon," said Nibs.

"We do?" said Slightly.

"What is it?" said the Twins.

"Well, we don't have it at the moment," said Nibs. "But we will. Tink will see to that. Right now our job is to get down to the fort and be in position by dawn." He started down the trail, Tink zooming ahead. The others followed Nibs with varying levels of enthusiasm. It was another hour before they reached the clearing that surrounded the pirate fort. Its outer wall was ten feet high and made of thick logs, from behind which came shouts and whoops, though the celebration seemed to be winding down. Every now and then a pirate would float above the fort, spinning in midair, giggling wildly—evidence that Hook was still dispensing starstuff.

"I hope they don't use it all up," Sarah whispered to J.D.

"I know," he answered. "He must have used a lot of it before to get the ship to fly."

They squatted in the undergrowth watching the fort,

swatting at insects, waiting for daylight. They were hot, tired, and thirsty. And afraid.

To the east, the sky began to turn from black to gray.

"Where's the weapon?" the Twins asked Nibs, for the dozenth time.

"It will be here," he answered, also for the dozenth time, although he sounded less confident than he had.

The sky grew lighter. The fort was quiet.

Then Tink arrived, chiming at Nibs with quiet urgency.

Then they saw what was behind her.

Sarah, stifling a scream, turned to run.

"It's all right," whispered Nibs, grabbing her arm.

"How do you know it's all right?" she asked.

"Because Tink says so," said Nibs.

"And you believe her?"

"I have to," said Nibs. "Come on."

Hook was the only pirate still awake. Smee and the others sprawled in the dirt all around him, drooling and snoring, exhausted from the night of revelry. But Hook was too elated to sleep. He stood amid the slumbering men, holding the gold box—the reason for his joy, the source of the power that had enabled him, at long last, to defeat the savages.

And capture the boy.

Hook ambled over to the center of the compound, where

a stout post was embedded firmly in the ground. There was an iron ring bolted to the post. Attached to this ring was a short, heavy, iron chain that ran to another iron ring fitted snugly around Peter's neck. The ring on the post was positioned just high enough so that Peter could not sit on the ground, but also just low enough so that he could not stand fully upright. He was forced to remain in an uncomfortable crouch; if he dozed and allowed his body to sag, the choking pressure of the neck ring jerked him painfully awake. To make matters worse, his hands were bound tightly behind his back. He had spent the night in hideous discomfort.

Hook had never been happier.

Peter's eyes were closed, but Hook knew he could not be sleeping. He gave Peter a sharp kick in the shin, which caused Peter's head to jerk upright until the chain stopped it violently. Peter glared at Hook with eyes reddened from exhaustion and pain.

"Been crying, have we?" said Hook.

Peter said nothing.

"You know," said Hook, conversationally, "I had intended to kill you as soon as I captured you. But it has been so much fun seeing you this way . . . I hate to see it end."

He touched his hook to Peter's neck. Peter drew back, but only a few inches before the chain stopped him. The hook found his neck again, its point just brushing Peter's skin.

"But know this, boy," said Hook. "You will die. And soon."

He twitched the hook slightly. A bead of blood appeared on Peter's neck. Hook saw pain in Peter's eyes, and fear. This pleased him.

Then he saw something else, just for a flickering instant, before Peter masked it. The boy had seen something. Hook whirled, and he saw it, too: a small, agile figure climbing over the wall near the fort's heavy gate. The boy dropped to the ground, followed quickly by a second boy.

"Intruders!" Hook bellowed, kicking the sleeping men around him. "Get them!"

The pirates were staggering to their feet, blinking.

"What is it, Cap'n?" said Smee.

"Intruders!"

Smee blinked. "Where, Cap'n?"

"There, you idjit!" yelled Hook, shoving Smee. "By the gate!"

As Smee and the others stumbled across the compound, Hook saw that the intruders were two of the Lost Boys. They ran to the gate, quickly slid aside the heavy plank that held it shut, then began opening the gate. Through the opening dashed three more Lost Boys.

"Get them!" Hook yelled again, but he was feeling less concerned now. If the Mollusks were attacking, he would have cause for worry. But the Mollusks were beaten. These were just children making a pathetic attempt to rescue their captured leader. They were no match for Hook and his men. Nobody was a match for Hook, as long as he had the gold box.

The gate was wide open now. The pirates were stumbling around chasing after the boys, who were so far eluding them. But the boys were making no effort to get to Peter. Hook frowned. What kind of rescue attempt was this?

Suddenly, it occurred to him: the scampering boys were a diversion.

"Close the gate!" he bellowed. "Close the gate!"

It was several seconds before the pirates heard him. Abandoning their pursuit of the boys, they headed for the gate.

Then they stopped.

Then they turned and ran back into the compound directly toward Hook, their faces white with fear.

Hook opened his mouth to order them back to the gate. But before he could emit a sound, he heard the sound he feared most in all the world—the steady ticking of a clock. It was the only clock on Mollusk Island; it had been infused long ago with starstuff, and since then it had never stopped, despite its strange location—inside the stomach of Mister Grin.

The gigantic crocodile lumbered into view, heading for the gate opening, its massive jaws gaping to reveal rows of jagged, spear-size teeth. For a few moments Hook was paralyzed with terror, and in those frozen moments he saw something that seemed impossible: there were three people riding on the crocodile's back.

"Hang on," said Nibs, from the front.

"Hang on to what?" said J.D., looking for something to grab on the giant croc's scaly back.

"I really, really don't want to fall off and get eaten by this thing," said Sarah, who was sitting between the other two.

"You won't," said Nibs. "I told you, Tink made a bargain with Mister Grin. We give him Hook, and he doesn't eat us."

"But he's a crocodile," said Sarah. "How do you make a bargain with a crocodile?"

"Tink speaks crocodile," said Nibs.

Ahead, through the open fort gate, Sarah saw pirates running away; beyond them, she saw Hook, who was holding the gold box and standing near Peter, who was chained to a post.

"Hang on!" shouted Nibs.

They clung as best they could to the broad back of the giant creature as it lumbered, with surprising speed, into the gate opening.

And then, with a thundering crash, Mister Grin stopped. Nibs, Sarah, and J.D. were hurled forward, just managing not to fly off the croc's giant snout.

"What happened?" shouted Sarah.

"The croc's too wide!" answered J.D. It was true: although Mister Grin's snout fit through the opening, his massive midsection was too wide. He had become wedged between the stout logs on both sides. Tink was a bright blur, zipping around the croc's enormous head, chiming furiously. Roaring in fury, Mister Grin swept his tail back and forth, shaking his monstrous body. The logs creaked and swayed, but the fort—including the narrow gate opening—had been designed specifically to repel Mister Grin; for the moment, the logs held.

Hook watched Mister Grin's struggle to get through the gate, and he knew two things. One was that eventually the giant croc would succeed. The other was that there would be only one way to escape the fort, and Hook held it in his hand. His men might not be so fortunate. But Hook had never been one to worry about his men.

There was a loud crack as one of the logs began to give way to the massive weight and strength of the croc. Hook gripped the gold box tight. He would use it in a moment. But there was one piece of business he had to take care of first.

He turned toward Peter.

Nibs and J.D. were both focused on Mister Grin's efforts to get through the gate. But Sarah kept her eyes on the gold box. Whatever else happened, they had to get the box back. Her fear was that Hook would simply fly away with it. The plan had been to catch him sleeping, but now they had lost the element of surprise. She expected him to use the starstuff at any moment. But so far he hadn't. As she watched, Hook began walking toward Peter, chained to the post, helpless.

Hook was raising his hook hand.

"Oh, no," said Sarah softly. And then she was scrambling forward on the croc's back, past Nibs.

"Sarah!" called J.D.

She didn't look back. On her feet now, she ran straight down the middle of Mister Grin's snout and leaped off the tip. She fell onto the dirt, rolling.

J.D. rose to follow her, but a sudden violent twist by Mister Grin sent him flying sideways. Sarah was on her feet now, running as fast as she could.

⚔️

Hook stood with his hook hand held high. His final triumph over the boy was going to be more rushed than he had planned, but he intended to savor, as best he could, this moment.

"Look at me, boy!" he said. "I want my face to be the last thing you see."

Peter looked at him, his face defiant.

Hook pulled his arm back for the final strike. He began an arcing swing, its target Peter's neck.

Sarah's flying karate kick caught Hook in his midsection. As he fell, spinning, his hook missed Peter by half an inch and kept going around his body.

It plunged into Sarah's chest, just below her collarbone.

Together they fell to the dirt. Sarah seemed unaware that she had been wounded until she saw Hook pull his hook, dripping red with her blood, from her body. She looked down and tried to scream, but what came out was more of a hideous gurgle.

Hook scrambled to his feet. With barely a glance at Sarah on the ground he turned back toward Peter, determined to finish the job.

"Get away!" shouted a voice. Hook turned and saw J.D. advancing on him cautiously, his eyes on the dripping red hook. He had no weapon. Hook swung the hook at him, and he jumped back.

Hook turned back toward Peter, but as he did he heard a roar and a crash. He spun back toward the gate: the beast had forced its way through and was coming fast. Hook made a quick calculation: there was no time for the boy. In one swift motion he raised the gold box, put the point of his hook on the wheel, and gave it a quarter turn as he tilted the opening toward his chest. During the night he'd had to tilt it farther and farther; there was no telling how much starstuff was left.

But there was enough for now; even with Mister Grin charging at him, Hook felt the now-familiar sense of elation as the starstuff lifted him in spirit as well as body.

Clutching the gold box, he began to rise. The croc roared, and Hook laughed: the beast would not reach him. His feet were four feet off the ground, now five, now six . . .

Suddenly, he stopped rising. He looked down and saw hands gripping his ankles; then he looked down farther and saw J.D. clinging to him desperately. Hook swore an oath and swung his hook downward, but it was difficult to reach with the gold box in his other hand.

The croc was almost to him.

He kicked his feet violently and at the same time strained to rise.

Somehow J.D. held on. And somehow Hook made them both rise another few feet. Hook's boots were ten feet up in the air now, J.D. dangling down, hanging on desperately as Hook thrashed his legs while still fighting to rise. They ascended another foot, but that was it; in the next moment, Hook sensed with horror that J.D. was dragging him down to the enormous croc's waiting jaws.

Hook knew he had to get rid of J.D. or die. With a desperate lunge he leaned over and swung his hook down as far as he could. But J.D. had been anticipating this. At the last second he released his right hand from Hook's ankle, and as the hook went by, he snatched Hook's wrist. Now he had

Hook by a foot and a hand; more important, he had neutralized the hook, at least for now. Hook tried to kick J.D. with his free foot, but his position was too awkward to get any force behind it.

They were starting to descend. Mister Grin was waiting.

Hook had one weapon left. He had to use it now, or be eaten.

With a roar of utter fury he hurled the gold box. J.D. saw it coming and moved his head just enough so that it did not hit him square. But a sharp corner caught his skull and he lost his grip on Hook's ankle. He now had Hook's wrist with only one hand. Hook gave a violent yank and pulled free. Freed of the weight, he shot upward.

J.D. fell to the ground, landing hard on his back. He couldn't breathe and blood was pouring from a wound in his scalp. He tried to rise but he was losing consciousness. The last thing he realized before he blacked out was that he was gripping something in his right hand.

It was his watch.

Hook, now drifting over the wall, looked back and saw a chaotic scene: his men, fleeing Mister Grin, had run out through the gate and were racing across the clearing toward the jungle. *Cowards*, thought Hook. The girl he had stabbed was lying on the ground, her face paper-white, her blood drenching her clothes. Peter, still chained to the post, was shouting urgent orders at the Lost Boys. One of them ran and picked up the gold box, then ran to the fallen girl and knelt next to her.

Hook didn't see what happened next; he had drifted too far away to see over the wall. He turned his attention toward his ship, anchored in Pirate Cove. Then he heard a roar and looked back. The crocodile had emerged from the fort and was coming after him again.

Hook strained to rise and aimed for the ship, praying he'd used enough starstuff to make it. From back inside the fort he heard a loud cry. Whether it was a cry of joy or a cry of anguish he could not tell.

CHAPTER 39

READY FOR ANYTHING

"NIBS! GET THE BOX!" PETER SHOUTED, straining against the chain holding him to the post.

Nibs stared wide-eyed at the motionless, blood-covered form of Sarah.

"*Nibs!*" repeated Peter. "Get the gold box!"

Shaken from his trance, Nibs looked around frantically.

"Over there!" said Peter, pointing. "The rest of you, find the key!" Peter rattled his chains. "Hook put it in his hut, I think. It's the one over there."

Slightly, Curly, and the Twins took off at a run toward Hook's hut.

Nibs had the box now. "What do I do?" he asked.

"Listen carefully," said Peter. "Set it on the ground next to Sarah. Now, twist the wheel on top. Just a little . . . good! Now, you mustn't look directly at the starstuff. Turn it 'round the other way . . . good. Now tip the box so the starstuff flows into the wound."

Nibs turned the box and lifted it over Sarah, his hands shaking badly. J.D., who had just regained consciousness, rose and stumbled over.

"Are you sure this is a good idea?" he called to Peter.

"I've seen it work before," Peter answered, remembering the time, long ago, when he had used starstuff to save the life of Fighting Prawn.

"All right," said J.D., reaching out his hands to steady Nibs's. Together they tilted the gold box, farther and farther, until finally there was a brilliant flash and the sound of bells as starstuff began to flow into the horrible wound just below Sarah's neck. Some spilled on Nibs's and J.D.'s hands. Nibs, unaccustomed to its effects, became elated and began to hum and giggle. J.D. concentrated, forcing himself to focus, through squinted eyes, on the box. The stream of starstuff was abating. He tilted the box farther, until it was almost vertical, but only the barest trickle came out.

Afraid of what he would see, he forced himself to look at Sarah's wound. His eyes opened wide.

"I don't believe it," J.D. whispered.

"Oh, my," said Nibs.

The wound had healed. Where there had been a deep gash in Sarah's skin, there was now only a faint redness—not even a scar. Only the hole in Sarah's bloody shirt indicated what had happened. Sarah's body was floating a foot off the ground; gently, J.D. pushed her back down.

Sarah's eyes blinked open. She coughed, then cried out as a searing pain shot through her chest. She was afraid to look down; her eyes shone with fear.

"You're gonna be okay," said J.D.

Sarah didn't believe him. She remembered the horrible sight of the red-smeared hook, her spurting blood . . . "I'm going to die," she whispered.

"No," said Nibs. He held up the gold box. "You're going to be fine." As he spoke, Sarah became aware of the warmth spreading through her.

Still, she didn't dare look down. Her eyes met J.D.'s. "Is it really okay?" she said.

He nodded. "As a physicist," he said, "I'm very reluctant to use the word *miracle*. But this was a miracle."

Sarah turned toward Nibs. "Thank you," she said.

"It was Peter's idea," said Nibs. "And I couldn't have done it without your friend."

"Well, then, thank you all," said Sarah. She frowned. "You didn't use up all the starstuff?"

"Don't worry about that," said J.D. "Just rest."

"But—"

"Just rest."

She lay back in the dirt and closed her eyes. They

brought her some water in a coconut shell and wadded up some big leaves to form a crude pillow. The Twins found the key in Hook's hut and brought it to Peter, who, with their help, finally freed himself from the ring around his neck. Sarah heard him walk over and felt his shadow as he stood over her. She opened her eyes.

"Are you all right?" he said. He himself had a raw, ugly, red line around his neck.

"I think so," she said.

"I think so, too," said Peter.

There was a moment of awkward silence, and then he said, "You saved my life. Hook would have killed me. I . . . well . . . thank you."

"And you saved *my* life, from what I hear," said Sarah. "I'd say we're even."

"No," said Peter. "You risked your life for me."

"I just . . . reacted," said Sarah.

"But why?" said Peter. "Why risk your life?"

Sarah shook her head. "I don't know. You were helpless there, chained to the post . . . it just seemed wrong."

Peter nodded again. He was silent for a few moments, then said, "You told me your brother is in trouble. With Ombra."

Sarah nodded.

"Then I'm going back with you," said Peter. "To help."

Tink chimed something.

"Tink, too," he said. "We've fought Ombra before. More than once. We can help."

"Peter, I really appreciate that," said Sarah. "But it's not a good idea."

"Why not?"

"Because our world . . . it's changed since you were there last. It's crazy there. You belong here."

"I'll come back here. When we're done."

"That's another problem," said J.D. "Assuming we can get over the bridge, I don't know how we'd get you back here."

Peter thought about that, then said, "We'll figure that out when the time comes."

"Peter," said Sarah, "I can't let you risk it."

"When Hook was about to stab me," he said, "and you stopped him—were you thinking about the risk?"

Sarah said nothing.

"So it's settled," said Peter.

Sarah sighed and closed her eyes. She fell quickly to sleep.

They went back to the Mollusk side of the island by sea after "borrowing" one of the pirates' longboats. The Lost Boys and J.D. rowed; Sarah, still weak, lay in the bow next to the gold box. Peter and Tink, high above, served as lookouts, but there was no sign of pirate pursuit.

As the longboat neared Skull Rock it was met by the mermaids, who used their powerful tails to greatly increase its speed. When they reached the Mollusk beach, they were greeted by Fighting Prawn and his men, who had worked through the night to repair their canoes in preparation for a rescue attempt. The Mollusks were relieved to see that the mission was unnecessary, although Fighting Prawn gave Peter a stern lecture about his foolish attempt to take Hook on alone.

After a hearty meal—food always came first with the Mollusks—Peter, Sarah, and J.D. described the events on the other side of the island. Fighting Prawn frowned when Peter announced his plan to go across the bridge with Sarah and J.D.

"Are you sure that is wise?" he asked.

"I'm sure it's what I want to do," answered Peter.

"It has been a long time," said Fighting Prawn. "That world has changed."

"A lot," added J.D.

Tink chimed something. The others looked to Peter for a translation. "She says Ombra hasn't changed," he said.

Sarah spent the rest of the day in the care of one of Fighting Prawn's daughters, Shining Pearl. Sarah's clothes were badly shredded and bloodstained, so Shining Pearl, with much pleasure, attired her in a traditional Mollusk dress made of material woven from grass fibers and dyed in a rainbow of colors. It took some convincing, but Sarah also allowed Shining Pearl to decorate her hair with shells.

Sarah slept that night in Shining Pearl's hut and awoke feeling almost fully recovered. She emerged to find J.D. deep in conversation with Fighting Prawn and Peter.

J.D. smiled at her outfit. "'Morning, Pocahontas," he said, happy he'd found his own jeans in Hook's hut.

Fighting Prawn said something in Mollusk, and Peter laughed.

"What did you say?" Sarah asked.

"I said you should be prepared to receive a boiled-jellyfish pudding," said Fighting Prawn.

"What are you talking about?" said Sarah.

"That's how Mollusk men propose marriage," said Peter.

J.D. laughed; Sarah blushed. "Have you guys made any progress?" she asked, eager to change the subject.

"We have," said J.D. "For one thing, we know where the bridge is."

"Where?"

"Skull Rock. The right-hand eye socket. Same as back in Disney World."

"Makes sense," said Sarah. "That's where we wound up when we came over the bridge."

"Yup. Fighting Prawn says that when Einstein and Pete

Carmoody went back, they had the Mollusks lower them to the eye in a sling tied to a rope."

"Is that what we're going to do?"

"Basically. But instead of being lowered in a sling, we'll be lowered in the ship from the Peter Pan ride."

Fighting Prawn chuckled at that; Peter blushed.

"I'm still trying to explain the concept of Disney World to them," said J.D. "They both have a hard time believing there's a ride named for Peter."

"There's lots of stuff named for you," said Sarah. "Peanut butter, for example."

"What's peanut butter?" said Peter.

"It's delicious," said Sarah. "But wait a minute . . ." She turned back to J.D. "I thought Hook dropped the little ship onto the Mollusk canoes."

"He did," said J.D. "But it was in shallow water. The mermaids found it and brought it to land."

"Do we really need it?"

"I think maybe we do," said J.D. "I think that when we activate the bridge, we're going to find ourselves in exactly the same place we left from."

"On the Peter Pan ride."

"Right. But here's where it could get a little weird. I also think it's possible that we're going to find ourselves there at exactly the same time we left."

"You mean at 9:07 P.M.," said Sarah.

371

"Definitely 9:07 P.M. But possibly at 9:07 P.M. on the same night we left," said J.D. "In other words, no time will have passed there at all."

"Wait a minute," said Sarah. "We've been here for, what, two days. Time has passed here. How can it be the same day there?"

"I don't have time to explain the physics of it," said J.D. "But time isn't what most people think. It's not a constant, and it's not linear. Does that make any sense?"

"Absolutely not," said Sarah. She turned to Peter and Fighting Prawn. "Does that make sense to you?"

They shook their heads.

J.D. smiled. "Yeah, it is counterintuitive," he said. "But humor me, okay? I'm just saying we need to be ready for anything."

"Okay," said Sarah. "So when do we do this?"

J.D. pulled out his watch. The band had broken when he'd yanked it off Hook's wrist, so he kept it in his pocket. He looked at the time. "A little under twelve hours," he said.

The ascent to the top of Skull Rock was perilous, especially at night—it required climbing a set of shallow footholds carved into the back side of the huge rock, which became increasingly steep until it was nearly vertical at the top. Sarah, still weak, had the hardest time, but Peter hovered next to her the whole way up, steadying her as needed.

J.D. also struggled with the climb, and was careful never to look down. The Mollusks, including Fighting Prawn, ascended the rock easily, despite carrying the gold box and coils of heavy rope, which they used to haul up the Peter Pan's Flight ship.

Far below, in canoes at the base of the rock, were more Mollusk warriors, along with the Lost Boys, who had begged to come along. Peter, after declaring that Nibs would be leader in his absence, had said good-bye and promised to come back soon. The Lost Boys believed him; they could not imagine Peter failing.

At the top of the rock, J.D. looked at his watch, easily visible in the moonlight.

"Fifteen minutes," he said. "Time to fill the locket." He pulled the second gold locket from his pocket and opened it. Sarah brought the gold box over and held its opening next to the locket.

"Please be enough," she whispered.

She turned the little wheel and carefully tilted the box toward the locket. Nothing came out. She and J.D. exchanged a worried look. She tilted the box more. Still nothing.

"Please," she whispered. She tilted the box as far as she could, the opening now pointing straight down.

Suddenly, the night was filled with light and music.

Just as suddenly, it was gone.

"Did you get it?" said Sarah, temporarily blinded.

"I think so," said J.D., snapping the locket shut. He realized he was floating, his feet six inches from the rock. In a few seconds he settled back down.

"That's all there is," said Sarah, her sight returning. "The box is empty. Do you think it was enough?"

"We'll find out," said J.D., looking at his watch, "in twelve minutes."

The Mollusks tied the rope carefully to the little ship. J.D., Sarah, and Peter climbed in, with Sarah in the middle, holding the gold box in her lap. It was a tight fit. Ten strong warriors held the rope, their feet braced firmly against the rough rock. Four more slid the ship to the edge.

"We'll tug twice when we reach the right level," said J.D.

Fighting Prawn nodded.

"Thank you," said Sarah. "For everything."

"You are welcome."

"I'm sorry for causing all this trouble," said Sarah.

"It was . . . interesting," said Fighting Prawn.

"Really?" said Sarah.

"Yes," said Fighting Prawn. With just a hint of a smile, he added, "Although that does not mean we wish you to return."

"Don't worry about that," said J.D.

The Mollusks began lowering the ship. As it disappeared from view, Fighting Prawn and Peter were looking at each other. Each knew it might be the last time he would ever see the other. Neither said a word. Neither had to.

The little ship descended slowly, bumping against the rock. The moon glinted off the water far below. Peter looked down, gauging the distance to the eye socket. He flew up once to tell the Mollusks to shift the rope about five feet to their right, then returned to the ship.

Finally, they reached the eye socket. It was much bigger than it appeared from the water, easily large enough for a man to stand upright in. When they were centered in front of it, Peter tugged twice on the rope, and they stopped descending. J.D. looked at his watch.

"Two minutes," he said. He handed the locket to Sarah, saying, "You've had experience."

Sarah took the locket. She looked at Peter and said, "Are you sure about this?"

He nodded.

"You can just fly away right now," she said. "We won't hold it against you."

"I'm going with you," he said.

"One minute," said J.D.

The little ship had twisted slowly on the rope and was now facing directly into the eye socket. Sarah leaned forward, the locket in her hand.

"Thirty seconds," said J.D.

They were utterly still. From far below came the sound

375

of waves slapping against the base of Skull Rock. J.D.'s eyes were on his watch.

"Ten seconds," he said.

Sarah clenched the locket.

"Five . . . four . . . three . . . two . . . *now*."

Sarah threw the locket.

For a moment, nothing happened.

Then the world went white. As before, J.D. saw nothing but the whiteness. As before, he heard the sound of his voice screaming, but this seemed odd because he was certain that he was not screaming. Then, with a chill, he realized that he was hearing himself—when he had come across the bridge the first time. Now he knew that his hunch had been right: they were returning to their universe at exactly the same moment they had left it.

Then he heard another sound, one he recognized immediately . . .

Caw! Caw!

And then he heard a blood-chilling groan.

CHAPTER 40

AIDAN'S CHANCE

ᴁVERYTHING SEEMED TO HAPPEN AT ONCE. The blinding whiteness suddenly vanished, replaced by the near-total darkness inside the Peter Pan's Flight ride; the little ship was once again suspended by a pole from the overhead track. In the first few seconds, J.D., Sarah, and Peter, their eyes unaccustomed to the darkness, saw only the ghostly glow of Skull Rock, to the right. Tink chimed urgently.

"Ombra!" said Peter.

They all felt him—a cold presence close by. J.D. and Sarah looked back; the last they'd seen Aidan, he'd been coming up behind them. Then Sarah felt something in front of her. She turned and screamed as, her eyes adjusting, she saw her brother perched on the little ship's prow, his face ghostly white, his eyes black holes.

He ducked under the sail and reached toward her.

"Aidan!" she said. "Please . . ."

His eyes were dead pools. His hands shot out. Sarah screamed again.

Then he was gone.

"Are you all right?" said J.D.

Sarah nodded. She looked down.

"He took the gold box!" she said.

"Was that your brother?" said Peter.

"Yes, but Ombra has him!" said Sarah.

"We'll get him back," said Peter, and before either Sarah or J.D. could say a word, Peter launched himself from the ship, with Tink right next to him. They flew back into the ride, disappearing in the blackness.

All this had taken only seconds, but in those seconds the little ship had reached the end of the ride. As they rounded the last corner and approached the moving walkway, they heard shouting and saw a crowd gathered on the Fantasyland concourse. In the middle of the crowd they saw people help-ing a big, dazed-looking man to his feet.

"That's the guy who tried to stop us," said Sarah.

"We need to get out of here before he sees us," said J.D.

They quickly stepped out of the ship onto the mov-ing walkway. They exited the ride down a hallway to the right, away from the big man, and plunged into the mass of visitors swarming through Fantasyland. Some of the people they passed pointed at Sarah, and she realized, with embar-rassment, that they were looking at the Mollusk dress she wore. But she didn't attract too much attention; this was the Magic Kingdom, where many people, including adults, wore costumes. All kinds of things went on here.

Peter, guided by Tink, flew back through the dark ride, past a line of miniature ships. Some visitors saw him and exclaimed to each other, marveling at this new wrinkle in the venerable ride. *He looks just like a real flying boy!*

Ahead somewhere in the blackness was Sarah's brother, inhabited and controlled by Ombra. Peter did not yet have a plan for rescuing Aidan. For now, he simply needed to find him and stay with him.

They flew through a maze of rooms with strange miniature vistas below—islands, mermaids, ships. They then entered a larger room, the floor of which was covered with a miniature city; Peter, who'd flown over the real thing, recognized it as London. Tink chimed, and he saw Aidan ahead now—a dark shape on foot at the other end of the room, moving with unnatural quickness. Peter pursued him through the Darling nursery. Aidan had now reached the beginning of the ride. Just beyond, Peter saw a mass of people waiting to board. He dropped to the floor, sensing that for now he would be wise to proceed on foot.

Clutching the gold box, Aidan ran the wrong way through the ride entrance, vaulted a railing, and pushed his way through the line of people waiting to get on the ride. Some of them complained; a Cast Member shouted something. Aidan ignored them.

Peter followed Aidan, also ignoring the protests, which were getting louder. Aidan climbed over several line dividers; he was now out on the Fantasyland concourse. Peter was only a few feet behind. Aidan turned left and began running through the dense crowd.

Peter was noticing his surroundings—more people than he had ever seen, so many dressed oddly. It was like a city, but with no vehicles or horses, and no real houses to speak of. Strange sights, smells, and sounds everywhere. And such bright lights! He was so distracted that he almost lost track of the running figure ahead.

He forced himself to concentrate. He had dealt with Ombra more than once, and each time it had been terrifying. But that was long ago. He assumed the shadow creature's power had been weakened—why else was he running?—but he didn't know how much. He didn't even know if Aidan was aware he was being followed.

They were now passing the Haunted Mansion. The crowd thinned out slightly. Peter moved a few steps closer to Aidan.

Aidan stopped.

Tink, hidden in Peter's hair, chimed a sharp warning. Peter stopped.

Aidan turned around. Where his eyes should have been were two black voids. They were aimed directly at Peter. Peter's blood ran cold; he had no doubt that the shadow creature knew exactly who he was. For a few seconds both of them stood utterly still. Peter struggled to control his rising fear, but he knew that if Aidan took a step toward him, he would flee.

Instead, Aidan suddenly turned and resumed running through the crowd.

Peter followed, a bit farther back than before, trying to understand what had happened. Clearly Ombra knew Peter was following, and yet he had not attacked. Why not? Where was he going? What did he plan to do? And how, if Peter was afraid to get close, was he going to rescue Sarah's brother?

He would have to figure something out. For now, all he could do was follow the running figure.

Armstrong shook his head, trying to clear it, trying to make sense of what had just happened. He remembered grabbing the boy, and then being engulfed by—it seemed impossible—birds. Hundreds of them. He'd been knocked down, and in the chaos he had lost the boy. Something else had happened in that furious swirl of feathers: he'd felt a presence . . . something cold, something evil.

He shook his head again. Whatever he'd felt, thankfully it was gone, along with the birds.

And the boy.

Brushing off the offers of help from the crowd around him, Armstrong scanned the concourse, looking for Aidan.

Where did he . . . wait a minute.

In the distance, he caught a glimpse of a tall man, moving away. The man's head turned. Armstrong recognized J.D.

"Excuse me!" he said, pushing his way past his would-be helpers. "Gotta go."

The Disney security guard was standing near the riverboat when he saw Aidan sprint past. He pressed the transmit button on his radio and said, "I got a Christopher Robin running through Liberty Square, heading for Frontierland."

"Copy," said a voice. "We're on the way."

Still holding the gold box, Aidan, with Peter twenty-five feet behind, ran into Frontierland; then suddenly, just before the Country Bear Jamboree, he turned left into a passageway that connected with Adventureland. Directly ahead was a popular "flying" ride, The Magic Carpets of Aladdin. Aidan swerved left onto the Adventureland concourse. He ran a few dozen yards and stopped suddenly. Peter braced, but Aidan did not turn around.

Instead he walked toward the Swiss Family Treehouse, an attraction built around a ninety-foot-high "tree" honeycombed with stairs and walkways. The crowd here was even thinner; many visitors, eager to watch the parade, had gone to wait along the parade route.

Aidan passed the entrance to the tree house and went to a rest area on the right, out of the flow of pedestrian traffic, where six benches were lined up against a curving metal fence. Beyond the fence was a sloping embankment leading down to a waterway; the whole area was covered with dense, tropical foliage.

As Peter watched, Aidan went to the fence and carefully set the gold box on it. Cautiously, Peter edged forward.

From his hair, Tink chimed a warning. Peter, keeping his distance, moved to the side so he could see the embankment below, where Aidan had set the box. The lighting was uneven, but after a moment he saw dark shapes moving in the foliage. He realized they were birds—large, black birds. The ground swarmed with them. There were hundreds.

The foliage moved as the birds crowded together beneath Aidan, who was doing something with the box. Peter edged a step closer.

What was he doing?

The thing was leaving.

This was Aidan's first real thought since the birds had descended on him and filled him with a cold, evil presence. After that, he had thought nothing, felt nothing, until now.

But he sensed the cold leaving him. And although Aidan had not yet regained control of his body, he was beginning to become aware again. For just a few seconds, his consciousness was somehow connected with the consciousness of the thing.

In those seconds, Aidan knew what the thing intended to do. Aidan knew he could not stop it. But he also knew that it was his chance to escape.

His hands were reaching out toward the gold box. Aidan did not control them; it was as if he were watching someone else's hands. His hands turned the box on the fence so that the opening was pointing toward the birds. His right hand found the little wheel.

Aidan knew that the thing was about to leave him. It had to go back into the ravens when the starstuff cascaded down on them. Then it would have the power it needed.

Aidan watched his right hand turn the wheel. At the same time, he felt the thing leave him completely, flowing into the birds.

Free now, he stumbled backward.

He felt someone grab him, keeping him from falling. He turned and saw a boy. He noted his filthy clothes, his bare feet.

Peter pulled his arm. "Come along," he said. "Hurry."

"Who are you?" said Aidan.

"I'm . . . a friend of your sister's. Come on."

Aidan, still dazed, nodded. He followed as Peter started trotting toward the Aladdin ride.

"There he is!" said the security man, pointing. "He's running this way!"

"That's the Cooper kid," said Agent Blight. "But who's the boy running with him?"

"I don't know," said Agent Gomez. "But let's grab 'em both."

Peter and Aidan stopped when they saw them coming—a half dozen Disney security people led by a man and woman in business clothes.

"We can't go that way," said Aidan. "They're after me."

They turned to run back the way they'd come, but stopped again. The ravens had taken flight and were now swarming near the Swiss Family Treehouse. The swirling black mass was forming into a shape that both Aidan and

Peter had seen before. A crowd of park visitors gathered quickly, gaping at the sight.

"We have to get away from here now," said Aidan.

"I know," said Peter. "Get on my back."

"What?" said Aidan.

The security people were almost to them. In the other direction, the raven mass was billowing.

"Get on my back right now," said Peter. Without waiting, he grabbed Aidan's arms and draped them over his shoulders. "Hang on!" he shouted. "When I say three, jump as high as you can. One, two . . ."

The closest security man was ten feet away; Gomez was right behind him, followed by Blight. Two more steps and they had them.

Then the boys jumped.

And they did not come down.

Gomez, Blight, and the security people stared, open-mouthed, as the two boys rose straight up into the night and disappeared over the roofs of the Adventureland buildings, heading in the general direction of Cinderella Castle. Around them the crowd of visitors cheered, enjoying this unexpected bit of Disney technical magic. They then turned their attention back to the swirling mass of black birds next to the Swiss Family Treehouse; the birds had formed into a shape that looked like a giant, hooded figure with glowing red orbs for eyes. The shape turned, as if searching, and then exploded in a furious burst of beating wings, streaming off in the direction the boys had gone.

The crowd applauded. Even the longtime veteran visitors, the true Disney faithful, were pumped. The Magic Kingdom seemed unusually magical tonight.

Peter flew in a low, wobbly swoop over the buildings. He was straining; he was very experienced at flying with another person—he'd taken the Lost Boys on countless rides over the island—but he'd never flown anybody as heavy as Aidan. It was all he could do to stay above the roofs.

Aidan's mood was equal parts terror and amazement— terror because of the buildings below and the birds behind; and amazement because this scruffy boy, who had mysteriously appeared to rescue him, was now flying him. Aidan could think of only one explanation for this, impossible though it seemed.

"Are you who I think you are?" he shouted into Peter's ear.

"What?" answered Peter, focused on flying.

"I said—" began Aidan, but at that moment Tinker Bell, annoyed by the shouting, poked her head out of Peter's hair. "Never mind," said Aidan.

CHAPTER 41

OMBRA'S PLAN

J.D. LOOKED BACK, SCANNING THE CROWD on the Fantasyland concourse. He quickly turned forward and ducked his head. "Bad news," he told Sarah. "The big guy must've spotted us. He's coming fast."

"Can he see us now?" said Sarah.

J.D. checked. "Not at the moment."

"This way," she said, turning sharply right past a herd of parked strollers and trotting toward the 3-D attraction, Mickey's PhilharMagic. They melted into the crowd milling around beneath the movie arcade. J.D. kept his face turned away from the concourse. Sarah peeked around him. She saw Armstrong, his head swiveling, walk past the strollers. He kept going.

"He went past," she said.

"Now what?" said J.D.

"Now we need to find Aidan," said Sarah.

"Any idea how we do that?"

"I guess we just start searching, and hope we find him before anybody else—what is it?"

J.D. was staring at the sky. "I found him," he said. "And Peter."

Sarah followed his eyes and saw them, unnoticed by the crowd on the concourse below—two dark shapes alighting on the arcade of the Peter Pan's Flight building, only a few feet from statues representing Peter Pan, Wendy, and her brothers in flight.

Sarah ran toward them, calling Aidan's name and shouting. Aidan, on hands and knees, saw her, and gestured urgently for her to stay where she was. Then he and Peter crawled along the roof in her direction. When they reached the side of the building, Peter dangled his legs over the edge and, with Aidan clinging to his back, they dropped to the ground. This did not go unnoticed—a small crowd, assuming this little drama had something to do with the Peter Pan ride, gathered, pointing, taking pictures and video, thrusting autograph books toward the bewildered Peter.

Aidan grabbed Peter's arm, pulling him through the crowd toward Mickey's PhilharMagic.

"Show's over, folks!" he said. "You'll see Peter in the parade!"

They made their way to J.D. and Sarah. Sarah gave her

brother a huge hug, much to his embarrassment. She turned to Peter.

"How did you—?"

"No time," interrupted Aidan, pushing his sister and J.D. toward the entrance to Mickey's PhilharMagic. "Hurry!"

They ducked into the building. Seconds later, the first dark, flying shapes appeared over Fantasyland.

Inside the movie, Aidan and the others joined a line of visitors flowing through the turnstiles. They passed bins filled with yellow 3-D glasses. J.D., Sarah, and Aidan took them; Sarah grabbed an extra pair and handed them to Peter.

"What're these?" Peter asked.

"Three-D glasses," said Sarah.

"I don't need eyeglasses," said Peter.

"Just take them," said Sarah.

They moved into a large waiting area, filled with families. Aidan gathered them into a little huddle for a whispered talk.

"We have a big problem," he began.

"The police?" said J.D.

Aidan shook his head. "Ombra," he said.

"But you got away from him," said Sarah.

"Yeah," said Aidan. "For now."

"What do you mean?" said J.D.

"Okay, listen," said Aidan. "I don't remember most of

what happened when Ombra was . . . when he was inside me. But when he left me, for just a second there, I could feel him. I knew what he was thinking." Aidan shuddered.

"What was he thinking?" said Sarah.

"He's weak. I mean, he still can do stuff—like the way he controlled me—but he doesn't have anything like the power he used to have."

"Thank goodness," said Peter.

"Because he's weak, he lives in the ravens," said Aidan. "He's spread out, a little bit of him in each one, so even if one bird is killed, most of Ombra is still okay. But he wants to bring the birds together."

"What do you mean?" said Sarah.

"Remember what the ravens did outside the hotel in London?" said Aidan. "When they formed into that giant Ombra shape?"

"Yes," said Sarah.

"He wants to be like that, only instead of a bunch of separate birds, he'll be one being. Like what he was long ago, only bigger. And more powerful."

"How's he going to do that?" asked J.D.

"Starstuff," said Aidan. "He wants to use it on the ravens."

Peter nodded. "It can change animals. That's where the mermaids came from." A chime sounded from his hair. "And Tink," he added.

"Exactly," said Aidan. "That's why he's been after Sarah

and me; he wanted the box. He's been waiting a hundred years to get hold of starstuff. He wants to use it to transform the birds, to bring them together with him inside them, so he'll become this new . . . thing. That's why he took the gold box. He had it all set up; he used me to turn the wheel, and when he did he left me and went back into the birds. The starstuff was supposed to transform them. Except—"

"There wasn't any starstuff," said J.D.

"I know!" said Aidan. "What happened to it?" He nodded toward Peter. "And how did *he* get here?"

"We went to Never Land," said Sarah.

"What?" said Aidan, drawing stares from people around them. Lowering his voice again, he said, "You *went* there? When?"

Before Sarah could answer, the doors to the theater opened and the crowd began to surge inside, carrying Sarah, Aidan, J.D., and Peter along. They sat near the back, put on their glasses, and leaned together to resume whispering. As the movie began, Sarah, with some help from J.D., quickly filled Aidan in on their trip across the bridge, their adventures on Mollusk Island, and their return to the same instant they left. Peter, meanwhile, stared through his 3-D glasses in openmouthed fascination at the screen, which displayed fantastic moving and talking images that sometimes flew toward him, coming so close that he could reach out and touch them—except that, oddly enough, he could not.

"So," said Aidan, after several minutes of sometimes-confusing explanations, "you came back with the box empty."

"Right," said Sarah. "We used up the last of the starstuff to get back over the bridge."

"But you're saying you came back at the same time you left—so it looked as if you never left."

"Right," said J.D.

"And that's when I grabbed the box," said Aidan.

"Yes," said Sarah.

Aidan nodded. "I get it," he said. "Ombra thought the box still had starstuff in it, because it did when you got on the ride."

"Who's that?" said Peter, pointing at the screen, where a cartoon figure was flying over London, clad in a green tunic, green tights, and a feathered green cap.

"That's you," said Sarah.

"What?" said Peter, drawing shushing noises from people sitting nearby. "I don't look like that! And who's the flying girl?"

"That's Tinker Bell," said Sarah. This drew a burst of bells from Peter's hair, and more shushing.

"What'd she say?" whispered Sarah.

"She says that looks like a flying cow," said Peter.

"Sarah, listen," hissed Aidan. "We have a big problem. Ombra really wants the starstuff. Since it wasn't in the box, he's going to think we still have it. He's going to come looking for us. The ravens are outside somewhere, right now."

"Not to mention the police," said J.D.

The movie was ending. Donald Duck flew off the screen and over their heads, face-planting in the wall at the back of the theater to the raucous laughter of the crowd. The lights came on; the doors opened; the crowd started shuffling out into the night.

"So what're we gonna do?" said Aidan, as they approached the exit.

J.D. stopped them. "Listen," he said. "Maybe I should just turn myself in to the police."

"What?" said Sarah.

"We don't need to keep running," said J.D. "We got the starstuff back to the island. Now we can explain that I didn't kidnap you guys. I mean, I'll probably get in some trouble, but . . ."

"No," said Aidan.

"Why not?" said J.D.

"Ombra," said Aidan. "He can get inside the police, get inside anybody. He is not going to rest until he finds the starstuff."

"But there isn't any," said Sarah. "Eventually he'll find that out."

"That's what has me worried," said Aidan. "He'll be angry. He'll want to hurt us. And he can. Sarah, you have no idea how evil that thing is. If the police have us, he can get to us."

"He's right," said Peter.

"So what do we do?" said J.D.

"We have to get out of here, away from the police and away from all these people," said Aidan. "And then we have to deal with Ombra."

"How?" said Sarah.

"We'll have to figure that out," said Aidan. "First, we need to get out of here."

They were almost to the exit. Ahead of them, the crowd in the concourse looked thicker than ever.

"All right," said J.D. "We're going to separate. We keep in sight of each other, but we don't walk together. There's a huge crowd out there; that's in our favor. We blend in, we head for the exit, and when we get outside we meet at the ferryboat landing. Okay? Watch for police and security guards."

"And watch the sky," said Aidan.

"I'll do that," said Peter. They had reached the exit.

"Ready?" said J.D. The others nodded.

"Okay," said J.D. "Let's go."

CHAPTER 42

A SUDDEN STORM

(P)EOPLE MOVED IN GROUPS IN THE PARK; anyone walking alone stood out. So Sarah, keeping her head down, stayed close behind a family of four as she left Mickey's PhilharMagic. Disney World had never seemed so big to her; the ferryboat landing had to be a mile away.

She peeked ahead through the crowd and immediately spotted the woman in the business suit—obviously some kind of police officer—who had been directing the security guards back at the Transportation Center. The woman was standing to the left side of the concourse; on the right side, Sarah saw the woman's partner, the grumpy-looking man. They were studying faces as the hordes flowed past them toward Cinderella Castle. She looked to her left, where Peter was moving with the crowd. Catching his eye, she pointed discreetly toward the female officer, then her partner. Peter nodded and darted back through the crowd; Sarah didn't know where he was going.

She looked to the right and found Aidan and J.D.; they had positioned themselves in the middle of a group of high-schoolers. Aidan fit in well enough, but J.D. stood out. They were heading straight at the grumpy man and apparently hadn't spotted him yet. Sarah tried to get their attention, but they weren't looking her way.

She looked ahead again and got more bad news: her "family" had veered left, toward the female officer. They were going to come within a few yards of her. Worse, the woman's head was turning Sarah's way . . .

"Hey!" the woman yelled. Sarah jumped, but then realized that the woman wasn't yelling at her; she was reacting to being hit on the head by a small object that had fallen from the sky. It bounced off and rolled on the ground.

A half-eaten turkey leg.

The woman grabbed her head and looked around angrily, trying to figure out where it had come from. Sarah, who had a pretty good idea where it came from, walked briskly past. She risked a glance upward and caught a glimpse of Peter's silhouette darting across the sky; a second later she heard a yell coming from the right. Sarah didn't look, but she figured Peter had targeted the male officer, too, which meant—she hoped—that Aidan and J.D. would also get past undetected.

Sarah picked up her pace, half trotting through the crowd descending the ramp next to the castle. Ahead she saw the end of Main Street, U.S.A.; it was lined with visitors, thousands and thousands of them, watching the brilliantly lit parade floats moving slowly up the street toward the castle.

Sarah's heart sank; the parade was blocking Main Street and the sidewalks were so crowded as to be nearly impassable. It would be very slow going to get to the park entrance at the other end of Main Street.

Sarah looked around and found J.D. about ten yards behind her; his expression told her that he, too, was discouraged by the obstacle course ahead. Her eyes searched farther back and picked up Aidan. He looked worried. When she made eye contact with him, he pointed up. She looked and saw the reason for his concern: high above the castle, the ravens were gathering.

Armstrong had a decision to make.

He knew where J.D. and the Cooper kids were. He had followed J.D. and Sarah to Mickey's PhilharMagic; he'd seen them meet up with Aidan and another, younger kid—a scruffy-looking boy in bare feet. Armstrong had almost tried to grab them then, but had thought better of it, remembering what had happened to him the last time. He had no idea where the birds had come from or what they had to do with the weird thing he'd felt. But he was now thinking that he might not want to tackle the kids alone.

He'd watched them go inside Mickey's PhilharMagic, then waited by the exit. When they came out he saw them split up. He'd been able to tail them fairly easily—they didn't get too far apart, and he was a pro.

Just a few minutes earlier, he'd seen them slip by the FBI agents, who'd been distracted when somebody—the scruffy kid, Armstrong guessed—threw turkey legs at them. Armstrong was amused by that: the mighty FBI, easily eluded by kids.

But now he was thinking he needed the FBI's help. He hesitated for a moment, then made his decision. He walked up to the male FBI agent, who was brushing turkey skin off his shoulder.

"They got past you," said Armstrong.

"Excuse me?" said Gomez.

"The Cooper kids, and the Aster guy. All three of them."

"And you are?"

"An interested party."

"And you're telling me this because . . ."

"Because if I show you where they are, you're going to tell their parents that I helped you rescue them. Do we have a deal?" Armstrong stuck out his hand.

Gomez looked at the seemingly endless mass of people—thousands and thousands and thousands of people—surging through the park. His feet were tired; he had turkey grease on his suit; and a few minutes earlier he and Blight had experienced the humiliation of having to call their boss and report that the Cooper boy had eluded them again, this time by flying. Their boss, of course, did not believe this; even Gomez and Blight had trouble believing it, and they had seen it. Their boss had informed them, using harsh words, that (a) people did not fly; (b) he wanted this case cleared now; and (c) if Gomez and Blight could not apprehend a pair of runaway kids inside an enclosed theme park, then perhaps they did not have a future in the FBI.

Armstrong still had his hand out. "Do we have a deal?" he repeated.

Reluctantly, Gomez shook the hand. He used his other hand to beckon Blight. "Show us where they are," he said.

✦

Sarah had reached Main Street and could barely move. Virtually everyone in the dense crowd on both sidewalks had camped to watch the parade. For every foot she moved forward, she had to excuse herself, squeeze between people, and risk stepping on others sitting on the curb. She glanced back—Aidan and J.D. were doing no better. She looked ahead—the end of Main Street might as well have been a million miles away.

And the ravens had moved. They were no longer massing above the castle; they were now flying in a circular pattern over Main Street. They were still fairly high up, and apparently had not attracted the attention of the crowd, which was focused on the parade floats.

Sarah felt a tap on her shoulder and jumped; she relaxed when she saw that it was Peter, who had an amazing knack for disappearing and reappearing.

"Thanks," she said, almost shouting to be heard over the parade music pouring from speakers all around them as spectacular floats, populated by Disney characters, rolled past.

"Thanks for what?" said Peter.

"Getting us by the police back there."

He smiled. "It was fun. Like dropping mangoes on Hook." The smile disappeared. "But we have a bigger problem." He nodded upward. "The birds have found you again."

"I saw them. You think they see us?"

Peter nodded. "They're following you. There's a lot more of them on the tops of these buildings, moving along with you."

Sarah looked up and saw dark shapes fluttering along the roofline. She shuddered.

"I don't think they can get you in this crowd," said Peter. "They'll wait until you're out in the open."

"So maybe we should stay in the crowd."

Peter shook his head. "The police are right behind you."

"So what do we do?" said Sarah.

Before he could answer, Aidan, with J.D. alongside, pushed through the crowd and caught up with them. Aidan was pointing up. "I think the birds found us," he said.

"They did," said Sarah. "Peter says there's more on the rooftops. And the police are right behind us."

J.D. looked back over the crowd.

"Yup," he said. "I see the two cops we saw before, and a bunch of security guys. And that big guy. We need to keep moving. Come on." Leading the way, he began pushing through the crowd.

"But when we leave the park, the birds'll be waiting," said Sarah.

Peter, who had been studying the passing parade floats, said, "Maybe I can take care of the birds." His hair chimed, and he added, "Tink and I."

"How?" said Aidan.

"It's the starstuff Ombra's after," said Peter. "He thinks you still have it, or know where it is."

"But we don't," said Sarah.

"He doesn't know that."

"What good does that do us?" said Aidan.

"Keep going," said Peter. "Don't go out into the open until I catch up to you." He turned and ducked into the crowd.

"Where are you going?" said Sarah.

But Peter was gone.

"Come on," said J.D., looking back over the crowd. "The cops are gaining!"

Sarah started moving again. She glanced up at the building roofline to her left. The shadowy shapes were moving with her.

Agent Gomez, annoyed by the parade music, was shouting into the ear of the head of security. "They're just ahead of us," he said. "I want your people to blanket the exits. We'll sweep them that way and your people will grab them as they come out."

"Got it," said the security man. He pressed the transmit button on his radio and relayed the orders.

Gomez shouted to Armstrong, "You still see them?"

The big man peered ahead over the crowd; in the distance, he caught a glimpse of the back of J.D.'s head.

"I see Aster," he said. "Maybe twenty-five yards ahead. Still heading for the entrance."

Agent Gomez turned to Agent Blight. "We've got them," he said.

"That's what we thought the last time," muttered Agent Blight.

It was one of the last floats in the parade, and one of the most popular. In front was a famous foursome, representing two classic children's stories—from *Alice in Wonderland*, the Mad Hatter and Alice; and from *Peter Pan*, it was Wendy, standing, and Peter, who sat cross-legged on a round pedestal. As the float rolled up Main Street, the crowd cheered and waved; the foursome smiled and waved back. Peter waved with his right hand; in his left he held a lantern, with panes of frosted glass. It was understood that Tinker Bell was inside.

Suddenly, a cheer went up; a figure was descending from the night sky. A boy! Everyone looked for the wire holding him up—there *had* to be a wire holding him up—but none was visible. Amazing!

The boy landed on the float next to Peter Pan, who appeared to be quite surprised. The crowd roared with laughter at the contrast between the natty Peter and the dirt-smudged boy in tattered clothes. For a moment, the two stared at each other; a thousand cameras flashed. Then, with a lightning-quick movement, the boy snatched the lantern from Peter's hand, crouched, and shot at impossible speed straight up into the sky.

The crowd went wild. There had been a rumor spreading in the park that the Disney Imagineers were introducing a spectacular new effect tonight involving a flying boy; now there was no question. The crowd erupted with speculation: How had they done it? Some said it was an incredibly realistic robot; some said it was done with lasers. All agreed it was utterly brilliant.

"I don't understand it either," said Aidan. "And I don't like it."

"You have a better idea?" said Sarah.

"No," they both admitted.

They had walked to the middle of the plaza. They stopped and watched as the security guards advanced warily toward them from both sides. The crowd—not so dense out here—swirled past them. Some people, weary from a day in the park, were heading back to their hotels; others were just arriving at the Magic Kingdom, hurrying to catch the legendary fireworks show. Occasionally somebody pointed to Sarah's long Mollusk dress, but for the most part the crowd paid no attention to the trio.

The nearest guards were only about fifteen yards away.

"Are you guys ready?" said Sarah.

"I'm not sure what we're supposed to be ready for," said J.D., "but yeah."

"I don't see Peter," said Aidan, scanning the sky.

"He'll be here," said Sarah. *I hope.*

The guards were within ten yards . . . five . . .

"Here we go," said Sarah. She reached into the shopping bag and pulled out Peter Pan's lantern. She held it up, and as she did the lantern lit up with a brilliant golden glow. The guards stopped, momentarily uncertain how to respond.

"Move in!" shouted a voice.

The guards started forward again. They had each taken

only a step or two when an ominous sound filled the plaza—
the sound of rushing wind, like a sudden storm, directly
overhead. They looked up to see a sky filled with dark shapes,
seeming to come from everywhere, flowing like a black aerial
river toward the center of the plaza.

Toward the lantern.

There was no time to escape, even if there had been
somewhere to run; in seconds, the first of the vast swarm of
ravens had reached the trio in the middle of the plaza. J.D.
and Aidan threw their hands in front of their faces; Sarah
closed her eyes but still held the glowing lantern aloft, determined to carry out the plan. The raven storm was all around
now, and Sarah heard nothing but the furious beating of
wings. She felt the air buffeting her, felt feathers brushing
her, and then she heard Aidan scream as she felt the same
awful cold she'd felt back in the ride . . .

And then the lantern was gone, snatched from her
hand. At the same instant she felt a shift in the movement
of the ravens. She dared to open her eyes, and saw that
the darting shapes were still all around, but now they were
pursuing something else, something moving too fast for her
eyes to focus on, a blur with a bright light that she knew to
be the lantern Peter had snatched from her. He was about
ten feet off the ground and flying in a gradually expanding
circle, with Sarah, Aidan, and J.D. in the center. Outside of
this strange hurricane Sarah could make out a scene of great

confusion—a growing crowd of park visitors, wildly excited by this spectacular post-parade show, rushing closer to take pictures and video, overwhelming the confused security force.

She felt J.D. grab her arm.

"Come on," he said. "This is when we get out of here."

He pulled her and Aidan toward the circling birds. As they reached them, the blur that was Peter shot past, then veered suddenly upward. The ravens followed, a geyser of blackness erupting into the sky.

"Now!" said J.D., pulling Aidan and Sarah with him as he plunged into the crowd. Overhead, Peter shot back and forth, drawing the ravens this way and that, sending the crowd below running in all directions.

J.D., Sarah, and Aidan, taking advantage of the chaos, ran toward the ferry.

J.D. glanced back at the milling crowd on the plaza; nobody was following them. They sprinted onto the ferry dock and through the gate seconds before the attendant closed it. Gasping for breath, they walked quickly onto the ship and found a spot at the rail from which they could see the plaza.

The blur of light that was Peter was rising higher and higher into the sky, darting back and forth with astonishing speed. Right behind was the vast cloud of ravens, not moving quite as quickly as Peter, but remaining close.

"Man," said Aidan. "There's so many of them."

Sarah nodded. "How long can he keep away from them?"

"I don't understand the physics of it," said J.D. "But he can't keep that up forever. He has to tire at some point."

"Then what happens?" said Aidan.

"I don't know," said J.D.

"He saved us," Sarah said softly.

They fell silent. The ferry horn sounded and the ship started to move. Sarah, Aidan, and J.D. stood utterly still, staring at the glowing light, growing fainter now, darting back and forth in the sky, pursued by the huge, relentless black cloud.

Peter was tiring, and he had no plan. He had thought it through to this point: putting Tink in the lantern to trick Ombra into believing it contained starstuff, then using it to lure the ravens away so Sarah, J.D., and Aidan could escape. But he hadn't had time to come up with anything beyond that. He'd assumed that he'd be able to figure something out when the time came. He always did.

But now the time was coming. The ravens were getting closer, and he was feeling slower and weaker. Tink, he knew, was exhausted from radiating the light that had fooled—and continued to fool—his pursuers.

If he kept flying much longer, the ravens would catch him. Ombra would have him, and Peter knew he would not be merciful. Time was running out.

And he had no plan.

He flew higher, higher; below was the castle, a spectacular sight from this altitude, had Peter been able to enjoy it. On all sides of the castle he saw people, tens of thousands of them. Many were looking skyward, although not in Peter's direction. Peter wondered what they were looking at.

Then he heard an explosion.

"Fireworks," said Aidan, pointing from the ferryboat rail as the first burst of color exploded in the sky near the castle, followed quickly by another, and another.

Sarah ignored the fireworks, squinting as she tried to keep track of the tiny, distant, glowing streak that was Peter.

"Maybe they'll help him," she said.

"Help him how?" said J.D.

"I don't know. Maybe he can use them as a distraction, to get away from the—wait a minute."

"What?" said J.D.

"He's heading toward them," said Sarah, watching the blur elongate. "He's heading straight toward the fireworks."

No mistakes, thought Peter. Even a single mistake meant death.

He could see the flashes of the mortars far below. Each

flash meant a fireworks shell had been launched into the sky, its fuse burning.

When the fuse burned all the way down, the charge inside the shell exploded, sending burning stars of molten metals and chemicals hurtling out in a predetermined pattern; some of them exploded in two, or even three, stages. The explosions were terrifyingly powerful, the shock waves buffeting Peter even at a distance of a hundred yards. He knew that if he got too close, he would be burned or knocked unconscious from the sky.

If he didn't get close enough, his plan would fail.

Either mistake would ultimately be fatal.

He glanced back; the birds were closer now than they had been. He veered slightly left, then right; the lead birds tracked him exactly. That was good. He was counting on the fact that the birds were focused on him, and not their surroundings.

He was over the mortars now. He veered left, circling, watching the mortars flashing below, tracking the shells hurtling upward, fuses burning. Peter had superb eyesight, but even he could not see well enough to tell exactly when a given shell's fuse had burned down completely. He would have to guess.

He felt something strike his feet and he kicked hard, knocking away a raven, which screeched in anger. The others were right behind. They were closing in on him. There was no time left.

He looked back at the mortars. He saw a flash, then another.

Perfect.

He veered sharply, heading to intercept the flight of the first shell. He flicked his eyes and caught a glimpse of the second, trying to gauge its trajectory. He did not look back, but he knew the birds were close. He slowed slightly, and felt one, now two, now three, striking his legs with their beaks. Ignoring the pain, he focused on the shell hurtling toward him. From this angle, almost directly above, he couldn't see the fuse. He wanted to veer now, to get away from the missile that was almost on him, but he forced himself to wait one more second . . .

Now.

With a desperate effort, he contorted his body and executed a sharp right turn away from the shell. For a tenth of a second he thought he'd turned too soon.

Then the night exploded into brightness. Peter was hurled forward, head over heels, barely hanging on to the lantern. White-hot burning stars shot past; he felt agonizing pain as one of them ricocheted off his left leg and another hit his arm. As he tumbled through the air he heard a piteous chorus of inhuman, screeching sounds; regaining control, he looked back and saw black shapes everywhere, some fluttering erratically, most plummeting toward the earth.

And some still coming for him.

413

Peter veered right, and the remaining birds followed. Peter looked desperately for the second shell, but could not pick it up; he knew it was close, but where?

He saw the flash an instant before he heard or felt the blast, and in that instant he knew he was much too close. As the massive shock wave hurled his body across the sky and the world went black around him, he felt himself falling through the night. Somehow he was still clutching the lantern, from within which sounded the urgent, but unheard, chimes of the much-weakened Tinker Bell, urging him to please, *please* wake up . . .

CHAPTER 43

A WAY OUT

𝒯HE FERRY WAS NEARING THE DOCK at the Transportation and Ticket Center, the announcer telling passengers to prepare to disembark. Sarah, Aidan, and J.D. remained by the rail, staring back across the Seven Seas Lagoon toward the Magic Kingdom. The fireworks show had ended, but they were hoping to see one light still in the sky.

It wasn't there.

The ferry docked. The announcer was asking the passengers to proceed to the exits.

Reluctantly, Aidan and J.D. turned away from the rail. Sarah didn't move.

"Come on," J.D. said softly. "We have to get off."

Sarah was staring out at the water.

"Where is he?" she whispered.

"He's a tough little guy," said J.D., putting his hand on her shoulder.

"Yeah, he'll be okay," said Aidan, not convincingly.

They were the last passengers along the rail now. A crew member called to them to please exit.

Sarah, with one last look at the sky, turned to follow her brother and J.D.

Behind them, they heard a splash.

Sarah was the first one back to the rail. She leaned over, eyes anxiously searching the water. She saw a glow beneath the surface, then bubbles, then . . .

"Peter!"

J.D. shouted for help; instantly, a crew member was there with a life preserver. In less than a minute Peter was sitting on the deck, coughing, dripping wet, somehow still clutching the lantern. Sarah gave him a hug; he responded with an embarrassed grin.

"I missed the boat," he said.

J.D. was able to convince the ferry crew that he didn't need any further attention, though Sarah wasn't so sure. "Are you okay?" she said, looking at Peter's clothes, which were even more ragged than before, and singed in places.

"I'll be all right," he said.

"What about Ombra?" said Aidan, softly.

"I think we've seen the last of him," said Peter.

"Thanks to you," said Sarah. From the lantern came a weak chime. "And Tink, of course," added Sarah.

They helped Peter to his feet and walked off the

boat, Peter leaning on J.D. and Aidan for support. The Transportation and Ticket Center plaza was filled with tired visitors heading home from a long day at Disney World.

"Where are we going?" said Aidan.

"We need to get Peter someplace where he can lie down," said J.D. "And he might need a doctor."

Peter waved that suggestion away. "Just some rest," he said. "I'll be fine."

"Once we get Peter settled somewhere," said J.D., "I need to contact the police. Might as well get that over with."

"I need to make a call right now," said Sarah, heading for a bank of pay phones.

"Who're you calling?" said Aidan.

"Mom and Dad," she answered over her shoulder. "Remember them?"

"Barely," said Aidan, trotting after his sister.

The wounded raven, its feathers badly singed, landed clumsily in one of the tree's upper branches. It could still fly—but not far, and not well. It could not remain in the tree for long; it was too exposed, too vulnerable.

It needed shelter. It needed to regain its strength. It needed to stay alive, so that the grievously weakened thing inside it could stay alive.

Below the tree was a large building. It had been crowded

earlier, but the people were gone now. From its perch, the raven could see a passageway alongside the building.

With a labored effort, it lunged from the branch and glided down. It fluttered awkwardly into the passageway, which led to an opening in the building. The raven flew inside. It was now in a large, dimly lit space. To the right was an archway, like the entrance to a cave. The raven, its strength waning, flew toward it. It landed on the floor just inside, exhausted.

The raven's head darted this way and that, looking for a safe refuge. Directly above, perched atop the archway, it saw a familiar shape—the shape of a large black bird, its wings extended.

With what little strength it had left, the raven launched itself from the floor and managed to flap its way up to the archway. The shape did not move; the raven sensed that it was not a bird at all, not even a living thing. But the raven was too weak to fly any farther, and the space atop the archway was high enough and dark enough to provide protection. The raven crawled behind the bird shape and huddled there.

It could stay there indefinitely. The thing inside it, though very weak, would keep the raven alive without food or water. The raven would stay there, a helpless host, for however long it would take for the thing inside it to grow strong again.

And then the thing would find a way out.

CHAPTER 44

SOMEDAY

Tom Cooper stood in the middle of the hotel suite's living room, his hands on his hips, a stern expression on his face. Natalie Cooper stood next to him, looking, if possible, even sterner. Their glares were directed at Sarah and Aidan, who sat on the couch, heads bowed, contrite and weary.

"We want an explanation," said Tom.

"Now?" said Aidan.

"Right now," said Natalie.

It was after three A.M. The police had finally released Sarah and Aidan into the custody of their parents, who had taken them to a hotel near Disney World. The Coopers had also agreed, reluctantly, to take temporary custody of Sarah and Aidan's new companion—the odd, unkempt boy Peter, who spoke with a British accent and whose hair made strange noises. Aidan and Sarah had begged their parents to take the boy, who they said was homeless and needed a place to stay. At the moment Peter was sleeping in one of the suite's bedrooms.

Tom and Natalie were very tired themselves. But they were also very, very angry. Above all, they wanted to know why—*why?*—their children had put them through this awful ordeal.

"Okay," said Sarah. "But it's going to take a while."

"We have all night," said Tom grimly.

"But it's really, really weird," said Aidan, shaking his head. "Even if we tell you, you're not gonna believe it."

"Try us," said Natalie.

So they did, telling the whole story from the day Sarah chased Aidan under the antique desk, through the adventures in England, then to Princeton, the strange journey to Disney World, and the even stranger odyssey to Mollusk Island and back. Tom and Natalie asked a few questions at first, but then simply listened, their expressions ranging from skepticism to open disbelief.

By the time Sarah and Aidan reached the end of their story, the sun was coming up.

"That's it," said Sarah. "That's what happened, we swear."

For several seconds the room fell silent. Natalie took a deep breath, letting it out slowly.

"I don't know what makes me angrier," she said. "The fact that you've decided to lie about whatever actually happened, or the fact that the story you're expecting us to swallow is so utterly, preposterously ridiculous."

"I knew you wouldn't believe us," Sarah said softly.

"Sarah," said Tom, "you just told us that you found a magical flying powder, and to keep it away from an evil spirit who lives in a flock of birds, you went to a fantastic island in another universe on a bridge built by Albert Einstein and came back with Peter Pan. Is that right? Is that the story you two want us to believe?"

Sarah and Aidan nodded glumly.

"All right, then," said Natalie. "If that's how you want it to be, your lives are about to become considerably less pleasant. I'm not just talking about being grounded. I'm talking about no allowance, no phones, no computers, no television, no sports, no clubs, no dances, no contact with friends, no social life of any kind whatsoever. You will go to school; you will come home; you will go to your rooms and do your homework. You will come downstairs for meals, and then you will go back to your rooms. That will be the extent of your activities, including on weekends, until you decide to be honest with us. Do you understand?"

Aidan's face was ashen.

"Mom," said Sarah. "Please listen. We—"

"Do you understand?"

Sarah put her face in her hands, weeping.

The sun was streaming through the window now.

"All right," said Tom. "We all need to get some sleep

now. We're going to head home tonight, after we figure out what we're going to do with your new little friend, whoever he really is."

"*Excuse me.*"

Tom, Natalie, Sarah, and Aidan looked over to see Peter standing in the entrance to the hallway. He looked small and skinny; the bright sunlight revealed cuts on his ankles and red burn marks on his arms and legs.

"What is it?" said Natalie.

Peter fixed his gaze on her. "They're telling the truth," he said.

"About you?" she said.

"About everything," he said.

"So you're Peter Pan," said Tom.

"I am."

Tom sighed. "Fine," he said. "Whoever you are, we're going to have to find a place for you, because we have to—" He stopped in mid-sentence. He felt Natalie's hand on his arm. She was staring at Peter's feet. Tom looked down.

"Oh my god," he said.

Peter had risen off the floor—a foot, now two. His body slowly rotated to the horizontal. He drifted slowly upward toward the ceiling.

"My god," Tom said again. He and Natalie moved involuntarily backward and sat down on the sofa. They looked at Aidan and Sarah, then back at Peter—who was now casually "lying" on the ceiling—and then back again at their children.

"Told you," said Aidan.

"I think she can come out now," Sarah said to Peter.

Tink's tiny, exquisite face poked out of Peter's hair. The rest of Tink emerged, and she fluttered gracefully down to the top of a table next to the sofa. Tom and Natalie stared at her, their mouths open.

Tink emitted a melodic burst of chimes, which Peter understood to mean, *They look like a pair of fish.*

"What did she say?" asked Natalie, enthralled.

"She says she's very pleased to meet you," said Peter, from the ceiling.

"I have bad news and good news," said F. Scott Turow, J.D.'s lawyer and old family friend.

"What's the bad news?" said J.D.

"The bad news is, the feds might—I say *might*—want to charge you with unlawful flight. But I'm thinking that even if they do, we're not talking about jail time, and we could be talking about charges being dropped down the road. I think it's just that, after all the publicity, they think they have to charge somebody with something."

J.D. nodded. "What's the good news?"

"No kidnapping, no abduction, nothing like that. The

Cooper kids are saying all the right things about you and their parents are adamantly opposed to pressing charges. I'm getting the feeling the FBI doesn't think this case will do its image any good. They want to put this behind them."

"What about the Princeton police?"

Turow allowed himself a small smile. "Same as the FBI, times ten. They're getting a lot of unwanted attention about their amazing flying police van, which neither they nor anybody seems to be able to explain. And apparently some of their officers were acting pretty strange the night you and the Cooper children, ah, disappeared. So bottom line, the Princeton PD and the FBI would both prefer to have this whole episode just go away."

"So what happens now?"

"Now we do some paperwork and you go home, at least for the time being. You'll probably have to present yourself for a deposition or proceeding at some point down the road. But for now you're a free man."

J.D. frowned. "Did you contact Mrs. Carmoody?"

"I did, and she's fine," said Turow. "Said she had the strangest experience—something about an unusual flock of birds on her front porch, and then a very odd daydream. But all is well, and she hopes you'll come back sometime for more lemonade."

J.D. smiled. "I'll do that."

"I also have a message for you from a Professor Macpherson at Princeton."

"What'd he say?"

"He said he's eager to hear if you found Rosey, and if so, how she's doing."

That got another smile from J.D., but no comment.

"I don't suppose," said Turow, "that you'd want to explain to me who this Rosey is, and whether she has anything to do with the flying police van and what you and the Cooper children were up to?"

"No," said J.D.

Turow nodded. "Probably just as well," he said.

Lester Armstrong dialed Tom Cooper's cell number and put the phone to his ear.

"Hello," said Tom's voice.

"Mister Cooper, this is Lester Armstrong."

"Oh, hi. I was just going to call you. The FBI agent, Gomez, said you were a big help in locating the kids. Natalie and I are grateful for all your efforts, although I guess we won't be needing your services any longer. I assume you'll be sending me a bill?"

"Yes, sure."

"Okay, great. Listen, we're getting ready to head for the airport, so—"

"Mister Cooper," interrupted Armstrong.

"Yes?"

"Um, look, I've done a lot of investigations in my time, tracked a lot of kids. I just want you to know there's something . . . weird about this case."

"Really? What do you mean?"

"I mean the birds and the flying kid. For starters."

"They do all kinds of amazing things at the Magic Kingdom," said Tom. "I believe they call it *Imagineering*."

"Mister Cooper, I was there. It wasn't imaginary. It was real."

There was a pause, then Tom, his tone suddenly guarded, said, "I'm not sure I understand what you want."

"I just want to know what happened," said Armstrong.

"I'm afraid I can't help you with that," said Tom.

"I see," said Armstrong.

"So you'll send me that bill?"

"Yeah."

"Great. Thanks again for everything. Good-bye."

"Good-bye."

Armstrong pressed disconnect, but continued staring at his phone. He would take the Coopers' money. He had earned that money. But he didn't like the way this was ending. He didn't like unanswered questions. And he hated the feeling that those kids—kids!—had gotten the better of him.

He stuck the phone into his pocket and made a promise to himself: someday, when he had some time, he was going to look back into this case. He was going to find out what the Cooper kids had really been up to. And he was going to find out what the story was with the flying boy. Something told him that the answers to these questions might be worth money. But even if he didn't make a nickel, he had made up his mind: he would find the answers.

Someday.

CHAPTER 45

THE CALL

$\mathcal{P}$ETER'S WISH—AND OF COURSE TINK'S—was to return to the island. Unfortunately, this was impossible, at least for the time being. Starstuff was needed to activate the bridge, and as far as anybody knew, there was no starstuff left on earth.

J.D. immediately got to work on this problem, along with Professor Macpherson, who was thrilled to have a project to work on again. They were certain they could figure something out, and although Peter didn't understand most of what they said—it had to do with "fusion," whatever that was—he trusted that they would ultimately succeed.

For now, though, he was stuck.

The Coopers insisted that, while Peter was waiting, he must live with them. This, they felt, was the least they could do. After all, Peter had left his world and come to theirs to save Aidan; in the end, he had done much more than that. They wanted to try to repay him by making him part of their family until he found a way home. He appreciated that; he liked the Coopers very much. Especially Sarah.

But the adjustment did not go well. It started with the airplane flight to Pittsburgh. Despite having spent much of his life in the air, Peter was not at all comfortable with being trapped inside a machine that was flying (in his opinion—and, of course, Tink's) *much* too high, and *much* too fast.

Peter also did not adapt well to the lifestyle of the modern suburban child. He was accustomed to making his own decisions about what to eat, when to sleep, where to go, and what to do. He preferred to be outdoors most of the time, and when he was outdoors, he generally preferred to be airborne. This soon became a problem. The first time he was spotted flying over the Coopers' neighborhood, the police were called, and the story wound up on the local TV news, with video taken on a cell phone. The TV station brought in an expert, who analyzed the video and declared that the "flying boy" was, in fact, nothing but a flock of birds. So the secret was still safe; but Peter was forced to accept that everyone would be better off if he flew only at night.

This meant that he spent most of his daylight hours feeling cooped up and adventure-deprived. He did enjoy being told stories, especially by Sarah, but he didn't care for television, which never looked real to him. He was utterly baffled by the Internet, and could not—despite Aidan's best efforts—see the point of video games. His feeling was, if you've battled real villains, it's hard to get worked up about fighting pretend ones.

And then there was the issue of school. Natalie and Tom felt strongly that Peter should attend; he felt, just as strongly, that he should not. The Coopers pointed out that he could neither read nor write, and that these were necessary skills. He pointed out that he had been without them for more than a century and had done just fine. They had not come up with a good counterargument for that.

It goes without saying that Tink detested almost everything about Pittsburgh. She had made only one new friend, a swallow. She considered the rest of the local birds to be idiots.

As days passed, then weeks, then months, Peter found himself more often feeling homesick for the island, the Lost Boys, the Mollusks, the mermaids—even, in some strange way, Hook. In fact, it was Hook he was thinking of—specifically, the time he had managed to swoop down and steal Hook's pants as he was taking his monthly bath—when J.D. called the Cooper house with the news. Sarah, who'd answered the phone, handed it to Peter. Peter held it gingerly; he did not care for telephones.

"Yes?" he said.

"Peter?" said J.D.

"J.D.?"

"Yes. Peter, do you want to go home?"

"To Never Land?"

"To the island. Yes."

"Of course! But . . . how?"

"It's a bit complicated to explain, but Mac and I have come up with something that we're pretty sure will work, if you're willing to try it."

Peter looked at Sarah, who was watching him intently.

"Yes," he said to J.D. "I do want to try it."

Tink, hovering by Peter's ear, listening, emitted a joyous burst of bells.

"We'll have to get you down to Florida," said J.D. "Put Tom or Natalie on the phone, and we'll figure out the logistics."

While the grown-ups made arrangements, Peter told Sarah what J.D. had said.

"So you're going back," she said.

"Yes," he agreed.

"That's . . . wonderful," she said. Then she started to cry.

Peter thought about hugging her, but settled for patting her shoulder. After all these years, he still didn't understand exactly what made girls cry.

CHAPTER 46

SOON

*T*HEY STOOD IN A LITTLE GROUP by the entrance to Peter Pan's Flight—Peter, J.D., and the Coopers. Peter wore a backpack, which contained the device that J.D. and Mac had made—a sleek black metal football, devoid of buttons or lights, which they called "the pod." The backpack also contained Tink, who was not thrilled to be in there with the pod.

J.D. looked at his watch, then the line for the ride.

"If you get in line in ten minutes, you should be just about perfect," he said. "You'll be at Skull Rock at 9:07. The pod will activate itself, so you don't have to do anything except hold on."

Peter nodded.

J.D. removed his watch and handed it to Peter. "Take this, so you can time it exactly right," he said. "When you get to the island, keep the watch safe. It's got a new battery, so it will last for years."

"Thank you," said Peter, "but we don't pay attention to time on the island."

"You will if you want to know when it's 9:07 P.M. here," said J.D.

Peter frowned. "Why would I want to know that?"

"So you can come back," said J.D.

"What?" said Peter.

"Really?" said Sarah.

"We think so," said J.D. "The pod should work at both ends."

"Wow," said Aidan. "So you can come back."

"And forth," said J.D.

"*Will* you come back, Peter?" said Sarah.

From the backpack came the sound of bells; it went on for some time, longer than Tink's usual terse pronouncements. Peter listened intently, his face solemn.

"What did she say?" asked Aidan.

"She says . . . she will miss you all," said Peter.

That was not, in fact, what Tink had said. What she'd said was that there was something bad nearby. She had felt it as they'd walked through the Magic Kingdom; at one point felt it quite strongly. What Tink was telling Peter—what she was warning Peter—was that if he returned to this place, he would be in danger.

"So," said Sarah. "You'll come back?"

From Tink, an ominous warning chime.

433

"Yes," said Peter. "I'll come back."

Sarah hugged him; he reddened.

"When?" Sarah said. "Soon?"

"Yes," he said, ignoring the now-noisy backpack. "Quite soon."

Sarah hugged him still tighter; his face grew still redder.

"I hate to break this up," said J.D. "But you need to get in line."

He stuck out his hand; Peter shook it, then Aidan's, then Tom's. Natalie gave him a hug that left tears on his shoulder. Sarah paused, looking at him. She seemed about to say something, then she stepped forward and gave him one last hug, even wetter than her mom's.

"Thank you," she whispered.

Then it was time. Peter got into the line. He attracted no notice from the other riders—just another child among the millions who'd shuffled through this fanciful arcade on their way to enjoy a magical make-believe flight. J.D. and the Coopers watched him as he moved slowly forward, glancing back at them often, each glance drawing a sob from Sarah.

They watched as he reached the boarding area. Just ahead of him, a dad with two young daughters boarded a little ship. Peter got on the next ship alone. As it carried him forward his eyes searched the crowd until he found his friends. He gave them a little smile, and a little wave. Then the ship was gone.

They all stared at the tunnel where the ships exited from the ride. Nobody said a word. A minute went by, then two . . .

They held their breath as the dad and his two daughters came into view. Then they saw Peter's ship.

Empty.

"It worked," J.D. said softly.

Sarah buried her face in her hands, her body racked by sobs. Natalie put her arm around her daughter, squeezed her tight.

"He's home, honey," she said. "It's where he belongs."

Sarah nodded, still sobbing.

"He said he'll come back," said Tom.

"Soon," said Aidan.

Sarah raised her head, and, through her tears, managed a weak smile.

"Soon," she said.

ONE YEAR LATER

𝒯HE NIGHT WATCHMAN believed it was nonsense, a case of overactive imaginations. For months now, visitors to the Haunted Mansion had reported feeling a strange chill as their ride vehicles—known as "doom buggies"—exited from the graveyard at the end. Even some Cast Members claimed to have felt it.

The night watchman didn't believe any of it. It was a big building; it got drafty. That was all there was to it.

Fed up with the rumors, the night watchman had finally decided to see for himself. Tonight he had switched rotations with the man who usually checked on the Haunted Mansion. (The man had seemed oddly happy about the switch.)

The night watchman made his way through the building, following the track of the now-still doom buggies. In the glare of the utility lighting he'd seen all manner of supposedly terrifying creatures—ghouls, ghosts, demons, monsters, a murderous bloodstained bride. But the watchman's coldly analytical eyes saw these things for what they were—clever stagecraft, nothing more.

He was in the graveyard, now, walking past a forest of tombstones, populated by a bizarre menagerie of animatronic spooks. The night watchman felt nothing, other than a sense of smug superiority. He could not for the life of him imagine how any rational person could be so weak-minded and easily influenced as to . . .

Then he felt it.

He was cold. Not the air around him; *he* was cold.

And there was something else—a feeling of dread, seeping into him . . .

Heart pounding, he walked quickly forward though the archway leading out of the graveyard. The building exit was just ahead. The watchman quickened his pace. He was afraid to look back, but he forced himself to. Behind him stood the empty archway. Above it, looking down, wings spread, was an animatronic raven. It did not move; the ride was not operating.

But the raven's eyes were glowing red.

It's a reflection, the watchman told himself, as he turned and hurried forward. A *trick of the light*.

He was almost running as he exited the building into the cool central Florida night. He stood still for a minute, sweating, catching his breath.

Perched on a tree limb high overhead, Peter watched the hurrying watchman.

"He looks scared," he whispered.

Tink chimed softly. *He should be scared.*

"You can feel it?"

Yes. It's stronger.

Peter stared at the Haunted Mansion. Tink nestled into his hair.

We have to go, she chimed. They were flying to Pittsburgh that night, not in a plane. They'd made the trip several times, and found that if they kept moving, they could just beat the sunrise.

"I know," said Peter. He stood up on the branch. "But we're going to have to keep an eye on this."

It's dangerous.

"Which is why we have to keep an eye on it."

We could stay on the island and be safe.

"We could," said Peter, stepping casually off the branch. "But where's the fun in that?"